THE NIGHT ENDS WITH FIRE

K. X. SONG

HODDERSCAPE

First published in Great Britain in 2024 by Hodderscape
An imprint of Hodder & Stoughton Limited
An Hachette UK company

This paperback edition published in 2025

The authorised representative in the EEA is Hachette Ireland,
8 Castlecourt Centre, Dublin 15, D15 XTP3, Ireland
(email: info@hbgi.ie)

3

Copyright © K. X. Song 2024
Map illustration by Alexis Seabrook

The right of K. X. Song to be identified as the Author of the Work has been asserted by her in accordance with the Copyright,
Designs and Patents Act 1988.

All rights reserved. No part of this publication may be reproduced, stored in a retrieval system, or transmitted, in any form or by any means without the prior written permission of the publisher, nor be otherwise circulated in any form of binding or cover other than that in which it is published and without a similar condition being imposed on the
subsequent purchaser.

All characters in this publication are fictitious and any resemblance to real persons, living or dead, is purely coincidental.

A CIP catalogue record for this title is available from the British Library

Paperback ISBN 978 1 399 72529 3
ebook ISBN 978 1 399 72527 9

Typeset in Tactile ITC Std by Manipal Technologies Limited

Printed and bound in Great Britain by Clays Ltd, Elcograf S.p.A.

Hodder & Stoughton policy is to use papers that are natural, renewable and recyclable products and made from wood grown in sustainable forests. The logging and manufacturing processes are expected to conform to the environmental regulations of the country of origin.

Hodder & Stoughton Limited
Carmelite House
50 Victoria Embankment
London EC4Y 0DZ

www.hodderscape.co.uk

Praise for *The Night Ends With Fire*

Sweepingly epic and tenderly romantic, *The Night Ends With Fire* is a fiercely feminist adventure about a young woman fighting to shape her destiny in a world of lore, magic, and war. One not to miss for fans of Mulan.

– Amélie Wen Zhao, NYT bestselling author of *Song of Silver, Flame Like Night*

As defiant and courageous as its protagonist, *The Night Ends With Fire* ushers in a stunning new fantasy world. I couldn't put it down – and I know I'll be thinking about it for some time to come.

– Nalini Singh, *New York Times* bestselling author of the Psy-Changeling series

An awesome, engaging fantasy that takes a hard look at the cost of being true to yourself. Adventure, romance and dragons abound in this fantastic tale.

– Patricia Briggs, #1 *New York Times* bestselling author of the Mercy Thompson series

The Night Ends With Fire is a cinematic tale of epic proportions, with jaw-dropping twists and a take-no-prisoners heroine yearning for freedom, recognition and glory. An explosive start to a captivating new series.

– Axie Oh, *New York Times* bestselling author of *The Girl Who Fell Beneath the Sea*

The Night Ends With Fire is what blessedly happens when the themes of Hua Mulan's legend are combined with wuxia principles and a powerful new voice in adult fantasy. K. X. Song's soaring, emotive prose takes the reader on an unforgettable adventure in a painstakingly realized world, laced with fascinating characters that effortlessly play off of one another and twists that leave us reeling. I devoured every page of this truly epic tale.

– Thea Guanzon, *USA Today* and *New York Times* bestselling author of *The Hurricane Wars*

ALSO BY K. X. SONG

An Echo in the City

To my grandfather, who laughed and cried to the stories of 三国演义. I wish I could tell you—I love them too.

致我的外公：我多想告诉您，曾经让您热泪盈眶的《三国演义》里的每个故事，如今也一样触动着我。

问古来将相可还存?也只是虚名儿与后人钦敬。

All those whom history called great left only empty names for us to venerate.

—CAO XUEQIN, *DREAM OF THE RED CHAMBER*

THE THREE KINGDOMS

- RUNONG DESERT
- Xianju
- **LEYUAN**
- RED MOUNTAINS
- Zhong Wu

PART I

ONE

An empire is like a cherry tree; if it is blooming, its petals must one day fall. If it is barren, its petals must one day bloom. Thus it has always been.
—BOOK OF ODES, 856

"War is coming..."

The rumors took wing and flew through the capital, leaving behind a trail of astonishment, fear, and, in some cases, a stirring hunger for glory. Only in my father's house were they met with apathy.

"I will not go," my father said, his face obscured by a cloud of smoke. The unaired room smelled of sweat and opium, but Father refused to let us open so much as a window. He claimed the sunlight would hurt his eyes. But I think he simply did not want to see the state of what he'd become.

His wife stood beside me, trembling. Xiuying was my stepmother, though we were only seven years apart. The servants had expected me to hate her upon her arrival, but against Father's increasing rage and lunacy, we bonded over a common enemy. As the years passed, we became more than allies; we became laotong. Old sames.

Now, Xiuying clenched her hands into fists, trying to conceal her emotions. "The draft is the heavens' mandate. To lie to the Imperial Commander is punishable by death—"

"For skies' sake, just tell them I'm unwell! Make something up. You're awfully creative when it comes to finding ways to spend money. Use some of that creativity to lie."

The injustice of this remark stole my breath away. How dare he accuse *her* of losing all our money? "It's your gambling habit that's brought us—"

Xiuying covered my mouth with her hands. "No, Meilin," she whispered.

Father blew out a delicate ring of smoke from his pipe; he hadn't even heard me. Lost in his thoughts, he murmured, "I won't go to war. I refuse. It doesn't befit me, a man of my stature." His hand trembled as he emptied his pipe against the old ashtray. The porcelain had once belonged to my mother's dowry. It was now chipped and stained, ruined like everything else in this household.

"Why don't you send the old footman in my place?" said Father, chuckling at his own idea. He set his pipe down at last, the full weight of his attention falling upon us. "He can pass for me."

"Father," I said loudly, unable to curb my tongue. "Zhou is not long for this world."

"Did I ask you to speak?" he snapped, his eyes lighting on me. Xiuying shot me a frightened glance, but I shook my head at her while Father laughed.

"Even better," he decided. "Two birds with one stone, as the scholars say. Better he die out there than waste our household resources any longer. These days even the dogs contribute more than he—"

"Uncle Zhou has done more for this household than you ever have."

The words were out of my mouth before I could think twice. Xiuying gasped; Father narrowed his eyes, then lurched to his feet, grabbing hold of the table to steady himself. He was advanced in years, but he was still a large man, several heads taller than me. They used to say he could command a room with his presence, before the opium commanded him.

He lumbered toward me now, his long hair loose on his shoulders, his gait sloping and precarious. With a snarl, he grabbed me by my chin, forcing me to meet his watery glare.

Our faces were inches from each other. I hadn't been this close to him in years.

Xiuying once confessed she'd thought him a handsome man when they first met, with his dark, luminous eyes, his straight nose and high cheekbones. "*You're blessed with beauty, like him,*" she'd said, trying to compliment me. I hadn't told her it felt like the worst kind of insult.

"That Zhou raised you to insolence," Father muttered. "After your mother died, I shouldn't have let him interfere." He turned my face from side to side, like a butcher inspecting a pig for slaughter. When I tried to pull away, his grip only tightened.

"How old is she?" he asked, glancing at Xiuying. His voice took on a mocking lilt. "How old is my dear, lovely daughter?"

Xiuying's voice quavered as she answered. "Only just past eighteen," she said. "I still have much to teach her in the ways of women's—"

"Silence." Father released me, his eyes roving down my body now. "Eighteen is far too old to be uncommitted. Have Zhou call for the matchmaker tomorrow. I expect a dowry by new moon."

The new moon was in a fortnight. "No," I bit out. "I refuse to marry."

I didn't see his hand until it smashed into my cheek, the force of the slap snapping my head to one side. I blinked, forcing back tears.

"You will do as you're told, Hai Meilin," he said, a lethal undertone to his voice. "And if you fail to fetch a handsome dowry as a first wife, I will sell you as a concubine."

"My lord, please . . ." I hated the pleading look in Xiuying's eyes.

"You will not intervene!" He raised his hand to strike her, but I grabbed her first, pulling her behind me. Xiuying was shaking so hard I could feel her tremors in my bones.

"My orders are final," he said. "Meilin has lived under my roof for eighteen years, using my name, partaking at my table. It is time to pay back her debts." His hand twitched, seeking his pipe. "Now get out of my sight."

Xiuying opened the door to flee before he could change his mind.

"And don't let any of the warlord's messengers into this house!"

The door slammed shut behind us. We didn't dare stop until we were down the hall, ensconced in the women's chambers at the other end of the courtyard. Only then did I allow myself to come apart.

"Mei Mei," Xiuying whispered. She tucked my face into her chest and rocked me back and forth as we both wept—quietly, for even in our own chambers the walls had ears.

"It won't be so bad," she murmured. "The matchmaker will find you a kind and decent man. He will treasure and protect you."

"I wager that's what the matchmaker said about Father too, when she paired you with him. They lie, all of them!" My voice was scraped raw. "I hate him."

Xiuying shushed me. "Don't blame your father. He's under much stress," she said. "The debt collectors come every day now."

I raised my head. "I thought you dismissed most of the servants."

She sighed. "Still, the way things are, the household cannot go on for much longer. Perhaps it is a good thing war is on our doorsteps." She paused, biting her lip. "Skies forgive me for saying such a thing."

I tried to wipe away my tears, the realization dawning on me. "You need my dowry, don't you?"

Xiuying opened her mouth, then closed it. "Well," she said, "with war approaching, I believe the debt collectors will be otherwise occupied."

"Jie!"

My little sister ran into the chamber, clutching her beloved rag doll. She was only five years old, but already she had an intuitive sense for knowing when conflict was brewing. Living in this volatile household necessitated it.

"Rouha," I said, drying my eyes and standing. Xiuying patted her on the head and smoothed her braids.

"I told Plum to hide in the nursery," Rouha said. "I can tell Father's in a foul mood."

"Clever child," said Xiuying. "Play with your brother and stay out of the way tomorrow, all right? Jie Jie and I will be occupied."

"What are you doing?" She clung to my legs, peering at me with dread and apprehension. So she had overheard.

"The matchmaker will be paying us a visit," I said, opting for honesty. "I'm going to bring home a big dowry for all of you. Then you'll have new silks for dresses!"

"I don't want silks," Rouha said. "I hate dresses!"

Xiuying forced a laugh. "You fear dresses like the phoenix fears iron."

"And I hate the matchmaker!" Rouha's cheeks were flushed crimson—the telltale sign of an emerging tantrum.

"Shhh." Xiuying pinched her cheeks. "They're nice people. They read the stars and bring good fortune to families across Anlai."

"Good fortune," I scoffed, though I tried not to sound overly critical in front of Rouha. She too would one day speak with the matchmaker, and the same fate would fall upon her. The thought sent despair coiling in my gut. No wonder Anlai mothers tried so hard not to love their daughters. It was like exiling a piece of your own heart.

"I'm thankful to my matchmaker," Xiuying said softly, meeting my eyes over Rouha's small head, "for she brought me to you, sister."

TWO

Men build cities; women tear them down.
—ANALECTS OF ZHU YUAN, 889

XIUYING FRETTED OVER ME THE NEXT DAY, DRESSING ME IN ONE of her remaining dowry pieces that she hadn't yet sold off. It was a pale blue silk embroidered with fluttering willow trees, once beautiful but now fallen to decay. The sleeves were worn and threadbare, and the hem unraveling. Still, it was the finest piece we owned, and Xiuying was determined to leave a good impression on the matchmaker.

I was only determined to survive the day.

At noon, I climbed the rooftops to watch for the matchmaker's palanquin. Outside the walls of our complex, the streets were in an uproar over news of the impending war. Travelers poured in from outside the city gates: merchants hawking their wares, young men reporting for duty, courtesans hoping to turn a profit before all of the soldiers left for the battlefield. The crowds were rife with anticipation and excitement, the feeling of opportunity in the air. Only our household remained unaffected—the atmosphere inside our walls as still and somber as a tomb. I was signing away my future, wasn't I? Not that I had ever had much of one to begin with.

The familiar panic settled in my bones. I forced my eyes closed and released the muscles along my jaw and neck, down my spine. Uncle Zhou's instructions echoed in my head as I breathed in and out, channeling my qi, my life force. *Wood, fire, earth, metal, water*, I recited, balancing each element within my own blood and breath. It was Uncle Zhou who'd taught me qi gong and kung fu from a young age, until my ability surpassed his, surpassed that of even our local grandmaster, who knew how to keep a secret. My natural gift did not stem from my physical strength, which remained middling at best, but my mental fortitude, which martial arts had only further honed, a whetstone to steel. Without the release of qi gong, I was not certain I could've endured my mother's passing.

They say a girl with an ill-fated mother is doomed to follow in her footsteps. For Rouha's sake, I hoped the superstitions carried no truth. My mother passed away when I was twelve, and Rouha too young to remember her. Uncle Zhou claimed it was due to her weak heart, but we all heard the other servants whisper about her madness.

A gaudy, lurid palanquin turned the corner, lurching from side to side until it stopped in front of our gate. The woman who emerged wore more expensive robes than I did. Her hair was seeded with gray, but she still bore the vigor of a woman in her prime. She brushed aside help from her palanquin bearers and hobbled through the gates on her own. Then I remembered myself. I was no longer a bystander to the outside world. She was coming for *me*.

I scrambled back inside my window and rushed down the stairs, nearly barreling into Xiuying.

"There you are! Uncle Zhou said the matchmaker's arrived."

Xiuying dragged me to the sitting room, which had been aired out in anticipation of the matchmaker's visit. Still, I could detect the rancid odor of opium in the air, impossible to entirely extricate. Father had left his mark everywhere.

"Thank you for coming all this way, Madame Shu," said Xiuying, before pouring oolong tea for the matchmaker.

Madame Shu's eyes were shrewd, calculating. "It's a busy season for weddings, and I won't waste time on small talk. Let's get to business," she said, in a brusque tone I hadn't heard many women use before. "The state of your home astounds even me. And I hear *all* the rumors. Lord Hai has a fondness for gambling, doesn't he?"

Xiuying gaped at her blunt words. Clearly, Madame Shu did not care to hold her tongue.

"Please, sit," I said, motioning toward the only sofa in the room. We'd sold most of our furniture to the debt collectors long ago. Through her eyes, I saw the barrenness of our home anew.

It wasn't always like this, I wanted to say. Father was from nobility, the eldest son of the Hai clan, and yet, in the wake of my mother's passing, his penchant for gambling and opium had sunk him far. And because he was the patriarch of our family, where he went, we all followed.

The matchmaker sat, then pointed at the folding fan hung across the wall. "Is that a likeness of your mother?"

I nodded. The fan was illustrated with an ink portrait done by a former friend of my mother's, too worn to amount to any money. We knew, because we'd tried to sell even that.

"Beautiful figure, that one," said the matchmaker, reminiscing. "Pity what happened to her." She leaned toward me. "I heard she claimed to be communing with spirits by the end of her days. Is that true?"

Xiuying interceded. "Of course not," she snapped. "No one in this household would ever invite such trouble."

"That's the sort of evil that lingers," said the matchmaker, raising a suggestive brow at the state of our house. "And your husband seems never to have recovered after her passing."

Xiuying's cheeks turned the color of a New Year lantern.

"My mother was very sick by the end," I said quietly, "but we've always obeyed the Imperial Commander in this household."

The matchmaker nodded. "Very good," she said. "Come here."

I first glanced at Xiuying, then inched closer. With little ceremony, the matchmaker took my face in her hands, pinching and prodding every part of my body from my earlobes to my breasts to the loose skin on my elbows. She tsked at my lack of curves but continued her thorough examination down to the arches of my feet. Finally, she perched on the sofa and pursed her lips. Her expression did not bode well.

"I have a man in mind." She sighed, flipping through her ledgers. "He's the best I can do for you."

Against all reason, I had hoped and prayed she would have no one for me. That all eligible men had gone off to duty or had no dowry prepared. All I'd wanted was one more year. To live.

"He's a merchant—"

Xiuying's inhalation was audible. The Hai clan might have fallen far from grace, but we were still nobility. To marry a common merchant was the ultimate act of diulian. Our whole family would lose face.

". . . which should be the least of your worries," Madame Shu continued. "What's important is that he'll pay a generous dowry for you."

"Of course," Xiuying said, recovering herself. "As the stars decree."

"Master Zhu is on the older side, but luckily for you, that means he'll have a dwindling appetite. Or so a woman can hope."

I shuddered. My vision darkened at the edges, warping the room around me.

"Will Meilin become First Wife?" Xiuying asked, her face pale with worry.

Madame Shu shook her head. "But she'll have the chance to become the mother of his firstborn. The other wives were unable to bear a son."

My voice came out hoarse. "What happened to the other wives?"

"Consumption," she answered curtly, avoiding my eyes.

"All of them?"

My skepticism was evident. Reluctantly, the matchmaker lifted her gaze from her ledgers to consider me. "You're a sharp one, aren't you?" she said. "Remember, *beauty is the wisdom of women*. You have a pretty face. Be grateful to the gods. Your mouth will be prettier if you keep it shut." Madame Shu paused, noticing her slip. "The Imperial Commander, I mean. Let his favor shine upon us."

"Surely, with her looks," Xiuying interjected, "she could secure at least a—"

Madame Shu slammed her hand down on the table. "Do you know how fortunate you are for me to even be willing to do business with your family? Your husband's name is a smear across all of Anlai. We've all heard the loan sharks are after him."

"But, this man, will he . . ." Xiuying trailed off, unable to continue. But I could hear the fear in her voice—fear that I might go the way of his former wives.

"You know how it is," the matchmaker said, her expression indefinable. "We women must make sacrifices for our families."

I understood Madame Shu's words all too well. There was no hope for our household. Father's addictions had only grown worse with age. And Rouha and Plum were still so young. I wanted them to live; I *needed* them to.

"Thank you, Madame Shu, for this honor," I said, bowing low to hide the tears in my eyes. By the time I rose, I'd regained my composure. "I look forward to meeting my betrothed."

"Very good," Madame Shu said, handing me my marriage contract. "Give this to your father. I'll see you in a week."

I smiled at the papers, the way one smiles at the gallows.

THREE

Emperor Wu, who is perhaps most renowned for establishing the imperial examination system, ushered in a new age of opportunity for the peasant class. Beginning in 825, anyone who passed into the highest rank could become a jinshi scholar, though it is worth noting that while all nobles were eligible for the test, the only peasants eligible were those with registration status within the capital city of Chuang Ning. Scholars thus attribute this legislation change as the catalyst for the ninth-century influx of migrant workers, as well as the creation of the Chuang Ning Slum Yards.

—REMEMBERING THE WU DYNASTY, 913

I WAS TOO ANXIOUS TO SIT STILL AFTER THE MATCHMAKER LEFT. I knew there was much preparation to be done prior to the wedding, but I needed to ascertain one thing first.

I needed to know if my future husband was a murderer. Xiuying would never agree to let me see him. It was bad luck, not to mention dangerous. But the feeling of a noose around my throat was tightening, and I felt I had to get out of the house. So I waited until Rouha distracted Xiuying with another tantrum, then escaped through my bedroom window.

I knew the approximate location of Master Zhu's house from skimming the matchmaker's ledgers, but to reach Wenxi District without trouble, I could not simply waltz down the street. Women were urged against traveling alone, and noblewomen were forbidden from it. But with my kung fu ability, I had other choices afforded to me. Jumping from rooftop to rooftop, I kept out of sight, crouching low whenever a passing pedestrian thought to glance toward the sky. The day was lovely: pigeons roosting on low-hanging eaves, festive red lanterns swaying above the streets. The New Year Festival had passed a few weeks earlier, and Xiuying had diverted Father long enough to let me take Rouha and Plum out to see the dragon dances. Plum had even tried to jump into the ring and play with them.

Outside Master Zhu's gates, I took shelter in the rooftop garden above a blacksmith's workshop. The streets in Wenxi District were cramped and narrow, with establishments squeezed together to utilize every inch of available space. Across the street, soldiers in uniform poured out of a gambling salon, drunken and laughing as if they hadn't a care in the world.

Master Zhu had high, painted residential gates to mark his wealth and status. Still, from this vantage point, I had a clear view of his courtyard below. Servants bustled through the open-air gallery, but I saw no sign of my betrothed. Hours passed and still he did not appear. Xiuying would be getting worried, I knew. She would assume I was practicing kung fu as I often did in the woods behind our residence, and send Uncle Zhou to look for me. But he would not find me there.

It was time to admit defeat and head home. I straightened from my crouch and stretched. That was when I heard the scream.

A serving girl was thrown out into the courtyard, her porcelain dish shattering against the stones. Seconds later, a barrel-chested man with long graying hair strode out of the hallway, straight toward the serving girl. At first, I thought he was offering her a hand, but then as she shot to her feet I understood she was trying to escape him. She was too slow. He grabbed her by the throat and shoved her against the wall. Then he struck her.

Involuntarily, my hand leapt to my own cheek. I could still feel the bruise where Father had struck me the day before. Even under multiple layers of ground pearl powder, the purple-green mark remained visible against my skin.

Master Zhu—and it must be Master Zhu, for only the patriarch of this house would dare cause such a public commotion—said something to the serving girl. She shuddered, and I wondered at his words. Then he released her, shook his head with disdain, and walked away, lifting the hem of his robe over the shattered remains of porcelain.

The girl was left alone in the courtyard, gulping down mouthfuls of air as she sobbed. Was that what I looked like, I wondered, when I thought I was all alone? How pitiful.

That was going to be me. I would flee Father only to fall under another master. And even if I were to bear him a healthy son and earn my status in this household, even if Master Zhu were to pass away, that son would one day grow up to become a man, and then he too would command me. He would dictate what I ate and where I slept, my comings and goings, my every word, perhaps even my thoughts. And I would be under the whim of men for the rest of my days.

No wonder my mother had chosen to give up on this world.

I sank to my knees, trying to swallow away the choked feeling in my throat. It would be easy, I thought. I could jump off this roof right now. I could take a running start, pretend I was about to fly. Perhaps that was what my mother had told herself, in her final moments before she'd drowned. Perhaps she had convinced herself she could breathe underwater. Perhaps she had wanted to see how far she could swim. Or perhaps she had simply yearned to be free.

It was selfish, undeniably. But generosity did not belong to slaves.

I rose to my feet. The gentle spring wind caressed my robes, toying with my billowing sleeves, my long hair. I could feel a wealth of qi flowing through me, my vital energy unencumbered and raw. I could do it; I could take flight. I could be free too.

But then I remembered Xiuying. And then Rouha and Plum. And I thought, *not them too*. They who were too young to remember Ma's passing. It would destroy them, as it had destroyed me.

I exhaled, deciding to head back. Xiuying was right; sometimes it was simply better not to know the truth of things.

And then I heard the second scream of the night.

This one was much louder, followed by many others. People shouted warnings; the crowd thinned like bats fleeing light. From my high vantage point, I spotted the source of the commotion. At the crest of the hill, an unhitched wagon was tumbling down the street, gaining momentum with every passing second. Shopkeepers flung their wares out of the way. Orphan children dove off the road; pigeons squawked and took flight. But at the far end of the street, I saw an old man who had tripped on the cobblestones. His cane had rolled down the slope, out of reach.

"Someone help!" screamed a gray-haired woman. She looked to be his age, more able than he, but too slow to assist him.

Burning qi coursed through my veins. I skidded toward the edge of the roof and dropped, not quite knowing what I would do. Just then, a young man in soldier's garb ran out onto the street to help the old man. How would he make it in time? I wondered. Baichi fool!

Heart hammering in indecision, I spotted the tall iron pole resting against the blacksmith's anvil. I knocked it from its post, then grabbed it before it struck the ground. I swore; the pole was much heavier than it looked. Focusing my qi, I gritted my teeth and lifted it in the air. I could not miss. The wagon was barreling down the street—it would thunder past me in a second. I could not strike too early, nor too late.

My eyes narrowed, my vision tunneling as I rammed the iron pole into the wagon's back wheel, aiming for the gap between the spokes. My aim was true. The pole slid through the spokes. Then the momentum jolted me forward, despite my firm stance. I flew into the street, smacking my head against the stone.

But unmistakably, the wagon had stopped. I raised my head, dazed, and saw the wagon lying on its side before me, as if it had only fallen asleep. Behind it, a few feet away, the young soldier stood in the middle of the road, his eyes wide. His gaze met mine; his astonishment only grew.

"You should be ashamed of yourself!" someone exclaimed. I turned around.

A bearded man was running down the hill, wailing. Bystanders shouted at him for leaving his wagon unattended. Some even picked up the squashed fruit from the road and lobbed it at his back. The wagon driver swore back at them—until he spotted the pale young soldier, who was now helping the old grandpa cross the street. His expression contorted and he fell on his knees before the young man, imploring him for leniency.

"Honorable Master Liu! May the spirits shine favor—"

"Remember the decree!" someone from the street hissed. The driver clapped his hands over his mouth as he kowtowed before the young master. The Imperial Commander's decree had only been passed a month ago, and most were still adjusting to the new norms. Under the mandate, all spirit worship was considered seditious. Even giving ritual offerings to your ancestors, much less invoking the old spirits and calling upon black magic, was considered illegal. The Anlai warlord had declared that as the Imperial Commander, he possessed the heavens' mandate, and therefore, the only religion allowed was worship of him.

"Please show mercy toward this poor beggar," the wagon driver continued, panicking now.

Master Liu held up a hand to silence him. I saw now that his clothing was finer than mine, finer even than what Father once wore. His long hair was pinned up with a ji headpiece made of ivory and pearl, and his left hand was adorned with a sparkling emerald ring. That ring probably could've fed my entire household for a year.

Whom had I just saved? And why were the commoners calling him Master Liu? With jewels like that, he must be at least a lord.

"I will report this incident to the magistrate," Master Liu was saying. "He will ensure justice is dealt."

The wagon driver began to wail in earnest, tearfully explaining that his only son was going off to war. Master Liu replied that for his own sake, he hoped the son was more mindful than the father. As the imperial guards arrived on the scene, I took my cue to leave.

FOUR

And in the void left in the wake of the Great Collapse, the Virtuous General Li Zhuo had no choice but to assume power, for he could not allow the duplicitous Ximing to rule.

—REMEMBERING THE WU DYNASTY, 913

I SLIPPED BETWEEN THE BLACKSMITH'S SHOP AND THE NEXT-DOOR gambling salon, hoping to find roof access at the end of the alleyway. I could smell the opium emanating from the gambling salon, thick and syrupy in the air. They would gamble away their coin, and then their lives, I thought, my lip curling. And the women would be left to pick up the pieces.

Without warning, the back door crashed open as two men fell out into the alleyway. I froze, standing not two paces from them. One man slumped to his knees and retched on the cobblestones, as the other watched with ennui and continued smoking his pipe. Then he spotted me.

"Pretty lady," he said, approaching. "What is your price for the night?"

"I am no courtesan," I replied, affecting disdain. I turned to flee back to the main road, but he seized me by the shoulder, then wrapped his other arm around me. I went stock-still.

"Would you begrudge a soldier his last night of freedom?" he asked me, his voice overloud and slurred. "We're forced to report for duty tomorrow. Don't you feel sorry for us?"

"It's the heavens' mandate," I choked out, trying to force myself into some semblance of calm.

"Then this is *your* duty to Anlai, my lady."

The other one stood now, wiping puke from his chin. "Dark-skinned," he commented, as if I couldn't hear him, "but pretty."

The one holding me pulled me closer against his chest. Then he whispered in my ear, "We'll be generous tonight."

I wanted to vomit.

"Get your hands off her," someone said at the end of the alley.

They turned to look at the newcomer. In their moment of distraction, I rammed my elbow into the man's stomach and felt his knees buckle behind me. Then I kicked him in the shins so that he released me, losing his balance and toppling onto the ground. I whirled around and took several steps back before he glared at me and leapt to his feet.

"I'll make you pay for that," he snarled, charging forward.

I anchored my qi, ducked, then used his own momentum to flip him over my head. I heard his body hit the ground with a resounding thwack, followed by a low moan.

The nauseated boy didn't put up much of a fight. He staggered away, gaping at me as if I had the face of the White Bone Spirit.

"Are you all right?" Someone cupped my elbow and I flinched, whirling around. It was Master Liu; he'd followed me into the alley. I nodded wordlessly, avoiding his probing gaze. I wondered if I was supposed to bow or get on my knees before him. Most nobles memorized the rank and status of each house so that they would know the proper decorum in every situation. But Father had not brought us to the palace in years. He had not been invited to the palace in years.

"Give me your names," Master Liu told the two soldiers. "If you do not report for duty tomorrow, I will remember."

As he spoke with them, I wondered if I could try running again. My robes were soiled and my carefully pinned hair loose on my shoulders. Xiuying would be so angry when I returned.

Something warm trickled down my brow. I touched my forehead. Blood. I hadn't even felt the injury with the excess qi coursing through my veins.

"Lady, I was looking for you."

I raised my head. The two soldiers had left. Master Liu stood before me, his brows drawn inward in consternation. Up close, I could tell he was only a few years my senior, perhaps nineteen or twenty. His complexion was pale, much paler than I was even with makeup, and his hair glossy and dark. He had a generous mouth and a strong, chiseled jawline, and tapered eyes like almonds. He was very handsome. He was also the warlord's seventh and youngest son, Liu Sky.

Now I fell to my knees in earnest. How could I not have recognized him—when I had seen him at the palace before? And what was he doing on the streets of Wenxi District, on the eve of war? Shouldn't he be in the imperial palace with his father, who had just declared himself ruler not only of Anlai, our kingdom, but also of all of Tianjia?

"Apologies . . . Prince Liu. I mean, Your Highness. I did not recognize you in the commotion—"

"Rise," he said, offering me a hand. There was a hint of a smile on his lips. "You'll ruin my disguise."

"You go by . . . Master Liu here?"

"To survey the city," he explained. "And learn the discrepancies between the official reports and the lived experiences of my people."

I nodded, not understanding but unwilling to pry. A woman's role was to be incurious. I recalled the old saying Father liked to use: *When a woman asks, smile but do not answer.*

"You're bleeding." He raised his hand at me and I flinched without thinking. Then his gaze darkened. "I won't hurt you," he said, in a different voice.

I nodded but did not lift my eyes from the ground. From his pocket, he withdrew a silk handkerchief and pressed it to my forehead. His touch was surprisingly gentle. This close, he smelled like sandalwood. Sandalwood and roses. I probably smelled like opium.

"What is your name?"

I looked up at him, frightened. "Why? Will you report me too?"

He laughed. His eyes crinkled into crescent moons, lending him a boylike appearance. "You saved my life, and several others. May I not know the name of the one to whom I owe a life debt?"

"You owe me nothing," I murmured.

"How can I repay you?" he insisted.

I opened my mouth, then closed it. There were many things I wanted. I wanted Xiuying to not be angry with me when I returned. I wanted Father to stop smoking opium and wake up. I wanted Plum to be able to attend school. I wanted Master Zhu to change his mind. I wanted not to marry. I wanted not to be a woman.

And Prince Liu could do nothing about that.

I bowed again, unwilling to look up into his bright, luminous eyes. "I am grateful to you for saving me from those soldiers."

"It seems like you had the situation handled yourself." An undercurrent of laughter ran through his voice. Was he mocking me? "If only my men riding out to war tomorrow could be half as fast and clever as you."

I blushed.

"And half as lovely."

My gaze flickered to his. He was staring at me, his eyes intent. We were still in a dark alleyway, alone and unchaperoned. I glanced at our surroundings and he seemed to remember himself.

"Let me escort you home at least," he said. "It's dangerous for a woman to be out alone at night. What were you doing here, anyway?"

Heat rushed to my face. "Are you also going off to war, then?" I said, hoping to divert his attention.

He took the bait. "Yes, but it is no burden for me." Perhaps we were both thinking of those two soldiers from the gambling salon.

"Why not?" Belatedly, I recalled I was not supposed to ask questions.

But he did not seem to mind. "In some ways, I've been preparing for war all my life. I always knew this moment would come." His expression darkened. "I was four when the Wu Dynasty fell. I still remember the warning gongs when the Chuang Ning walls were first breached."

The Wu Dynasty was the former empire that had united Tianjia. Now, the Three Kingdoms lived separate, each ruled by a different warlord who had assumed power in the void left by the fallen emperor. I was only an infant at the time of the Great Collapse, too young to remember anything more than stories of that time—stories of terror and unimaginable violence.

"For fifteen years, the Three Kingdoms have never been tied together by more than an uneasy truce." Prince Liu's voice turned hostile. "Ximing is a worm among birds, thinking it can grow wings and fly. Despite having no army and no gold in their coffers, they clamor for war. And Leyuan . . . Leyuan is run by fools."

My heart pounded as he spoke. The world of men had always felt like a locked door to me. Father was not interested in politics, and the little he did know, he would never share with his daughter. *A happy woman is one who does not involve herself in the affairs of men*. I was meant to trust my master in all matters, and not seek to understand the world beyond my immediate household.

But apparently, Prince Liu felt no such qualms. Perhaps they did things differently in the Forbidden City, the imperial palace at the heart of Chuang Ning. Or perhaps as the seventh son of the warlord of Anlai, he could disregard rules that no one else dared break.

Prince Liu stopped in front of a snow-white stallion, so tall my head barely reached the horse's torso. A light brown streak ran down his forehead, and his huge eyes were dark and intelligent. "Can you ride?" he asked, as he adjusted the bridle.

"Of course," I said, before hesitating. "I-I mean, yes."

"I should have expected no less, from a master of kung fu. Who trained you?"

"Uncle—I mean, a household servant." At his look of skepticism, I added, "His brother is a grandmaster of martial arts."

He seemed to find this more reasonable. "Even my best men would be hard-pressed to match an ability like yours," he said, as he helped me onto his horse. Moments later, I felt him swing up behind me, startling me stiff. But of course. I couldn't have expected him to lend me his steed and let me ride off alone. But now he would know where I lived.

"Where to?"

I exhaled, dread closing in. "Willow District. At the . . . Hai residence."

"Hai?" he repeated. I could not see his expression, but I could hear the surprise in his voice. "You belong to the Hai clan?"

I nodded, shifting in my seat. I was unused to his proximity, to his unmistakable *maleness*. Apart from Uncle Zhou, I had little experience with men. Here was one now, not a hand's breadth apart from me, his chest strong and warm, his thighs braced around my own, the scent of his skin like heady sandalwood and late-summer air. I could feel his curious gaze on me, but I could not meet it, instead staring down at my own threadbare dress.

"What is your name?"

My throat was tight; I did not know why. "Hai Meilin."

"Hai Meilin," he repeated, enunciating the vowels carefully. And now I knew why I wanted to cry. Because in a fortnight, that name would no longer be mine. I would belong to the Zhu clan instead. I would belong to Master Zhu.

His horse was so tall and steady I could barely feel the potholes in the street. "I hope to see you again one day, Lady Hai. Perhaps when this war is over."

He was so bold with his words, I thought. I could not say yes, for I would be a married woman when he returned. But I could not say no, for that would be an offense against a prince.

So instead, I asked, "When do you think the war will be over, Your Highness?"

"If only I knew," he said with a laugh. "But I don't believe it will last long."

I felt his arms tense around me. "There is much posturing at the start of war," he continued. "Who has the most men? Whose army is the best equipped? From there, it's simple calculations. The warlord with the best hand or the greatest bluff can propose a treaty in his favor. And then the others will follow suit, depending on the hand they've been dealt. Then we'll end up back where we started. Another truce. More tiresome dinner parties. The Three Kingdoms unchanged."

"So you don't believe in the Imperial Commander's mission, then?" I asked. "To unify Tianjia, I mean."

There was a beat of silence, and I wondered if I'd misspoken. But I felt him shrug behind me. "Once Ximing's warlord declared reunification, the other warlords were forced to follow suit, or risk looking like cowards."

"Ximing was the one who first declared war?" I asked, astonished.

I felt him nod. "They claimed the terms of the Three Kingdoms Treaty were unfair. But they were responsible for the last war, and they lost. My father had to make an example out of them. They had to be punished—for the sake of justice." He paused. When he spoke again, his voice was changed, no longer ruminative. "Regardless, I don't believe there will be another emperor over all of Tianjia again. Look at us. We're so different now. We could never be unified again."

"I've never met anyone from Ximing or Leyuan," I said honestly. "Not even the ambassadors." For they stayed in the Forbidden City.

"You're not missing out on much, I'll tell you that," he said. "Anlai is the most beautiful place in the world." I could hear the smile in his voice. "With the most beautiful women."

Was he ... flirting with me? I had no idea how to banter like this, to trade flattering words as light as feather fans and silk sashes. Uncle Zhou had taught me kung fu and Xiuying had taught me herbal remedies, but no one had schooled me in the world of court, of pretty compliments and easy smiles. My mouth dry, I did not respond.

"I've made you uncomfortable. I apologize."

"I-I'm not used to meeting princes." I cringed; I sounded like a country bumpkin.

"That's all right," he said, pulling the reins as we neared a crowd. "That means I have less competition."

Back-to-back palanquins blocked off the main thoroughfare that led out of Wenxi District. Another reason I preferred the rooftops: no traffic. Prince Liu hissed with annoyance but could do nothing to pass, save reveal his royal identity.

"Please!" a woman cried from beyond the crowd. I saw then why we were stopped: imperial guards had surrounded Magician's Square, where common street illusionists showed off for tourists, and silver-tongued fortune-tellers told the gullible what they wanted to hear.

"We've done nothing wrong!" the woman screamed. "Help us—they'll feed us to the dogs, or worse—"

She broke off with a gasp. Through a gap in the crowd, I caught sight of the sobbing woman, struggling against a guard as he dragged her into a cart, loaded with other pseudo-spirit mediums in their characteristic bright garb. All of them were blindfolded, gagged, and bound, unable to move, speak, or even see. Motionless, they looked like puppets without their strings, inanimate.

The sight turned me cold.

"By order of the Imperial Commander," the soldier announced, "we are removing all spirit mediums to protect the state from the evils of black magic."

"If Auntie Tien has 'black magic,' I have a tail," a commoner within earshot muttered. "Have any of her fortunes ever come true?"

"When she predicts sunshine, I bring an umbrella," his friend replied.

I glanced back at Prince Liu, who was watching the public display with an inscrutable expression.

"They're not—they're not going to execute the spirit mediums... right?" I whispered.

Prince Liu shook his head, then turned his horse and left, taking the long route around Magician's Square, through the Slum Yards. Neither of us spoke after that. I was thinking of the woman's panic as she struggled against her captor. But what frightened me most were the other fortune-tellers and their silent acceptance: sitting bound and blinded, awaiting their fate.

Was that how I was to be carted off to Master Zhu's?

And why this sudden attention on spirit mediums? Although spirits were often blamed for poor weather or bad luck, most in

Anlai did not actually believe in their existence. They were considered children's bogey tales, ghost stories.

While much of the history of black magic had been erased, somehow, my mother had known what others did not. She had told me that Emperor Wu banned the practice of black magic at the founding of the Wu Dynasty a century ago, because he blamed spirit mediums for the rampant chaos of the Warring States Period, which preceded his reign. During the Warring States Period, my mother said, there were dragons and birds of fire roaming the earth, as plain to the eye as the imperial gates rising above us.

But those stories were mostly lost now. And what my mother told me—I never could quite believe.

Toward the end of her life, my mother had begun to say things. Things that did not follow reason. Things that, if the Imperial Commander had caught wind of them, would have ensured she was not alive, one way or another.

"Why?" I asked the prince, when I could bear the silence no longer. "They have no real power. They're just trying to make a few coins."

I felt Prince Liu adjust his hold on the reins. "In truth, I agree with you."

I waited. When nothing followed: "Then . . . ?"

With some reluctance: "You see, on the eve of war, my father was visited by an old seer from the south. Part of the Ruan minority group." His voice took on a scornful edge. "The seer told my father a spirit would spell his demise, and the demise of Anlai itself."

I inhaled sharply.

"Father ignored the threat, of course. He had the seer punished, and I thought that was that. But later, he had a certain room in the imperial treasury checked, for the first time in decades. And that was when he discovered"—Prince Liu hesitated, shifting behind me—"a certain jade seal stolen."

"A jade seal?" My brows crinkled.

"Never mind," said Prince Liu, shaking his head as if to clear it. "You're very easy to talk to, Lady Hai. I forget myself with you."

"I—apologize, Your Highness."

"No," he said. "It is I who must apologize, for filling your ears with such nonsense."

"Nothing you say is nonsense to me," I said earnestly, twisting in the saddle, before coloring at the way his eyes took me in. He smiled crookedly, his hand brushing my own, before reining his horse at the end of my street. I hadn't realized we were back in Willow District.

From where we'd stopped, I could see the gates to my home a little way away. He clearly did not know which one it was. That was good, I thought. Perhaps he hadn't heard the rumors, then. I would die of mortification if he met Father in his current state.

I moved to dismount but he beat me to it, dismounting first, then offering me his arm. Just then, the gates opened. "Meilin!"

Xiuying and Uncle Zhou hurried outside. Xiuying was dressed in her gardening clothes, her skirt soiled and patched, and Uncle Zhou wore a motley assortment of jackets piled on top of one another, for he felt chills at night. I flushed, seeing our humble household through the prince's eyes. Xiuying staggered to a halt upon noticing Prince Liu. She most likely did not recognize him but could tell he was from wealth.

Uncle Zhou did. "Your Highness." He bowed. Xiuying followed with an elegant bow of her own.

"Thank you for returning Meilin to us," said Xiuying. "We were so worried."

"It was my honor," he said, smiling kindly at me. "I hope—"

Through the open gates, a pig ran out onto the street, dodging both Xiuying and Uncle Zhou. Prince Liu lunged for it—and got a kick in the leg in return. I muffled a laugh while Xiuying cried out, apologizing profusely. Laughing, the prince limped after the pig and finally seized it, returning the resigned creature to Uncle Zhou. The pig was fat and near adult age. I had no idea where it had come from.

"Apologies, Your Highness," Xiuying said, breathless but smiling. "We're not accustomed to livestock in our house. Meilin's dowry began arriving today, you see."

Dowry. I saw the word sink into him. Prince Liu's expression changed from surprise to disappointment to polite indifference. He turned to me and bowed once more, stiffly this time.

"Apologies for my forwardness, Lady Hai. Congratulations on your upcoming nuptials." His voice was cool and impassive. "I shall take my leave."

We all bowed, not daring to lift our heads until he was on his horse and down the street. Then Xiuying turned to me, her cheeks flushed. "What was that about?"

"He was impressed by my kung fu abilities," I hedged.

She shot me an incredulous look as Uncle Zhou chuckled. "How can you get into so much trouble in one day?" Xiuying complained. I prepared myself for a scolding, but instead, she grabbed me, wrapping me in a tight embrace.

"Oh, Meilin," she said, burying her head in my shoulder. "How I will miss you when you're gone."

FIVE

The Tian word for slave *is made of two characters: girl and hand. For the girl is the slave, and the hand is the means with which she serves.*

—BOOK OF RITES, 829

THAT NIGHT, I COULDN'T SLEEP. PRINCE LIU'S WORDS WHIRLED IN my head like a haixiao wave gathering power. *If only my men riding out to war tomorrow could be half as fast and clever as you.*

In the privacy of my chamber, I could admit it. Yes, I was fast. I was clever too. Not with words, surely, but in other ways. I had managed to stop that moving wagon with only an iron pole at hand. I could best Uncle Zhou in hand-to-hand combat by the time I turned thirteen. Though I had never touched a sword, I was skilled with the staff.

Outside of fighting, I knew how to scavenge for food and how to fashion a tourniquet. Xiuying had grown up in southern Anlai, the daughter of an herbalist in a rural farming village. She had taught me how to counteract poisons and brew herbal remedies against pain.

If those soldiers I had met outside the gambling salon were any indication of what I'd be facing, I could take them on.

In the darkness, the possibilities took hold of me. Sweat trickled down my back at the insanity of my own idea. Could I really go through with it? Could I leave this life behind, and everything I had ever known? In the looking glass, I saw my nightgown loose around my thin frame. The matchmaker had frowned at my lack of curves. But in a different life, perhaps they could become my means of escape.

Quietly, so as not to wake Rouha and Plum next door, I stripped my sheets from the bed and laid them next to the window. The moon was waning, and little light filtered in through the lattice window. No matter. Using the knife I hid beneath my bed, I cut long, uniform strips of linen.

By the time I was done, dawn was breaking. I had little time if I was to go through with my plan. In the dark of the night, the idea had felt surreal, like a dream. Like the consequences of my actions would not fall on my own shoulders. But with the light of day, the weight of what I was about to do struck me anew. I hurried to Xiuying's room with equal parts fear and exhilaration in my heart. When I entered her chambers, she was bleary-eyed but awake.

"You're here," I said, relieved. "I was afraid you'd be in Father's bedchamber."

"Oh, he hasn't called for me in months," Xiuying said with a yawn. "The opium tires him. Why? What's wrong?"

Hesitantly, I moved closer to the window, so that she could see me in the light of dawn. Her mouth fell open.

"Meilin!"

"Shh," I said. "You'll wake the children."

"You can't be serious."

"I am," I said. "I must go." She could see in my face that I wasn't bluffing.

Xiuying rose and rubbed her eyes. "But why? You've seen the dowry, Meilin. Master Zhu is wealthy. You won't go hungry anymore."

I had wanted to spare her, but... "I saw him beat a serving girl," I said, not wishing to go into detail. "He's just like Father. And I... I can't live like this anymore. I can't. I can't become what my mother—" I broke off, suddenly out of breath.

Xiuying's face changed, taking on a fierce, protective cast. I knew then that she was on my side.

"You are not your mother, Meilin. You do not have her madness."

"I know."

She worried her lip. "If you're caught, they'll believe you're a man. Enter *any* village and they'll impress you! Uncle Zhou told me they send deserters to the front lines."

I shook my head. "They won't need to impress me. I'm going to enlist."

She gaped at me.

"You know it's safer this way."

"Safer?" she repeated, her temper rising.

"If I'm a man, then I must enlist—or risk impressment. And if I'm a woman..."

Her eyes flashed with grim understanding. If I was caught as a woman, death would be preferable. "Yes, all right," she said. "But, Meilin, the dangers—"

"I won't get caught," I interrupted, trying to sound more confident than I felt. "Besides, Prince Liu said the war will be over in the blink of an eye."

My words only further agitated her. "Even if you survive the war, do you think they'll let you live?" Xiuying hissed. "They would never let a woman get away with something like this."

I tried to take her hand, but she drew away from me. "Something like what?"

She swallowed hard. "They would never let a woman hold on to power."

I shook my head at her. "Sister, I know all these things. My ambitions are small. I only wish to have a little more time. A few months, maybe more. Then I will be satisfied."

I had wished to spare her, but now she understood. Her eyes welled with tears. "You would rather death out there in the wild, than death here, enslaved."

I nodded.

"And I will never see you again."

She didn't let me answer her with false promises. Instead, she embraced me without restraint, something she almost never allowed herself to do. Muffling her sobs so that she wouldn't wake the household, she cried into my hair, then rubbed my back. I was unsure who was comforting whom.

Outside the window, song thrushes were waking and trilling their morning greetings. I was running out of time.

"I'm going to enlist in Father's place," I told her.

Xiuying disentangled herself from me. "No. I already told the Imperial Commander's messengers he's ill." Her voice still sounded congested, but she was alert now. "You can go as his son."

"But there's no record in the annals—"

"A bastard son," Xiuying clarified. I absorbed this idea, then nodded; Xiuying's ideas were usually better than my own.

She left the room, returning a few minutes later with supplies for me. "Wear these instead," she said. "They'll fit you better."

I'd been wearing Uncle Zhou's old clothes, but she'd handed me a new set of tunic and breeches. "Where did you get these?"

"I'd been saving them for Plum," Xiuying answered, businesslike. "I'll rewrap your bindings. You did a good job, but you'll need to make sure the bandages don't peek through your neckline. And I'll tie your hair up. I do your father's hair quite nicely, don't I?"

The weight on my chest began to lighten. "Sister," I said. "I . . . thank you."

"There's something else," Xiuying said abruptly, and by the way she spoke, I could tell she already regretted what she was about to say. "I don't know if I should be giving this to you, but it's your choice to make. It's your choice what you do with it."

"Do with what?"

With trembling hands, Xiuying withdrew a delicate necklace from her pocket. The cord was simple, nearly invisible in the dim light, but the pendant was not. The jade was unlike anything I had ever seen. Emerald green, dark, light, it seemed to change color every second, flickering like sunlight upon water. Engraved in the base of the stone, in tiny lettering no larger than a single grain of rice, were two characters: 青龍. *Qinglong*. Azure Dragon.

As if drawn by a magnetic force, I reached out to touch it, my fingers closing around the necklace before I realized what I was doing. *It is greed*, I realized. I was covetous for it.

"Your mother gave it to Uncle Zhou before she passed," Xiuying explained. "She wasn't in her right mind at the time. You know how she was . . . different then."

Xiuying had never met my mother, but she had heard the stories. How my mother had once claimed to hear voices. How she had told my father that a powerful spirit lived in her ear. How in her final days, no one could enter her rooms. No one but me.

One serving girl had tried. Against instruction, she had tried to bring my mother tea and mung bean cakes. I was not present when it happened, but I'd seen the girl in the aftermath: collapsed on the ground, writhing like a snake in heat, her eyes white, her words nonsensical.

After that, no one else dared enter my mother's rooms.

When my mother passed, we locked the door to her chamber. When the debt collectors came, we dismissed the remaining servants. Gradually, the memories became stories, stories like fiction. We moved on. We forgot. But still, there were times when I passed my mother's locked door and felt the glittering dark of the space beyond, the weight of that air. Like an inhaled breath, *waiting*.

"Your mother gave Uncle Zhou strange instructions." Xiuying swallowed, her expression pained; yet she was determined to go on. "She told him, '*Give this to Meilin when she is ready to die.*'"

Despite myself, I shivered.

"That's why we didn't want to give it to you," Xiuying hurried on. "But it's presumptuous of me to make the decision for you. It should be your choice what you do with it. Throw it into the sea for all I care. Or sell it in the market. By the quality of the jade, it could be worth several taels of gold."

Xiuying wasn't remotely superstitious. Most in Anlai were like her, believing that dragons and other spirits were nothing more than tall tales, meant to scare children into behaving. As for me, I did not know what to believe, but I'd known my mother; I'd seen how far she'd fallen into madness. I'd seen the way she'd convulsed with fear at the sight of the lily pond in our garden, which was barely deep enough to swim in. The way she'd refused drink in her last hours, though her lips cracked and her voice thinned to a sliver of a whisper. And then—how they'd found her drowned body in the Wen River, so bloated and decayed she'd become unrecognizable. Uncle Zhou had not let me look at her, but I'd seen the funeral shroud slip off one bare foot before the burial, revealing a swollen, rotted blue.

We never did find out why she'd gone for a swim.

Now my hand tightened around the necklace. The wise choice,

undeniably, was to listen to Xiuying and throw it into the sea. And yet, looking at its flickering, iridescent beauty, its subtle sweet fragrance like my mother's, I knew I would not—*I could not*—give it up.

Instead, I tied it around my neck, tucking it beneath my bindings so that the pendant hung between my breasts. I could feel its strange sentient warmth thrumming against my sternum, its gentle pulse as rhythmic as the lapping of tides. In the dark, I imagined it was my mother's heartbeat.

Xiuying had turned her face away from me. She busied herself with my hair, tying it into a topknot high on my head, then securing it with a wooden ji pin. "I'll tell your father that you've left for Master Zhu's house early because of the war. I doubt he'll even notice your absence. He's sated with the fats of your dowry and hiding from the warlord's messengers as it is. I have a feeling he won't leave the house until the war is over."

Xiuying's tone was casual, but I could hear the hard edge to her words. She was trying to be strong, for my sake. If things were to go wrong, she would bear the brunt of the aftermath at home.

She patted my shoulders and turned me toward the looking glass. "There," she said. "That's you."

Under Plum's tunic, my body was transformed. I was short for a boy—no disguise could change that—but my dark complexion and slender frame helped me. I smiled.

"It's a good thing we spent all that time in the sun, foraging for roots," Xiuying said jokingly. I could tell she was holding back tears. "Be careful, Meilin. Even if you don't value your own life, know that I do."

I turned toward her. We had little time before the sun rose, before I had to report for duty. There were so many things I wanted to tell her, so many feelings I wished to convey.

But I had never been good with words. I squeezed her hands with my own. "I'm sorry for leaving you alone with him," I said quietly.

Xiuying's eyes were full. "I'm sorry for letting you take his place."

We embraced once more, both of us reluctant to draw away. "Go," Xiuying finally said. "Before your father wakes."

I lifted the traveling bag she'd assembled for me. She'd only had a few minutes to prepare, and yet she'd packed it brimful with supplies. It dawned on me that I would no longer have her steady optimism and wits to rely on. Out there I would truly be on my own.

In the hallway, I opened the door to Rouha and Plum's room, peering inside. Their small figures were peaceful under the pale beams of early sunlight. As I looked in, Rouha muttered to herself and shifted in her sleep. Plum had his fist in his mouth, his hair mussed over his forehead.

I smiled at their sleeping figures, then closed the door softly. *I should go*, I told myself. But following a different impulse, I glanced down the hallway instead. My feet drifted toward the final door at the end of the corridor, shrouded in a thick layer of dust.

Perhaps it was the knowledge that this was goodbye. Or perhaps it was the insanity of the night. I did what I had not done in almost six years: I reached for the handle.

"*You called for me.*" A strange, lilting voice broke through the gloom, at once familiar and foreign. "*I heard your call.*"

I could feel the weight of the air beyond the keyhole: heavy, suffocating, like the sky before a lightning storm. One step, and I could drink from that well, feel its shimmering heat upon my skin...

"Meilin!"

Xiuying's voice broke through my trance. What was I thinking?

I bit my tongue and fled for the stairs. It was a strange lucid dream, brought about by the stress of goodbye. Nothing more.

"Coming!" I called, hurrying to the gate to find Xiuying waiting with Father's draft letter.

"Take this." She thrust the scroll toward me. "You're his bastard son, yes?"

I nodded.

"Trust no one with your secret," she said. "Men are wolves, remember this."

I nodded again.

"Try to keep quiet. The nail that sticks out gets hammered down, remember."

"Xiuying—"

"Go!"

She pushed me out the door and slammed it shut. But before it closed, I heard her muffled sob.

SIX

Find a man of strength and one will win a battle.
But find a man of honor and one will win a war.

—BOOK OF ODES, 856

THE ARMY CAMP WAS CHAOS. HORSES UNTETHERED AND ROAMING about, tents half-erected—some caught in the spring wind, floating away like billowing kites. Men everywhere. Laughing, sleeping, eating, fighting. More men than I had ever seen in my life.

Registration was over in a flash. All my prepared lies went unused; the army official barely even bothered to look me in the face. He documented my information with a few chicken scratches, then handed me an identity tag made of rough-hewn wood. "Seventh Company, Third Platoon. Your lieutenant will decide your squad at the end of the training period."

I cleared my throat. "Could you place me in a platoon not based in Chuang Ning?" I asked, knowing I'd have a higher chance of being recognized in the capital city. "Anywhere else is fine—"

He didn't spare me a glance. "Next!"

I was shoved out of the way. Clutching my identity tag to my chest, I wove through the crowd, looking for Company Seven on the signs above each mess hall. I hoped I would get to see Leyuan or Ximing, somewhere I had never been before. Unlike most soldiers, who hoped to stay in Chuang Ning, where it was likely to be safest, I hoped to leave.

Seventh Company had set up camp on the outskirts of the western fields. It was quieter over here: some men napped under the shade of an oak tree; others sharpened their blades or roasted chestnuts over a fire. Their commander had clearly not yet arrived. *Our* commander.

A cook had left a pot of hot water on the table outside the mess hall. I decided to make tea, not because I was particularly thirsty but because I wanted something to do. I took out dried zhua barley roots from the outer pocket of my bag; Xiuying had truly thought of everything. I had not made it one step out of the tent when someone stopped me.

"Are those zhua roots?" The boy was absurdly tall and thin as a stork, with a pointed chin like a sparrow's. I had to crane my neck just to see his face.

"Yes," I said, my voice coming out as a squeak.

"I haven't seen zhua barley in years. Makes me homesick." Something about his voice felt very familiar. "Are you from the south too?"

Then I understood—his accent. It reminded me of Xiuying. Though Xiuying had worked hard to correct it, her southern accent still came through when she was caught off guard. I'd always liked it—it was warmer and smoother than the harsh dialects of the north.

He was waiting for my response. "No," I said, after a pause.

He peered at me. "You don't talk much, do you?"

"No."

He shrugged, unbothered. "Good for you. I talk too much. Ma says it gets me in trouble all the time. 'The tree that grows tallest in the forest . . . is the first to be toppled by winds,' you know?" Privately, I thought it an apt metaphor, considering he was probably the tallest boy in our platoon. "I'm Sparrow, by the way. What's your name?"

"Oh . . ." It took me a while. "Ren."

"Ren! So, where'd you buy them? I didn't know we could get dried herbs like that in Chuang Ning."

"I-I got the seeds from a friend," I said, trying to subtly edge toward the exit. "And grew them myself."

"Oh? Where's your friend from?" He'd fallen into step beside me.

"A small village called Huang Ju," I muttered. "You probably don't know it—"

"Huang Ju? *I'm from Huang Ju!*" Several bystanders turned to look at us in dual amusement and irritation. Xiuying's warning about not standing out echoed in my head. "I've never met anyone from my province since I moved to the capital, let alone someone from my village! Who's your friend? Is he in our platoon too? Oh, skies, my dialect is so rusty now, I hope I can still practice with him."

"Oh . . ." *How do I get myself out of this mess?* "My friend's not a soldier."

"Is he too young? Too old?"

"She's a woman."

"A woman!" He grinned at me. "A lady friend?"

I flushed down to my toes. "N-no. She's . . . married."

"How do you know her, then? What's her name? I wonder if I know her too?"

I shouldn't have said it, but in the face of his direct, pointed questions, I lost my ability to lie. "Xiuying. Her maiden name was Yu Xiuying."

"Yu Xiuying," Sparrow repeated, a dreamy look crossing his face. I seized the moment to cross the grounds toward the fire. He trailed after me like a missing tail. "I knew Xiuying all right," he said. "The prettiest, nicest, smartest girl in the village. In the whole province."

I made a noise of agreement, before realizing that gave the wrong impression. Sparrow didn't notice.

"She married into some noble family, didn't she? We all saw it coming. If anyone was going to get out of Huang Ju, it was her. It was the best marriage to ever come out of our village."

This unmoored me. I had pitied Xiuying when she first arrived, betrothed to a gambler with a growing opium addiction, about to become second wife to a low-tier noble family. But to her, in comparison to the poverty of her village, it must have seemed like a stroke of good fortune.

"Which platoon are you in?" Sparrow asked. "You're in Prince Liu's company too, right?"

"Prince Liu?" I repeated, trying not to panic. *Calm down*, I told myself. *There are seven princes. What are the chances that I'll be in the company of the one who recognizes me?* And regardless, yesterday he had seen me in a dress with pale makeup and rouge. He wouldn't recognize me like this—tan skinned and unadorned.

Sparrow had plucked my wooden tag from my jacket pocket. "Thought so. We'll be in the same platoon." He grinned. "We'll be seeing a lot of each other, then. I mean, every second of every day. Marching together, fighting together, even sleeping together. It's exciting, isn't it? I think we'll all be best friends by the end of this war. Unless we die first."

His words registered in my head, slowly, like water seeping through a fine net. The tent behind the mess hall—our dormitory. The razed field to the north—our practice grounds. The trenches farther north—latrines.

How am I ever going to get away with this?

"Attention!"

Everyone shot to their feet as our commanders arrived on horseback, dismounting before the fire pit. Others filed into order and I hastily copied them, squeezing behind Sparrow. This had the unfortunate consequence of blocking my view. I could only see three giant stallions, two white and one black.

The larger white stallion had a light brown streak running down his nose.

"At ease." It was, unmistakably, the voice of the seventh Prince Liu.

Sparrow shifted to one side and I caught a glimpse of the three of them. The seventh Prince Liu had taken off his ornate jewelry and now wore practical riding attire. The sword at his side was engraved with a flying dragon—the mark of the Anlai warlord.

Behind him was another prince, there was no doubt about it. The man's slender yet tall stature reminded me of a willow tree, graceful and elegant. He had not removed his jewelry or tied back his hair, so he looked more suited for a tea drinking ceremony than an army campsite.

"Who's the pretty one?" whispered Sparrow.

The boy next to us shushed him, but someone else replied: "The sixth prince. He's supposed to be leading a different company, though. I've heard he doesn't fight."

"I bet he doesn't," Sparrow snorted.

"They're sloppy," said the third and oldest man, who gripped the reins of a black stallion. "We'll need to change that."

"That's Lieutenant Fang," whispered Sparrow. "He's a war hero. He fought in the Great Collapse."

Sparrow was shushed yet again.

Lieutenant Fang looked to be in his late thirties, his hair already strewn with salt and pepper, his face scarred from battle. From the lieutenant's expression, I suspected that he saw himself to be the true commander of this platoon, and Prince Liu the honorary figurehead. *Power dynamics will be at play, then.*

"Our company will be stationed here until we are deployed to Ximing," said the seventh Prince Liu. "Until then, Lieutenant Fang will supervise your daily training regimen."

I watched Lieutenant Fang surreptitiously touch his right hand to the armlet on his left. The armlet was inlaid with ivory, but made of iron, which was thought to ward off evil spirits. So he was superstitious, I thought. He probably believed the rumors that corporeal spirits roamed freely in Ximing, heralded as gods by southerners.

"Ximing?" Whispers rustled through the crowd. Sparrow looked delighted; we would be traveling through his province to reach the southern kingdom. Other soldiers looked less than pleased. The freckle-faced boy beside me whispered about how the Imperial Commander must not favor his sixth and seventh sons, to send them so far from the capital, and to Ximing of all places.

"I hear in the south," the freckle-faced boy continued, "they eat their wives after they've borne children. There's a special dish for it—bitch stew."

"I heard they carve out the eyes of all captured Anlai soldiers," someone else added. "Even if the soldier's already dead—just to make sure he can't see in the afterlife."

The elder Prince Liu whispered something in his brother's ear. The seventh prince narrowed his eyes in a now-familiar expression. It was the same way he'd looked at those drunken gamblers outside the salon. I felt his gaze fall over the crowd and ducked behind Sparrow.

"I expect discipline and restraint from each of you. There will be consequences if you fail to obey. This is war," said the seventh prince, his voice low and imposing. "Life is dispensable. Honor is not."

SEVEN

Men are like wolves: drawn to fear.
—ANALECTS OF ZHU YUAN, 889

LIEUTENANT FANG SENT US TO RUN THE CAMP PERIMETER RIGHT away.

"You thought because today's our first day we'd have no training?" Fang scoffed. "Did you think Ximing would give us a welcome parade too?"

Sparrow detoured to gulp down water before taking off on the six-li run. He asked me to wait for him, which I did hesitantly, first making sure Prince Liu was nowhere in sight.

But Lieutenant Fang saw us. He marched toward Sparrow and grabbed him by the scruff of his neck, no small feat considering Sparrow was over half a foot taller. "What do you think you're doing?"

"Getting water, sir. Before the run."

"Did I say you could get water?" He threw Sparrow with so much force the boy landed on the ground. I jumped in fright.

Sparrow got to his feet wincingly. "Spirits, don't you think that's a little—"

"Don't invoke the name of evil!" Fang snarled.

Sparrow raised a brow at the rather heated reaction. Was Lieutenant Fang simply a stickler for obeying the warlord's mandate, or did he actually believe in the existence of evil spirits?

Sparrow cleared his throat. "Sorry, sir, I was just—"

"And don't talk back to me."

Sparrow bowed his head. I hastily bowed as well.

Fang shook his head. "Southern trash," he muttered, rubbing his iron armlet once again. "They raise you like animals and expect you to perform as men..."

I could see Sparrow's ears turning red. I nudged his boot before I saw, over Lieutenant Fang's shoulder, one of the untethered mares charging toward us.

"Sir—" I squeaked.

"And you," he said to me, his upper lip curling with disdain. "Do you think—"

"Sir!" The horse was only a few meters away; it would bowl him over unless he moved. Propriety be damned, I reached for him and tried to push him out of the way. I wasn't strong enough and he looked at me as if I had turned into a sea slug. Then Sparrow recognized the imminent threat and dove toward both of us, so that we all toppled to the ground.

The horse stampeded past us moments later, charging into the nearest tent and tripping over the many folds of cloth. Thankfully, there were no soldiers inside.

Lieutenant Fang swore as he disentangled himself from our mess of limbs and got to his feet. He smoothed his short beard as he surveyed the scene, trying to preserve the remnants of his dignity. I jumped to my feet and Sparrow followed moments later, pocketing something with a wicked grin on his lips. I did not know why he was smiling, but I wanted to warn him to wipe that smirk off his face. Fang looked like he needed a pummeling bag for his anger and would choose the closest target. I recognized his expression because I had seen it often on Father.

At that moment, bashful soldiers from Second Platoon came running to collect their escaped mare.

"How dare you lose control of your mount!" Fang shouted, storming toward the Second Platoon soldiers. Sparrow and I looked at each other and took our cue, darting off on our run.

"I can't stand northerners like him," said Sparrow, his pace increasing with his frustration, much to my chagrin. "They think they're so much better just because they hide in the shade all their lives." He made a low noise in his throat. "Anyway, I'll show him."

Alarmed, I stopped running. "Don't do anything to call attention to yourself!"

Sparrow winked at me, a feral look in his eyes. "I'm just returning the favor," he said slyly. His words didn't exactly reassure me.

RUNNING WAS TOLERABLE, BUT LIFTING BUCKETS BRIMFUL WITH WAter up and down the mountain was not. And we hadn't even touched a blade yet. Despite my kung fu training, I was woefully behind everyone else with regard to physical strength. It became painfully obvious that I lacked the sheer muscle the other boys possessed. And Fang remembered me. A look of irritation crossed his face every time he saw me, which wasn't often. I was taking pains to avoid his field of vision.

We were all exhausted by nightfall. I had dreaded trying to sleep with a company of male strangers, but now the thought barely alarmed me. I was just looking forward to the rest.

After a dinner of buckwheat noodles and salted pork—Fang warned us the rations would worsen once we left Chuang Ning—we headed off to our dormitory. Sparrow nabbed two bedrolls for both of us and secured me a corner spot in the tent. I was beginning to see how helpful an ally he was. Though he was clumsy and talked too much, his towering height gave him a natural advantage in training, and his cheerful demeanor earned him easy friends. Next to him, my reticence went unnoticed, since his chatter took up all available space.

"Did you hear they're giving all the squad leaders personal mounts?" someone was saying. "They'll choose those soldiers by the end of spring—the best of the best."

Sparrow had told me squad leaders were the top soldiers of every platoon, recognized for their superior skill and bestowed with status and honor. Each company had twenty squad leaders, who each led squads of ten.

"Twenty mounts for each company?" Sparrow joined their conversation with the ease of water flowing downhill. "I wonder how much that costs."

"It's war!" the boy laughed. His muscles must not have ached as bad as my own did, for him to be able to smile so. "Business does splendidly in war. I would know."

Sparrow was asking him about his family trade when the tent flap opened. Lamplight filtered inside as two tall silhouettes filled the opening. The stature of the man on the left sent me shrinking back. It was Prince Liu.

"Out." His order left no room for contradiction. "Now."

Sparrow shot me a look of bewilderment before obeying. We all filed wordlessly out of the tent.

"Line up." Out in the open field, I could see the harsh lines of his face, stern and unyielding.

In contrast, Lieutenant Fang stood beside him positively fuming. I had no idea what had happened, but I knew I wanted to be as far from that radius of anger as possible. I positioned myself at the far end of the line.

"I did not think I would have to repeat myself on this matter: we do not tolerate thieving in this army. We do not tolerate dishonesty of any kind."

Soldiers traded looks of astonishment around me.

"I'm certain it was this platoon, Your Highness," Fang said, glaring at us.

Prince Liu nodded. "Search their tent."

Only then did I notice the line of guards behind the prince. They nodded and filed into our tent, and seconds later, I heard sheets being overturned, bags opened, containers dumped upside down. I winced, thinking of my extra pair of chest bindings, and the tea leaves Xiuying had given me to prevent monthly bleedings. If asked, I could pass off the bindings as underclothes for chafing, I thought quickly, and the teas as medicinal.

"I don't understand." The boy excited about the horses spoke up. "What was stolen?"

"My armlet," Lieutenant Fang snarled. "Which was a family heirloom, passed down from the Wu Dynasty!"

"He's not even from a noble family," someone muttered.

"He probably thinks he'll need it when the phoenix spirit sets him on fire in his sleep."

One boy giggled, before someone else whispered, "Shut it! Remember the warlord's mandate."

Sparrow coughed but did not chime in, which was odd for him. I recalled the events of this morning—how Sparrow and I had knocked Fang over to avoid the charging horse. In the tangle of our limbs... had something gone missing then? I didn't dare glance in Sparrow's direction, but I did wonder. Sparrow had said he hated being bullied as a southerner. It was a chip on his shoulder, just like it was on Xiuying's.

Minutes passed. After an agonizing wait, Prince Liu's personal guards filed out. "No armlet found, sir." And no mention of any other eccentric items found either. I breathed out in relief.

Lieutenant Fang hissed in exasperation and pointed at us. "Search them! They're probably wearing it as we speak!"

A low thrum of panic filled my ears.

Prince Liu motioned the guards forward, starting at the end farthest from me. This did nothing to quell my rising hysteria. Neither did Fang's next words: "Strip! Now!"

Grumbling, the soldiers complied. Sparrow looked unconcerned, yawning. He shucked off his pants first and I blanched, looking away. But then I saw everybody else in the line, all fifty men, in various stages of undress. Only I was still standing there, gawking like a chicken about to be plucked.

I felt my mother's pendant thrumming against my chest, hot and pulsing. Or maybe that was just my own heartbeat.

"*How humiliating,*" a voice purred in my ear, "*to not last a single day in the world of men.*"

I whirled around. There was no one behind me.

Had I only imagined that strange, sinister voice? And yet it was not the first time I'd heard it. I recalled the eerie trance I'd fallen into outside my mother's locked door, as I'd sought to say my goodbyes. "*You called for me,*" the voice had said. "*I heard your call.*"

Was this it—the madness I had been waiting for all my life? Passed down from my mother to emerge moments before my inevitable death?

I dug my nails into my palms, forcing myself to focus. Almost everyone had undressed now. I was at the end of the line, but I would soon be noticed. My heart was ratcheting so loudly I thought it would burst out of my chest. If I was caught, they'd kill me.

And then I understood what I must do. Thievery was considered criminal, but it was not a capital offense. The punishment would be severe, but I wouldn't be executed. Not like I would if . . .

Fang spotted me. "You! What are you waiting for?"

The rest of the world faded away. I could hear nothing but the ringing in my ears. I took a step forward and it was a miracle I did not fall, for my knees were trembling like a newborn doe's.

"I—" My voice came out like a squeak. No one heard me above the commotion. Louder: "*I* stole your armlet."

This time, my voice rang out across the field. All motion ceased. Prince Liu raised a brow, laying eyes on me for the first time since he'd arrived.

"I knew it!" Fang rushed me, grabbing me by the shoulder as if he thought I would make a run for it. Sparrow stared at me, open-mouthed. "Where is it?" Fang demanded, relief evident in his voice. He truly missed his superstitious token, I saw. I felt pity for him in that moment. But no more pity than I felt for myself. "Hand it over."

"I-I lost it."

"What?" he squawked. "Where?"

"I don't know. During training, I think?"

"Why, you—" He grabbed me by the throat, lifting me clean off the ground. I grasped at his hands, choking.

"Stop," ordered Prince Liu. "Since the soldier has admitted to his crime, his punishment will follow protocol."

Fang released me, and I slid to the ground, sputtering.

"What is your name, soldier?" Prince Liu stood over me, his silhouette harsh against the lamplight.

"Ren," I rasped. "Hai Ren."

"Hai?" he repeated, confusion twisting his features.

Fang stepped between us before he could continue. For once I was glad of his interruption. "You know the rules," Fang told me. "I hope you enjoy a good flogging."

He looked like he was about to relish the experience. Sparrow noticed this too.

"Sir!" Sparrow said. "Isn't it the case that when the commander is present, he should administer the punishment?"

Fang looked at Prince Liu, who nodded. "Take him into solitary confinement," said Prince Liu. "He can await his sentence there."

EIGHT

A traitorous man must be judged according to the motive of his crime, for between black and white are countless shades of gray. But a duplicitous woman can never be redeemed. Her only punishment must be death.
—ANALECTS OF ZHU YUAN, 889

I COULD FEEL ALL EYES ON ME AS I WAS LED AWAY, FLANKED BY TWO guards. My cheeks burned with shame and terror. The adrenaline had left me, and now all that remained was the sick, queasy anticipation of my punishment.

They led me to a small barn at the edge of camp, then bound my hands together and lifted them above my head, tying them to the rafters. Somehow, despite my dread and discomfort, I fell asleep, dreaming familiar dreams of empty landscapes and barren hills, empty but for faint, glowing lights, blinking in and out. As a child, when I'd confessed these recurring dreams to my mother, she'd told me they were visits to the spirit realm. When I'd asked her why I saw no spirits, then, she told me it was because I lacked a key.

My eyes had gone wide—how could I find a key?—but then she'd burst into laughter, and I realized I'd been tricked, again. My mother liked to make false promises: *"I'll always stay by your side, Meilin."*

She liked to shock people, to astound them: *"I've never liked men,"* she once told Uncle Zhou, much to his discomfort. *"Not in that way."*

With my mother, it was hard not to feel like a ball of yarn in a cat's paw, to be toyed and tampered with. She had the power to unravel me, wholly, and the power to wind me back together. She did not lie in the way that other people lied, to obscure the truth, but rather, her own forms of reality were so twisted, so bent, that they became misshapen lies.

Footsteps sounded outside, rousing me from my stupor. The barn door opened; I expected to see Lieutenant Fang, but only Prince Liu entered.

It was the first time we'd been alone since yesterday, in the Wenxi marketplace. But he did not know that.

His cold eyes fell over me, his gaze flicking from my arms tied up to the ceiling rafters, to my face, bruised and dirtied. If he had any ounce of recognition, he did not show it.

In his hands was a cracked leather whip.

Blood drained from my face.

He did not speak. It was so silent in the barn that I could hear the bray and whinny of horses outside. He stepped toward me, his mouth pursed. His lips looked purple in the dim lamplight, his hair dark as newly ground ink. His handsomeness was unchanged, but fatigue now lent a gray tinge to his face.

He watched me as I watched him. "Where is it?" His voice was like iron, immovable.

"S-sir?"

"Where did you hide Lieutenant Fang's armlet?"

"I told you, sir. I lost it." But I could not meet his eyes.

His jaw clenched. He stepped around me so that he faced my back. I could not see him, but I could feel his presence like a volatile flame.

The first lash came without warning. I heard the whistle in the air, then gasped, less in pain than in shock. The second lash followed moments after, then the third. I forgot how to breathe.

I had experienced pain before, many times over. When Father hit me, or when I'd broken my ankle falling from a rooftop with loose tiles. Those instances were nothing like this: premeditated, methodical, dehumanizing. I felt like an animal, trussed up and caged. Was this to become the narrative of my life?

But they do not know, I reminded myself, my teeth gritted. They did not know my secret. And that knowledge was power. I was still free.

The realization gave me strength. After the first lash, I forced my mouth shut and barely breathed as lash after lash fell across my back. I understood that this was not personal; this was protocol. Prince Liu's force was not particularly light or heavy, only standard. Still, I hated him for doing what I perceived to be cruel.

I was not guilty of this crime. My crimes were far worse.

I did not know how much time had passed. It took me a long while to realize the lashes had stopped. Prince Liu was cleaning the whip, his mouth puckered with distaste. If yesterday he had seemed like a free spirit with his boyish, easygoing personality, today he looked the prince he was: unapproachable, out of reach. Dangerous.

"I hope you've learned your lesson," he told me. "This place won't be like what you're used to; I can see that." He paused. Beneath his sternness, I sensed a taut thread of emotion to his voice. What it was, I did not know. "Your punishment is not yet over. You will spend the next twenty-four hours in solitary confinement. I will return in a day."

Then he shut the door behind him, and I realized he wasn't going to untie me. The real pain began now.

HOURS LATER, THE DOOR FLEW OPEN WITH A THUD, STARTLING ME from my stupor. Morning light flooded the barn. If it was still day, then I shouldn't yet be released. Confused, I squinted against the light to see someone stride inside.

"Your friend found the missing armlet," said Prince Liu.

He cut my ropes with a single swift slash. I fell forward, my limbs impossibly weak. Everything ached.

To my surprise, he crouched beside me. "You'll need to visit the infirmary," he said. "Let me see if—"

I realized he was moving to check my back and shoulders. I shrank away from him, panicking.

He stopped. The expression on my face startled him; he recognized my fear.

He moved away from me, rising to his feet. "Your friend said he found it lying outside the mess hall. He said you must have dropped it. That is, if you ever had it in the first place."

He suspects me.

"Sir?"

He glowered down at me. "If you want to put a target on your back, make sure you're strong enough to carry the target first."

With that, he strode out the door. I sighed. In the span of a day, I'd managed to attract the ire of not only my platoon lieutenant but also my company commander.

Sparrow came barreling in moments later. He'd most likely been eavesdropping outside, waiting for an opportune moment.

"Ren!" Instead of appearing shocked at my sorry state, he grinned. "I suspected our commander was a softhearted prince. He didn't even lash you unclothed."

I gaped at him. "You mean, normally . . ."

Sparrow nodded. "Your scars won't be half as bad as mine. That is, if you even scar at all."

As I limped toward the door, Sparrow warned me, "I doubt our dear lieutenant will let you take the day off from training."

"I know," I said. "I don't want the day off."

I had decided in the cold darkness of my isolation—I didn't want to just survive. I wanted to prove myself here. I needed to.

Squad leaders were the best of the best? Then I'd be a squad leader. I had until the end of spring—I'd show them I didn't just belong here. I'd *excel*.

Sparrow looked impressed. "Then you didn't miss much. We're on archery."

I hastened my pace across the field. I'd never held a bow before.

"Oh, and Ren," said Sparrow, scratching the back of his neck. "Thanks. For . . . you know . . ."

Sparrow thought I'd taken the blame for his sake. Well, I certainly wouldn't correct him.

In the back of my mind, I heard that unnatural, silky-smooth voice purring. *"Well done,"* he hissed, and I recoiled, chilled to the bone. Only now did I notice the way my necklace hummed in response to the voice. *"I'll see you soon."*

NINE

The madness, they saw, was catching. Like a tree poisoned at its roots, the corrupted ones could not be saved.
—LEGENDS OF THE MOUNTAINS, 754

MY BRAVADO LEFT ME ON THE TRAINING FIELD. ARCHERY WAS a disaster; I could barely string a bow, much less hit the bull's-eye. Fang was distracted during archery practice, but as we moved on to strength training, he homed in on me with a predator's focus.

"Trainee Hai!" he bellowed, never mind that he was only a couple feet behind me. "Don't even think about cheating. Fill your buckets to the brim."

But the other soldiers had only filled their buckets halfway. I glared at the ground and filled both my buckets brimful with water. They were much heavier now. Panting, I tried to balance both on my carrying pole and staggered beneath their weight.

"You're splashing water on the ground," Fang said. "That disqualifies you. Start over."

I trudged back to the well. I filled the buckets once more and leveled them on my pole. I took one step forward. A droplet of water spilled onto the dirt.

"Start over," said Fang.

I slammed the buckets on the ground. "It's impossible."

"You'll climb the mountain twice for disrespecting your superior."

"But—"

"Three times."

"Sir!"

He shoved me and I lost my balance; I fell. "Talk back to me again and you'll earn your second flogging. Is that what you want?" He shook his head at me. "I can tell you're used to getting pampered, pretty boy, but you won't find any of that here. My word is law. Understand?"

My cheeks heated. "Yes, sir."

"Now, begin again. I expect three trips from you. You can join us when you're done."

He strode away to berate some other hapless trainee. I struggled to my knees but could barely find the strength to stand. Before me, Mount Niang Pu rose infinitely tall. The task felt inconceivable. I could hardly climb it once, much less three times. How could I have believed I would survive this place?

"You're weaker than I thought." The voice was back. *"Get up."*

Choking with surprise, I did what I was told. I stood. *You're not hearing voices*, I told myself. *You're just tired.*

"But madness is catching," the voice chuckled. *"Is that not what the skeptics say?"*

The voice I'm hearing isn't real, I insisted again, but this time I recalled my qi gong training, concentrating my vital energy and focusing it inward to clear my mind. *Wood, fire, earth, metal, water.* I cycled through each element, balancing the weight of each breath.

"Who taught you such mind tricks?" The voice sounded surprised now, and peeved. *"Surely not your mother?"*

I ignored him as my mind slowed and settled into an impenetrable stillness, allowing no intrusive thoughts. On my feet now, I told myself to just lift the buckets. Then I told myself to take one step. Then another. And another.

I fell into a numb trance, not thinking of the pain, not thinking of how many more li I still had to go. My mind fixed on the present moment, on the ground beneath my feet, on the step I was taking. On and on.

And then I was done. Every muscle in my body felt as if it were on fire. I nearly collapsed by the well, but I knew once I sat, I wouldn't be able to stand back up. So I trudged to the training ring instead.

By this time, the platoon had moved on to sword practice. I entered the tent and went to stand in the back. Sparrow found me and furtively passed me a cool cloth, dampened with water. I wiped my face and straightened my shoulders, trying to dredge up some excitement for sword fighting. Noblewomen were forbidden from holding a sword, much less learning how to use one. I had often wondered what it would be like, especially since Uncle Zhou told me I was skilled with a staff. Surely there was some overlap between the two?

I chose a longer training sword, despite Fang's warning that beginners would fare better with the shorter blades. I figured the long sword would more closely resemble the staff. They were both made from wood, with the edges blunt and thick. I lifted mine in the air, marveling at its heft. With a real blade, one day I could kill. And be killed.

I lowered my practice sword. It was blasphemy for a woman to have such thoughts. And yet no spirits had struck me down. Fire had not fallen from the sky. I was bruised, bloodied, and half-dead on my feet, but my secret was safe.

My grip tightened around the hilt. "*You are not your mother, Meilin.*" Xiuying's voice rang in my head. "*I know,*" I'd told her. For my mother had given up on this world. She had chosen to stop fighting, to succumb to the madness in her mind. I thought of the voice I'd begun hearing and ignored the pounding of my heart, instead evening my breaths, honing my qi. Even if I too was cursed with madness, I would not yield to it. I would remain sane, self-sufficient, and I would prove my worth to everyone who thought otherwise. I looked out at the crowd of men before me: some eager, some weary. Some strong, some feeble. *I will best each and every one of you*, I promised myself, *until* no one *can look down on me*.

"How many of you have used a sword before?" Lieutenant Fang asked. About a third of the platoon raised their hands. Fang's hawklike gaze fell over me and my long sword, and his face tightened with disdain.

"*Pride comes before a fall,*" Lieutenant Fang recited, sneering at me. "Trainee Zhao." He motioned toward Zhao Zilong, who had raised his hand. "And Trainee Hai. Enter the ring."

With all eyes on me, I had no choice but to obey. Privately, I wished I'd let Lieutenant Fang get run over by that charging horse.

"A practice duel," Fang explained. "To show us what true swordsmanship looks like. From two . . . *veterans* in the practice."

My cheeks burned. He wished to humiliate me. Stealing his iron armlet was more than insubordination. It had been a personal affront.

Zhao Zilong started to circle me; I mirrored his steps, not knowing what to do myself.

Zilong did not have Sparrow's height, but he was taller than me. Everybody was. He was also stocky in build, and his stance was wide and planted; it would be difficult to knock him over. He switched his sword from his right to his left hand, then back to his right, causing me to squint. Was he ambidextrous or merely feinting?

Then he attacked. He swung at me, and I understood that for the purposes of this duel, I was supposed to bring my blade up to meet his. Instead, I panicked and ducked, running to the other end of the ring. The onlookers laughed. "Are you going to run from Ximing too?" Fang called, baiting me.

My topknot had come loose. I blew a stray hair out of my face, glaring at my opponent. He was relaxed now, recognizing how inexperienced I was. I gripped my sword with both hands and charged forward.

My attack was sloppy; he parried, then slid his sword forward along my own until I was forced to retreat, but not before he got in a glancing blow to my sternum. I felt something warm and wet pool there but did not look down. Pain was temporary, I told myself.

And yet the stress of the day was getting to me, and I was lagging badly. Zilong came in fast for another strike. I tried to dodge and used my sword for balance, but its weighting was different from a staff's. I tripped, losing control for a few precious seconds. Zilong saw his opening and knocked my sword from my hands, the force of his blow throwing me to the ground. He pressed his wooden blade to my neck. "Point."

The other soldiers whooped and cheered.

"That," said Fang, "is the difference between an experienced swordsman and a novice." Zilong lowered his sword and offered me a hand up. "By the time we arrive in Ximing, I expect none of you to give me as catastrophic a performance as Trainee Hai did today."

"You're bleeding," Zilong told me. I looked down at my chest. The wound was shallow, but the blood had seeped through my bindings and tunic.

"Sir," Zilong said, to Lieutenant Fang. "Should Trainee Hai go to the infirmary, or . . . ?"

I thought Lieutenant Fang would refuse straightaway, but he only arched a brow. "If you want to skip training with your level of skill, then please do."

Which meant leave and lose face, or stay and suffer. I stayed.

Throughout sword practice, even though my knees felt like they would give out, even though my head hurt so badly I could barely keep my eyes open, I kept going through the motions, rehearsing the same maneuvers time after time. My body betrayed me; it set me apart as different. So I would work twice as hard to compensate. In my head, there was room for only one thought: *You must prove yourself. You must.*

Lieutenant Fang thought I didn't belong here. The difference between him and me? I *knew* I didn't belong here. And so I had to prove both of us wrong.

That night after dinner, Zilong brought out a jar of sorghum wine from home and earned the goodwill of our entire platoon. I stayed long enough to remain inconspicuous before sneaking out of the mess hall to retrieve my training sword. Then I returned to the practice ring. At this time of night, the tent was silent but for the susurration of grasses. Distantly, I could hear laughter pealing out from the mess hall.

The other trainees were not like me, and I was reminded of this every second I spent in camp. They had the luxury of simple, unquestioned camaraderie. The platoon was like a family, with the tacit expectation that everyone had each other's backs.

But I belonged only so much as I fit in. Only if my secret remained safe. And I could not let myself forget it, despite the kindness shown by Sparrow and Zilong and even Prince Liu. I looked at the blade in my calloused, sun-darkened hands and swallowed.

Only alone, with nothing but the crickets to hear me, I let myself voice aloud what I had lacked courage to admit in the day. "Ma," I said to the skies, "I don't want to just survive. I want to be the best."

I wanted others to respect me—to *fear* me. To know my name and know it with awe.

Something deep within me, long dormant, stirred, like a creature coming out of hibernation. I felt a visceral thrum of approval, an assured *rightness* in my bones. Was it my imagination, or did my mother's necklace quiver in response, hot against my bare skin?

I shook myself awake. The fatigue was getting to me. With a sigh, I moved my feet into starting position. Despite my aching shoulders and ringing ears, I harnessed my qi and lifted the sword in my hands. I brought it down. Again. Again. Through the night.

I did not realize someone was watching me.

TEN

So the gods of old broke their own bones and scattered them across the skies. The people below found the gods' bones and called them imperial jade, for there was no stone on earth as lovely or as divine.

—WINTER AND SPRING ANNALS, 417

DAYS BLURRED INTO WEEKS AS WE SETTLED INTO THE TEDIOUS routines of camp. Despite the monotony, we were too exhausted for boredom. Every morning, we rose before dawn, and every evening, we slept long after dusk. Individuality was condemned; differences purged. At the start, Zilong drank too much; Sparrow slept too much; Red complained too much. Others, like me, had less trouble with excess than insufficiency. I didn't speak enough. I didn't weigh enough. Every criticism highlighted my lack thereof. But gradually, over the following month, the differences between us shrank, until we became one. One platoon, one company. Each the same as the others. This was the strategy of the Anlai army.

But the others did not see what happened at night, after the oil lamps were extinguished. It was then that I carved out my separateness from the others. Every night without fail, I practiced by the light of the stars.

It was during the night of the new moon, a month into training, when I crept out after a night of boisterous drinking to commence my solitary practice session. Archery was proving to be problematic. I had recurring nightmares of the prior week, when Lieutenant Fang had balanced an apple on my head, forcing me to stand in as target practice to realize the stakes of poor archery. Luckily, he'd chosen Zilong, who was the top performer in our platoon. Zilong had carved the apple in two, leaving me breathless but unharmed. Still, I dreamed of that arrow flying toward my face, my limbs locked in fear. What I would do to have an ability like Zilong's, to loose an arrow as easily as plucking the string of a pipa.

At the archery butts, I gathered discarded arrows from the line of scarecrows, then took up position ten chi from my target. I lifted my bow, inhaled, then aimed.

"You're holding it wrong."

I jumped, dropping my bow. Whirling around, I came face-to-face with my company commander, Prince Liu. I hadn't seen him since that first night, when he'd punished me for thievery.

I bowed low, cheeks burning. "Sir."

His topknot was disheveled, his cheekbones touched by sun. His hanfu robes were now simple and unadorned, no different from the robes Lieutenant Fang wore. Yet he stood like a prince, his posture straighter than a staff.

He motioned toward the bow. I picked it up hastily and restrung my arrow. Then Prince Liu closed the distance between us and placed his hands over mine. His hands were warm and calloused, the span of them almost twice as wide as my own. I gulped at our proximity, trying not to reveal my nervousness.

"Widen your stance," he said. "Your feet should be shoulder width apart. And perpendicular to the target. Right now, you look like you're trying to charge directly at it." He guided my bow with his hands over mine. "Loosen these fingers," he said. "Don't grip so hard here. Now align the arrow with your target. Exhale as you release the string, so that your qi and arrow are in unison." He loosed the string and I felt its whiplash course through me. The arrow landed in the scarecrow's head with a clean thud. My mouth fell open. I had never managed to achieve that before.

"Now try again," he said, letting go of me. When I only stared at him, he nodded at me. "Go on."

Turning toward the target, I tried to concentrate on my task at hand, but I could feel his gaze like the heat of the sun. Why was he here? How long had he been watching me? Where had he gone this past month? How many other companies did he command? What did the war front look like in Leyuan? In Ximing? I forced myself to let go of these buzzing thoughts, focusing on his directions.

I loosed my arrow. It struck a tree behind the scarecrow. My whole being flushed.

"Try again," said Prince Liu, unperturbed. "Your technique is getting better."

I couldn't believe he was wasting his time on me, an unranked soldier. Then again, his supervision made me feel as if I were doing something illegal. Were soldiers not allowed to practice on their own? Had I committed a crime without knowing it?

I shot again. And again. My fifth arrow finally struck the scarecrow's leg.

I turned to catch Prince Liu's reaction. He was smiling. The sight made my stomach flip.

"Good job," he said, and my heart leapt. His praise felt like a drug. "You improve quickly. And you have remarkable control over your qi." He clapped me on the shoulder then, hard enough to make me wince.

"I was trained in qi gong from a young age, sir."

"I thought so," he said, before eyeing me. "You're shorter than most. Compensate by aiming upward. You'll injure a soldier by shooting him in the thigh, but you're aiming to kill, not injure."

"Yes, sir."

I bowed again, expecting him to walk away, but he only stood there, studying me with an air of curiosity. "Have we met before?"

"N-no, sir," I said in a rush, so quickly my words came out in a garbled mess. "I-I mean, I'm new to the capital. I'm a bastard son of the Hai clan, and grew up in the east, so I've never met anyone from the royal family before..."

He nodded. I didn't know if he understood me. "I've seen you out here several times," he said, jerking his head at the empty fields around us. "Do you train every night?"

I bit my tongue, wondering if I should conceal the truth. But beneath his clear, sharp-eyed gaze, I felt as if he would discern my lies immediately. I nodded with reluctance.

"Do the others know about this?" By others, I assumed he was thinking of Lieutenant Fang.

Even more reluctantly, I shook my head.

A line creased between his brows. I thought he would tell me off, but he only said, "Carry on, then."

FROM THEN ON, PRINCE LIU SUPERVISED MY TRAINING SESSIONS AT night. He watched most of the time, only occasionally intervening to point out bad form. When I moved on to sword practice, he dueled me, but not as Zilong had done. He fought not to win, but to teach. One night, I arrived late after Sparrow had tried to engage me in conversation and found Prince Liu waiting by the barracks, two staffs in hand. I had mentioned in passing that I knew the staff, and he had jokingly said I should teach him. Or, I had assumed he was joking. That night, we trained long past midnight.

On our twelfth night of doing this, I finally summoned up the courage to ask. We had just finished staff practice, which appeared to be a personal favorite of his. It was still early in the evening, and he seemed in no hurry to return to his quarters. He sat on the grass and drank from his canteen, then held it out to me. I sat tentatively beside him.

"Don't you have . . . something better to be doing with your time?" I asked.

He grinned, leaning back to look up at the star-strewn sky. He appeared to be in an unusually good mood tonight. "I'll tell you a secret," he said, with a carefree manner, "since you've told me yours."

I stilled, before remembering our conversation earlier, when I'd confessed to being a bastard son. That was the secret he assumed he knew.

I pulled my knees up to my chest, facing him. A shaft of pearly moonlight fell across his cheek, highlighting the sharp, defined planes of his face, which were so fine they felt like art to me. He was so handsome, and I was just supposed to ignore it, as if it never even occurred to me.

He cleared his throat. "I'm an insomniac," he said simply. His eyes cut to mine to catch my reaction.

I squinted at him. "Is that a disease?"

He laughed, unruffled. "Sort of," he said. "I have trouble falling asleep."

I absorbed this novel piece of information. "Even when you're tired?" I asked, with some wonder.

"*Especially* when I'm tired." He stuck a blade of grass in his mouth, as if he were a country boy, then lay back on the field. I had never seen him so at ease, completely changed from the strict commander who had demanded complete obedience. I saw now that Prince Liu wore many faces. Like me.

"Why?" I asked him, my curiosity piqued. Sleep was something I wanted more of but never had enough time for. I'd never questioned not being able to sleep even if I tried to.

He shrugged one shoulder. "Hungry ghosts. Evil spirits. That sort of thing."

My eyes widened, thinking of his own father's mandate.

"I'm joking," he said, a smirk unfurling on his lips. "Besides, I like it out here at night. It's calm. Peaceful. Not like it is in the day."

"I don't know," I said with a small smile. "My platoon gets pretty loud at night sometimes."

"Ah, yes," he said, still chewing his blade of grass. "You've developed quite a reputation already. They call Third Platoon the Drunk Platoon."

"Really?" I said, astonished. Boys from other platoons sometimes joined us at night, but I barely interacted with any of them. There were so many new faces all the time, I couldn't keep up. Not like Sparrow, who seemed to be bosom friends with the entire company already.

Prince Liu propped himself up on one elbow. "One of your comrades owns a family brewery, right?"

I thought of Zilong and his endless supply of alcohol. How had Prince Liu come to learn such a trivial detail? "You knew that?"

"Soldiers"—he flashed a crooked grin at me—"are the most incurable of gossips."

We both looked out into the dark fields, blanketed by night. A warm spring breeze drifted across the campground, carrying with it the scent of blooming jasmine. Almost forty-five days had passed since I'd left home. Xiuying would soon begin making preparations for the Qingming Festival. And Rouha would be clamoring for glutinous rice dumplings. The thought left me oddly homesick.

Not that I wished to go back.

"You'd almost forget we're going off to war," I said quietly, "with how high-spirited everyone is."

Prince Liu ran a lazy hand through the grass. "It's easy to forget, when no one wants to remember reality."

I looked at him then. Without his searching gaze, I felt freer to look. His topknot had loosened, so that locks of black hair framed his face. He had long, curling lashes; they gave his eyes a youthful, boyish look.

"Are you afraid?" I asked.

"It's my duty," he said, "to lead this army."

His eyes were faraway. "You didn't answer my question," I said softly.

His gaze locked against mine. "It's not important." The timbre of his voice changed. "What's important is duty."

So that was how it was with him, I thought. Duty first, always. Fitting for a warlord's son.

"And you?" he asked.

I considered his question. I was afraid of many things. I was afraid of being discovered as a woman. I was afraid of being set apart from the others, of trying my very best and still failing. I was afraid of spending the rest of my days chained to the women's quarters, to serve at Master Zhu's beck and call. But was I afraid of dying out there on some foreign battlefield? The truth was, I couldn't fully imagine that reality, and so the idea of it did not leave me frightened.

"No," I said after a pause. "Perhaps it is only my ignorance of war, but I find I am not afraid."

He appeared unsurprised by this. "I knew you were brave," he said, "when you didn't make a single sound."

I cocked my head at him, bemused. "What do you mean?"

His mouth twisted ruefully. "When I lashed you that first night, you didn't make a sound." I stilled at the awful recollection. "I knew then that you'd survive." He shot me a wry smile. "You're small, Ren, but surprisingly strong."

"Surprisingly?" But I smiled back at him. "Thank you . . . sir."

"Call me Sky."

HOURS LATER, AS I LAY IN MY BEDROLL, A SLOW WARMTH SPREAD through my chest as I recalled my conversation with Prince Liu. *Liu Sky*. I let myself smile, unseen in the dark.

But I had forgotten I was not alone. A voice hissed in warning, and I felt my blood curdle. *"Don't trust him,"* said the now-familiar disembodied voice. *"He will betray you."*

"How do I know I can trust you?" I whispered furiously.

The ominous voice grew distant, as if he were slinking away. *"You can't."*

Beside me, Sparrow shifted in his sleep. I stilled, praying no one had woken. If they knew I was hearing voices in my head, even my few friends wouldn't defend me. Was the voice imagined—somehow the same disease that had afflicted my mother? Or perhaps worse—was the voice real, and my mother had been telling the truth all along?

Mother once said a powerful spirit lived in her ear.

I shivered at the thought, at the blasphemy of it all. If I was caught, it'd surely be the end of me. A sentenced lunatic had few options in Anlai. At best, they were confined to an asylum. At worst, they were labeled a black magic practitioner—and their corpse fed to the dogs.

Was this punishment from the heavens, I wondered, for forsaking my predestined fate? Or had this always been in my cards—to follow in my mother's footsteps?

Disquieted, I reached under my tunic to loosen the necklace from my chest bindings. I clutched it in my palm for the first time since Xiuying had given it to me, wishing for relief from my anxiety. It occurred to me then: the voice had only begun speaking to me after I'd obtained my mother's necklace. After I'd worn her jade pendant.

I studied the jade in the dark. I couldn't make out the characters, but I could feel them, engraved in the stone: 青龍. *Qinglong*. Azure Dragon.

Could it be, I wondered, could it truly be a spirit seal? A way to commune with fabled creatures beyond the physical realm, worn by the spirit summoners of legends past? But the old seals had been locked away since the rise of the Wu Dynasty, over a century ago. The only known jade seal in Anlai belonged to the ruling Liu family, where it was stored in the imperial treasury . . .

"*Father ignored the threat, of course,*" Sky had told me, the day before I'd enlisted. "*But later, he had a certain room in the imperial treasury checked, for the first time in decades. And that was when he discovered—a certain jade seal stolen.*"

Could this be that stolen seal?

Could my own mother have been the thief?

But if she'd truly stolen a spirit seal, if she'd truly borne the power of a genuine dragon, how could she have drowned in the Wen River when she'd always loved to swim? Taking the growing abuse of my father without protest. Confining herself in her rooms, as if she *had* to be locked away.

I had never once seen her perform any kind of black magic, much less summon a dragon. My memories of her were mostly from her final days, when she would mutter to herself or to me, start stories with no beginning or end, walk in circles, or even disappear for hours at a time, before locking herself in her rooms and refusing to come out.

How could it be true: my mother, a spirit summoner? No, it was absurd, to believe that my mother would have dared break into the imperial treasury, to harness the power of the sea dragon. I was lonely and delusional. I only wanted to convince myself that I was not alone, that my mother had also been like me—covetous, full of greed, desiring more than her appointed lot in life.

I closed my eyes in disappointment. Against the darkness of my eyelids, I was confronted by a memory, or a vision. I saw a girl, running as fast as her legs could carry her. *Ma?* I wondered. But then she came to an abrupt halt, turning with a jagged, stifling violence. It was not my mother. It was . . . me.

Her face, once familiar, was transformed by rage. She drew her sword as her attacker whirled at her, their blades decisive and furious. Their shared hatred was evident in their thrusts and parries. They were fighting to kill.

And as the girl lost her sword and the boy brought his down to her throat, I finally caught sight of his face. *Liu Sky*.

ELEVEN

> *Of spirits they are as numerous as men, but none so great as the Cardinal Ones, who shape the four directions and balance the elements of the world. Like lightning after thunder, when a Cardinal Spirit emerges, war and destruction follow.*
> —LOST JOURNALS OF AN 8TH-CENTURY LIXIA SCHOLAR,
> DATE UNKNOWN

MY EYES FLEW OPEN. IT WASN'T A VISION OF THE FUTURE. IT was just a nightmare. And yet I couldn't let go of the image, of the hatred in Prince Liu's face.

Disturbed, I picked at my scabs before hissing in annoyance as fresh blood began to flow. Without warning, my mother's pendant flared with light, bright enough to wake the others. I smothered its glow with my hand, pressing my bloody palm against the jade. The light blazed all at once—blinding me—and I felt as if I were falling, tumbling through the air. Then all went dark.

WHEN I OPENED MY EYES, THE SLEEPING TRAINEES WERE GONE. EVERY sense of pain in my body had vanished. A cool numbness settled over my limbs, as if the body I wore no longer belonged to me. Dazed, I saw that my jade still glowed. But it was less noticeable now, for everything within this strange place... *shone*. Where was I?

A coaxing, whispering breeze fluttered across my body, murmuring, somehow also sentient. The trees here were gold and feathered, leaves like wings about to take flight. The ground moved with my every step, so that I wasn't sure if it was I who was moving, or the earth.

This place was foreign to me, and yet I felt a tremulous *knowing* in my body, like the tuning of an instrument; this was the pitch I'd been looking for.

You've been searching for this place all your life.

"I've been waiting for you."

I whirled around, then gasped.

The sea dragon spirit stared down at me. He was a snake the size of a hundred men, with iridescent blue-green scales and glittering gold-flecked eyes. His tail flicked impatiently in the air as he waited for me to understand. My gaze darted from his razor-sharp claws to his jagged, pearl-like teeth. At last our eyes locked. "Qinglong."

His voice was blistering, cold as ice. "One of my many names."

"You've been speaking to me," I said, still in shock.

"And finally you deign to reply."

"H-how can I see you?" I said dumbly. "Where are we?"

"Where do you think we are?" he asked, vaguely amused. A humming firefly drifted too close to my face and I swatted at it; I felt qi course through my veins as the air suddenly fogged with mist.

I stumbled back, startled. Had *I* done that?

"It is much easier for human vessels to harness their lixia in the spirit realm. You will not find it as natural in your world."

The . . . *spirit realm*. But of course, I thought, scanning my surroundings as the mist cleared. There were the fields we had trained in this morning, now an ethereal emerald instead of a dull brown. There were the forests bordering Chuang Ning, now wondrous hues of gold and amber, sparking with vitality, flickering with lights that could have been fireflies or something else. It was an eerie reflection of the world I knew, both familiar and alien.

Familiar in more ways than one, I realized. For I had been here before. The shape of this place had appeared often in my childhood dreams, though never as vividly as this. I had glimpsed the shadow of this place, its echo, but never so directly—never before had I been allowed inside.

All along, I only needed a key.

I turned my jade over, reading the miniature characters inscribed there. 青龍.

Xuanwu, Zhuque, Qinglong, Baihu—they were fables, all of them, meant to teach children of the four directions. North, south, east, west. Tortoise, phoenix, dragon, tiger. Each Cardinal Spirit represented a wind, a time of day, a season, and an element. But it was make-believe, nothing more.

Mother once said a powerful spirit lived in her ear.

"This is . . . real? All my life . . ." I trailed off. All my life, I'd believed my mother to be afflicted with madness, and I perhaps cursed with the same dormant affliction. But what if she'd truly never been mad? What if, all along, she'd simply never been believed?

"We don't have much time," growled the dragon. "Zhuque's seal is close to being found. You must learn to harness your power. You must test the boundaries of what you can do."

He opened his mouth and out flowed a river of such force its currents thrust me off my feet. I struggled not to sink as the waters flung me about, and swallowed bucketfuls of water, choking. "Help!" I screamed. But the dragon only laughed.

The waves engulfed me, sweeping me farther downstream. I felt water invade my entire being, suffocating me, blinding me. In my panic I opened my mouth to scream; water filled my lungs, and with it, consuming fear. This was it. This was how I would go. Just like my mother.

"The might of the sea is yours."

The water vanished. I hit the ground with a sob, then curled in on myself, shivering with cold and misery. "This must be a mistake," I said hoarsely. "I can't command the power of the sea. I should return the seal to the treasury, or..."

"You desired me, hungry one," the dragon snarled, as he wrapped his massive body in a tightening coil around me. "I only answered your call."

"M-my call?" I stuttered.

"Your greed is unending," he hissed. "An ocean's hunger."

My eyes skipped up to meet his. In their golden depths, I recognized the ruthlessness in them, the cruel, unconcealed ambition. For it reflected my own.

Buried deep within me, acknowledged by no one, not even me. Because it was depravity, for a woman to desire more than her lot in life. To aspire to more than safety, protection. To aspire to *power*.

"No," I said, my heart rate ratcheting. "No!"

I would belong, I told myself. I would not be cast out, the ugliness of my true nature revealed. As the dragon's body coiled tighter against mine, I willed myself to even my breaths, to cycle through the elements in my body and find balance, control. This time, I imagined myself in a different world, one without dragons or mythical beasts, one where I was safe on my pallet, in a tent with other sleeping soldiers, where I was no different from any other. I would belong. I would belong. I would belong.

I WOKE ON MY PALLET, CURLED ON MY SIDE AND SOAKED IN SWEAT. Dawn light penetrated the tent canvas. I unfurled my palm and found dried blood smeared against the surface of the jade, which appeared innocuous in the early-morning light. I considered throwing away the jade, or even hiding it somewhere on the training grounds, but the thought of someone else discovering it sent waves of revulsion down my spine. Deep down, no matter how foolish it was, I knew I could not bring myself to give up the jade and its irrevocable connection to my mother, the mother I had never known.

The morning gongs sounded. I tucked the jade back under my tunic and scrambled out of bed. Against the humdrum chatter of gossiping soldiers, last night's events became nothing but a strange dream.

But what if it had been more than a dream?

No. I shook myself awake. *Remember your mother. Remember how no one believed her. Remember—she went mad.*

I gritted my teeth and strode toward the barracks. I was already different enough as it was. If I started raving about spirits, I would be past the point of redemption. Even now I could barely maintain my facade; I was only clinging to the brink of conformity. I had to purge my differences so wholly that I couldn't afford to even *think* of the possibility of difference.

So I forgot about the golden-eyed sea dragon. I forgot about the eerie beauty of the spirit realm and the strange inner workings of that dreamworld. I forgot even about the pulsing warmth of my mother's necklace, which, when it called to me in the nights after, I told myself was simply the beating of my own deceitful heart.

TWELVE

One army must have one mind. To commit unjust violence
against a fellow soldier is to betray the army and the state.
—EDICT OF THE IMPERIAL COMMANDER, 923

CHERRY BLOSSOM SEASON ARRIVED, SCATTERING PALE PINK PETals across the surface of the Wen River, as if in lieu of the offerings usually left to the heavens. Over three months had passed since I'd enlisted, and still there was no talk of our departure for Ximing. Soldiers had begun to gossip; apparently, the battalions due for Leyuan had left weeks ago.

I for one rarely thought of our impending departure, fixated instead on making it through each day. I had become an insomniac like Prince Liu, not because I couldn't fall asleep but because I feared the consequences if I did—of returning to that sinister dreamworld and finding the dragon waiting for me. No matter how tired I was, I never gave in to the urge to hold my mother's necklace, to answer the lure of the spirit—if there even was a spirit. Instead, I used qi gong to discipline my mind, to focus on my task at hand, and to become stronger, indisputably. I learned the lie; I became the lie.

It was late in the spring when Sky disclosed to me that the troops were preparing to muster for the southern front. Seventh Company would follow shortly. When I sat up, nervous, he laughed and told me to relax. He claimed I was more than ready for battle and suggested I rest before the muster orders came.

"You can ask for a day's leave," he said, wiping his forehead. We were both sweating hard from our nightly training session. "If you have family you want to visit. Before we set off for Ximing. Winter's even asked for a week off."

"Winter?"

"My brother," he explained. "The sixth prince. He had some business in the palace, I think. That or he just missed his bed."

Preoccupied, I cracked my knuckles one by one. "Are they going to choose squad leaders now?"

"Shortly before we set out," he replied.

Within Third Platoon, there were five open positions. And I wanted one of them.

I must have looked distracted, because Sky boxed me on the ear. "You can stop trying so hard all the time, Ren." Sky had gotten increasingly comfortable with me, to the point that sometimes he felt no need to wear a shirt. Not that I didn't enjoy this. It just made things . . . challenging for me. "I see you," he continued, mopping his sweat with the hem of his tunic. "You're keeping up now."

"I don't want to just keep up," I said without thinking. "I want to be the best."

Sky raised a brow. "Why?" he asked plainly. "I didn't see you as the arrogant type."

"That's you," I retorted, and he laughed. Sky laughed easily, always quick to find a reason to smile. It was one of the reasons I enjoyed spending time with him. He didn't put on airs like other nobles. In fact, the only moments I remembered he was Prince Liu and not my training partner were when he gave speeches as commander to our company. Then I could hardly recognize him on the dais, his bejeweled figure glinting in the daylight.

"Then why?" he pressed, not easily diverted. He had a constable's intuition for knowing when I was hiding something.

"I need to prove myself," I said, looking down. "I need to prove I deserve this."

I needed to prove that I, as a woman, could be better than the rest of them. That I too could belong. That I too could be free.

LIEUTENANT FANG DELIVERED THE NEWS AT BREAKFAST. "PACK YOUR bags, boys. We're mustering for the southern front."

The news was met with mixed reception. Red, the platoon bully, groaned and left the mess hall to sulk. Zilong sighed and returned to his bowl of bone broth. Sparrow caught my eye, plunking down beside me with a second helping of noodles. "It's really happening," he said. "We're going to be war heroes!"

"We have to survive first," I said realistically. I also wasn't a morning person.

"It's a small kingdom, but a vicious one," said Zilong grimly. "The Ximing people are known for being barbarians. If you're captured, don't bother praying for escape. My father told me to just—" He mimed slitting his own throat. We all winced. "Otherwise, they'll experiment on your body, tear you apart limb by limb. Sometimes the death takes days. Sometimes months."

Sparrow's noodles slipped from his chopsticks.

We started packing after breakfast. When Zilong tried to bring an entire case of rice wine, Lieutenant Fang's face turned purple.

"Which part of 'pack only essentials' do you not understand, boy?" Lieutenant Fang looked harried, his hair sticking up at odd angles above his head. It was clearly not his first confiscation of the day. "We are traveling *light*, do you hear me? This is war, not a parade."

This was one of his favorite sayings, which we had all heard many times by this point.

"But, sir," Zilong protested, "this is necessary for the morale of our troops..."

"Silence!" Lieutenant Fang shouted. "Everyone, give up your packs for inspection."

We filed out of our tent in a single queue, the practice now ingrained. Of course, Fang chose to begin his inspection with my belongings. He dumped the contents of my pack on the dirt with little regard. A water canteen, an extra uniform, and... his prying hands stopped at a carefully folded piece of silk. Xiuying's mosquito net, which she had lent me in case I was sent south. Lieutenant Fang sneered, holding up the cloth with two fingers as if it were a stinking carcass. "Do you think you're too good for our army-issued pallets?" he asked. "Get rid of this. You don't need an extra sheet. It's cursed hot down south."

"It's for mosquitoes," I protested.

Fang's mouth twisted. "Are you afraid of bugs now, pretty boy?"

"The insects down south carry malaria and yellow fever. If our troops contract the disease..."

"He's right," Sparrow chirped up, which only further aggravated Fang.

"Silence!" His eyes were livid. "I ordered you to get rid of it. What will you do?"

I swallowed hard. *One army, one mind.* "Get rid of it, sir."

THAT AFTERNOON, IT WAS TIME TO DECIDE SQUAD LEADERS. THREE months of training had led up to this point—the determination of the best men.

Nominating yourself for the selection process was voluntary. I knew Xiuying would advise I stay out of it. Even loudmouths like Red had chosen to opt out once they'd seen the competition. So everyone was shocked when I'd volunteered the day before.

The gossip ran wild. Even Sky had heard the rumors, which he'd raised during our nightly practice session. "Make me proud," he'd said.

"I thought commanders didn't play favorites."

He'd smirked then. "Prince Liu doesn't. But Sky certainly does."

Within Third Platoon, Lieutenant Fang officiated the tournament. The squad leaders would be chosen via a single-elimination tournament bracket.

But of course the system was rigged. Apparently, Lieutenant Fang hoped to squash my ambitions before they rose any higher. In the very first bracket, he placed me up against Zhao Zilong, the top performer in our platoon. Sparrow protested at that, but Zilong merely shrugged. "Luck is luck," he said. He clearly didn't expect me to put up much of a fight.

Zilong's many friends jeered at me as we entered the training ring. Zilong and I hadn't dueled since that first week, when I'd humiliated myself with my inability to hold a practice sword. Now, as we entered the ring and bowed to each other, we could both see that the other had changed. I for one no longer gripped my sword as if it would fly from my hand. Zilong, meanwhile, had gained bulk in these past three months of training. I could not take him on in strength; I would have to rely on speed. Speed and surprise.

So I attacked first. I leapt toward him, feinted, then struck out with my sword. He faltered, catching the blow at the last second. I had nearly drawn blood; if only I had been a moment faster. His eyes narrowed as he appraised me anew. He had not known about those hours spent training at night, but now he, and everyone else watching, could see that I was different.

The mocking jeers had stopped; the room was silent and still now.

We circled again, birds readying to take flight. Zilong was tense, alert. He tried a flying dragon maneuver on me, but I had learned this same technique and anticipated its end. I dropped and rolled away, then jumped to my feet and lunged at him from behind. His sword met mine with a brilliant clang, the force of it reverberating up my arm. Against his strength, I could not hold his blade for long, so I disengaged and danced back. He tried to counterattack, as did I, relying on my superior kung fu ability to leap across half the ring and deliver a perfect spinning thrust. He dodged, just barely, falling over himself but getting up in the nick of time. He wiped a sheen of sweat from his forehead, breathing hard.

I had the advantage. Everyone could see it, even Zilong. He was going to lose.

Victory coursing through my blood, I tried a move Sky had taught me—wayward crow. I ran forward at a diagonal, feinted, used my footwork to throw him off-balance, then tried to bring my sword in close for a finishing blow. Yet I misjudged Zilong's reaction time, for he managed to parry my sword with his. While we were locked in close proximity, Zilong's superior strength gave him the advantage. And in a single second, he disarmed me.

In disbelief, I staggered back. *I lost*, I realized. *I actually lost*.

A gong vibrated the earth. My surroundings returned to me as I looked beyond the training ring to the watching audience. The crowd gaped at us in shock, before beginning to cheer. "Zhao Zilong! Zhao Zilong! Zhao Zilong!"

"You thought you could become squad leader?" Lieutenant Fang sneered at me, his low voice cutting through the cheers. "You'll never be good enough."

Zilong picked up my practice sword for me. "Nice try, Ren."

I stared down at my calloused hands, trying to ignore the sounds of the cheering crowd, cheering for Zilong, never for me. Trying to ignore Lieutenant Fang's casual malice, Zilong's gloating smirk, even Sparrow's look of resigned acceptance. No one had believed I would actually win. No one had believed in me.

I knew, objectively, I was good enough to become squad leader. I knew I was more competent than most of my platoon. But that wasn't enough. It wasn't enough that I knew it; I needed everyone else to recognize it too.

I needed them to acknowledge *me*.

My hands clenched into fists by my sides. The pressure built in my head, as if I were climbing a mountain, rising in elevation. I felt the dragon's voice flicker in the recesses of my mind, and I was too distracted now to use qi gong to block him out.

"Make them acknowledge you."

I hissed in frustration, trying to tamp down my pride, my anger, my desire for recognition. It wasn't right for a woman to feel such things, but I felt them, and I was a woman. What did that make me?

A perversion. Someone who would never belong.

My body hummed like a tuning fork, my vision blurring as if tears filled my eyes. I looked up and found Zilong's gaze on me. He was still smirking.

And then the water buckets exploded. Zilong—directly in front of them—got hit by the brunt of the force. He was knocked backward, his head slamming into the corner of the weapons rack. And when he raised his head, I saw blood coursing down his cheek.

That was the last thing I saw. My vision, already blurry, went dark. I blinked; nothing. I could see nothing. I rubbed at my eyes, as if expecting to find a blindfold there. There was nothing.

All around me, soldiers were talking. Someone seemed to be taking Zilong to the infirmary; others were discussing how the wood must have rotted, for the buckets to have collapsed. Someone pushed me to the side and I stumbled but caught myself, groping blindly until I found a wall to lean against. Why couldn't I see properly? What was *wrong* with me?

"*You used too much power at once,*" said the dragon in my ear. "*When you overuse your spirit power, your mind and body will attempt to compensate by giving up another one of your senses.*"

So I gave up my sight? I thought, horrified as I clawed at my eyes. But all I could see was pressing darkness. No. I didn't *want* this. I didn't want this power that hurt people, that manifested my cruelty, my jealousy, all the parts of myself that I tried so hard to keep hidden. Minutes that felt like hours passed. The tournament continued, and it was only near the end of the final duel that my vision, at last, began to clear.

A tall hazy shape stopped before me. "Ren? There you are." I recognized Sparrow's voice. "You're white as a ghost."

"Is Zilong . . ." I cleared my throat. "Is Zilong okay?"

Sparrow shrugged. "Bad luck, right? Though maybe it's a good thing those water buckets got to him first. By the look on your face, I could've sworn you were about to sucker punch the poor man."

"I did nothing!" I protested.

"*Liar,*" whispered the dragon.

"You're not real," I whispered, my voice cracking with fear. "I'm *not* mad."

"Sorry?" said Sparrow.

"*It felt good, didn't it?*"

I had not done that. That was not me. I was *normal*. I was like everyone else.

I would claim my place through my sword alone. I would belong.

"Ren, are you . . . crying?"

I ran.

THIRTEEN

Those with spirit power possess an excess, which disrupts the balance of all living things. The excess draws spirits like flies to honey. That is why spirit wielders entail a danger to humanity at large; they disrupt the balance of a proper and equitable society.

—COMMENTARY ON THE WARRING STATES PERIOD, 822

I DREADED SEEING SKY AFTER THAT. HE WOULD HEAR OF MY FAILURE, and it would reflect on him, though no one else knew he was the one who'd trained me. I felt as if I had failed twice, once on my behalf, and once on his.

I arrived early to the training ring and sat on a bench with a staff propped up between my knees. In my head, I replayed the duel with Zilong from earlier that day, remembering when he'd disarmed me. I went over that split second with a fine-toothed comb. I had been too slow; I had miscalculated the distance; I had failed.

I closed my eyes, but the scene repeated over and over in my mind, impossible to ignore. With a groan, I thunked my forehead against the staff. I could feel Zilong knocking the sword from my hand, the hilt flying from my grip, the breathless sensation of loss. I knocked my forehead against the staff again and again. After all my hours of hard work, I had still lost. And following my defeat, with my emotions running high... but I couldn't think about that. What happened with the water buckets was nothing more than a coincidence.

It was a simple accident, I told myself. For the alternative was too distressing to consider.

"Stop or you'll hurt the staff." Sky's voice was teasing.

I raised my head as he nabbed the staff out of my grasp. "Don't be a sore loser."

"Easy for you to say." I folded my arms crossly. "You've never lost in your life."

"False," he said, tossing my staff in the air, then catching it. "I lost against you yesterday."

"In a game of rummy." I rolled my eyes. "The stakes weren't exactly high."

He considered me, balancing the staff over one shoulder. "I've lost before," he said, more quietly. "When the stakes *were* high. It hurts every time." His voice took on an infuriatingly superior tone. "But there's no use dwelling on it."

My face heated. "You don't understand. I'm good enough to be squad leader. But . . . the bracket was rigged. Lieutenant Fang placed me against Zhao Zilong in the first round. And Zilong is the best soldier in our platoon." I kicked the bench. "Lieutenant Fang is a vindictive fool."

"He's your superior in command."

"And we're all going to sicken and die because of him," I muttered, storming off. Sky was no comfort. He was all *duty this, duty that*. He believed you should accept the cards you'd been dealt in life and be satisfied. Well, easy for him to say. He was born a prince of Anlai, and I was born a girl.

"Wait." Sky ran up to me and caught me by the shoulder.

I glanced back, my ill humor like a dark cloud around me. "What."

He had two staffs in hand now. He threw one at me, which I caught instinctively. "Fight me."

Boys, I thought disdainfully, *they think everything can be solved with a fight.*

Then he swung at me, and I whirled back into the ring. We lashed out at each other, leaping and spinning and dodging. Neither of us fought to end the match, only to prolong it.

Surprisingly, it was exactly what I needed. My blood racing, qi coursing through my nerves, sweat pouring down my back—it felt good. My qi wanted to center itself, and my body wanted to move again.

"What were you talking about?" Sky shouted, as we parried back and forth. "About Lieutenant Fang?"

"It's—never mind," I panted, dodging his blow and lunging forward with one of my own.

He frowned as our staffs met. "Is he still picking on you? The necklace debacle was months ago."

"Armlet," I corrected. "He . . . has a good memory."

"I can talk to him, if you wish—"

"No!" I rammed his staff with too much force and accidentally knocked his clavicle. He winced, falling back a step. "It's a small matter," I said. "I'm just letting off steam."

He shrugged, rubbing his collarbone. "Let it out, then."

We circled again, both dripping sweat. I recalled the events of this morning, when Fang had thrown out my mosquito net.

"You know . . ." I trailed off. How was I to explain this? "I have family down south," I started.

"You do? I thought you said you were from the east."

"Well, from my stepfamily's side."

"Hai Meilin." He looked up eagerly, curiosity piqued. "Is she your stepsister?"

I fumbled with my staff and dropped it. Flushing bright red, I pressed my foot against one end and caught the lifted edge with my hand. "No," I said. "It's my stepmother who's from the south."

Sky looked like he wanted to ask more, so I cut him off hurriedly. "She's warned me of yellow fever before. I'm worried..."

"Yes?" His eyes were narrowed. I realized this could come off as a criticism of his command.

"Maybe your army isn't adequately prepared." I bit my tongue. "Forgive me for speaking so openly. I know it's not my place."

He set his staff down, leaning against it as he considered me. "Speak."

"Most of the soldiers don't have mosquito nets. Or coils." I swallowed. "If we catch disease, our army is useless against Ximing."

Sky nodded, understanding. "Father assigned Winter and me to the southern front, knowing that Ximing's forces pale against Leyuan's. But both of us are nescient of the dangers in the south." He eyed me. "It's a fair point you've raised."

"Oh. I... Thanks."

He handed me his staff, then strode toward the tent flap. "Put that away," he said. "I need to confer with my generals. We don't have much time before we set out."

I stood there like a log as I watched him stride into the night. He'd sounded like a commander again in those final moments. It was the first time Sky had ever given me an order.

"*But it won't be the last*," the dragon hissed. I jolted angrily.

I didn't want to admit it, but it wounded my pride to hear Sky order me about like a common foot soldier. I wanted to be his equal, worthy of his attention and respect. I wanted to be able to speak freely with him, without worry of recrimination, or punishment.

If I were captain, or even commander, Lieutenant Fang would not be able to bully me as he did. The other soldiers might not like me, but they would respect me; they would *fear* me. *What would that be like?* I wondered. *What would it be like to have that kind of power?*

My mother's necklace throbbed in response.

"Hey, pretty boy. You're up late."

I spun.

Red meandered toward me. "Who were you talking to?" he asked lazily. "Were you . . . praying?" He grinned. "Disobeying the warlord's mandate, I see."

On closer inspection, his eyes were unfocused and his pupils dilated. Then I smelled the noxious scent on him. Though he held no telltale pipe in his hand, I could recognize that odor from a mile away. *Opium.*

"Were you smoking?"

"Are you going to report me?" He smirked. "My apologies, squad leader." He bowed mockingly. "Oh, wait. You're not squad leader."

But he did not see how furious I was. There was nothing I hated more than this, this waste and indulgence. I shoved him hard, and in his intoxicated state, he couldn't put up a fight. He fell flat on his back, splattering mud everywhere. It had rained recently, and the grass was soaking wet. When he tried to rise, I pinned my boot against his chest, pushing him back into the puddle.

"Listen, Red," I told him, my voice a low snarl. "We're going to war tomorrow. And I'll be damned if I die because one of the soldiers who was supposed to have my back was off getting smashed instead. You can sabotage yourself in your own time. But don't bring the rest of us into this."

Once again, I felt that eerie humming in my body, the weight of something not quite human churning through me, driven by my visceral desire to be obeyed. It felt like qi and yet nothing like qi, like comparing the glow of the moon to the light of dawn.

"*It is spirit power*," said the dragon. "*Lixia.*"

You don't want this, the rational side of my brain told me. But it was too late. I'd lost control.

"*Use your greed,*" the dragon whispered. "*Draw upon that well of hunger.*"

A ring of water rose from the puddle beneath him, encircling his throat. Red started to choke, gasping for breath. I drew the ring closer. Not enough to kill, but enough to hurt. To invoke fear.

And why not kill him? I thought. *To get rid of the evidence.*

"*No, killing him will raise suspicion,*" advised Qinglong. "*Make him forget instead. Compel him—make him abide by your will.*"

"*Listen to me,*" I told Red. It was undeniably my voice that had spoken, but beneath it, layered like an echo, was the voice of another. The dragon's?

Red's eyes went wide and then, strangely, blank. That jarred me. I awoke as if from a trance and realized what I was doing—I was torturing someone. I was inflicting pain on someone and enjoying it.

I was like my father.

"*Forget this,*" I told Red, before things could escalate. "*Get out of my sight.*"

At the command, I felt the elusive jolt of spirit power leave my body, tunneling into Red. His expression vacant, Red straightened and hurried away, not making a single sound of protest.

Had I somehow... forced him to follow my will?

Overcome by nausea, I squatted down in the mud, making sure I wasn't about to keel over or vomit. My vision had gone blurry again, but thankfully, I could still see the grass under my feet, the trees in the distance. Then I looked down at my arms.

My veins were corded black.

My stomach heaved and I barely had time to aim for a nearby bush before the contents of my stomach came up. I retched until there was nothing left. Then, waiting for my nausea to settle, I rested my head between my knees.

"*You did well,*" whispered the dragon. "*But next time, remember to also conserve your qi. You cannot use one without the other.*"

"There won't be a next time," I hissed, before blocking him with my mental shields. I'd had enough.

Alone, the misery of my circumstances struck me anew. The sea dragon and his spirit power were real; I could deny his existence no longer. But this would simply remain one more secret I could tell no one about.

For a human to wield spirit power—that was *black magic*. Praying to spirits for divine intercession was one thing; black magic was entirely another. If before I had toed the line of acceptability, now I was completely out of bounds.

My stomach clenched, nausea rippling through me once more. Though mostly forgotten and disbelieved, black magic was still strictly forbidden. My mother, in her most anxious and unwell moments, had voiced aloud her nightmares of discovery—fearing imprisonment, torture, even death by dragging.

Now they were my fears too.

The loneliness constricted in my chest, burying itself deep in my body like a parasite. My lies continued to pile on top of one another. I had comrades now, *friends*—but still there were parts of me they could never know.

I was an abomination, a thing not meant to exist in the Three Kingdoms. Even I recognized my own depravity and loathed it. How much more would others loathe me?

My instincts remained the same: *Lie, hide it, maintain your disguise. Don't let people know who you really are, or they'll cast you out. Your hard-won belonging is as delicate as a hummingbird's wing.*

I would do anything to protect it.

FOURTEEN

During the Warring States Period (798–820), usage of black magic grew rampant, reaching new heights at the turn of the century. Notably, the land grew barren during this period, and over one quarter of the population succumbed to famine, disease, or infighting. Following the unification of Tianjia in 820, Emperor Wu's first edict passed was the ban on black magic, which at the time was defined as any manifestation of spirit power visible to the human eye. Thus, while fortune-telling remained in vogue in the capital, most spirit wielders were forced to relocate south, where the emperor did not keep as close a watch.

—A COMPREHENSIVE OVERVIEW OF LIXIA-INDUCED DISORDERS, 910

"YOU SPOKE WITH PRINCE LIU ABOUT THE MOSQUITO COILS?" Sparrow found me at breakfast, where I was drowsily contemplating my congee.

"What are you on about now?" I asked, reaching for a youtiao fried breadstick from his bowl.

Sparrow slapped my hand away. "Everyone's talking about it—how Prince Liu credited *you* for coming up with the idea!"

"What idea?" I sat up, unpleasantly roused.

"I didn't even know you talked to him. And now it seems like you're best buds."

"Don't be absurd. He's the prince," I said. "I'm not even a squad leader."

"You're still hung up on that?" Sparrow guffawed. "Prince Liu's issued mosquito coils for every platoon."

Mosquito coils were incense sticks shaped in spirals so that they burned for a longer duration. Xiuying had once shown me the ones she'd made from scratch, using leftover ingredients like orange peels and chrysanthemum. Last night, I'd suggested mosquito nets to Sky, but he had made the better choice—coils would be more cost-effective for an army of fifty thousand.

I spooned a mouthful of congee, thinking. Sky was smarter than I gave him credit for.

"Bragging already?" A tall shadow fell over us. I didn't have to raise my head to recognize Lieutenant Fang's glowering demeanor. "You think you're so clever. Let's see how clever you are on the battlefield, boy."

With that, he walked away, leaving me with an ill feeling of foreboding. "He's just jealous," Sparrow muttered. "He's probably afraid you'll replace him, and then he'll be out of a job."

I stirred my congee before it congealed. I had no head for politics.

Fang stopped at the head of the mess hall, issuing orders. "Check the fresh water supply," he told Zilong. "Make sure the buckets are secure this time."

I stiffened, but no one so much as glanced my way. As long as no one connected the collapsed water buckets to me, I was safe.

After breakfast, we assembled in our assigned squads. In an ironic twist of fate, I was assigned to Zilong's squad. Sparrow was assigned to Wolf's squad, which caused him to bid farewell to me as if he were leaving for a faraway kingdom. "Don't forget about me," he said, affecting a plaintive voice. "You'll always be like a brother to me," he announced, punching me on the arm. "There's no greater bond than that."

"What about your future wife?" joked Zilong, who was unabashedly eavesdropping.

Sparrow regarded him seriously. "Women and children are like garments, but brothers are like limbs. If you lose a piece of clothing, you can get another one. But if you lose a limb, you'll always feel its loss."

WE MARCHED FOR THREE WEEKS TOWARD XIMING. IN MY FORMER LIFE, I'd never realized how vast Anlai was, how far its borders stretched. The seasons passed from late spring to early summer, and we celebrated the Dragon Boat Festival by trudging thirty li through a narrow gorge. And yet Sky told me we were lucky. We hadn't heard of Ximing making any defense preparations. It was almost sinister—how negligent they were. As if they were fools. Or... as if they were unafraid of us.

It made no sense, Sky told me one night, after we had passed Mount Fuxi and were nearing the southern border. Leyuan was the largest kingdom with the greatest armed forces, but Anlai was the wealthiest; it held the most natural resources—and controlled the capital of the former dynasty. And yet the kingdom that had broken the truce and first declared war was Ximing—the weakest kingdom of the three and the smallest by far. Ximing lacked both population and arable land. The kingdom had starved and emptied its storehouses during the last famine, so that Ximing had been forced to go to Leyuan and Anlai to broker trade agreements that greatly disfavored their own people.

"Our spies report that their armies have yet to mobilize. Instead, their chancellor seems preoccupied with hiring out local bandits and monks. Apparently, his monks are searching for precious stones, as if they hope to enter the jewelry trade." His brows furrowed. "It makes no sense."

I spun my staff with one hand. I didn't like to think about things that lay beyond my control. "Let's get back to training."

ON THE NIGHT BEFORE WE REACHED XIMING, I COULDN'T SLEEP. SKY was occupied with endless strategy meetings; he'd skipped increasingly more training sessions as of late. The busier Sky was, the more idle I became. The nights he didn't come to training practice, I played games of rummy with my squad instead. Endless days of marching had left me lethargic and inert. Even my dreams had grown tedious—repetitive visions of an empty spirit realm, empty but for me.

The dragon did not appear again.

No matter. Tomorrow we would reach Ximing. There I would cross into a new land, step foot into a kingdom separate from my own. I wanted to tell Xiuying so she could share in my excitement. But I knew Xiuying would not be excited for me. She would be afraid.

There would be enemy soldiers across the border, with every intent to kill me. And I would have to fight back. And I would have to kill.

With restless energy brewing beneath my skin, I dressed in the dark and went out to train.

The forests down south were much louder than the ones surrounding Chuang Ning. These forests hummed with perpetual motion and verve, at all hours of the day. I could hear cicadas screaming from the treetops, their calls loud and unceasing. And in the distance, I could make out the steady crashing of waves, for beyond the forest lay the sea.

I stayed far away from the sea.

Lighting an oil lamp, I headed for the outer edge of the clearing, not close enough that I would wake my sleeping platoon, but not far enough that I couldn't see the tent line. I began moving through crow formation, each step methodical and memorized. By now, my sword felt like an extension of my arm, its weight as familiar as my own limbs. As I lifted my blade and slashed it through the air, the metal caught the lamplight and reflected it into the gloom.

Something moved in the trees.

I froze, breathing heavy from exertion. Slowly, I raised my blade again, then tilted it at an angle, so that the yellow lamplight refracted. Nothing. Just shadowy trees swaying in the breeze.

But I could have sworn I'd seen something.

Unnerved, I glanced around. Soldiers were assigned to patrol the camp perimeter every night; tonight, it had been Second Platoon's responsibility. Where were they?

Without sheathing my sword, I turned in the direction of that wayward shadow. I couldn't be certain, but I thought it had moved west. To my relief, the commander's tent lay in the opposite direction. Sky wouldn't be in danger. Though quite probably, there was no danger at all, and I was imagining monsters in the dark.

I prowled along the camp perimeter, pausing by the village well. There was nothing wrong with it, only Lieutenant Fang had ordered us to leave the pail on the ground after drawing water, rather than on the edge, to ensure that the pail did not slip and fall inside, leaving more work for the next soldier.

But the pail was lying on its side now, balanced on the rim of the well. I hesitated, then moved closer. That was when I saw the boot.

The heel of a worn boot peeked out from behind the well. A soldier had been drawing water, and then . . . I gasped as I saw the body. The boy was lying prone on the forest floor, unmoving. He wore Second Platoon garb.

Then I felt a cold intrusion in my mind. Though it had been weeks since he'd last spoken to me, I recognized Qinglong's voice at once: *"Watch out!"*

FIFTEEN

When the phoenix called, the spirit of bronze answered. The spirit of copper returned her song. Only the spirit of iron, stubborn to the end, despised her beauty, and resolved to forever defy it.

—BOOK OF CHANGE, 207

I WHIRLED AROUND AS A BLACK-CLOTHED MAN BROUGHT HIS SPEAR down on me. My training took over as my blade met his with a vicious crack. He tried to parry, but his spear was shoddily made and splintered under the weight of my sword. I kicked him in the chest. He stumbled back and I thrust my sword forward into his gut. The resistance of flesh shocked me, but momentum forced my blow through. With gritted teeth, I pulled my sword out, and the man fell soundlessly, the forest foliage carpeting his body. His eyes were blank and unseeing, his expression frozen in a perpetual grimace. I staggered back, nearly dropping my sword. I had just killed a man.

I had imagined this moment so many times before. Not this stranger, but always—Father.

It was during his moments of hysteria, when my father would slap, strangle, wrench at my hair like I was an animal. All those times, I never fought back. I never lifted so much as a finger against him. And yet, in my mind's eye, I had imagined so vividly—the act of killing him. I knew it was blasphemous to imagine such a fate befalling your father. I knew it made me a monster. But I thought, like a coward perhaps, that because I had never acted on such impulses, I could still claim innocence.

I felt a flicker of impatience and recalled the presence of another, living inside my head. My stomach curled in revulsion. "Why did you warn me?" I hissed.

"*Believe it or not, our goals are one and the same,*" said the dragon dryly. "*However vexing your methods are.*"

"I don't trust you."

"*At least you've stopped ignoring me.*"

Because you're real, I thought. *Or—because I'm like my mother.*

"*Your thoughts are circular.*" A sound like a yawn. "*I tire of them.*"

I heard voices in the distance and shook myself awake. With adrenaline coursing through me, I couldn't even bring myself to be afraid of the spirit.

I had more urgent matters at hand. Running toward the supply line, I confirmed my worst suspicions. The patrol soldiers were missing—captured or dead. In their place, I saw black-clad men moving through the gloom, rummaging through the covered wagons, entering soundlessly, and leaving only moments later. I counted at least four dozen of them.

What are they doing to the supplies? I wondered. *Are they . . . poisoning them?*

"*What else?*" Qinglong replied, as if I'd spoken aloud. "*Did you think they were leaving gifts for you?*"

By their nondescript clothing, they looked like thieves. I recalled what Sky had mentioned about the Ximing chancellor hiring bandits. Bandits did not have the advantage of numbers. But they had stealth. And unlike us, they knew this terrain.

One of them glanced over his shoulder, and I ducked into the undergrowth, my heart hammering in my chest. I gripped my sword so tightly my hands burned. I had to stop them, I thought.

But there were too many. If I tried to take them on at once, they'd kill me.

"Fool! Go mobilize your men."

Somehow, that felt more frightening than taking on faceless bandits. I imagined trying to get Zilong and Wolf and Lieutenant Fang to obey me. "I can't," I whispered. "No one will listen to me. I'm not even squad leader." That sparked an idea. "I'll tell Sky! He'll issue the order."

"Go right ahead, take your sweet time with it," Qinglong said, voice ridden with sarcasm.

I edged away from the supply wagons, half-crouched, then made a break for it, sprinting through camp. When I arrived at the commander's tent, out of breath and panting, Sky's personal guards looked at me with undisguised disdain.

"I need to speak to Prince Liu," I said breathlessly. "Now!"

"Prince Liu is currently indisposed, soldier. You can report to your lieutenant in the morning. He will submit any requests for—"

"It's an urgent matter!" I tried to push through them, but they immediately raised their weapons, pointing their swords at me.

"Stand down," the more senior one said, a new note of warning in his tone. I'd seen him around before; he was one of Sky's longtime personal guards. "If you do not comply—"

"Let him through, Captain Luo." A weary voice, rough with sleep, came from within. "I know him."

Captain Luo glared at me as if I were to blame for every one of Prince Liu's sleepless nights. I shouldered past him and hurried inside.

"What is it, Ren?" Sky asked me, his voice raspy from being woken. He was shirtless, wearing only a pair of breeches. As he sat up in his pallet, I watched the corded muscles in his chest flex and contract, the planes of them hard as hewn stone. I blinked forcibly and dragged my gaze away. I was touched to see that he'd been using a mosquito net and burning a coil. He'd taken my advice.

But as I observed him, he observed me. Now he cocked his head at me like a bird. "You know," he said, rubbing sleep from his eyes. "Sometimes you remind me of..."

I shrank from him as if struck. What if he formed the connection between me and the eccentric girl he'd met in Wenxi District?

"Bandits!" I cried out, startling both of us. "They're poisoning the western supply line. I'm not sure if they're planning an ambush too..."

Sky shot to his feet, brushing past me out of the tent. "Sound the alarm now, Tao," he told Captain Luo, who hastened to keep up with Sky's furious strides. "Send reinforcements to the western food stores. And assemble the general council."

I stared at their backs as they moved farther and farther away. Then Sky glanced over his shoulder at me. "Ren, aren't you coming?"

I gulped and followed. I thought I'd been dismissed.

Belatedly, the younger guard ran after him, clutching Sky's uniform to his chest. "Commander! Your clothes!"

Soldiers had begun stumbling out of their tents, bleary-eyed and bewildered. Some even headed toward the trenches, as if going about their usual morning routines.

"Second Platoon is unaccounted for, sir," Lieutenant Tong of First Platoon was briefing Sky. "We've sent for—"

The first wagon exploded not ten yards from us. I sensed the hiss before the fuse caught and dived in front of Sky, shoving him to the ground. We both fell as debris sprayed everywhere.

For a breathless moment, our eyes locked, our faces mere inches from each other. I met his startled gaze, felt his hands tighten instinctively around me. Then the world returned. I jumped to my feet and Sky rolled off the ground as Luo Tao and a dozen other guards converged around him, guarding their commander. "Get the prince to safety!" Lieutenant Tong ordered. "Take him north—"

"No," Sky said, his voice like steel. "I need to see Winter now." Winter commanded Sixth Company, which was stationed west of ours.

"Now do you wish you'd listened to me?" Qinglong had returned.

"Don't rub it in," I said, flexing my ankle to make sure it wasn't sprained. "What are they targeting? Is it just the food stores?"

"Oh, so you trust me now."

"I don't trust you, I'm just gathering opinions," I hedged.

I could've sworn I heard a snort. *"Use your head and put out the fire before it spreads. And stop thinking about Prince Liu's shirtless physique."*

I choked. "Stop reading my mind!"

I grabbed blankets to suffocate the fire, which had spread in small flames across the supply line. More people converged in the clearing with every passing moment. There were Anlai soldiers everywhere, and few bandits. But this couldn't be the sole purpose of their attack, could it? I had estimated over fifty bandits earlier, when they had presumed themselves to be unwatched.

The dragon had told me to use my head. But it was hard to think with the fire crackling and hissing around me, soldiers running in every direction and horses spitting and rearing. I mulled over what Sky had told me days earlier. Ximing didn't have a standing army. If I were the warlord of Ximing, and I suddenly declared war and drafted a handful of fishermen and sailors, what would I need? How could I send them off to fight?

First of all, teachers—to train them. But that was dispensable. They could learn on the job. What else? I recalled the poor quality of the bandit's spear. It had been shoddily made, using cheap materials. If I lacked resources in my own kingdom, then I would steal. *The armory!*

I eyed the eastern quarter of camp, which was decidedly less on fire. Because the bandits didn't need to steal our food stores, I thought, but they did need to take our weapons, intact.

Before I could take off running, I collided with Sparrow.

"Ren!" he exclaimed. He too was shirtless. Why had no one bothered to put on their clothes? "What's going on? They told us to rally around the western supply line—"

"Forget that. We need to protect the armory," I said. "Can you find Zilong? Bring Twelfth Squad. And Thirteenth, if you can manage it."

"What about you?"

"Meet me at the armory. I need to confirm their intentions."

"It's dangerous, Ren! You can't go alone."

"I'm not alone," I answered without thinking. Then I ran, before Sparrow could question my sanity.

"*I would not advise such forthcoming speech,*" said the dragon. "*And I am* not *your chaperone.*"

"I didn't know you had a sense of humor," I retorted aloud, zigzagging through camp. In the chaos, I figured no one would notice one soldier talking to himself.

"*All spirits do. Or else we'd be subjected to an eternity of boredom.*"

The armory was noticeably emptier than the western quarter. I heard the clink of metal and ducked behind a tree, just as a trio of bandits scurried out of a covered wagon with their arms full of small cloth bundles. Strange, I thought, for I'd imagined they would be stealing weapons. Spears and swords and bows would not be so small.

I waited a beat longer, then saw another few bandits emerging from a different wagon, also with what looked to be small parcels in their arms. By the way they carried them, the bundles appeared heavy. A third emerged, this one with a giant axe, which made more sense, but why take an axe and not a sword, which was probably the most expensive and prized weapon in the armory?

Bewildered, I waited until I was sure the coast was clear, then quickly darted inside the deserted wagon where the thieves had come from. And I wasn't a moment too soon, for just as I entered the safety of the wagon, I heard more bandits converge in the clearing, entering a wagon directly behind mine. By the sound of their voices, there seemed to be over a dozen of them.

Careful not to make a single sound, I peered into the gloom, my eyes adjusting to the dark. I saw the steel swords stored in their usual place, untouched. The longbows too, were arranged neatly in wooden racks, coils of bowstring still folded in oiled paper. *Strange and stranger*, I thought, before my gaze drifted to the spears and discovered most of the spearheads missing.

They'd taken the iron spearheads and left the bronze ones behind. So too with the axe; they'd taken only the iron axe-head. Why were they stealing our iron?

Strident voices grew outside the wagon, until one voice, loud enough to be discernible above the rest, cut through the quarrel. "We have time—they haven't even noticed us. Let's do a final sweep through," the bandit leader ordered. His Ximing accent was smoother and more tonal than our northern dialect, though still possible for me to comprehend. "Sima will have our heads if we miss anything."

Belatedly, I realized what this meant for me. I shot to my feet just as the wagon flap lifted, and a bandit hopped inside without carefully inspecting its interior. He didn't notice me until it was too late, and I struck him in the temple with the hilt of my blade.

The blow had been silent, but the sound of his body slumping to the floor was not. There was a dull thunk, and I swore under my breath; I should've thought to catch him.

"What was that?" The bandit leader's voice was sharp. "Little Frog?"

The wagon flap lifted, and the sudden glare of the lamp blinded me. I recoiled, then tried to take advantage of their surprise by leaping over them. I was too slow. As I jumped from the wagon, I felt a knife slash my sword arm and I fell, dropping my blade. I rolled to my feet seconds before the bandit leader threw a dagger where my head had just been. The dagger landed in the dirt, and he chuckled, largely unworried.

Because they had me surrounded. I staggered back as bandits closed in from all sides, kicking my sword out of reach. There were over a dozen here. I wondered where the others had gone. Had they taken the iron and run? What were they planning to do with it?

I needed to tell Sky. I needed to warn him that Ximing was a threat, that something was terribly wrong. Something that we had not prepared for. But my throat closed as I realized I would never have the opportunity to tell him, because I was going to die here.

SIXTEEN

On the subject of Cardinal Spirits, much is known about elemental magic, namely, the ability mediums possess to wield the natural elements of their spirit. But beyond elemental magic, it is a lesser-known fact that the mental abilities of spirits transfer similarly onto their vessels, so that the more powerful of these mediums also learn the ability to read and control the human mind.

—LOST JOURNALS OF AN 8TH-CENTURY LIXIA SCHOLAR, DATE UNKNOWN

"HOW MUCH IS SIMA PAYING YOU?" I BLURTED OUT, MY VOICE shaking as I stood there, defenseless. I had no idea who Sima was, but I assumed he was the man behind their mission. "I can pay more."

"You?" The bandit leader guffawed. He stepped toward me; his gait was odd, lurching. "You're just a foot soldier."

"I-I have the ear of the prince," I said. "I can arrange for you—"

"We'll have the ear of the prince soon enough, won't we, boys?" he crowed. "We'll have his ear and the rest of him too."

"Listen, I have more iron," I invented wildly. "Storehouses full of it. I can trade it to you—"

The bandit leader eyed me with curiosity. *He didn't realize I knew about the iron.* "We don't want it," he said. "We're trying to get rid of it."

I stored this new piece of information in my head. "Then how will Sima react when he realizes you've left behind a whole storehouse full?" I asked, changing course quickly. "Do you think he'll be pleased with you then?"

The bandit threw back his head and laughed. "You're a clever little fox, aren't you? You're funny." But he brandished his axe, and I realized I'd somehow unwittingly revealed my ignorance. He would dispose of me now. "Pity we can't leave behind eyewitnesses."

He walked toward me, swaying. As he raised his axe in the air, I cringed back. Instinct screamed at me to shut my eyes, but I refused to resign myself to my fate—

An arrow whistled through the air and embedded itself in the bandit leader's neck. Only one person I knew could shoot like that.

Zhao Zilong leapt into the crowd seconds later, swapping his bow for a curved steel blade. I had never been happier to see him.

"You came!" I shouted. He threw me the spear of the fallen bandit and I caught it in the air, spinning around to stab the bandit behind me.

"You looked like you needed the help," Zilong said, as steady as always. "Next time don't take off without your squad. That's an order."

"You can lecture me after we survive!" I yelled back, before beheading the bandit closest to me. I soon lost myself in the fighting.

Thirteenth Squad arrived on the heels of Twelfth Squad, and Wolf led his men to surround the armory. With the added reinforcements, the bandits were being overwhelmed, and they recognized this too. We would win this fight.

Out of the corner of my eye, I noticed a bandit take advantage of the chaos to slip into the forest. I grabbed a bow and quiver from the overturned wagon, fired an arrow, missed, then chased after him.

He was injured. His tunic dripped blood on the forest floor, leaving a clear trail for me to follow. I decided to change my approach. I followed soundlessly, watching as he limped and swayed, clinging to trees for balance. He followed a small creek into another forest clearing, one I hadn't known about. My sense of direction was skewed without the sun to guide me, but I thought we were on the side of the forest closest to the seaside fishing village.

As I trailed the bandit, the gentle sounds of the forest replaced the ruckus of battle. The air smelled of running water, of sweet cexi blossoms, but also—of blood. My tunic and trousers were sticky with it. Perhaps some of it was my own, but most belonged to those whose lives I'd taken. My adrenaline waned as I ruminated on the past few hours, on how many men I'd killed. What had frightened me was not the killing itself, but how *easy* it was. Mindless almost, as if it were only a natural course of action. My sword arm knew what to do; it knew how to kill. But of course, for I had practiced these maneuvers again and again. Somehow, during all those hours of training, I had not realized this.

I had spent so many nights practicing my fighting technique, not with the aim of killing but with the aim of proving myself. I had wanted to show my platoon how skilled I was. I had wanted them to fear and respect me. But I had not thought beyond it—to the consequences of my actions. I had not thought of what being in this army, in this war, would mean.

Xiuying had known. And that was why she had looked at me with such fear in her eyes. Because she had known what I would become.

And she had known that I would never be able to get away with it.

"Do you think they'll let you live?" she'd asked me, on our last night together. *"They would never let a woman get away with something like this."*

"Something like what?"

"They would never let a woman hold on to power."

THE BANDIT STOPPED SUDDENLY AT THE BASE OF A LARGE TREE, JOLTING me from my thoughts. I went still, not wanting to alert him to my presence, but then he bent and reached inside the tree trunk. I did not want him to pull out a sword, not when I only had a bow and a single arrow with me.

Making a split-second decision, I crept up to him and struck him with my boot, catching his shoulder with a high kick. He fell face-first to the ground, narrowly avoiding the stones lining the creek. I turned him over, then pressed my boot to his throat. "How many of you are there?" I asked him, raising my voice to be heard over the gurgle of the stream.

He gaped at me, stunned. Then—assessing.

"Answer me!"

"A-about a hundred of us, give or take." *A hundred*, I thought grimly. So I had not encountered the full extent of their forces.

"What is your mission?"

"You know—to raid your armory."

I studied him; he didn't blink. *He's lying.*

So many men, and for what? To poison our food stores? To steal our iron? Why hire a hundred bandits when you could accomplish those tasks with fewer men? Their leader, this man called Sima, had sought considerable manpower for this mission, and he'd been willing to pay for it . . . because his goals were manifold.

The bandit leader's words returned to me. *"We'll have the ear of the prince soon enough . . . We'll have his ear and the rest of him too."*

"The prince. You want the prince," I realized with mounting horror. "Why?"

His answering smile was crude. "Figured that out, have you? Too bad you don't know his little secret, then."

"What secret?"

The fear on my face must have shown, because he began to laugh. "Your precious prince is a liar." He wheezed for breath, and I loosened my grip on him. "You Anlai folk are all hypocrites."

"Wh-what are you talking about?" My voice was shaking.

"Sima wants him because he's... touched." The man's eyes glittered. "You know, we've been following your company for three days now. Last night I caught sight of him, before dark. He's a pretty thing, isn't he? No wonder he doesn't fight. Sima told us to strip him naked, to make sure all his belongings were taken from him... he just needs to be kept alive..."

I recoiled. The images were too violent, too horrific. Cold sweat broke out over my skin. I looked at the bandit and could barely see him; my vision had begun to dim, blurring at the edges.

Quick as a shadow, the bandit withdrew a hidden knife and slashed me in the calf. I screamed and fell to my knees, and he quickly pinned me to the ground and brought his knife to my throat. I struggled against him, but he had my arms and legs locked in place. I was defenseless against his attack.

A small, simple mistake—one that would lead to my death. But I couldn't die. Not like this. Not now.

The rush of running water roused me. *"Your greed is unending,"* the dragon had said. *"An ocean's hunger."*

I called upon that greed, that well of desire. I felt the familiar humming in my limbs, the gathering of qi and spirit power. I wanted to live. I wanted to live. I wanted to—

The bandit raised his head, awestruck. I followed his gaze and saw the dozens of water droplets hanging in the air between us, floating.

"Release me," I ordered, keeping my eyes on him. I could feel the weight of his elemental threads, the unique energy that made up

his inner being, and I let my qi mirror his. Earth and metal; my qi conformed.

His grip loosened, but his expression wavered, fighting my control. "*Release me*," I said again, and this time I felt the deep echo in my bones.

He obeyed.

He looked from the stream to me. "You're touched too," he said, and there was a new emotion in his voice.

Fear.

I felt my vision beginning to flicker. I clenched and unclenched my fists, willing myself to stay awake, to endure. The power running through me was too much. My lungs were closing; I was going to hyperventilate.

"Tell me, why do you fight for Anlai? Why do you fight for Anlai when you know they'll butcher you for your lixia?"

"Li-lixia?" The dragon had used that word too.

"What your ilk calls—*black magic*." He leaned forward, his fear lessening in the face of my panic. "For humans to take the abilities of gods—and make them their own."

"You're wrong! I don't— I wouldn't—"

"How weak you are," he sneered, reaching for me. "I should take you with the Anlai princeling. Perhaps Sima will reward the extra catch—"

I did not understand the laws of spirit power, but I knew the rules of kung fu. Focusing my qi as I did before combat, I concentrated on my target and then, following instinct—let go.

The water droplets condensed in the air and merged, then flew into his mouth, choking him. I started in alarm, watching as his eyes rolled back in his head. Foam rose from his lips until he turned limp and, finally, went still.

He'd . . . drowned.

I'd drowned him.

My limbs were trembling, uncontrollably now. I took a ragged breath but drew little air. If this kept up, I was going to keel over. My skin was slick with sweat, yet I felt a deep chill in my bones.

My vision went dark. I lost my balance and fell, then cried out as I felt the bandit's limp body beneath me. Crawling away from him, I tried to stand but toppled, this time landing on my wounded leg. The noxious scent of blood, everywhere. I felt my consciousness slide . . .

No, no, no. I couldn't faint. Not when Sky's life was in danger. I exhaled slowly and concentrated on rebalancing my qi. *Wood, fire, earth, metal, water.* I looped through each element, forcing my mind to settle.

Slowly, the world returned. My gaze flickered to the bandit before I turned away, disturbed by the sight of his corpse. But now I recalled why I'd followed him in the first place, and went back to the tree trunk where he'd stopped.

I peered inside the hollow, then pulled out several heavy cloth bundles. Immediately a sharp lancing pain went up my arms. I dropped them with a gasp, feeling as if I'd been burned. I felt lightheaded, dizzy. For a second, my head had felt strangely . . . *empty*.

As if a presence long burrowed there had, for a moment, disappeared.

Fearing I would lose my balance, I knelt on the ground. The contents of the bundle had tumbled out in the dirt. Inside was a motley assortment of iron tools, weapons, and household items. It wasn't just stolen goods from the armory, as I'd expected. They'd taken the head of a hammer, horseshoes, iron blocks, and other oddities that had no purpose when removed from their wooden counterparts. Why had they done this? I assumed Sima had paid them to get rid of all the iron they could find.

I had no time to mull this over now. I had to find the other bandits; I had to find Sky. If Sky was still at the camp, he would be safe, surrounded by our army. But if he'd been taken already... I had to find him. Why had the bandit claimed he was... "touched"? Sky was not like me. Sky was good; he was pure; he would be the hero of every story. Perhaps I had simply misheard. Regardless, it was not my priority now.

Where would they have taken him? And for that matter, how had the bandits traveled here? On foot? But they had waylaid us so suddenly, and even outwitted Prince Liu's spies. By horse, then? But where were the horses? And surely bandits could not afford horses for their entire crew.

I looked back at the fallen bandit. His face was tanned and weathered with sun. I recalled the way he'd swayed when walking, as if perpetually off-balance. Sea legs, I realized with a pang. I strode toward the bandit and looked more closely at his shoes. Deck shoes.

They'd come by boat. That was why we hadn't anticipated the ambush.

I only had one arrow left, and no blade. I ripped a piece of cloth from my tunic and tied it around my calf to stanch the wound. Then I swiped the bandit's flint knife—this would have to do—and ran in the direction of the sea.

SEVENTEEN

> *As to how the new chancellor has managed his unprecedented rise to power, some suspect a secret deal undercut with Warlord Cao. The exact nature of the deal is unknown, but it is alleged to be an offer no man could refuse.*
>
> —MINISTER JIA, IN A PRIVATE MISSIVE TO PRINCE LIU, 923

THE SUN BEGAN TO EMERGE. PALE RAYS OF DAWN LIGHT PENEtrated the canopy overhead to grace the forest floor, and gradually, birds awoke, trilling morning greetings.

I did not know if I was too late. My body was failing me, my legs burning and begging me to slow down. Stubbornly, I maintained my breakneck pace, praying I would not faint before I found Sky. Then, on the verge of collapse, I heard voices in the distance. I veered in the direction of the sound, slowing as I caught sight of the growing crowd.

Here were the bandits I had not accounted for. Through the trees, I couldn't make an exact estimate, but there looked to be at least two dozen. They were dragging a prisoner with them, someone who wore fine silk robes, with long dark hair flowing loosely down his back. I caught a flash of his face. Pale, like the moon. *Sky!* My heart threatened to spill out of my chest.

Then I noticed another contingent pursuing them, this one nearly twice the size of the bandit crew. At the front, I recognized

Sky on his stallion, charging toward the bandits. His personal retinue of guards surrounded him.

Confused, I darted closer, crouching beneath a clump of dense huya bushes.

"Stop!" Sky's voice resounded through the woods. I couldn't make out his expression from this distance, but he sounded furious.

"I don't believe you're in a position to command me, prince." The bandit who spoke held the captive, pressing a knife against his throat. My blood crept.

I recognized the captive then. It was Sky's brother Winter.

Has the bandit been speaking of Winter all along?

"We're taking him with us. He'll be treated like an honored guest by the chancellor," the bandit leader said, voice mocking. "But Chancellor Sima was clear about our orders—if you intervene and try to stop us, we'll kill him. Then we'll just dispatch a body. Saves us some trouble, don't you think?"

Sima is the chancellor of Ximing?

One of the bandits in the rear turned, and I immediately ducked, breathing hard. This was bad. I stood between the bandits and their ship, and the bandits stood between me and Sky.

Then Sky dismounted from his horse. "Commander!" I recognized the voice of Sky's guard, Captain Luo, pitched high with distress.

Sky did not heed him. He dropped his sword on the ground before advancing toward the bandit leader, his hands raised in surrender. What could he possibly be thinking?

"Take me instead," he said. "I will go in his place."

You baichi idiot! I wanted to shake him and knock some sense into him. But he was out of reach, and I could not think straight. I was going to watch Sky get taken prisoner by bandits and carted off to the Ximing chancellor. And I would never see him again.

The bandits conferred with one another. I couldn't make out their words from this distance. I edged closer, scrambling from one tree to the next. I was within earshot now, only thirty feet away. *Thirty feet*, I realized. That was the standard distance for target practice.

I had not thought of it earlier, because I did not trust my archery abilities. No one in my platoon would've called me a superb archer by a long shot. And the complexity of this shot was unparalleled. If I missed, and struck the sixth prince instead . . . I swallowed, my mouth dry as sand. I had one arrow left. I could not miss.

I would get only one shot.

I watched and waited as Sky left his guards behind and advanced alone, defenseless and vulnerable. He stood in the gap between the two parties, his face carefully impassive. He was staring at his brother.

For Sky, I could not miss.

I strung my bow with trembling hands, repeating Sky's advice in my head. *Widen your stance. Don't grip so hard. Align the arrow with your target.* Holding my breath, I waited for an opening. The man holding Winter was obscured by his crew, but he was turning slowly, ever so slowly.

The bandits finished conferring, before their leader turned to Sky. "Actually," he said, voice dry, "we don't want you."

The crowd shifted in surprise. Winter came into view then, along with his captor.

Now. Qi flooded my veins. I released my arrow and let it fly through the air, forcing myself not to blink as if my sheer stubbornness could will it in the right direction.

But as the arrow veered closer, I saw my mistake. I had been aiming for the neck, but I had aimed too low. With a clean thunk, the arrow struck the bandit's leg.

I swore. The man was still alive, only screaming. He whirled around to seek the arrow's source—

Sky leapt forward, capitalizing on his distraction. He twisted and kicked his brother's captor in the stomach, then rolled to the ground to dodge a flying spear. The prince's men followed, Lieutenant Fang falling into the fray and fighting with the ferocity of a dozen soldiers. I had never seen him in action before, and now I understood why he was respected in the army, despite his illogical and absurd temper.

Captain Luo pulled Winter out of harm's way. I breathed out a sigh of relief before noticing a bandit staring at me; after firing, I'd forgotten to duck back behind cover. He charged and I swore; I had no arrows left. Using my bow, I managed to disarm him, before he jumped me and we both went rolling down the forest slope. The bandit was slow but huge, over twice my size. We wrestled, sliding, before I felt him pin me to the ground, wrapping his meaty hands around my throat. I choked, but with the last reservoirs of my energy, I remembered my flint knife and stabbed him in the side. He groaned, his grip loosening but still tight, and I stabbed him again, and again. He collapsed on top of me. My muscles burning, I tried to push him off, but I could not. It felt like a ton of bricks had just caved in on top of me.

From above, I could hear that the fight had ended. Without their valued prisoner to protect them, the bandits were no match against the sheer size of the Anlai contingent, which only continued to grow as more soldiers joined the fray. Lieutenant Fang was barking orders now; I could recognize the wrathful tone of his voice anywhere. It was usually my cue to run.

I summoned the last dregs of my strength and tried once more to lift the man off me. He didn't so much as budge. Had he gotten heavier in death?

"Ren?" someone called. It was Sky.

I heard his footsteps treading down the forest slope. "Over here," I answered weakly.

Moments later, I felt the massive weight lift off my chest as Sky heaved the corpse off me. He looked down at me, bruised, bloodied, but alive. Wonderfully alive.

Tears sprang to my eyes. He offered me a hand, pulling me to my feet. I smiled at him, before considering something. "How did you know it was me?" I asked, brows creasing. Surely he hadn't seen me in the ensuing fight.

"Only you would be clever enough," he said, before grinning, his eyes twinkling with merriment. "And only you would shoot him in the thigh."

EIGHTEEN

And on the harvest moon, the full moon glows red, shining light on long-concealed secrets. Those who have nothing to hide may celebrate and make merry, but those with secrets would do well to stay close to home.

—BOOK OF RITES, 829

I SENSED THE WHISPERS ABOUT ME AS I RETURNED TO CAMP, BUT I was too tired to care. Sky had given the order to delay our journey by a day, to assess our losses and regroup in the aftermath of the ambush. There was no use trying for stealth now; we knew that the Ximing chancellor was aware of our impending arrival.

Sky asked if I wished to join the council meeting, but I declined, telling him I had no head for politics. Instead, I returned to bed. When I awoke, hours later, the sun was low in the sky. I felt groggy and disoriented but mostly uninjured. My arm and calf wounds had already begun to scab over, as had the many peculiar nicks and scratches dotting my body. Some of these surface-level cuts, clustered mostly along my left side, had appeared prior to the ambush, though I had no memory of how I'd gotten them. It didn't bother me much. With the amount of training we endured every day, it was no surprise my body often felt like one giant bruise.

Outside our tent, Zilong was leading our squad through his daily practice regimen. I wondered if I could duck back inside and pretend I hadn't yet woken.

"Ren!" he shouted, spotting me with his hawklike vision. "Come join us."

Grudgingly, I retrieved my sword and obeyed. I soon became grateful that Zilong treated me no differently than before, because he was the only one. My other squad members watched me curiously. During our breaks, I could hear them whispering my name.

"What's happened?" I asked Zilong, as we ate our supper by the campfire. Today's menu was fish, and more fish. I was sick of seafood, but it seemed we would only have more of it once we crossed into Ximing.

"You really don't know?" he asked, frying his mackerel with the meticulous care he did everything with. "Lieutenant Fang was livid."

I shuddered. "We haven't crossed paths yet."

"Thank the skies," he said, turning the spit. "Prince Liu recognized you for your valor this morning. Apparently, in front of the whole general council."

I stilled, too astonished to be entirely pleased. I tried very hard not to move a single face muscle and give away my reaction. "He did?"

Zilong cast me a sidelong look. It was only then that I saw he was jealous. "Lieutenant Fang lost his temper. He even tried to condemn you as a black magic practitioner." At the look on my face, Zilong chuckled. "Don't worry. Everyone just laughed."

I couldn't breathe. "No one believed him?"

He raised an incredulous brow. "No one believed in a children's bogey tale, if that's what you're asking."

I exhaled in relief. And yet—how had Lieutenant Fang known? Had it only been a wild guess?

"I'm not trying to take his position," I said, scratching at the many scabs on my left arm, so numerous they looked like haphazard tally marks.

"Everyone knows that."

"Everyone except him."

Zilong nodded reluctantly. "You're a good fighter, Ren," he said. I could tell he was taking care to keep his tone neutral. "You use your head in battle. And you don't let emotions cloud your judgment."

He clapped me on the shoulder, then stood and left, saving me the embarrassment of receiving a compliment. Zilong was jealous, I saw, but he didn't let that cloud *his* judgment. I respected him for that.

Left alone, I indulged myself. *Prince Liu recognized you for your valor.* Was this what opium felt like—this rush of pure, unadulterated euphoria? Because it was addictive too. I wanted more. More praise, more recognition. Prince Liu believed I was worthy. And so did Zilong, in his own way. His envy meant he saw me as a worthy rival for the first time. In that moment, I didn't even care that I'd garnered Lieutenant Fang's enmity. *I belong here, Ma,* I told the stars. This was only the beginning. I would get better; I would do better. Until *everybody* recognized me.

As I got ready for bed, I recalled Zilong's words: *You don't let emotions cloud your judgment.* I stifled a laugh. The irony was not lost on me. Women were yin—weak and fickle, governed by their flighty emotions. Men were yang—rational, calm, and unyielding. We were told as children that women could not lead, fight, or govern, for they were too easily swayed, prone to hysteria and fitfulness.

But I had proven them wrong.

I had escaped Chuang Ning wanting nothing more than scraps. As I'd fled from my childhood home, I'd only wished for a little more time—just to breathe, to see, to live. I had not thought beyond survival.

But now my waking dreams were filled with ambitions of glory and power. I wanted Prince Liu to recognize me before my platoon, before my company. Before the warlord himself. I wanted to become captain, even commander, so that no one could belittle me again.

I was a woman, and I had dared go after more than my allotted cards in life. I had disguised myself as a boy, and I had gotten away with it. And now, like a novice gambler who bets once and wins, I was hungry for more. I felt ready to slide all my chips into the beckoning pot.

Distantly, I heard a low purr of approval. I ignored the sound.

I didn't question why my hand gripped my mother's necklace.

"MEILIN..." THE VOICE WAS SOFT, WAVERING. "*I DO NOT WISH FOR YOU to repeat my mistakes.*"

I awoke with a start, sitting up on my pallet. "Ma?" I asked aloud, before registering the sleeping trainees around me. Only a quarter of the tent was full; Sky had given us the night off for the harvest moon, but most of the soldiers had elected to stay up and drink, rather than prioritize a good night's rest. Outside, I could hear bawdy, tuneless singing, led by none other than Sparrow.

Had I been dreaming? Was I *still* dreaming? Beyond the drunken voices, I could hear another sound, this one pitched at a different frequency. It wasn't higher or lower, just... *separate*. As if emanating from a different plane of existence.

My mother... had she been looking for me?

Ignoring reason, I rose and dressed in the dark. I could feel the dragon's restlessness in the corner of my mind, his pressing emotions perceptible just beyond the boundaries of my mental shields. Gripping my mother's necklace, I let its pulsing warmth guide me. I knew it was irrational, but it felt like the spirit of my mother, trying to lead me somewhere, somewhere that I needed to go.

My jade led me out of camp, in the direction of the sea. The crimson moon lit my steps as I descended into the undergrowth, the forest floor sloping gradually downward until I came upon a small clearing lit by moonlight. What looked like a mound of moss lay in the center of the clearing, until I neared and saw that it was not moss but algae. Beneath it was a still pond, its shallow waters invisible beneath the thick coating of green.

The energy of this place reminded me, oddly enough, of my mother's chambers. In the stillness, I could make out a vague haze floating in the air, like a heat ripple when the sun was out in full force. And yet the haze was not caused by sun or heat. It was simply wrong, out of balance with the natural order of things.

The tinny sound built in my ears. The darkness above the pond seemed to beckon, that eerie, rippling haze drawing me forward. The ripple disturbed the stillness of the place. It did not belong.

I made my way down the bank, slipping in a patch of mud. The call grew insistent, a hummingbird's thrum in my bones. I could see that haze of shimmering black, undulating in the air like a mirage. It was so familiar, like breathing in my mother's old perfume.

And so I stepped through the black haze, and its warm mist coated me, like my mother's embrace. I felt the change in the air immediately. The world that greeted me felt lighter, more distant from reality. This time, I recognized the way my emotions grew sparse and thin here. I had entered the spirit realm.

There were other people now, wandering the same eerie, flickering forest, lit by elemental threads. Some appeared dazed and lost in a trance. Others wept, clutching at their hair, though their sounds were barely audible. Who were these people? What were they doing here?

Then I saw a girl swimming in the pond, and my blood crept. Her long hair fell over her shoulders, which were tanned from sun.

She treaded water absently, each stroke careless yet powerful. She was clearly a confident swimmer.

Her face was turned away from me, but I felt the knowing in my bones. As I took a step toward her, she glanced my way.

She wore my face.

"Meilin?" she asked. "You're here."

"Who-who are you?" It was hard to look at her. This pond, unlike the stagnant, algae-infested pool of the human realm, was clean and glittering with yellow and blue light, like the polished surface of a sapphire. Against the light's brilliance, it was hard to make out the girl's face. *A trick of the light*, I told myself. *Just a trick of the light*.

"Meilin," she said again. Her voice was younger than mine, sweeter. "Mark my words: *never trust a dragon*." She lowered her voice, speaking in a whispered rush. "He will use you, just as he uses each of us. And if you let him in, he will never let you go."

"But—"

A rush of icy wind surged past us. The girl cringed inward, as if anticipating an invisible attack. "I should go."

"Wait!" But when I tried to grab her hand, it slipped through mine as if made of smoke. She was gone.

I whirled around. The other strangers were staring at me now, unmoving. Even the weeping one had stopped crying, only watching me with wide, waiting eyes. No one made a sound.

The hair on the back of my neck rose. What were they waiting for? Could it be . . . Qinglong?

I did not wish to speak with the dragon. Even though he'd saved my life, I did not trust him. I did not trust what I could do with his powers, nor who I was becoming under his influence.

I had to get out of here. I had to get out of here *now*—before he came for me.

Without a second thought, I ran straight toward the haze—which I perceived as a door.

I fell out onto the other side. Gasping with relief, I collapsed on the grass.

Only to discover I was no longer alone.

NINETEEN

The spirits fought and fought and fought, until the world was but a remnant of what it once was. And out of the ruins rose the four Cardinal Spirits, the Azure Dragon of the east, the Vermillion Bird of the south, the Ivory Tiger of the west, and the Onyx Tortoise of the north. No lesser spirit could defy them.

—WINTER AND SPRING ANNALS, 417

"I SENSED YOU WERE NEAR. HAIYANG."

I scrambled upright. A man stood on the other side of the clearing, tall and golden-eyed. His voice was warm and low, with a natural lilt to it that made the words sound like song.

Around his neck, he wore a gleaming jade pendant.

"Lovely," he said, and I wasn't sure if he was talking about my pendant or me. But his eyes were not on my face. "May I hold it?"

"N-no." My voice came out as a croak. "Who are you?"

He smiled. He had a high forehead and a wide mouth, which, when smiling, made one want to smile in return. Though his features were pleasing to the eye, his face was marred by one imperfection: a jagged scar, running from brow to jawline.

"If you are Haiyang, one of the sea, then I am Taiyang, your inverse."

Taiyang—one of the sun. "You wear a spirit seal," I said, carefully.

I had thought I was the only one.

"One buried. One drowned," he began to recite. But I knew this poem too.

One buried.
One drowned.
One stolen.
But none so pitiful—

"—as one forgotten," he finished.

My mother had taught me that poem. Yet even when pestered, she had not bothered to explain its meaning. She had been like that, my mother: elusive, distant, someone who withheld even as she gave.

"Zhuque's seal was buried. That is, until today," he said, his hand rising to toy with the pendant at his throat. "Which is yours? I presume . . . the one stolen?"

"I-it was my mother's!"

"Ah, so she was the one who stole it?" His eyes penetrated me then, turning vague and remote. My spine prickled with unease as I felt a subtle coldness slide across my consciousness.

"What are you doing?" I demanded, reaching for my qi.

His mouth quirked with surprise. "Your mental shields are astonishingly strong, for someone so untrained in lixia. How?"

I glared at him. "Why should I tell you anything?"

He smiled. "Fire and water are lifelong rivals," he said. "They do not meld easily." Then his smile vanished. *"Tell me how,"* he ordered, and I heard it then—the unmistakable echo. A feminine voice, soft yet potent. *Zhuque*, he had said. *The phoenix of the south.*

I could do nothing but obey. "Q-qi gong," I stuttered. "I believe it's because I've trained in qi gong from a young age."

"It seems you are used to shielding," he said. An unwanted caress against the back of my mind. "Perhaps you owe your natural inclination to your parents. Shielding your true thoughts and feelings from them for so long . . . it couldn't have been easy."

"You-you read my . . ." The thought was so vile, I couldn't finish it. "How could you—"

"But so can you." And to my astonishment, he closed the space between us and took my hand. Up close, his golden eyes were gleaming, open as clear skies. "Follow me."

Not skies. *Seas*. Open seas, waves that swallowed one whole. With a gasp, I fell, and all space between us vanished. Not even the separation of consciousness remained, for I was within him, and his memories became mine.

A TWIN, PART OF A MATCHED SET, YET THE OTHER HALF DIED YOUNG. Both drank from a forbidden pot of tea, far too hot, but the tea burned his brother's throat, while Taiyang lived. After, his parents never spoke of his brother, but Taiyang suspected his hungry ghost followed him wherever he went.

A childhood friend, a girl he'd known since infancy—grown into a lovely woman. Their reunion at eighteen: shy, admiring, each in awe of the other. Love bloomed easily between them like the fruits of a yinhua tree, requiring little persuasion to grow. Within a year, they were wed. A child soon followed—a girl. His parents were displeased, but privately, Taiyang was delighted. The girl took after her mother.

War came. No one was surprised—no one save the fool Taiyang. Enthralled by the bliss of married life, he'd allowed heady optimism to buoy him forward, believing that in his complete happiness, misery could not touch him.

War laughed in his face.

A general dressed in red and gold, his face far more lucid, more remembered than any other, gave Taiyang his disfiguring scar. Bleeding out on the floor, certain to die, he watched as his wife was dragged out of hiding, pinned down, her skirts lifted with one hand, her throat choked with the other. After the general was done, he killed her first. This was his only mercy, for her child was next.

Taiyang watched, unable to speak. He was nineteen in age, but he felt as if his life had ended before it had begun. He understood then the cruel nature of fire; it spared him alone, granting no heed to those he loved.

The child's body was too small to bury. He could not find her bones in the ashes.

The years passed with the indifference of time. As if it was tattooed into his skin, Taiyang recalled the general's face with crystalline, razor-edged clarity. He saw the general every night as he closed his eyes for sleep, and every morning as he rose in the dark before dawn. The general's face lay in the sun, in the sky, in the sea.

The world moved on; Taiyang never did. Every day, he plotted the general's ruin. A hunger for vengeance grew within him like a malignant tumor, laying bare everything in its path. With one aim in mind, he made his way across the Three Kingdoms, searching for a way into the spirit realm, a way to bargain with the spirits. As a dreamer, he could perceive its existence, but he could not enter without a key.

"One buried, one drowned, one stolen, but none so pitiful—as one forgotten."

Taiyang never forgot. In the dark, lonely nights after the Collapse, the key called to him, sensing the sheer depths of his hunger. When other scholars learned of his quest, they laughed at him, calling him a fool. They tried to warn him: walls exist for a reason. What was the reason? Even they did not know. Unlike their ancestors, they had forgotten. Yet they were enshrined in their tired traditions, uncurious to learn of the real power beyond their stale books.

So Taiyang went alone, as the sun rising in the sky. He traced the ancient poetry of the lixia masters, which led him from the Ximing delta to the wastelands of Leyuan. And on the eve of the harvest moon, nine years later, Taiyang dug deep into the red dust and unburied a key. The long-missing jade was scarlet in color, its radiant light flickering like the flames of a warm hearth, a safe place. As he held the seal in his hand, something within him stirred, something he thought had forsaken him long ago. The feeling of home.

He was home.

Walls exist for a reason, they had said. But walls had not stopped the general from bringing ruin to all Taiyang held dear, had not stopped his life from ending nine years ago, had not stopped his family from abandoning him, just as his twin brother had once abandoned him.

Without hesitation he drew upon the phoenix's fount of power, tearing a rift in the veil between realms and setting in motion what he had dreamed of every night since the Great Collapse.

First an apparition in the sky, then a living beast. Slowly, the Vermillion Bird took shape before him: growing great wings of fire, eyes of black coal. Zhuque's immense beauty was breathtaking, terrifying. Taiyang fell to his knees before her. Even though he had believed in the Cardinal Spirits all along, seeing her in the flesh humbled him. He felt like a long-lost child, discovered far from home.

"I've been waiting for you, hungry one," said the phoenix. "Here is your choice: Would you surrender yourself to the world, or would you make the world yours?"

She extended her seal toward him.

He took it.

I GASPED, SURFACING FROM HIS MEMORIES TO FIND MYSELF BACK IN the clearing. The sounds of the forest had quieted, as if even the creatures of the night eavesdropped with bated breath.

Taiyang, one of the sun, watched me, his eyes wet with suppressed tears. To my surprise, so were my own. The sheer rage and suffering and grief of his memories—what a torment it was to live inside his head. I had thought myself angry, but my anger was like unformed ore to his steel.

"What did you do to me?"

"I opened my mind to you," he replied. "But it was you who followed. It seems you have a natural talent for it—for impulsion. Your mental control is strong." He smiled sadly. "But you are lacking in other ways." He hesitated. "I could ... train you."

I opened my mouth, then closed it. My first impulse was to accept. Not because I trusted him, not because I even thought him a worthy teacher, but because deep down, I did not wish to be alone. To find someone like me, someone cursed, someone who defied the natural order of things—I did not have to be alone.

"Hungry one," I wondered aloud. "She called you hungry one."

The dragon called me the same thing, I did not say.

Taiyang considered how to answer this. "Do you know of the Cardinal Spirits?"

I nodded. Most children knew of the fabled dragon, phoenix, tiger, and tortoise, who controlled the four directions and winds.

"But do you know where the phoenix gets her power? What she craves above all else?"

I hesitated, not wanting to meet his gaze.

"Vengeance," he said at last. "She wants vengeance."

I'd felt the intensity of Taiyang's desires, felt his torturous need to enact revenge on that general. How much of that was him? How much of that was Zhuque's influence?

"Just as the phoenix feeds off vengeance, the sea dragon feeds off greed," he continued. "That's why Qinglong's been waiting for you, all this time."

"*Your greed is unending*," the dragon had told me. "*An ocean's hunger.*"

"Then why—"

I broke off as we both heard voices in the distance, nearing.

"Join me," he said, more urgently this time. "If you're discovered, Anlai will butcher you for your so-called black magic. I can provide safe haven for you. But you must come with me now. I can't stay here."

"Now?" I balked. "I can't—go—"

"Why not?" he asked. "You know I could make you."

It was the wrong thing for him to say. I drew my sword, letting its polished blade catch the crimson moonlight. "Try it," I hissed.

His face changed. "I don't want to fight you, Haiyang." He studied me, but this time I made sure my mental shields were impregnable. "The world will not survive it."

Behind him, a sudden flicker of movement caught my eye. I raised my head above the line of trees and saw, on the mountain, a shadowy figure standing at the crest of the cliff, twin blades strapped to his back. His long billowing robes rippled in the wind as he surveyed the sleeping forest below. Though I knew we were hidden by tree cover, though I knew he could not possibly see us in the dark, I felt his gaze land directly on us.

A cold shiver ran down my spine. This forest was crawling with predators tonight.

"I cannot help you here," said Taiyang, drawing my attention back to him.

"And I cannot go with you."

The voices were growing louder. I could make out laughter now, and banter between a large group of rowdy soldiers from the Anlai army. Taiyang turned to flee, but as he strode away, he spared one last glance in my direction.

"Fire and water do not meld easily," he said quietly. "But, Haiyang, we need not be enemies."

TWENTY

In the nineteenth year of the Warring States Period, the Runong Desert Champion buried the seal of the Vermillion Bird under one thousand li of hard sediment, so that her power would not terrorize the human people again. And thus, peace was restored to Tianjia.
—COMMENTARY ON THE WARRING STATES PERIOD, 822

I HURRIED BACK TO CAMP BEFORE ANYONE COULD GROW SUSPICIOUS of my absence. But just as I was reaching for my tent flap, Sparrow emerged from within.

"Ren? You're awake?" The hour was long past midnight. "Come with us!"

I registered his uniform then. I'd assumed he'd been heading out for the latrine, but he was fully dressed. He'd even slicked his hair back with grease.

"I met a lady friend in Ji Zong," Sparrow explained, grinning from ear to ear. Ji Zong was the name of the fishing village a few li west of our campsite. "She said to come back for the harvest moon, and to bring friends this time."

Sparrow bounced on the balls of his feet. "We'll be back before dawn. No one will even notice we're gone," he explained, as Wolf, Jibo, Little Pig, and Zilong joined us. They were all smirking and shushing each other, making lewd jokes under their breath.

"I'm pretty tired," I said, feigning a yawn that morphed into a real one. "I think I'll pass this time."

"Are you sure?" he said. "Village women aren't like uppity Chuang Ning shrews. They're mostly unschooled, dumb as rocks really, but talented in other ways." He winked.

This side of Sparrow unnerved me. "You're disgusting."

"Why? They're willing. All they need is a *little* encouragement..."

"What are we waiting for?" Wolf interrupted, saving me from a response. "Let's hurry."

"Should we wash first?" Zilong asked, running a self-conscious hand through his hair. "At the hot springs?"

Jibo made a face. "I don't think we have enough time," he said quickly.

"You hate washing, huh?" Sparrow said, peering at the boy.

Jibo flushed.

"Jibo fears water like the phoenix fears iron," his squad leader, Wolf, said knowingly. "Let's get out of here. We'll need to return before dawn."

"You go on." I pushed Sparrow away as he was trying to take my arm.

"What is it?" Zilong teased. "Do you have a sweetheart back home?"

"Yes!" I pounced on this idea. "And I promised her I'd stay loyal."

"Not like she'll know the difference," said Little Pig.

"Besides, who's to say we'll come home in the spring?" Jibo chimed in.

"I'm just ... not interested, okay?" My cheeks heated.

"Ren doesn't lean that way," Wolf snickered. "He spends his nights with the prince instead."

The others laughed. Face flushed, I watched them disappear into the night. I did not know how to keep up with their banter. At home, Xiuying teased me, but always with good humor. In turn, I teased Rouha, but it was not hard to outwit a five-year-old. Though I had significantly improved my swordplay, I was still slow-witted in conversation, and this was my weakness. While others could wield words like knives, to me they remained millstones.

I sighed, wide-awake now. I wondered if I should train again, but my muscles, still sore from the previous night's events, balked at the idea.

I thought of what Zilong had said about the hot springs. I hadn't dared go earlier, with so many soldiers frequenting the springs, but at this time of night, most would be sleeping, and the ones that weren't were off gallivanting in Ji Zong with their lady friends.

I knew the general direction of the springs, but the forest seemed to have shifted in the night, becoming contradictory and labyrinthine. I retraced my path several times before I eventually heard the trickle of running water and felt the rising temperature in the air.

The hot springs were not large—only two pools of shallow water, surrounded by low-hanging vines and ferns, so that the tips of their leafy tentacles floated in the water. Where the first pool met the second, someone had rolled a large boulder over to cover a small geyser, but the boulder had come loose. The geyser erupted intermittently, spouting brilliant jets of steaming water, which scattered like music over the pool. It was a beautiful sight, but it would probably disrupt my bath. I undressed and eased myself into the steaming waters, then rolled the boulder back over the geyser hole, covering the spurts of water.

Goose bumps pricked my exposed arms, so that I submerged in the water, up to my neck. I let out a breathless sigh of exhilaration. All around me, steam rose as thick as a curtain. No wonder Xiuying had once mentioned hiding in the springs to avoid completing her chores as a child. No one could possibly spot you through the filmy mist.

I let my hair out of its perpetual topknot, and my scalp tingled with relief. I ducked my head underwater, thinking of practicing a few strokes, but immediately came up for air instead. The feeling of water closing in from above was too much.

As a child, I'd loved to swim, to float weightlessly along the river currents. But that was before my mother had drowned. Before I realized that water could embrace you, and in the same breath strangle you whole.

My mother, too, had loved water. A small stream ran behind her childhood home in the countryside, and there she had taught herself how to swim. As the only daughter of a jinshi scholar who'd tested into the highest rank of the imperial examinations, my mother had grown up between her family's ancestral land and the Forbidden City. She spoke often of her childhood: teaching the other noble girls how to swim, stealing into the imperial library to read forbidden texts, writing obscene poetry under a pseudonym that grew notorious. She loved reminiscing on her childhood . . . and then glossing over the years that followed.

And yet, what I remembered most vividly were her final years. And in her final years, she was not herself.

I remembered how she would disappear into her chambers for days at a time, refusing to emerge for food or even water. Once, as a ten-year-old, I stuck my ear to the door of her chamber and waited, listening for any signs of life within. I waited there for so long my legs fell asleep. Still, I heard nothing. Not a murmur, a rustle, or even a single footstep. I was terrified this time she would not emerge. This time my mother would be found dead.

But then the next day came, and with the sun she emerged. I never told her of my silent vigil, but from then on, I began to question if she was truly staying in her rooms during those long isolations.

As time passed and her madness worsened, she allowed me inside and I witnessed the extent of her deterioration. In her last days, she could hardly get out of bed, much less escape the house. Because no servants could enter her rooms, I was the one who fed and cleaned her, who listened to her meaningless rambling, her mind hanging as if by a single thread.

That was the problem with freedom, I thought. Once you'd tasted it, you couldn't live without it, ever again.

What did that mean for me? Was there a way I could ever live freely? For that matter, did anyone in this world ever live free, unbound from their countless duties? Duty to your family, to your emperor. Duty to enlist in the war, to marry for your dowry, to care for your husband's children. Was there such a thing as living for oneself? The mere thought of it felt selfish, immoral.

The only way to escape was to die. That was the choice my mother had made.

Flushed, I pulled myself up from the water and sat on the bank. My cheeks were overheated and my long hair a sodden mass around me. As the water settled into stillness, I peered down at my reflection. *"She looks like her mother."*

Was it I who'd voiced that thought, or someone else? The dragon... against all odds, I had grown accustomed to his presence.

I shivered despite the heat. *"Your greed is unending,"* Qinglong had told me. *"An ocean's hunger."*

My shadow self had always been there, lurking just beneath the surface. Ready to ruin me with her ambition, her lust for power. She had been the one to fantasize about fighting back against Father, torturing him, even—sometimes—killing him. She had been the one to envision escaping this life, fleeing Master Zhu's grasp and enlisting in the army instead. She had been the one to conceive of achieving rank and glory, of becoming the most revered and respected soldier of her company, of her kingdom.

Her greed was unending. Her greed was mine.

I stared down at my reflection; my reflection stared back at me. *Her eyes*, I realized with a jolt. *Her eyes are golden*.

I kicked at the water, disturbing its surface. A trick of the light, I told myself, but my heart was pounding. I slid back into the water, finding solace in its warmth. I resumed washing and, gradually, my pulse settled. Until I heard voices filtering through the trees.

By the sound of their footsteps, there were many of them.

TWENTY-ONE

The ghost of the fair maiden haunts the springs, so that on a moonlit night, some claim to see her shapely figure hiding in the mist.
—WINTER AND SPRING ANNALS, 417

I DUCKED INTO THE WATER, HOLDING MY BREATH. TO MY HORROR, I watched as Sparrow, Zilong, Wolf, and Little Pig all descended down the path that led to the hot springs, engrossed in their conversation.

"What a stick in the mud!" Sparrow groused. He jumped onto the bank and began to strip. I backed as far away as possible, careful not to disturb the water.

Wolf was calling Lieutenant Fang a few choice words. I gathered that he'd caught them before they'd made it to the village.

Little Pig muttered, "If he can't have fun, then none of us can—"

Zilong dived into the pool, upsetting the waters and sending a wave straight into my face. I sputtered before I could catch myself.

Zilong looked around. "Did you hear that?"

I shrank behind a low-hanging fern. I needed to retrieve my clothes and run. *Or should I wait until after they leave?* My heart was pounding like a war drum in my chest. This was worse than chasing bandits.

Zilong's gaze roved across the hot springs. But before he could come closer to investigate, a new set of footsteps approached. "I thought I'd find you here."

"Commander!" Zilong straightened and saluted.

With abject alarm, I watched as Sky leapt from the tall boulder overhead to the bank of the spring. "At ease," he said.

The others relaxed but did not return to their former conversation, which had involved belittling their superior in command.

Sky seemed to intuit this. "Lieutenant Fang was not the one who curtailed your evening plans," said Sky. "That was me."

"You?" Sparrow said, nonplussed. "But, sir, Lieutenant Fang was the one who caught us heading to Ji Zong."

"He reported the incident to me first. And I agreed with him. You shouldn't go." He turned to Sparrow. "Soldier Wang." Sparrow seemed flabbergasted by the fact that Prince Liu knew his name. "I heard you visited Ji Zong yesterday. How much information did you give your friend?"

Though his voice was light, there was an unmistakable thread of accusation in his words.

"Biyu was curious about the war efforts," Sparrow admitted. "It affects her business, you know. Apparently, there was an unusual fire in the greater Yun region yesterday, one that couldn't be doused despite the summer rainfall. She was wondering if the military could help. She wanted to better understand how our army—"

"Did you tell her our land route? And the number of our forces, and our military formations?"

After a weighted pause, Sparrow said, "I only told her how many soldiers are in each platoon, I swear it, sir!" He gulped, then rushed on. "But she's an Anlai civilian! She wouldn't betray us to Ximing—"

"This close to the border, the loyalties of these people are imprecise. Do you know we're nearer to the Ximing capital now than to Chuang Ning? Anlai's borders are too far-reaching, and the southern villages are known to grumble against their tributes." Sky cracked his knuckles, an air of casual nonchalance about him. "We can't afford to take that risk."

"Sir..." Sparrow looked like he wanted to cry.

Sky lifted a hand. "What's done is done. Don't blame yourself too much, Sparrow, is it?" He smiled kindly. "Beautiful ladies have a way of getting us to talk, don't they?"

Something that Sparrow had said was nagging at me, like a pebble in my boot. But try as I might, I couldn't shake it out into the open.

"Join us, Commander?" Zilong asked boldly. "The water's a balm for sore muscles."

"Why not," said Sky. And then, to my mounting distress, he pulled his shirt off over his head. He did not leave his clothes on the ground like the others had. Instead, he laid his on the shelf of rock, where I had placed mine earlier.

I felt my life flash before my eyes. Sky whirled around to look over the soldiers in the water. "Who else... Ren?"

How did he know immediately?

My breath hitched in my throat. "Y-yes?" I asked, not leaving my shelter behind the ferns.

"Come over," said Zilong. "What are you doing in the corner?"

"Oh... the water feels better over here," I fibbed.

"Does it?" Zilong approached my side of the pool. "I didn't know the currents caused—"

"Stop!" I exclaimed. "It's... quite hot." My voice grew increasingly flustered. "It takes some getting used to."

Beyond the ferns, Sky was looking at me strangely, a suspicious set to his mouth.

"How is Winter?" I asked, trying to change the subject. "I mean, Prince Liu."

"He's recovering." With a rueful smile, he added, "It's mainly his pride that's injured."

"We heard you were willing to give yourself up in his place," said Zilong.

"Yes," Sky replied, without elaborating.

"You must be close," said Sparrow, who could make conversation with a rock.

"As close as brothers vying for the same throne can be."

I hadn't thought of it that way. Then again, I had assumed Sky was exempt from court politics. After all, he was the seventh son, the youngest and furthest from power. I'd assumed that was the reason behind his carefree humor and lighthearted antics, because he did not bear the weight of a potential crown. But perhaps I'd been mistaken. Perhaps all princes were prey to ambition.

"Use your power. If you're caught—"

I ignored the dragon's voice, shielding my mind against him. Instead, I scanned my surroundings and shoved the boulder with all my strength. It came away from the geyser hole, which erupted with a huge surge of water. Little Pig shouted in surprise. Water flew everywhere as I vaulted out of the pool, snatched my clothes, and ran. I couldn't be sure if anyone had seen me beyond all the steam and mist, though they certainly heard me.

"Ren?" Sparrow called. "Where are you going?"

"Let him go," I heard Sky say. "I'm sure he has his reasons."

TWENTY-TWO

Thus the ancient people worshipped the spirit of the Dian River, for there was no other force as beautiful as it was lethal.

—WINTER AND SPRING ANNALS, 417

PRINCE LIU INSTRUCTED OUR COMPANY TO PREPARE FOR BATTLE as we crossed into Ximing the following day. According to his scouts, Ximing forces awaited us at the mouth of the Dian River. They would try to thwart our advance there.

"Ximing has the advantage of fighting on their home ground," Prince Liu said, looking out over his troops. "They chose an apt location. Not only is the terrain uphill for us, but the river will prove treacherous to ford." His hand moved unconsciously to rest on his sword. "Once we've secured a foothold on the river, it will be an easy victory. Our numbers are more than triple theirs."

From new intelligence reports, we'd learned that the Ximing army was suffering from mass defection. And without the manpower to discipline and penalize the defectors, the Ximing generals could not impose order within their own forces.

The Anlai army had no such problems. Only this morning, we'd watched as Lieutenant Tong dragged a convicted traitor before our assembled forces. The man, who'd been a member of Winter's personal guard, had been caught dispatching information to the Ximing capital.

"Please," the man said, on his knees. "They have my family. They threatened my children... I didn't have a choice."

Sky's face was unrecognizable, unfeeling as stone. "You had a choice," he said. "You chose to betray your kingdom and forsake your duty."

"You don't understand the power they possess. If you interfere... the fire will come for us all—and the Three Kingdoms will be reduced to ashes!" he cried out. "The veil between realms—it's disappearing... and the spirits will soon walk among us." He started to sob as he babbled on, his words losing coherency.

The hair on the back of my neck stood on end. *Surely it's nothing more than a dying man's pleas for mercy*, I reasoned, looking for cues from the soldiers around me. My platoon appeared mostly bored, some even hiding laughter. To them it was mere nonsense.

But they had not traversed the spirit realm as I had.

"My son, my only son," the man cried. "They threatened to kill him, then me."

Sky drew his sword. "Then you should have died an honorable death, instead of shaming your family name." Sky strode toward him. "There is no mercy for those who forsake their duty."

With that, he beheaded the man with one clean slice. I flinched, looking away as the head rolled in the dirt. Sky cleaned his blade, his expression cold, before he turned back to look at his brother. Winter appeared unusually pale, though it was hard to tell, since the Liu princes were so light in complexion. Then Winter strode away, and I knew he was upset. I did not blame him.

Sky's words left me uneasy. I disagreed with everything he said, not for the sake of that man, whom I did not know, but for myself. I could see now that Sky cared about duty more than anything else. He was kind until he was not. He was easygoing until he was not. As for me, there were oaths that I had forsworn, duties that I'd failed to uphold. I'd wielded a sword, though it was forbidden for women. I'd practiced black magic, forbidden for all. Even beyond these ghastly crimes, more simply, I'd broken my betrothal to Master Zhu; I'd forsaken my filial duty to Father, who—by the law—owned me and my livelihood.

Daughter, sister, wife. I'd given up these names by taking on a new identity, deceiving my fellow soldiers and my commander. That night at the hot springs had been too close a call. I shuddered to think of what would have happened if they'd caught me then, or even before that, if they'd seen me threatening my squadmate with black magic. My gaze returned to the beheaded man, who was being carted away by guards, his arms limp and dragging in the dust. I feared both men and spirits now. I had no allies, only enemies on all sides. *What would I do*, I wondered, *if they came for me next?*

AFTER SKY DISMISSED US, LIEUTENANT FANG GATHERED THIRD PLAtoon together. I had tried to avoid him since the night of the ambush, though I suspected his ire toward me had not diminished. He'd simply been waiting for an opening to attack.

"Soldier Hai," he said. "Such a commendable, exemplary soldier should lead by example. We shouldn't miss an opportunity to put you to good use on the battlefield—so you may earn greater rewards from your commanders. Maybe even from the warlord himself!" He offered me a disparaging smile. "I'm placing you in the vanguard. You will help establish a foothold on the river before our platoon crosses."

Sparrow shoved through the crowd. "Sir! It'll be a massacre out there. Shouldn't the more experienced—"

"It will be a difficult task," Fang agreed. "For that reason, we should leverage our most commendable soldiers, who can take the challenge."

With no choice but to obey, I nodded and saluted stiffly.

Zilong stepped forward. "Twelfth Squad will go with him."

I turned to him in shock, but he did not acknowledge me. Swallowing the lump in my throat, I watched as Zilong saluted Lieutenant Fang, whose face had taken on a gray cast. And thus, Twelfth Squad became the unlucky ones. Because of me.

Zilong caught my eye at last, then glanced over at the other soldiers under his command. We were both thinking the same thing. We did not know how many of us would be alive by this time tomorrow.

THE RIVER WAS CALLED DIAN FOR A REASON. TWO RIVERS CONVERGED into one at the base of the Ximing army camp, then flowed on to the sea, not ten li away. The rapids were swift and brutal, threatening to steal the lives of any who endeavored to cross it. Not only would we have to face the full force of the river, overflowing from monsoon season, but we'd also be subjected to Ximing arrows and cannons. Ximing had the higher ground, but once we secured a foothold on the banks of the river, according to Fang, we could plow through the rest of the army.

"If we live that long, anyway," Zilong had said under his breath.

It was a poor day for battle, on all sides, but Ximing had forced our hand. We could not afford to delay any longer and risk meeting reinforcements from the Ximing capital. The day began gray and overcast, but as we reached the river and saw the waiting army beyond, rain started to drizzle, making for low visibility.

The Ximing army had already spotted us. Soon arrows flew through the air. I watched them soar toward us with a certain degree of detached awe; they were numerous and in concert, like birds migrating south. Then they struck. Soldiers died. And I remembered myself.

We had no choice but to continue. The riverbanks were slick and treacherous. I slipped in mud and fell flat on my back, narrowly missing an arrow by sliding backward in the sludge. By the time I staggered to my feet, Zilong and the rest of my squad were already racing ahead, nearly indiscernible in the thicket of soldiers. I sprinted forward, my grip on my sword clumsy. It was not at all like the neat and focused duels of the training ring. This was messy and chaotic and lawless. Sky had been wrong; there was no order in war. No one was thinking of duty here. It was kill or be killed.

Under Ximing's arrows, our army was falling like wheat stalks at harvest. The only solution was to ford the river and meet them head-on. I recalled what Sky had taught me and ran at a zigzag, darting from left to right as I made for the river. I jumped and slid down the river rocks to land in shallow water. Despite the summer heat, the water was icy cold. I gritted my teeth and waded forward. An arrow zinged past me; I ducked and swore as it scraped my ear. Hot, viscous blood trickled down my neck. The force and speed of that arrow had sent my heart into my throat, but I steeled myself not to dwell on the near miss.

All around me, dozens of men were getting swept away by sudden, abrupt currents, or decimated by arrows. The river water began to run red; the nauseating scent of blood hung heavy in the air. Ahead of me, I spotted Zilong moving eastward. I didn't understand his motivations—he was taking an indirect route, wasting precious time—until I realized he'd found a safer path through the river. The currents were shallower farther from the river mouth, easier to cross. Little Pig trailed him, knowing that wherever Zilong stepped was probably his safest bet. I agreed with Little Pig. I followed.

Gradually, other soldiers took heed and moved up the river, trailing our path. The river up here was stymied by a natural rock wall, which slowed the trajectory of the currents. More of us began to cross, using Zilong's path. Up ahead, I caught sight of Zilong—he'd made it onto the other side! Soldiers began to cheer as Zilong bounded up the riverbank with astonishing agility, dodging arrows left and right. He mowed down the first Ximing soldier awaiting him, and the others fell back, knowing now to be afraid. Little Pig and the others soon followed in his wake.

"Watch it!" the soldier behind me cried. I ducked just as an arrow hurtled past me. But the sudden motion caused me to slip on a loose rock, and I nearly fell in the river.

The man behind me grabbed my arm. "Thank you—" I started, just as an arrow landed in his neck. I watched in horror as he collapsed, nearly taking me with him. I wrenched myself out of his grip and staggered onward. I started to run now, not caring if I fell in or not. I was trying to run from the ghost of that man's eyes, from the ghost of death. There was so much death all around me, and it made me afraid. If fear turned men into monsters, I thought, then what did that make me?

I scrambled up the banks, then squinted through the thickening sheets of rain, seeking out archers. There. A cluster of them on the embankment. I swung up to meet them, and up close, they were defenseless. I slashed, parried, stabbed. All sound turned dull and distant in my ears as I fixated on battle. Faces blurred before me until I no longer saw them as people. I saw moving limbs, targets, *enemies*.

The rain had transformed from a drizzle into a torrent. Water soaked my clothes, but the cold did not penetrate my bones. Qi was coursing through me too fast for that, as fast as the river rapids. The qi built and built until it needed an outlet, it *required* it, and if I had not had enemies to kill in that moment, I think I might have turned on my fellow comrades.

A giant horn blared, the sound cutting through the lash of the storm. I surfaced as if from underwater, turning to see the full force of the Anlai army descending on the riverbanks. *We are going to win*, I saw. The younger Prince Liu helmed the charge, his sword drawn and raised in the air as he rode atop his white warhorse. He shouted a command to his soldiers, but his words were indiscernible through the heavy rainfall.

Without warning, a disconnected emotion flooded through me, overwhelming in its intensity. A thrill down my spine, a lightness in my being. It was, strangely, *exhilaration*.

Confused, I reached for my mother's necklace, which pulsed against me like a second heartbeat, out of rhythm with my own. The seal was hot, painfully so. *A warning*.

Too late, the air thickened to fog, and a visceral sense of foreboding tore through me. Disoriented, I lost sight of Prince Liu in the haze, barely able to see the soldier I'd been fighting moments earlier. The amount of steam in the air befitted a hot spring, not an open battlefield.

"Retreat!" someone shouted, but I could not recognize the voice. I could see nothing, only a red-hot light that pierced through the mist. A flame. How close was it? It looked near, but I could not feel its heat. No, it had to be several li from here. Then how could I see it? Unnatural, that a wildfire could break out in the midst of a downpour.

Because it was enormous. And it was growing, so rapidly it could not be natural. Now the flames spread across the entire northern bank of the river, creating a wall of fire so tall it looked like a red cliff.

Screams followed. I did not know if it was our men or theirs burning.

Another link in a chain of unnatural occurrences.

I had no time to ponder this now. A man stabbed me in the calf and I cried out, returning my attention to the fight at hand. Swearing, I disarmed him and slit his throat, then used his body to block the next attack. The new enemy soldier impaled his sword on the corpse, grunted, then pulled back to free his blade. One step was his undoing. I watched in confusion as he tipped backward, then fell, disappearing from sight.

Horrified, I peered down through the fog, realizing that I'd backed onto a narrow ridge. I had to get out of here, but I couldn't go in the direction of the fire, which was only growing. I made for higher ground, then cursed as I ran straight into a squad of Ximing soldiers.

"Ren! Behind you."

I spun as Zilong made his way to me, so that we fought back-to-back on the promontory. We both trusted each other, knowing the other's strengths and weaknesses. The soldiers began to back away from us, sensing the threat. Unintentionally, we created a small clearing around us.

But this attracted too much attention. The fog lifted momentarily as I spotted an archer on the mound overhead, aiming his bow in our direction.

"Zilong!" I screamed, just as another soldier hurtled toward me, locking me in close combat. I could sense the arrow whizzing through the air, but I couldn't break away from my attacker. He was trying to angle his spear into my gut. I pretended to weaken, then used his momentum to flip him over me, off the cliff.

I looked back—Zilong was gone.

"Zilong?" I called. And then I saw him through the mist.

He'd fallen into the river, the arrow embedded in what looked to be his shoulder. It was hard to tell through the waves that were trying to shove him under. I caught sight of his face—lanced with pain.

And then I heard the heavy footfall of an enemy soldier behind me, one I hadn't spotted earlier. I only had a moment to turn before he was upon me, and then it was too late. He pushed me over the edge.

I fell.

I hit the water headfirst, swallowing a mouthful of river water. Panicking, I couldn't make sense of up or down as I was shoved downstream. In my mind's eye, I saw my mother's bloated purple foot, her rotted corpse. I watched her open her mouth underwater; I watched her soundless scream. I watched the Wen River consume her whole, merciless, unforgiving. *Water is unforgiving.*

The currents propelled me up. I broke through the surface of the river, gasping for breath. *Focus, Meilin!* I tried to channel my qi, but I couldn't grasp it; my attention was too scattered. Then I spotted Zilong, who was farther downstream.

He was going to die, I realized, unless I did something. He *needed* me. I forced my terror back and swam toward him, letting the waves buffet me forward as I reached out and attempted to grab hold of his arm. He was struggling to remain upright, to breathe. I noticed his blood seeping into the water with a terrifying velocity.

"Zilong!" The currents were stronger than I thought possible. In mere seconds, we'd been swept past the battle, past both the Ximing and Anlai contingents.

"It's too late for me!" he shouted. "Save yourself!"

"You're not going to die!" I said. "Just—hold on!"

I tried to lunge forward again. I managed to catch hold of his sleeve before the currents ripped us apart once more. We'd been thrust into a dizzying whirlpool. I could barely see through the spray of foam and mist.

"Ren—" Zilong said something else before his head went under. He was too weak in his current state. He couldn't fight the rapids. *Think, Meilin!* I scanned my surroundings as I fought to keep myself afloat, then caught sight of the low-hanging branches over the southern bank.

"This way—" Without warning, the currents shifted and Zilong barreled right into me. I choked, swallowing a gallon of water. We both sank into the river, but I grabbed his hand underwater and tugged him to the surface. We had to get out of this whirlpool. Gripping him, I summoned my qi and swam upstream, seizing an overhanging branch with one hand.

"Take—take it," I bit out, panting from exertion. Painstakingly slow, he forced himself forward and let go of my hand to grasp the branch. My momentary relief faded as I saw his wound up close. It was not in his shoulder as I had assumed. It was a chest wound. Close to his heart.

The branch creaked, unable to bear our combined weights. Frantically, I seized on to a nearby branch, this one thinner.

"Zilong—"

My branch snapped; I was thrown back into the river as a wave swallowed me whole.

"Ren!" Zilong shouted. "Watch out!" There was a ragged note of desperation in his voice. I struggled to fight my way to the surface, the waves beating down on me relentlessly, and then, when I did surface, it was too late. I saw what Zilong had been staring at with abject horror. The roaring sound that filled my ears belonged to a waterfall.

I heard Zilong scream my name, before I sailed over the edge.

TWENTY-THREE

Never trust a dragon.
—LEGENDS OF THE MOUNTAINS, 754

I FELL WITH NO END. FALLING, FALLING, FALLING, I FELT DEATH wrap its cold arms around me. I did not know if I was in the air or underwater or below ground. I did not know if I was flying or sinking or swimming. I heard sounds all around me: rushing water, pounding currents, the caw of birds... seagulls?

Was this death? Then why did I feel so numb?

I sank deeper, until the birdsong faded, the light faded, everything I knew faded within the total, pressing darkness. Time passed indefinitely; seconds or years or centuries elapsed. I lost my name, I lost my sense of self. Floating in the darkness, I waited.

For I sensed he was coming to me then. He had been waiting for a very long time.

"Hai Meilin," said Qinglong, and in the dark depths of the sea, his voice had power like never before. The words boomed through me, rattling through my bones. I felt as if every syllable would strangle me in its power.

I shrank back, delirious. "What do you want from me?" Dimly, I registered that it should be impossible to be speaking underwater, yet the thought did not faze me.

"Open your eyes."

"I don't want to."

"Open your eyes!"

The voice reverberated through me, so that I had no choice but to obey. As I blinked one eye open, the water did not hurt my eyes as I'd expected. Instead, I could breathe easily, as if the water around me was a figment of my imagination. And yet my body felt weightless—I floated as easily as a feather.

Only one source of light broke through the pressing darkness— Qinglong. His iridescent scales gleamed as moonlight on pearls. Despite myself, I recognized the spirit creature's undeniable beauty.

"Where . . . where am I?" I looked up but could not see the surface of the water. No light penetrated from above. Was I in the human realm, or in the realm of spirits?

"You fool," he said. "You did not use your power."

My memories rushed back to me with the force of a gale. "Zilong!" I cried out. "Is he all right? Is he—"

"He's dead," Qinglong snapped. "Because of you."

I stared at him, then shook my head. This must be some sort of peculiar dream. Likely, we had not yet set out for battle, and soon I would wake, the day not even begun. In no reality could Zilong be dead.

"This is no dream," said the dragon. "Ten thousand men will be dead before this day is over. Their deaths are irreversible—the consequences of war. Do you understand now what is at stake?"

I'd just had breakfast with Zilong the day before. I'd stolen his youtiao and he'd gulped down my congee in retaliation. Zilong was the best soldier in our platoon. He was the strongest, quickest, smartest... and yet all of that hadn't prevented him from getting killed in battle.

"I tried to save him! I—I fought—"

"With your sword," Qinglong sneered. "I gave you an ocean of might and you chose a drop of rain instead."

"I can't use spirit power," I said frantically. "My platoon—they'd turn against me—"

"Your platoon is dead!" he snarled. "This is not a war of men. And if you insist on fighting as a common foot soldier, then you may rejoice in your upstanding scruples and embrace the ashes of all you hold dear."

It took me a moment to register his words. *The ashes?*

Someone else had mentioned ashes. Someone... someone who'd tried to warn us. *"The fire will come for us all—and the Three Kingdoms will be reduced to ashes!"* The traitor Sky had beheaded.

So much death. And for what? The traitor was dead; Zilong was dead; my platoon was dead; and we all had blood on our hands. Tears welled in my eyes, but I blinked them away, unwilling to give in; despair was a river too deep to ford.

My mind itched; I was on the cusp of a revelation. Yesterday, I'd dismissed the traitor's words as nonsense. And yet Sparrow's friend in Ji Zong had mentioned a fire too: strange, unquenchable flames ravaging the southern countryside. I'd seen it myself at the battle at Dian River. The unnatural fog streaking the skyline in mere seconds. The fire so striking I could spot it from miles away, before it grew into a wall of pure flame.

I recalled the odd orders of the Ximing chancellor—to steal all iron from our armory. *"We don't want it,"* the bandit had said. *"We're trying to get rid of it."* Why?

Iron was heavier than steel, easier to break. Cheaper to craft. And yet, in stories of old, it was always iron the heroes wielded.

A bright knife of memory plunged through my chest. The night at the hot springs, when Jibo had been reluctant to bathe—Wolf had made a joke of it: "Jibo fears water like the phoenix fears iron."

The one who fears iron is the phoenix.

A wave of nausea swept over me. How could I have missed such an obvious connection?

Because . . . I knew who possessed the phoenix's seal. Taiyang, one of the sun. The golden-eyed stranger.

"Chancellor Sima," I whispered.

He'd known. He'd always known we were on opposing sides. "*Fire and water do not meld easily,*" he'd said, back when we'd first met. "*But, Haiyang, we need not be enemies.*"

"You're full of surprises today," said the dragon, startling me. "You've met him, haven't you?"

This too surprised me—that he didn't already know.

The dragon sneered. "Zhuque's vessel must have concealed the memory from me. He borrows the old scholars' tricks."

He said *scholar* like one said *swindler*.

"So you don't know everything," I said, jutting out my chin.

His voice took on a scathing tone. "No, I don't know everything. Because my supposed vessel, who should be my eyes and ears in the human realm, instead ignores me, and even goes so far as to shield her mind from me." His eyes narrowed then. "I will tell you this— you will lose this war without me. Against Zhuque's power, your pathetic army does not stand a chance."

I had seen Sima wield his lixia today—that wall of fire he'd created, so high I could not see the mountains behind the northern riverbank.

"That is only a fraction of his true power," Qinglong replied, as if I'd spoken my fears aloud. "His seal was stolen from him yesterday. If he'd possessed the full might of Zhuque's strength, no one in your army would be alive right now. Even your dear Prince Liu would not survive the—"

"Is Sky alive?" I demanded, my heart surging into my throat.

"Your prince is alive," Qinglong replied, and my shoulders slumped with relief. "For now. But his life—as does yours—hangs in the balance by a fraying thread."

My head hurt from trying to imagine the possibilities. I tried to walk away, to put distance between us, but with every step I took, Qinglong only seemed to grow closer, bigger. He was manipulating me, I realized. I could not trust my field of vision here.

The dragon laughed. "We are in the spirit realm, Hai Meilin. This world abides by my rules."

I tried to contain my anger. "If you want me to work with you, if you want me to be your so-called eyes and ears, then you need to help me too! What do you mean, that's only a fraction of Sima's power? What do you mean, Sima lost his seal—I saw him only yesterday! He showed me his seal—I saw the mark of the Vermillion Bird."

The dragon sneered at the mention of the phoenix's name. "At last you are asking the right questions. Sima lost his seal because he was betrayed. By someone he believes to be a friend."

Unbidden, my thoughts jumped to the man on the mountain, the way he'd surveyed the forest below, as if he'd been looking for something. *Somebody.*

"On the eve of the harvest moon, Sima retrieved Zhuque's seal. It was no easy feat. He required hundreds of men to excavate the buried jade. They were given to him by the warlord of Ximing, in exchange for his support in the Three Kingdoms War. But neither the warlord nor the chancellor could have foreseen the traitor. Even the whisperers among the spirit realm do not know the thief's true identity. But it is known that they are clever. And fast. Only two days after Sima retrieved the seal, the thief stole it from him. Then they smashed the jade and threw the pieces into the sea."

My mouth fell open. "Then it's as good as gone."

"Do you think a spirit seal can simply disappear?" The dragon sniffed. "Like a misplaced coin? Why do you think the Wu Dynasty buried Zhuque's seal under a thousand li of sediment?"

I gaped. A thousand li?

"Mark my words, the pieces will turn up soon. The lixia will make itself known, and nature will obey. Clearly, Sima has already recovered the first piece." I thought of the fire at Dian River, shuddering. "But you must find the remaining pieces before he does."

"Me?" I squeaked, starting to back away.

The dragon's tail lashed out, so suddenly I could barely cry out. But when it touched my cheek, there was no impact, no pain, only a cool dampness like mist.

When I blinked, the world was changed.

Sima Yi stood on the bank of the Dian River overlooking the battlefield. His eyes were triumphant as he observed the fires raging below, watching as Sky tried in vain to ride through the flames. "Pull back!" Sky shouted at last, conceding defeat. "Pull back!"

Sima slid one hand into his pocket. Though I could not see it, I sensed he gripped the jade shard in his hand, rolling it across his fingers like a marble. The first piece had washed ashore on the Dian River, and now he waited for the second and third piece to follow.

"Do you see how destructive his power is? It is but a shadow of what it could be, once the seal is made whole." The dragon spoke into my mind.

The world shifted. Now I watched as Xiuying tried to pull Rouha and Plum from our burning house. "Meilin," she screamed, throat ragged. "Help me!"

I tried to run forward, but I was as insubstantial as a ghost. I passed through her, unable to lend a hand. The flames engulfed the gates. "Run!" I screamed at her, but she stumbled and fell to her knees instead, coughing.

"I-I'm sorry," she wept, holding her son. Rouha, I saw, was already dead. She had suffocated amid the smoke, her blank, unseeing eyes trapped in fear.

I screamed, desperate to escape this vision. Instead, the dragon led me to the Forbidden City in Chuang Ning, where I could do nothing but watch as Chancellor Sima dragged a bound Sky to the dais.

"Your father will pay for what he did, up to the tenth generation," said Sima Yi. His eyes were bright gold, twin suns. I could feel Zhuque in his aura.

Chancellor Sima—Zhuque—drew his sword. I was screaming so loudly I could not hear what he was saying. Sima did not go for Sky's throat, but instead stabbed him in the stomach—a slow, painful death for his enemy. Sky fell but did not die. The blood oozed from his tunic. He shook but did not make a sound. I watched his face drain of color, his eyes slitted in pain. I screamed until I could not scream anymore.

Death would've been a mercy then.

Qinglong was still not satisfied. He took me last below the imperial palace. I had never seen such a place before. But from the tang of sweat and fear emanating from within, I knew nothing good could come of it.

In the corner of the room was a cage, no larger than a pig's pen. Imprisoned inside the iron bars was a girl, stripped naked, her back emblazoned with wrathful scars. She was forced to sit because the cage could not sustain her full height. Long unkempt strands of hair covered her face, but already I recognized her. It was impossible not to.

"This is the price of your failure. During the war, you will be spared—to watch everyone you love die an excruciating death. Then, driven to madness, you will, at last, die alone."

I could feel the bars pressing against my chest, my ribs. I could feel myself diminishing with time, becoming a specter of my former self. It was my greatest fear, realized.

I felt the dragon's tail flick against me once more. I had no strength left to protest.

"But there is another possibility." The taste of blood and ashes disappeared from my tongue, replaced with fresh water and new life, sweeter than anything I'd ever before tasted. "If you succeed in your quest, if you retrieve Sima Yi's jade before he does, you can change the fate of the Three Kingdoms." The world spun. "Power and glory will be yours, Hai Meilin. You will be accepted by your people, and loved for who you are."

In his final vision he offered me, I was no longer a ghost to the world, but an inhabitant within it. Within this strange reality I breathed in the fragrance of plum blossoms, early spring. Outside, I heard the front gate swing open. I rested one hand on my sword hilt before hurrying out into the courtyard.

It was Sky, stepping across the freshly painted threshold. His face lit up in a smile as he caught sight of me.

"What are you doing here?" I asked. Behind him, I could hear Sparrow telling a joke in the rock garden, Rouha laughing so hard she was hiccupping. When had Sparrow arrived?

Sky closed the distance between us and caught me around the waist. "I like this dress on you," he said, fingering the silk of my fluttering sleeve. "*Meilin*." I stilled, marveling at the sound of my true name on his lips.

"Sky—"

"Your Highness." I turned to see Xiuying bowing, Plum hiding behind her skirts. Xiuying's expression was somber, but her eyes twinkled. "It's an honor."

Sky straightened beside me. "The honor is mine," he said. "Jie."

The dragon released me. This time, I was reluctant to let go. The whiplash of these disparate visions had left me breathless, faint. "What must I do?" I whispered, clinging to the sweet remnants of that dream.

"Find the remaining two jade pieces," he said, and now I clung to his every word as a lifeboat. "You cannot allow Zhuque to restore her seal to wholeness. She is our greatest threat."

I nodded, before recalling how the jade thief had tried to smash the seal into pieces. It was what I would've tried, logically, but it had proven ineffective. "But how do I destroy the seal?" I asked. "You said even throwing the jade in the sea won't work!"

"Once you find the jade," said the dragon, "give it to me and I will take care of it."

I let out a breath, heart still pounding from the heady promise of my final vision. That future—I would make it mine.

Reality crashed back into me. "And what of Chancellor Sima?" I demanded, thinking of the complexity of the mission ahead. "He knows vastly more than me; besides, I think he can sense his own seal!"

"Learn to use your power, Hai Meilin. Learn, before it is too late."

Before I could protest, I felt my body propelled forward, so fast I could barely breathe as I shot through the surface of the water. Gasping in fright, I fainted.

When I woke, I was lying on a beach, the tide trickling into my boots. I sat up too quickly, inducing a splitting headache, then grimaced at my surroundings. There was no sight of civilization for miles. I felt numb all over, chilled to my bones, and yet—I was, undeniably, alive. I had fallen off a cliff and drowned in the sea. And lived.

In my hand, clenched so tightly it left an imprint on my palm, was my mother's necklace. It had saved me. The dragon's power had saved me. I contemplated it for a while, then slid it back around my neck.

Why had I shied away from my spirit power before? I had seen it as taboo, as black magic, another way to separate me from my friends, to thwart my goal of conformity. But it was a fool's errand. Try as I might, I could never be one of them. I was a woman.

I was more than that. Anyone could have found my mother's necklace, but my spirit affinity was stronger than most—even Sima had recognized this fact.

"Would you surrender yourself to the world, or would you make the world yours?"

I got to my feet shakily.

In truth, it was not the threat to Anlai that changed my mind. It was not even the foretelling of my own demise. Death was coming for me regardless; I'd always known this. Ever since my mother had taken her last breath in the Wen River, I'd always seen death as an inevitability, guaranteed as thunder after lightning, winter after fall. And yet, what had never been guaranteed to me was freedom.

I had never known that another possibility existed, a chance at everything I wanted. That if I won this war for Anlai, I could be known and accepted for who I was. In victory, I could have my sword, my name, my freedom. I could protect those I loved. I could, in turn, be loved for it.

My power, I recognized it now for what it was. A gift.

I would make this fate mine.

PART II

TWENTY-FOUR

*And if I ever write "Tonight the moonlight is strong,"
I am trying to say that I miss you.*
—THE CLASSIC OF POETRY, 532

THE JOURNEY BACK TOOK THREE DAYS. BY THE TIME I REACHED the mouth of the Dian River and saw the remnants of the battlefield, I was weak with infection and fever. My head felt as if it were on fire, and my toes felt as though they were swollen pieces of ice.

"Couldn't you have deposited me closer to camp?" I grumbled. I'd started talking to myself on day two. The dragon, of course, didn't deign to answer me. I'd begun to notice he was only present in my head at certain times, usually when I least needed him.

When I saw the first signs of my platoon's camp, I would've cheered out loud if I hadn't been so dehydrated. As it was, I could barely bring myself to lift one foot in front of the other. I had the queasy feeling that the dragon's seal was the only thing keeping me from keeling over entirely.

Night had descended hours earlier. It was getting so dark I could barely make my way through the forest. I hoped I wouldn't run into a patrol solider, who might mistake me for a Ximing bandit in my current state.

A light flickered in the distance. Someone was practicing alone in the clearing, a mile out from camp. That was dangerous, I thought, and went against protocol. If the soldier was caught, his lieutenant would penalize him. The oil lamp winked and guttered as the soldier lashed out with his sword, his movements so forceful they swayed the fire.

As I stumped closer, he straightened, peering into the gloom. "Who's there?" he asked sharply. And the sound of his voice brought tears to my eyes. I'd thought I would never hear that voice again.

"It's me," I said, unhelpfully.

His face went blank with shock. "Ren?"

I staggered out of the trees into the clearing. "Sky," I said. "I—"

Overcome, I fell forward, and he caught me around the waist. "Ren!" He lowered me gently to the ground. "You-you're alive. We all thought . . ." His voice broke.

I'd never heard him stumble over his words before.

My eyelids flickered. All my willpower left me as I saw that I was safe now; I no longer needed to cling to consciousness. "I nearly died," I told him. "But the dragon . . ."

He put his hand to my forehead, his touch cool and gentle. "Tian ah, you're burning with fever," he said. "I'll take you to the physician."

"No!" I tried to push him away, but I was too weak. "I can't see the physician. I can't." I couldn't remember why; I just knew this was a cardinal rule. "Listen to me . . . the dragon said . . . the fires . . . because of . . ."

"Shh," said Sky. He was still holding me. "It's okay. You're safe now, Ren."

I wanted to tell him it wasn't okay. I wanted to tell him I had news of the utmost urgency, that we had to set out for southern

Ximing immediately. But I could hardly speak. Darkness pressed at the edges of my vision.

"Infection," he said, as it dawned on him. "Where are you injured?"

I couldn't answer. He shoved aside the rags of my jacket, then ripped my tunic open. And then his hands fell away. His face turned from confusion to total disbelief. In my fevered state, I could not comprehend the source of his astonishment.

He tried to speak. "Y-you—"

I fainted.

I LAY IN A FUGUE STATE FOR THE NEXT FEW DAYS. DIMLY, AT THE EDGES of my awareness, I sensed movement and sound, but I could not make meaning or sense out of them. I felt as if I were watching myself from within a dream.

In this strange, dazed state, I felt someone carry me into a tent and lay me on a bed. This bed was softer than my own, and I slept as I hadn't in a long time—soundly.

I woke to a voice telling me to drink. Cool water was pressed to my parched lips, yet I lacked the strength to raise my head. A hand steadied the back of my neck, supporting me. I drifted off into darkness.

Another fever dream in the middle of the night. Gentle hands lifted a towel off my forehead, replacing it with a new one, dampened with water. Above me, a shadowy figure sat beside my bed, watching me. I fell asleep once more.

It was night again. All was quiet outside. I heard a bullfrog croaking in the distance, a horse munching on grass. Despite the multiple blankets piled on top of me, I'd never felt so cold in my life.

The chill penetrated my bones. I shook so hard it felt involuntary, like I couldn't stop. This frightened me—the notion that I didn't have control over my own body anymore. There was little else I had control over.

I willed myself to stop shivering, but this only made me shake harder. I wondered if we were in the northern ice channels, surrounded by snowbanks on all sides. I saw snowflakes in the air, falling on my frozen lips. I was going to freeze to death, wasn't I?

I turned and saw someone watching me. It hadn't occurred to me that I was not alone. He was studying me, his brows drawn inward in concern. I wanted to tell him it was okay, I was okay. I wanted to lie as I always had. And yet, somehow, I knew that he knew. That my lie was no more, evanesced. And strangely, though I had tried so hard and agonized for so long to keep it hidden, the thought relieved me. I no longer needed to lie.

The fever dream was surely a dream, for this could not be happening. The boy got into bed beside me and tentatively put his arms around my shaking limbs. He pulled me into his warm, solid chest and held me tightly, as if trying to lend me his warmth. I lay there, shivering and trying not to shiver, listening to a stuttering heartbeat in the dark. I wondered if the heartbeat belonged to me, or to him. And only then did I fall asleep, cold and warm at once.

TWENTY-FIVE

Depending on the strength of the spirit, and the degree of spirit affinity the vessel possesses, mediums may be able to harness the abilities of the spirits they commune with. The most obscure, and perhaps abhorred, of these abilities is compulsion. Compulsion enables the medium to compel his subject to obey his bidding, through manipulation of the mind. In contrast, its less stigmatized cousin, impulsion, forces a subject to yield their emotions, and to a lesser extent, their thoughts, to the spirit medium.

—LOST JOURNALS OF AN 8TH-CENTURY LIXIA SCHOLAR, DATE UNKNOWN

THE SPIRIT REALM IS COLD.

Blood coated the roof of my mouth. I spat in mild distaste, then stretched. *"The spirits demand blood,"* my mother had once said, murmuring to herself before falling asleep. Only now did I understand what she meant.

When the dragon had last summoned me, the spirit realm had appeared empty. Now there were throngs of people, some wandering, some standing rooted to the ground. Though some appeared to be talking, no one seemed to perceive each other's presence. Yet I could feel them—and I could feel the familiar presence of the one I sought. Taiyang, one of the sun.

I pushed through the masses of people, in a hurry to reach him. One of them bumped into me, a tall, slender man with long, gleaming hair. His delicate, pale features appeared vaguely familiar, but he turned away too quickly, and I lost sight of him in the crowd. I returned to my objective.

Chancellor Sima. No longer did he burn with the power of the Vermillion Bird. Instead, he appeared like a ghost of his former self. Older, fatigued, eyes sunken and knuckles raw. I could feel the lack in him—the void Zhuque had left behind. Could I read him now, I wondered, as easily as he had once read me?

Up close, I saw that his face was streaked with tears. I thought of his dead wife, his dead child. *Death follows him*, I thought. Then I recalled my mother.

Like it follows you.

Last time, I'd taken his hand to see into his memories, but he had not needed my touch to see mine. He'd simply stared into my eyes, even from a distance, and known my thoughts. With Red too, I recalled, it had been through his eyes that I'd invaded his mind.

"*I opened my mind to you*," Taiyang had told me. "*But it was you who followed. It seems you have a natural talent for it—for impulsion.*"

Our eyes met, striking against each other like the clash of steel. Suddenly, I became aware of my own body, of leaving it.

This time was not like the last. If previously Taiyang had fed me a narrative, a predetermined memory, this time, he did not know I was inside. I was in his head with him; *I was him*.

I WOKE ABRUPTLY, MY HEAD EMPTY, SLOW WITH FATIGUE. OUTSIDE, THE sky was still dim, awash in stars. Had I been drugged? I tried to rise and nearly fell over, my sense of balance awry. A subtle yet foreign fragrance permeated my chambers—cedar and jasmine. I held my breath, sensing the wrongness in the air.

Then I perceived the silence. It was not the silence of the night; it was the silence in my head. The Vermillion Bird said nothing.

My hand leapt to my throat. And here was the answer—the cord around my neck had been cut. Someone had stolen Zhuque's seal.

Without warning, a loud crack echoed through the halls outside. I heard doors banging open, guards calling out. "Who's there?" someone shouted.

I threw open the doors to my chambers. The open-air gallery was empty, empty but for an iron dagger lying on the floor. I touched it, then flinched. The iron was searing hot. They'd used it to destroy the seal. But they hadn't succeeded; they couldn't have.

They could not destroy the seal without me. Its vessel.

Beyond the hallway, the balcony door lay ajar, curtains fluttering in the breeze. Dreading what I'd find, I stepped outside, looking out over the calm horizon, where the sky met water. I understood what the thief had done—short of forcing a vessel to destroy his own seal, they'd simply gotten rid of it. Hidden it, in the best place they knew. The sea.

The waves lapped greedily beneath me.

I could no longer hear the phoenix's voice, but I could feel the broken pieces of my jade, calling out to me like birds seeking their way to shelter. They would come back to me, their master.

Soon the sea would return what the thief stole, and until then, I would bide my time.

I GASPED, SURFACING FROM THE MEMORY AS IF FROM A DEEP BODY OF water. Taiyang no longer stood before me; he'd fallen to his knees, his head in his hands. The contrast between his memory self and his dream self was stark. In his memories, his initial reaction had been one of calm sensibility. But in this dreamworld, he'd lost his inhibitions, his spirit seal, and he was no longer calm now.

"They took *everything* from me," he whispered. I crouched beside him; his voice was so weak, I could barely hear it. "How can you stand it?" he asked me, lifting his head. "I'm so . . . so angry now. Without an outlet . . . it's consuming . . ."

Vengeance, I recalled. *The phoenix feeds off vengeance.* Without the outlet Zhuque provided him, Taiyang was left to bear it on his own.

"I can't think, can't breathe, can't—"

He was hyperventilating, I saw. "Slow down." I did not know why I was helping him. Perhaps because in his loneliness, I saw my own. "You're breathing too fast."

He looked at me, squinting at my face. I inhaled; our eyes met, sparking. I saw his pregnant wife lying on their bed, asleep. She woke to see me bringing out a bowl of congee for her.

"You shouldn't be cooking," she said. "That's my responsibility—"

"Shh." I laid a hand against her forehead. This baby was killing her. "You need to rest."

"Your mother already hates me, Yi," she whispered, voice hoarse. "If I lose the child too . . ."

"Limei." I drew her into my arms. "You will live. Our family will live."

Our connection came in and out. I could feel Taiyang shaking beneath me.

"A girl?" My father paced before me, his arms crossed over his chest.

"Yes," I said. "A strong, healthy child."

"Who is still a girl," he finished. "There's nothing to be done about it now. Abide by the healing period, then try again. Limei looks like she's had a hard time with it. She'll most likely only last a second time."

"Don't you dare—"

"Sima Yi!" the midwife called, urgency in her voice. "Your wife needs you."

I dragged myself away, letting go of him. My fingertips felt seared, as if I'd touched hot iron. "Do you practice qi gong?" I asked him, thinking of what I did in moments like these.

He gave me a shallow nod. I guided him into a sitting position, watching as he centered himself. Slowly, he regained control, his breaths evening.

"The ancient lixia masters also used qi gong to harness the mind," he said, after some time.

So he wished to change the subject. But I could still see Limei in my mind's eye, still see the way he'd cared for her, defended her, lost her all the same.

I knew how this story ended. She died. Their child died. Leaving only Taiyang behind, a shadow of his former self. Alone with his guilt, his regret, his loneliness.

I knew what that felt like.

"You never told me we were on different sides of the war," I said.

His eyes were sad. "I thought you didn't have a side."

I considered this. My fate was inextricably tied to the war, not because of the geopolitical infighting between Anlai and its rival kingdoms, but because of the spirits pulling at the strings of men. I cared little for the Anlai warlord, insomuch as he was the father of my commander. I cared even less for my kingdom, which traded and sold women like livestock at the marketplace. And yet, when I thought of my family back home, and my platoon, my friends, my prince—I knew that had never been true.

"Perhaps I don't care for politics," I told him. "But I care about my people." I looked him in the eye. "I think you can understand that."

He seemed to shrink into himself, no longer the cold, unfeeling man he'd been on the battlefield at Dian River. "You must know—I can no longer hear the phoenix's voice," he confessed. "She brought me comfort, Haiyang. And now, even that has been taken from me."

I released a hard breath. "Can't you see that Zhuque is using you?"

His smile was equally embittered. "Can't you see that Qinglong is doing the same to you?"

We were both miserable people, but in our misery, we understood each other. I needed Qinglong, for my own goals, but I would never let myself reach the state of desperation and dependence that Sima now found himself in.

I straightened, making my choice. It was true, I pitied him, but my compassion had limits. When it came to those I loved, I was selfish to my core.

"Fire and water," he said softly. "Fate is so easily predictable, is she not?"

He said something else, but I was no longer listening. I took a step toward him, peering into his faintly yellow eyes, and conjured the sensation of falling.

What had Sima called it—impulsion? It was as easy as learning to float in water. Even when I felt his qi resisting the intrusion, I pressed my own fire and metal against it, recalling the inclinations of his elemental being. His qi embraced me, an old friend.

I was Taiyang; I was within him. His presence coated me, anger and pain and grief. I shook off his insistent emotions and concentrated instead on my surroundings. *Salt spray. Waning moonlight. A bustling port, ships waiting to dock.* And . . . a new emotion—one I hadn't sensed before. *Anticipation.*

The second jade piece is about to wash ashore. I can feel it. Drifting closer every day. Nearing Xi Lan on the eastern coast.

Xi Lan?

I felt Sima stir, his consciousness growing suspicious. I broke free immediately.

"So it must be this way, then. You made your choice," he said, his face hard. "Know the consequences, Haiyang."

"As should you." I met his gaze, letting go of any lingering remorse. "Know that the next time we meet, in the human realm, *I will kill you.*"

TWENTY-SIX

Qi gong, or the practice of energy cultivation, enables its practitioners to maintain balance of the body and mind. Perhaps this is why, during the Yong Dynasty—frequently known as the Golden Age of spirit wielders— lixia scholars mandated the practice of qi gong prior to accepting a bargain with a spirit. Unfortunately, much of the text from this era was lost during Emperor Wu's purge of black magic.
—A COMPREHENSIVE OVERVIEW OF LIXIA-INDUCED DISORDERS, 910

WHEN I AWOKE, SUNLIGHT STREAMED IN THROUGH THE TENT walls, scattering the dust motes and turning them golden. My fever had broken, and I felt largely clearheaded. My memories were still wobbly and illogical, but I disregarded this, confident they would return to me eventually.

I didn't recognize the tent I was in. Confused, I touched the fine quality of my linen blankets before it hit me—this was the prince's tent. What was I doing here?

I stood hurriedly, finding a clean uniform folded beside me. My strange dreams had left a bewildering echo on my memories, so that I couldn't parse fact from fiction.

I dressed, then tied my hair back in its customary topknot. Outside, I could hear soldiers going through their midmorning routines. I felt for my necklace before I left the tent. To my relief, my mother's pendant was still there, tucked safely beneath my tunic.

But that reminded me of more urgent matters.

I strode out of the tent, then jumped in surprise at the guards stationed outside. Bowing clumsily, I stammered that I was lost. Strangely, they needed no reason for my presence. They simply nodded and let me walk away.

I hurried back to my platoon in the eastern quarter. At the archery butts, Wolf found me.

"So the rumors are true!" Wolf exclaimed, jogging toward me and clapping me on the back. His affection surprised me; he knew me because he was Sparrow's squad leader, but he'd never shown anything more than a vague curiosity about me before. "Back from the dead, Hai Ren."

"It's Pretty Boy!" said Red, dropping his bow and whooping. Beyond him, I saw that Sky had been teaching Little Pig how to properly string a longbow. Despite the fact that everyone else had noticed me, Sky refused to so much as glance in my direction. He'd put his back to me, his shoulders stiff.

Before I could think more of it, I felt an enormous force barrel into me from behind. "Ren!" Sparrow shouted in my ear, blasting my eardrums. "You're back!"

"How long has it been?" I asked, rubbing my ears. "You're acting like I've been gone ten years."

"Close," Sparrow replied. "Ten days."

"Ten days?" I shrieked. I cursed my sickly body and its inconvenient sense of timing. A new thought dawned on me as I looked around. Why was Little Pig training with Wolf's squad? "Where's the rest of Twelfth Squad?"

Everyone exchanged dark looks. "Twelfth Squad's disbanded," Wolf said, not one for mincing words. "Only two survivors remained. Well, now three, including you."

I took this in. So only three of us had made it out of the vanguard. Sparrow had been right; it was a massacre. I looked from

Little Pig to Red and nodded. A hard-won camaraderie had formed between us, though we'd never cared much for each other before. We were the only survivors of our squad, of the people we'd marched with for over a month.

Sparrow cleared his throat. "Zilong..."

"I know," I said.

"That's why we all thought you were dead too," Sparrow explained, voice thick with guilt. "That's why we didn't look for you."

I shook my head. He didn't owe me any apologies. "I would've thought the same."

"He tried looking for your identity tag among the bodies," Red chimed in, pointing at Little Pig. "And he cried." He pointed at Sparrow, who pouted.

"Why'd you have to tell him that?" Sparrow's ears were turning red.

"And *he* was mopey and brooding for days," Red continued, pointing at Prince Liu, who was still by the archery butts, shooting arrows alone. His aim was off; he fired straight into a tree.

I squeezed Sparrow's shoulder, then edged out of the circle. I had to speak with Sky. "Prince Liu!" I called. I was certain he'd heard me, but he pretended not to. "Prince Liu!"

Without retrieving his arrows, he stalked off into the woods. Exasperated, I quickened my pace. "Sky!"

I caught up to him in a thicket of trees. Sky whirled around with such fury and violence, the trees shook. Mating songbirds took off in a flurry, properly afraid.

I took an involuntary step back. But no matter what personal vendetta Sky had against me now, this was bigger than the two of us.

I swallowed, determined to say what I'd planned to. "When I

was in enemy territory," I began. On my long journey back to camp, I'd thought over how I would explain this to him. "I gained intelligence of the utmost urgency. The Ximing chancellor has assembled a weapon capable of terrible destruction. That's why Ximing declared war; that's why Chancellor Sima knew they could win." I predicted his next question and quickly said, "But he hasn't been able to use it yet. At least, not to its full extent. One of his allies betrayed him after the harvest moon and tried to destroy the weapon... but wasn't entirely successful." Sky wasn't paying attention to me; I could tell by his expression. "Listen to me! Chancellor Sima is on his way to Xi Lan as we speak—"

"This shouldn't concern you." Sky's voice was cold as steel.

"What?" Had he heard anything I'd just said? "If Chancellor Sima gets there before us, Ximing will be able to burn down all of Chuang Ning in days! This could mean the end of war as we know it, the end of—"

"You need to leave."

I recoiled. The indifference in his voice hurt like the sting of an old wound, never fully healed.

"Once you've recovered, pack your bags and return to Chuang Ning. You can go with the supply crew. They'll make the journey next week." He spoke with no feeling or kindness.

I opened my mouth, then closed it. I didn't know what to say. Never had I imagined an outcome like this. "You need me," I tried. "Only I know the location and the logistics of Sima's plans. Sky, listen to me. You need to assemble a small group of your top men—"

"That doesn't include you."

I exhaled in utmost exasperation. "I thought I'd proven to you by now that I—"

"My top *men*," he repeated. "You know very well that does not include you."

I went utterly still. My memories rushed back to me with the violence of the river rapids. When I met his eyes, they spoke volumes. "You know," I said.

This was the final straw—his temper exploded. "How long were you planning to get away with this?" he burst out.

Our eyes met, and suddenly I felt the shape of his elemental threads—water and wood—and I felt myself mold to them. Then I was inside his mind.

Get rid of her, thought Sky. *Get rid of her now—*

I pulled out of his thoughts as if escaping a burning building. *I don't want this*, I thought, as I felt the hot prick of tears behind my eyes. It was too much to see the loathing in his face; to hear his thoughts was unbearable.

"Your crimes are punishable by death!" he snapped. "Did you think this would be all fun and games?"

I swallowed my emotions and glared back at him. I loathed the patronizing intimation of his words. "Don't presume to know my circumstances," I said. "My alternatives were worse than death." I walked away from him and then changed my mind, spinning back around. "You would never understand. You are and have always been a prince of the wealthiest kingdom in all of Tianjia. But not everyone was born like you, Sky. Life at home for me was worse than death out here."

His lip curled. "Your emotions are getting the better of you."

And now my temper blazed brilliant and searing, hot enough to match his. "Oh, so now that I'm a woman everything I say is due to my emotions?" My voice trembled with outrage. "Fine," I said. "Let's decide this through logic and reasoning, like real *men*. If I beat you in single combat, then I stay. If I lose, I leave."

I drew my sword. Another frantic bird emerged from the treetops and took off for the clouds. Prince Liu drew his.

We were both furious, unable to remain levelheaded. I swung at him first, but I sensed him holding back. This made me even more furious, if that was possible. I pressed him harder, and soon our swords were a flurry of motion, silver steel glinting in the dim forest light. He hissed as I drew blood, his eyes narrowing. And then he gave up his restraint.

He leapt toward me. I was still sore and stiff from my bout of sickness. I was slower than usual and too angry to be cautious. He found an opening and had his blade up to my neck in seconds. He glared down at me, then released me, shoving me back.

"Best out of three," I said, panting, giving him only a moment to register my words before I attacked once more. We spun, flew, parried. This time, both of us were hungry for a fight. I dived at him but he tripped me, and then we both rolled to the ground, tumbling, our swords left behind in the dirt. I struggled to get him in a choke hold, but in close combat, he didn't need technique to pin me, only sheer strength. I tried to twist out of his arms, but he forced me to the ground, using his knees to keep me trapped. "It's over, *Meilin*."

He said my name as if it were a curse.

With that, he stood and retrieved his sword, turning to go. My blood was boiling beneath my skin. I watched him retreat, then grabbed my sword from the dirt and ran at him from behind.

He heard me coming and ducked instinctively. But I had the element of surprise. Although he brought his sword up to meet mine, his balance was off. I disarmed him with one swift blow, then leveled my blade at his throat. I pressed the cold steel against his skin. I could feel his every breath, pulsing beneath my blade.

"You already lost," he said, teeth gritted.

"No," I told him. "I don't give up until I win."

TWENTY-SEVEN

In the times of old, spirits roamed freely among men, until humankind was all but blotted out. The ancient gods, missing their incense offerings and ritual worship, sought a way to protect humankind and restore balance between the realms. Thus, they used their own bones to fashion seals that would limit the power of spirits, forcing them to coexist with men.
—WINTER AND SPRING ANNALS, 417

S**KY GLARED AT ME AND STORMED OFF. WE DIDN'T TALK UNTIL** later that evening, when we'd both cooled off from our fight. He found me at dinner, then motioned for me to leave the others.

I followed him into the woods. I brought my sword with me, just in case.

"You said the Ximing chancellor has some sort of weapon," he said stiffly, without looking me in the eye. We sat on a fallen log, with enough distance between us to seat several others.

So he'd heard *some* of what I'd said, at least. Could I tell him everything?

The yearning was so fierce it hurt, physically. I wanted to reveal every secret I'd hidden from him, to give up every lie that kept us apart. I wanted Sky to know me, to see me for who I truly was. And yet I knew it to be an impossible wish. To people like Sky's father, lixia was black magic—evil at its core. If I told Sky the truth now, he'd be forced to imprison or even execute me, for I posed an unprecedented threat to his men.

Instead, I reminded myself of Qinglong's vision, of the long game I was playing. I had to win this war, to save my family and my kingdom. Only after I'd proven myself could I reveal the truth of who I was.

So I held my tongue. I made up an unconvincing lie about eavesdropping on several high-ranking Ximing generals in the aftermath of the battle. I told him this was how I'd learned of Chancellor Sima's spirit power and his stolen jade seal. I'd never been a good liar, and yet Sky listened without question.

"I knew things were not as they seemed," said Sky, after I was done.

"You believe me?" I said, startled, for although I'd come to him asking for his trust, when indeed given, it bewildered me. Most in Anlai placed lixia in the same category as mythical beasts and magical alchemy. Something acknowledged in old fables and ballads, but not to be believed in the modern age.

And of course, those who did believe in its existence—like the Imperial Commander of Anlai—seemed only to fear and abhor it.

"Why wouldn't I?" Sky snapped. "While you were gone, we received more reports of fires at the southern border. Inexplicable wildfires that burn with no end. Whole villages razed to ash. The flames persist even under heavy rainfall. You saw for yourself what happened at the Dian River battle. It's unnatural." His voice was thick with noticeable disgust; I had to hide my shudder. Though his repulsion was not directed at me, it felt like a personal affront. "Our losses were staggering. They held their ground with only a third of our numbers."

"How many?" I asked. "How many did we lose?"

Sky let out a breath. "Ten thousand."

Qinglong had been right all along. The dragon had known the future, seen it before it had come to pass: *"Ten thousand men will be dead before this day is over."*

Qinglong had not been bluffing.

"Those fires—those are likely just experiments," I said, forcing calm into my voice. "Sima's testing the range of his returned abilities. But with every jade piece he reclaims, his powers will grow. And then he'll set his sights on more than villages. He'll aim for Chuang Ning."

I thought of my family back home, wondering if news of the southern war front had reached them yet. Compared to Ximing villagers, most Anlai civilians, especially those in Chuang Ning, had been thus far removed from the brutalities of war. But when the fighting came to their doorstep, would they be ready?

Qinglong's vision crept into my mind's eye—of my family's horrific death. I could not lose Xiuying and Rouha and Plum as I'd lost Twelfth Squad. That would be a loss that would break me.

Sky was toying with a gnarled twig, his jaw clenched. I wondered if he was thinking the same thing. Chuang Ning was his home too.

"Chancellor Sima is already on his way to Xi Lan," I told him. "I don't know when his jade will wash ashore, but we have to get there before he does. If he manages to secure another piece of his seal, his powers will grow twofold." I leaned forward. "We must set out immediately. Tomorrow."

"You saw what happened at the Dian River. I can't move that many men—"

"Not the whole company," I cut him off. "Speed matters more than strength right now."

"With such numbers, we won't be able to take on the chancellor and his men."

"Not yet," I agreed. "But his jade is the priority—for now." I thought of my promise to Chancellor Sima in the dream realm. My mental abilities might be comparable to his, but Sima's elemental magic far surpassed my own. To stand a chance against him, I needed to remedy that. "I'll come back for him next time," I finished.

Sky shot me a look, his expression inscrutable. At last he said, "Xi Lan is a two-day journey from here." He sighed, breaking the twig under his boot. "The army's waiting for supplies as it is. If all goes according to plan, we'll be back within a week."

I startled. "You're coming too?"

He eyed me. "Did you think to go alone? *You?*"

It went unspoken, but we both heard it—what was left unsaid. *You, a woman?*

"I would've asked fresh horses of you, and perhaps several men," I said carefully. "But I wouldn't have presumed..."

"I'm coming too," he said, in a voice that was final. But we both knew this was no easy declaration. For the commander of Seventh Company to leave on a secret, undisclosed mission... no matter how skilled his deputy, our army would fall into some level of disarray.

And yet a part of me was all too happy for him to join me. Sky was the best swordsman I knew, and I trusted him with my life. I wanted him with me in enemy territory, of course, but also—this would make things even more difficult for me. If the plan failed and Sima and I came head-to-head, how would I be able to hide *my* spirit power from Sky?

Sky ground the remains of the branch into dust. "I'll need to discuss matters with Winter first. He may know more about the source of the chancellor's power—and how to destroy it." He grimaced. "And I'll need to find someone to lead the army while I'm gone."

I frowned. "Couldn't Winter—I mean, Prince Liu—"

Sky sighed. "He could. He won't be pleased with it, though."

Liu Winter had long been a source of confusion for me. "Winter is . . . your *older* brother," I started.

Sky nodded.

"He doesn't always act like it," I said, before wondering if I should've kept my mouth shut.

Sky shrugged. "He doesn't enjoy killing. He is the better of me in many ways." He glanced sideways at me. "He would not have lost his temper with you as I did."

I wondered if this was as close to an apology as I was going to get.

"Why did your father send him off to Ximing?" I asked instead. "If he doesn't enjoy fighting?"

Sky scoffed. "He's a warlord's son," he said. "He doesn't have a choice."

Duty, again. But did a warlord's son really have no choice but to follow in his father's footsteps? In a similar manner, did a gambler's daughter ultimately become a gambler as well? I toyed with the cord of my necklace and thought of all that had transpired thus far. I had taken many risks since leaving Chuang Ning. Even joining the army had been a gamble, a wager with the highest of stakes.

So yes, maybe we did inherit the tendencies of our parents, no matter how hard we tried to do otherwise. Or maybe, some of us tried harder than others.

"Keep this between us," said Sky. "Tell no one of Sima's black magic. Morale is low as it is—particularly after Dian River. Some may already suspect the truth, but I don't want my men deserting in hysteria."

I nodded, then looked up at him. "Have you told anyone?" I asked, flushing deeply. "About . . . who I am?"

"You're still alive, aren't you?" He arched a brow, his expression hostile.

So he hadn't. And he was furious with me for it, for taking him down with me. I knew it wasn't fair to him, when he prized honesty and integrity above all else. "Thank you."

"Don't," he bit out. "Don't thank me." Abruptly, he rose to his feet. "I'll have nothing to do with the ruination of your life."

TWENTY-EIGHT

According to my spies, there is much discord between the three Ximing princes, for they are as different from one another as night and day. The eldest is known for his filial nature, for he is his father's favorite and the clear front-runner for the throne. The middle son is as ruthless as he is indomitable, prone to battle and bloodshed. As for the youngest, well, less is said about him. He is known to be spoiled and vapid, renowned for his beauty and little else. I wouldn't worry about him.

—MINISTER JIA, IN A PRIVATE MISSIVE TO PRINCE LIU, 923

WE LEFT THE NEXT DAY. OUR TEAM WAS SMALL, AND WE TOLD no one who did not immediately need to know. I convinced Sky to let me bring Sparrow, who I knew would be useful when gathering intelligence from the southern fishing villages. Not only could Sparrow strike up a conversation with anyone, but he also knew the southern dialect that Sky and I couldn't always comprehend. Sky brought along his personal guard, Luo Tao, who remembered me from the time I'd barged into Sky's tent yelling about bandits. Tao was older than us, in his late twenties, and he'd traveled through Ximing before. He'd even met Chancellor Sima once, though at that time Sima had only been a lowly court official. Since then, he'd climbed court like the roots of a fengshu tree, overtaking everything in its path.

"There was always something distinctly *wrong* about him," said Tao, after Sky had informed them of the true goal of our mission.

"Even in Ximing, the man had no friends, no allies. I'd wondered how he'd ascended to chancellor."

"Now we know," answered Sky grimly. "Because Warlord Cao wants a puppet with supernatural powers."

I looked away from Sky, my face heating. The prince's words stung, though I couldn't articulate why.

"First that cursed fire, now this," said Sparrow. "No one's going to believe me back home."

"They will soon enough, when Ximing forces reach Chuang Ning," said Tao unhelpfully, as he toyed with his necklace. I'd noticed that since the battle at Dian River, a few soldiers had taken to wearing dark-colored pebbles around their neck, as if that would help against spirit corruption.

"This feels like a bad joke," Sparrow muttered. "Like I'll turn around one day and realize you all were pulling my leg."

Tao clapped him on the back. "You're not that important."

Sparrow laughed, grinning back at Tao before a new thought occurred to him. "Though if it's all true, why are we only going to face Sima with three men?"

I choked; Sky's eyes bulged.

"I mean, four—including you, Your Highness. Sorry, I didn't know if you'd join us in the dirty work."

"Our first target is the jade," I insisted.

The jade. My thoughts were as circular as hawks orbiting prey. *Retrieve the jade.* Ever since the battle at Dian River, I'd thought of nothing else.

Soon it would be within my grasp.

"We'll come back for the chancellor later," Sky said grimly. "And take him as prisoner then."

Sparrow shuddered. "I won't feel right until that man is butchered and burned." He made a noise of distaste. "Even then, death is too easy for a black magic practitioner like him."

I had to conceal a shudder of my own. Not because I agreed with Sparrow's sentiments, but because I feared that almost everyone in the Anlai army shared them.

No one will find out, I promised myself. *And if they do—I'll stop them.*

In the back of my mind, Qinglong hummed with approval. At last, the two of us were in alignment.

As we set out along the eastern coastline, descending deeper south, we passed villages stricken with poverty. Children ran up to us begging for money, their bodies gaunt and their clothing ragged. Sparrow and Tao were unmoved, but I saw Rouha and Plum in every one of these children. It made me sick inside.

Yet Sky suffered the most. At first he tried to stop and help, but Tao warned him against it, for fear of attracting unwanted attention. As we rode on, ignoring them, he seemed to grow more and more distant, closing himself off from the outside world.

He's idealistic, I thought, *and despite his princely manner and confidence, he knows little of the world outside Chuang Ning.*

By nightfall, we'd made good time, and stopped on the outskirts of New Quan, the last large trading port before we reached Xi Lan. Tao led us to a modest inn just outside the port center, next to the sea. He introduced Sky as a minor Ximing noble, and the rest of us as his entourage.

Though the innkeeper was awkward and shifty-eyed, the inn itself was comfortable. In comparison to the campsites we'd grown used to, even simple commodities felt like luxuries. Rice paper shielded the lattice windows, which offered a pleasant view of a banyan tree in bloom, its gnarled branches close enough to touch.

Beneath the lattice windows was a simple table, along with two beds positioned on either side.

Sky looked at the beds, then looked at me.

"I'll share a bed with Ren," Sparrow piped up. "Prince Liu, would you and Tao want to—"

Sky stiffened like an affronted peacock. "Ren, you're not sharing a bed with—"

I glared at him. "I'm sleeping on the floor, okay?"

We didn't talk after that. But late in the night, after I had finished first watch, Sky got up and gave me his pillow. So I guess he didn't hold grudges for long.

TWENTY-NINE

While one should strive for balance of the five elements, true balance is impossible to maintain. Just as no two personalities are alike, no two bodies carry the same elemental composition. Dangerously, overuse of lixia heightens this imbalance, intensifying the overrepresented elements of the body.

—LOST JOURNALS OF AN 8TH-CENTURY LIXIA SCHOLAR, DATE UNKNOWN

"M EILIN . . . I DO NOT WISH FOR YOU TO REPEAT MY MISTAKES."

I awoke as if struck, shooting to my feet. "Ma?" I asked aloud. Only Sparrow's wheezing snore replied, from where he sat slumped over by the side of the door.

The sky was still pitch black, and I knew I should return to sleep. And yet I couldn't shake the creeping itch along my spine. Halfheartedly, I tried to shake Sparrow awake—it was his watch—but rousing him had always been harder than rousing a sleeping panda. Giving up, I strapped on my blades and snuck downstairs.

Despite the late hour, I found the innkeeper awake and pacing the anteroom, as if waiting for something to happen. I took one look at his nervous expression and knew—*he sold us out.*

Across the room, the innkeeper turned; his eyes found mine. I reached for my sword just as he opened his mouth to shout.

"*You won't make it in time.*" I could feel Qinglong's urgency, melding with mine. "*Remember your lixia.*"

I made a snap decision. I sought the innkeeper's gaze and held it, tunneling my awareness toward him. "*Stop,*" I ordered, and to my sheer delight, I felt the dragon's echo in my command. Reaching for my qi, I sensed the composition of the innkeeper's elemental being—and let my qi become his. "*Do not warn the others,*" I ordered. "*Tell me—what is your aim?*"

The man could not move, much less speak. He stared at me, glassy-eyed and distant.

"*Conserve your qi,*" hissed the dragon.

Perhaps I was channeling too much energy into him. Instead of harnessing the full might of my power, I eased back, intertwining my qi and lixia, before letting a single thread trickle into the man's mind.

In a deadpan voice: "They want the Anlai prince."

"To take him as prisoner?" I demanded, thinking of our last run-in with bandits.

"To kill him."

My blood ran cold. I needed to go, *now*. But surely, the only way the Ximing assassins could enter our chamber was through this stairway, which I was currently guarding. Then I remembered—the banyan tree.

"Stay here," I ordered, before realizing I did not know how long my command would hold. "*Go to sleep,*" I told the innkeeper.

He looked at me with panicked bewilderment. As my attention strayed, I realized, my control on him lessened. *Focus, Meilin!* I centered my qi, forcing my breaths to slow. "*Go to sleep,*" I said again. And he slumped over.

So did I. I felt depleted, as if I'd just run a hundred-li race. Catching my breath, I forced myself upright and ignored my ink-black veins, which crept past my wrists, up my forearms. My vision had begun to blur, but I refused to lose concentration, refused to panic. This was no time to be sensitive.

I crept around the side of the inn. Sure enough, I spotted a black-clothed assassin climbing the banyan tree, and a crowd of a couple dozen others below him on the ground. The tree climber was positioning his bow in the direction of the lattice window. His target was asleep, unmoving, and he had a clear view into our room. It was a shot even I could make.

He reached for an arrow. I had no time. I had only my sword with me, and a few knives. I could scream; that might wake the others, but it would also alert the assassins to my presence.

Qinglong growled. "*Remember—*"

"I know," I hissed.

I knew I needed more practice with my elemental magic. *Now is as good a time as any*, I tried to tell myself. Grimly, I recirculated my qi, feeling for what dregs I had left.

I oriented myself east, in the direction of the sea, and then, remembering how I reached for my qi before any martial arts move—I did the same now. I reached, calling for water.

Nothing happened. The assassin strung his arrow. He aimed.

Why isn't it working? I thought desperately.

"*You need to let the sea in,*" Qinglong growled. "*I can do nothing for you if you're afraid of that which you try to wield.*"

"I'm not afraid . . ."

But I was. I did not want to go near the sea, or let the sea near me. My mind kept conjuring the memory of my mother's rotted corpse, her bloated purple foot.

Water was a mercurial beast, one that could aid just as easily as it betrayed.

"*Let the sea in,*" Qinglong snarled.

I felt the rumbling of the sea in my bones. Its dark, never-ending expanse, its fickle tides, its foaming currents. I felt the great depths of its power, like a well that drew and drew and drew. And though I was scared of it, though I wanted *not* to want it, the simple truth was that I did. I desired that power—not for the welfare of the state, and not even for the good of humanity. Simply for myself.

I let the sea touch my selfish greed. Its swelling waves called to me, raising the heights of my secret ambition. I felt my lungs expand with heady desire, with pure want.

It was no secret to the sea.

I called; the sea came. Water crystallized in the air before me. Conserving my qi, I shot the barest sliver of water around the archer's ankle, forming a chain.

Then I tugged.

The archer lurched sideways, before falling headfirst to the ground.

"Big Knife!" his companion cried out, running forward as a puddle of blood welled around Big Knife's head.

They did not notice the blood mixing with seawater, which pooled beneath their feet. I exhaled, letting my resolve harden. As did the water—into ice.

The men slipped and fell on the ice like majiang tiles. Chaos descended. At the commotion, a blurry figure peered out of the lattice window. Sky? But I could not make out his face. My vision was going out, like ink spilling over a scroll, blotting out every word. *Not now*, I thought in panic, clawing at my eyes. *Not now*.

Help me! I begged, but all I heard was overwhelming silence. I counted out three seconds, then five. My sight did not return. I tried to take a step back, to hide, but I hit a raised root and fell, landing badly on one knee. Blind, I started crawling, moving away from the commotion.

"Who are you?" one of the men shouted, his voice coming dangerously near. "What are you doing here?"

I tried to rise to my feet to run, but he reached me first, grabbing me by the scruff of my neck. Then I felt his entire being tense. "Golden eyes," he breathed. He released me.

I landed on my feet. And started to run.

"What are you doing?" A voice from farther back. "He's with the Anlai party! Kill him!"

"He's a spirit medium," the man who'd held me said.

"Then kill him *now*!"

I felt an arrow whiz past me, barely missing the rim of my ear. I could hear bandits pursuing me, too many to take on my own. I wondered if I could compel them, but my qi was almost entirely depleted, and mind control required eye contact.

I ran into the forest. I slowed, afraid of hitting a tree or losing my balance. I was beginning to see hazy shapes again: the outline of a boulder, a tree trunk. Then the tree moved. Too late, I realized my mistake. What I'd thought a tree was a man, waiting for me.

He threw his dagger at me and I dodged in the nick of time, my training kicking in as I rolled away, whipping out my own blade in the process. I aimed low—at his gut. I heard rather than saw the knife meeting its mark. The assassin howled in pain, a guttural sound, one that surely everyone and everything in the forest heard. I cursed his booming voice, thinking to retreat before the others found me. But already I heard their approaching footsteps.

I blinked rapidly, willing my sight to return faster.

"Qi and lixia go hand in hand. If you don't learn to conserve your qi, someday your sight will never return." The dragon's voice was faint, as if coming through a long, windy tunnel.

"Thanks for the moral support," I snapped, before catching sight of what I'd missed earlier—a familiar, rippling black haze. Near the tree trunk where the bandit I'd knifed was bleeding to death. The tree had been hollowed out with time, forming a natural shelter from wind and rain. But no birds or forest creatures occupied the tree, and only now did I notice I heard no birdsong *anywhere* in this forest, despite the early-morning hour. The glimmering black haze that filled the space within the tree appeared exactly like the one I'd found in the Yun clearing the night of the harvest moon. And that eerie tinny sound—the same sound I'd heard within my mother's chambers.

It must be a gate, I thought. A gate between realms. If I were to step through, it would lead to the spirit realm.

"*It is a tear in the veil,*" the dragon said, sounding curiously delighted. "*So that any human, not just those with seals, can enter our realm. But only those with strong enough spirit affinity can survive such a place. The rest...*"

My eyes widened as another assassin headed straight past me for the portal, walking as if hypnotized. His eyes were bright with desire, his shoulders shaking with nervous energy. But when he reached the black haze, instead of disappearing inside as I'd expected, he began to scream. An inhumane, animal sound, as if he were being consumed alive. His eyes rolled back in his head as his body convulsed, twitching like a beheaded chicken's. I couldn't watch. I turned away, just as I saw more men approaching the gate.

"Get back!" I yelled, not because they weren't my enemy, but because no one deserved such a fate. Yet they ignored me as if I hadn't spoken at all.

I considered using force to persuade them, then decided to better pick my battles. I ran back toward the inn, trying to ignore the guttural screams that I left behind in the clearing. I couldn't have helped them, I told myself, my skin pricking with gooseflesh.

"*You could have compelled them,*" the dragon pointed out.

"Are you trying to persuade me to help my enemy?" I demanded.

"*I'm trying to make you see the truth. You could have helped them, but you chose not to,"* said Qinglong. *"Because you are not noble or tenderhearted. You are pragmatic and self-serving; you are a survivor. That is why you continue to survive."*

I tried to ignore the visceral discomfort that rose at the dragon's words. For these were qualities I desired in myself. Xiuying was benevolent and tenderhearted. Sky was noble and kind. These were traits I tried to mimic, strengths I knew that heroes of every legend possessed. But who was I deluding? I was not the hero of this story.

My ambition was the secret, ugly kind, the kind that nurtured villains and tyrants. But I would not become like my mother or father; I would keep my madness in check, and I would maintain my guise for everyone else. *What I want*, I reminded myself, *is to belong*. To be treated as an equal in the Anlai army. Nothing more.

The dragon sniffed with distaste. *"Your self-deceit is... Watch out!"*

Someone lunged at me and I bit back a scream, dropping into a roll. Two bandits converged upon me from both sides, before a third joined them; all seemed to have been fleeing the inn.

I drew my sword first, slashing one across the chest before he had time to recover from his surprise. Two others leapt at me in tandem; I dodged one attack only to take the brunt of another across my lower ribs. I staggered back in pain as the other disarmed me and kicked me to the ground. I tried to rise, but he pinned me in place, nudging my own sword against my throat.

"You'd fetch us a pretty price," the man said. "Pity we don't take prisoners."

"I know the chancellor!" I choked out, trying to buy time. "He'd want me—"

But without further preamble, the assassin lifted my blade. I felt my eyes fill with hateful tears—

The man gagged, blood splattering from his mouth as a knife

impaled him from behind. He lost his grip on me and I rolled out from beneath him just as Sky cleanly beheaded the remaining bandit.

Sky's furious glare severed me in two. "Skies, could you be any more stupid? You thought you could take on over two dozen assassins on your own?" he shouted at me, before stringing together a slew of curses I didn't expect a highborn prince to know.

My hand dropped to my ribs, coming away bloody.

He froze. "Are you hurt?" he asked, his voice changed.

I tried not to sway. "It's a shallow cut," I said hoarsely.

He closed the distance between us with three angry strides. And yet when he reached for me, his touch was careful. "How bad is it?"

I fumbled for the ties on my tunic, my hands clumsy. "May I?" asked Sky, and the gentle resonance of his voice sent chills of another sort down my spine.

I nodded. "It's nothing you haven't seen before."

A stain of red crept up his neck. "Only in the most imperative of circumstances—"

"Sky," I interrupted, gritting my teeth against the dull throbbing in my head. "I don't care."

His anger at me evaporated as he saw my pain. Carefully, he untied my tunic to examine the wound. A dark cloud passed over his face as he took in the shape and measure of the wound, and the slightly concerning amount of blood I'd lost. Then he met my gaze.

"Get on my back," he ordered.

I made a sound of protest. "I will not!" I sputtered.

"You can barely stand on your own," he pointed out. "Get on my back or I'll pick you up." He made to reach for my waist and I jerked back, before blood rushed to my head and I nearly fell with dizziness. His jaw clenched. "Get. On. My. Back."

I could tell he was in no mood to argue. With a sigh, I let him bend down before I wrapped my arms around his neck, feeling like a small child again. He hoisted me up as if I weighed nothing, then walked back to the inn, his steps even and steady. This close to him, I could feel his heat despite the cold morning air, and smell the faintly smoky scent of his skin. He smelled so good I wanted to press my nose against his neck. Mortified, I kept my body rigid against his. I hoped he couldn't tell how irregularly my heart was beating.

Thankfully, we ran into neither Tao nor Sparrow in the inn. Even the innkeeper had vanished, though Sky seemed unsurprised by this. He set me down in the receiving room before disappearing in the direction of the kitchen. Returning with a jug of alcohol and a swath of clean bandages, he pulled the damask curtain closed behind him, so that we would have some pretense of privacy.

"Where are Tao and Sparrow?" I asked.

"Interrogating the innkeeper and the remaining bandits," said Sky, his mouth puckering with distaste. "The innkeeper recognized me from his time as a traveling merchant in Anlai. It was bad luck, but at least we stopped the news from getting out." He knelt down before me. "If you sensed something amiss last night, you should've woken me earlier. You're a good fighter, Ren, but you're a *terrible* soldier. You think for yourself. You don't obey orders. And you look out for your own agenda over your platoon's."

"That's not fair!" I argued, even though I recognized the truth in his words. Even now thoughts of Zhuque's seal swam in my mind: *Retrieve the jade.* This goal superseded any of Sky's, any of Anlai's. But to him I said, "I don't have any choice but to obey. I'm just a common foot soldier." I tried to keep the resentment out of my voice.

"*You don't have to be,*" whispered Qinglong. "*You could be so much more.*"

It occurred to me then, looking down at Sky: *What if I were commander of this army,* I wondered, *instead of you?*

Sky sliced off the bottom half of my tunic. "You shouldn't be even that," he replied.

I rose in indignation, and he sighed, gently pushing me back. "Stay still," he said, but not unkindly.

I wasn't mollified. "If not for me—"

"I know," he said. "If not for you, our army would be in much worse shape today. In fact"—his expression turned ruminative—"I might not even be alive right now."

I quieted at that. *And your life still hangs in the balance*, I told him silently, remembering Qinglong's vision. *More than you know.*

Sky uncorked the jar of liquor. "This will hurt," he warned, his mouth drawn in a grim line. Then he poured alcohol over my open wound.

I screamed, fighting him, but he grabbed my wrists and held me down until the first shock of pain subsided. "I'm sorry," he said lowly. "I'm sorry."

I wiped at the involuntary water leaking from my eyes. "A lot of people want to kill you, you know."

His jaw ticced at that. He said nothing as he finished bandaging my wound, his hands meticulous yet quick. Above all he was gentle, painstakingly so.

Even after he had finished, he did not release me. His grip only tightened, before he looked up into my face and said, "You shouldn't be here." The lines around his eyes deepened with worry. "You're so . . . *breakable*."

One of his hands had shifted up to skim my bare waist. I tried not to concentrate on the sensation of his touch, which felt warm and gentle and profoundly *right*. I cleared my throat. "You once said my martial arts ability rivaled that of your best men."

"In the training ring," he replied, "not in war." He rose to his knees and then, to my infinite surprise, let his forehead drop to mine. "I wish I could protect you," he admitted, so quietly I couldn't be sure I'd heard him correctly.

I held my breath. My heart stuttered at his proximity, at the way his scent washed over mine, voiding all other thoughts. "You *are* protecting me," I said breathlessly.

"I'm risking your life by letting you stay."

At that, I tried to jerk out of his grip. Sky had a certain skill for provoking me. "Is my life not my own to risk?" I demanded.

"Ren." The knot at his throat rose and fell, a curious vulnerability. "Please—try to understand. I would give anything to bring you back to Chuang Ning, to keep you safe behind the imperial gates. I can't protect you out here. Half the time I can't even concentrate— I'm only fighting with half a mind because . . . the other half is looking for you, making sure you're okay, wondering where you are . . ."

"That's your problem," I said. "Not mine."

"I know." He released me. "And I hate it." I looked away, guarding myself from the inevitable. I thought he would step away then, but instead, his other hand drifted up to cup the back of my neck. His searching gaze felt like a brand against my face. "I can't lose you again," he whispered, as if the words were an oath. "When I thought you didn't make it after Dian River . . ."

"I'm not so easily gotten rid of," I said softly, giving him a small smile. I watched as his eyes dipped to my lips, and I noted the bright heat in them. I drew in a breath and instinctively let my eyelids lower. Through my lashes I watched as he leaned in, his own lips parting—

The front door to the inn slammed open. Sky and I sprang apart as Tao's and Sparrow's voices filtered in through the anteroom.

Sky stood stiffly, turning his back to me. "Stay here," he ordered. "I'll bring you a fresh set of clothes."

THIRTY

Impulsion is chameleonic in nature; one must attune and mold themself to the elemental threads of another's mind and inner being, in order to then infiltrate their thoughts and memories. Thus, until the Yong Dynasty it was believed that only female spirit mediums could practice impulsion, because women, as yin, are less strong in character and more easily influenced by their environment.

—LOST JOURNALS OF AN 8TH-CENTURY LIXIA SCHOLAR, DATE UNKNOWN

WE ARRIVED IN XI LAN IN THE EARLY EVENING, AS SILVER FOG swept over the coastline. I had seen the ocean from afar before, but I had never come so close to it, the crashing waves sounding as if directly in my ears. The wind was both violent and seductive, frenzied one moment, gentle the next, bringing with it the caw of seabirds and the spray of briny salt water.

To find the jade, Tao suggested visiting a jeweler, and Prince Liu proposed scouring the oceanside, but Sparrow suggested visiting the local tavern first. "Gossip is our single most powerful tool," he told us. This sounded much better than spending hours in the dark dissecting fish carcasses or overturning seashells in search of a tiny jade shard. Sparrow's plan won.

We found the tavern easily enough—it was at the center of downtown, directly overlooking the pier. At this time of night, the place was packed. There were fishermen getting off from work, traveling merchants bringing news of the war, and sailors blowing off steam with rowdy games of little sparrows.

As Sky crossed the threshold, his shoulders squared and his head lifted high, he garnered plenty of attention from the regulars. The crowd thinned around him as naturally as water breaking from rocks. Sparrow and I shared a grimace, before Sparrow ducked to whisper in my ear, "Let's split up. You can stay with Prince Liu."

"I'm not his babysitter!" I protested, but Sparrow had already taken Tao and hastened to the other side of the tavern.

Frustrated, I followed Sky. He'd marched straight up to a table occupied in a heated round of little sparrows.

"You," Sky said, his eyes narrowing on the man dressed in brightly colored merchant's garb. "You're a trader, aren't you?"

I swore under my breath. Sky was terrible at blending in.

"So what if I am?" the merchant asked, bristling.

"Have you bought or sold any precious stones lately?" Sky paused. "Discovered in these parts?"

The man sat back in his chair. "Are you interested as a buyer or a seller?"

"Both," Sky answered decisively. *What is he doing?*

The man next to the merchant leaned forward. By his weathered skin and sun-bleached clothing, he looked like a sailor. "Why do you ask?" said the man, his eyes glinting with greed. "What sorts of precious stones are we talking about?"

Just what we need, half the town on our trail.

Before Sky could open his mouth and tell everyone he was the prince of Anlai and searching for jade of incalculable worth that coincidentally Chancellor Sima was also searching for, I jumped in.

"There you are!" I said to Sky, feigning relief. I turned toward the onlookers. "Apologies if my lord disturbed you. We've just paid a visit to the fortune-teller—who informed Lord Fish he would meet his dearly beloved once he discovered a precious stone in Xi Lan."

Everyone laughed at this. Sky glared at me. I pretended not to notice.

"I've got a daughter!" one man volunteered. "Lovely as diamonds."

"But you've got no diamonds," said his friend.

"Mind if we join you?" I asked, sliding out a chair for Sky. "Drinks are on my lord!"

The men cheered at this, welcoming us to their table. "Lord Fish?" the trader next to me asked. "I've never heard a name such as this."

"Ah," I said, stalling. It had been the first word I could think of. "It comes from his childhood name—Little Fish."

"My true name is Lord Feng," Sky interjected.

"Little Fish it is!" the old man across from us exclaimed, winking at me.

I slid my elbows onto the table, pretending not to notice Sky's growing irritation. "Is it true the chancellor's here?" I asked, as they resumed their game of little sparrows.

"Oh, he's here, all right. Arrived yesterday and caused quite the stir. We thought he'd come to punish deserters—or worse, conscript the rest of us leftovers. Instead, he spent all day strolling the shoreline and squinting at the sea, as if waiting for some sign from the skies."

A thrill ran through me. I'd sensed Sima's impatience in the spirit realm and hoped for the best. Now I knew my intuition to be correct—Zhuque's jade hadn't yet washed ashore.

"I bet he has a secret lover," mused a young boy with ruddy cheeks. "Many years ago, she promised she'd find him on the beach at summer's solstice. He remembers her promise..."

"Oh, sing your love songs elsewhere, will you?" said the fisherman. "Though I do wonder what he intends to do *here*."

"I heard even the New Quan scholars are flummoxed," said the trader. "They call him the Blessed One and think he's some voice of the deities. Apparently, they invited him to peruse their ancient lixia collection, but he went straight to Xi Lan instead."

My eyes grew wide. "Their lixia collection is *legal*?"

He snorted. "It's funded by the state."

In Anlai, most imperial scholars used science and logic to refute the power of spirit mediums. Although there might have been banned books on lixia passed around the Chuang Ning black market, there were certainly no established library collections dedicated to the subject.

What I had taken as an immutable way of life was actually just an Anlai custom. Here in Ximing, things were different. Chancellor Sima wasn't labeled as a dangerous black magic practitioner. Here, the scholars called him blessed.

Because the people of Ximing didn't see lixia as black magic. They saw it as power.

The trader lifted his drink before realizing he'd finished it. I scanned the table, noticing the empty cups. A few more drinks would set them at ease and hopefully help them forget us and our nosy questions. I got to my feet. "I'll order another round for the table," I explained, as Sky glanced at me.

I pushed through the crowd toward the bar. So Chancellor Sima was waiting for the jade to wash ashore, as was I. How long would it take? Two hours, two days, two months? No, because time was not on his side. Ximing was losing, and Sima knew this. He needed the phoenix's power to turn the tide of the war.

The tavern was too loud, too crowded. Struck by a wave of nausea, I paused to lean against the wall. In my anxiety, my traitorous mind called forth the visions Qinglong had shown me. Xiuying running into the fire, screaming. Rouha begging me to save her, her hand outstretched as it withered to ash. Sky falling to his knees, his face ravaged with blood.

I shook myself awake, pinching the soft inside of my wrist.

The jade was still at sea, I reminded myself. I had to trust my instincts, trust my ability to read Sima Yi. Without his seal, Sima was like an open book to me, powerless to guard his emotions and thoughts. And yet he possessed other abilities that I lacked. The lack left me vulnerable. It left me weak.

With a shudder, I thought of that naked girl crouching in her cage, helpless and alone. Her future was so close to becoming my own; I could feel it, the way I teetered on the edge of defeat.

"No," I whispered aloud. I would find Zhuque's seal. I would change my fate.

"What can I do for you?" said the barmaid, smiling toothily at me as I approached the bar.

I felt as if I hadn't seen another woman in years—I blushed down to my toes.

"Just ordering a second round for my table."

"Generous, aren't you?" She was still smiling.

"I-I'm not the one paying," I replied. Skies, why was I stammering?

"My, you're a sweet one," she said, sliding her fingers onto my wrist. She leaned in and whispered, "Watch out for patrol soldiers. They were here earlier—looking for deserters."

I swallowed. She could tell I was of draft age. "Thank you."

She winked at me. "I'll be right out with those drinks."

I nodded and left. As I wove through the tavern, I felt a prickling sense of discomfort at the back of my neck. I glanced around, then struck eyes with a broad-shouldered man sitting in the corner, alone. Instead of looking away when I glared at him, he smiled at me.

Maintaining eye contact, he raised two fingers in the air, then beckoned. An unmistakable challenge.

My hackles rose. Yet the tavern was crammed with customers, and my companions were all nearby. There could be no harm in talking. Something about this stranger intrigued me. I sensed he possessed secrets.

He sat with his head tilted against the wall, his legs sprawled out beneath the table, an air of casual nonchalance about him. He carried no weapons, at least not ostensibly, and though his robes marked him as a commoner, his hair was far too glossy and smooth, and his topknot impeccable, not a strand out of place. As I stopped in front of him, he looked up at me and smiled, revealing even, pearly white teeth. Definitely not a commoner.

"Hello, stranger," he said. His voice was a low baritone, rich and lilting.

"What do you want?"

He kicked the chair opposite him. "Do sit."

I stayed where I was.

Up close, I could tell he'd tinted his lips a deep rose hue. The color accentuated his tawny complexion and emphasized the fullness of his mouth. I swallowed. It was impossible not to notice: he was the most beautiful man I'd ever seen.

By the crooked slant of his grin, he seemed to know what I was thinking. I flushed with irritation and glared at him.

"I've never seen you here before," he remarked.

"I'm not from here."

"I know," he said.

I tried not to let that catch me off guard. "By the looks of you, neither are you."

His smile widened. "What makes you say that?"

I crossed my arms over my chest. "Your nails are manicured,

your face is unlined, and you look like you spent an hour on your hair this morning."

"Two hours," he answered amicably. "Did I do a good job?"

I didn't know what to make of him. "You spent that much time on your appearance, only to sit in a dark corner and mope."

He laughed. "Am I moping?"

"Hiding, then," I guessed.

"Hiding from who?" he said, playing along. He seemed to be enjoying himself.

"Patrol soldiers, perhaps," I said. "You look to be of draft age."

He made a scornful noise. "No one heeds the draft."

"So you're a deserter."

He leaned in as if to confess a secret. "You can't desert if you never enlisted in the first place."

I lifted a brow. "Then how do you spend your time instead?" I asked. "If the draft is so undesirable."

He raised his glass at me. "The usual frivolity," he said. "Drinking, flirting, hunting for hidden treasure." He seemed to say the last word with a slight emphasis, or perhaps that was my overactive imagination.

"What sorts of hidden treasure?" I asked, my curiosity piqued. Finally I slid into the seat offered to me. He smelled pleasant, of jasmine and cedar. I breathed in the scent, then frowned. There was something hauntingly familiar about the fragrance, though I couldn't place the memory. Had I met this man before?

"Oh, you know"—he gave the barest of shrugs—"opal, amber, *jade*." He smirked. "The usual."

Jade. "Any luck so far?"

"Yes." His voice took on a suggestive lilt. "Running into you."

THIRTY~ONE

The tide of war is like a flame in the wind;
it can turn in an instant.

—BOOK OF ODES, 856

I STIFFENED. "I DON'T KNOW WHAT YOU'RE TALKING ABOUT."

He sipped his sorghum wine—pale, like his eyes. "Aren't you also hunting for precious stones?"

Perhaps he had overheard our conversation at the other table. Skies knew we weren't being discreet about it. "That's my master," I lied. "Not me. I just follow him."

"Something tells me you're not a follower."

"Something tells me you're not a deserter," I shot back. He looked too much like a noble for that.

He laughed, unperturbed. "So I lied," he said lightly. "So did you."

I shifted uneasily in my seat. What was he referring to? And how did he know so much? I forced myself to look him in the eye. "Then tell me this," I said. "Why are you seeking precious stones?"

He leaned toward me, and my heart raced despite myself. By the openness in his expression, I thought he would reveal the truth.

But I was overly trusting. "I like pretty things," he said in a conspiratorial manner. His eyes flickered across my face. "I have a weakness for them."

Coldness trickled down my spine, though I was careful not to show any outward reaction. "That's surprising," I replied.

"Is it? I find that vanity and an appreciation for beauty go hand in hand."

"Perhaps," I said, an edge creeping into my voice. "Or perhaps there's another motive you don't feel inclined to share."

I caught his jaw muscle pulsing. *He's hiding something.*

Calling upon my lixia, I leaned in, holding his gaze with mine. Yet strangely, though I could feel the nature of his elemental threads—water and earth, and fire too—his mind was a locked door to me. I could no more enter his thoughts than walk through walls.

"Golden eyes," he said, holding my gaze. "Interesting."

I blinked, looking away. The bandit too had claimed that my eyes were golden.

"What's your name?" he asked.

"Zhao Zilong," I replied quickly. "Yours?"

"Lei," he said, with his southern lilt.

"Just Lei?" I asked, wondering if it was a false name. *Lei* was usually half of a shuangming. "Which character?" I asked him. "Lei—to build from the earth?"

"No," he said. "Ming Lei—as in the buds of a flower." His smile was wry. "Perhaps my mother wished for a girl."

I swallowed. "Your mother was a fool, then."

"Was she?"

I did not answer him. He tilted his head like a bird, studying me.

"I wonder if our paths will cross again."

A hand slammed down onto the table between us. "His paths have nothing to do with yours," Sky hissed, taking me by the shoulder. "Let's go, Ren."

"Ren?" A crooked grin twitched across his lips. "I thought you said your name was Zilong."

I tried to hide my blush. "I have many names," I said, aiming for insouciance.

Sky started to lead me away. Lei raised his glass to me in farewell. "As the best of us do."

Sparrow and Tao waited for us by the tavern door. "What was that about?" Sparrow asked me.

I shook my head, flustered. "I have no idea."

"I didn't like the look of him," Sky muttered.

We gathered under the low-hanging eaves of the tavern. Although some noise drifted through the door, a layer of silence coated the summer air. The night breeze was cool, scented with brine and sulfur.

"We're too early," I said. "The jade's still at sea."

"This whole mission is madness," said Sparrow. "How in the skies are we supposed to find one piece of rock floating in the middle of the ocean?"

"It's not a rock," said Sky, to my surprise. "It's a powerful lixia seal—and it will make itself known."

I eyed him with certain suspicion. Sky had disproved all my initial assumptions, if only for the sake of being contrarian. He knew the meaning of *lixia*, a word most Anlai citizens never heard. He rarely used the term *black magic* and seemed to regard Sima's power not with the fear and superstition that Tao embodied, nor the disbelief and incredulity that Sparrow exhibited, but instead with calm, rational calculation, as if this was just another majiang piece in a game he was playing to win.

It irked me—that he could earn my respect, even while being his usual infuriating self.

"But on whose schedule?" asked Tao. "The sea is vast. If your intelligence is accurate"—he looked at me—"and the thief threw the seal into the sea, the jade could've gone in any direction. How are you so sure it's here?"

"Well, Chancellor Sima is here too," Sparrow pointed out.

"Yes," said Sky. "We target the weapon or its source." I recalled his original idea—to go directly after Sima. "We give it a day. If the jade doesn't turn up by then, we leave."

I started. "But—"

"And return with more men," Sky continued, as if I hadn't spoken. "We launch an attack on the warlord's residence in New Quan. We kill Chancellor Sima. And we end this."

Sparrow shuddered. "Pardon my disrespect, but you'll have a hard time finding soldiers to volunteer for that job. That Dian River fire was something unnatural."

Sky's face was hard. I knew he had no compassion for men who forsook their duty. Instinctively I reached for my mother's necklace, before remembering I'd sewn it into the lining of my tunic the day before. I wouldn't make the same mistake Sima had; I wouldn't let anyone steal it from me.

"Sacrifices must be made" was all Sky said.

Sparrow and Tao nodded, as did I. Inwardly, I'd made up my mind. The others might leave, but I would stay. I would stay and wait for the jade.

THIRTY-TWO

I have found the Ximing people to possess weaker constitutions, which is perhaps why they are predisposed toward lying, treachery, and duplicity. In my extensive travels, I have been careful never to do business with the Ximing, for a Ximing son would gladly slaughter his own father if it meant personal gain.

—THE EXPEDITIONS OF MA CUI PO, 879

I WOKE IN THE MIDDLE OF THE NIGHT, SKIN SOAKED WITH SWEAT. My dreams were fleeing fast; I clung to them like trying to grasp at water. I recalled the spike of exhilaration, an end to indefinite waiting. The jade! It had washed ashore at last.

And yet that wasn't the extent of Sima's thoughts. There had been something more in my dream, something more difficult to grasp. Surprise, pain, a faltering of strength. Sima had been planning to set out at once, I'd been sure of that. But something had stopped him. A cold lancing down his throat.

I stood, before remembering the cup of tea poised precariously beside me. It toppled over, spilling cold tea across the straw mats. A wave of déjà vu crested through me. *Poison*, I recalled. Sima had been poisoned.

"What time is it?" Sparrow asked groggily, as I woke the others. "I thought we weren't leaving until tomorrow?"

"No," I said. "We're not going back yet. The jade. It's here." Meticulously, I strapped on every blade I owned. "I was out for a walk when I heard the news. Sima's ordered his guards to retrieve the jade. It's in Xi Lan."

Sky whirled on me, his eyes glittering in the semidarkness. "You went for a walk alone?" he hissed. "Are you mad?"

I bristled. "I would've been alone regardless. If you'd left tomorrow as planned." It was unwise to speak the truth, but I was tired of obeying orders like a dog. "I wouldn't have gone back with you. My priority is the jade. We have to destroy it."

"And you were planning to tell me this when?"

I didn't reply. Sky's voice turned deadly. "You would have disobeyed a direct order from your commander?"

I stared at him and slowly nodded. *It wouldn't have been the first time.* "My priority is the jade," I repeated. *And why must you be my commander?*

Sky's hands were clenched. He wanted to hit me, I knew, and perhaps he would've if he still saw me as his soldier. Anger mounted within me. "We don't have time for this," I snapped. "You can lash me later for my disobedience."

Sky flinched. He did not reply.

We left in a hurry, waking the stable hand to retrieve our horses, and paying him handsomely for the inconvenience. Our steeds were eager, ready for blood. But they could not help us when we reached the sea.

A mile south of Xi Lan, we saw a small crowd of fishermen gathered at the cliff's edge, lit by moonlight. Dismounting, we left our horses a safe distance from the bluffs and went on foot to meet the crowd. Sky led, forcing his way through. Following him, I gasped as I caught sight of the jade, understanding why it had drawn a crowd.

The jade shard was visible even from a distance, for it shone, as if calling to its vessel. Yet no one had thought to retrieve the precious stone, because it was suspended at the end of an unnaturally long, narrow ridge. At its base, the ridge was no wider than the width of a sapling tree. At its tip, it was hardly the width of a blade.

"Stars above." Sparrow's jaw hung open.

None of us had ever seen a cliff face like this. "How could this have happened?" I asked aloud.

"Nobody knows," the nearest fish boy said. "But it wasn't like this yesterday, I can tell you that. This all used to be cliff that got sheared away overnight. That thing out there—that's no ordinary rock."

I shook my head and turned to my companions, who were gathered near the precipice, huddled against the wind. Despite our being so close to the edge, the angle of the cliff made it hard to see below. If someone fell, no one would make out where they landed. Not that it mattered—it was surely death.

"What if we tied a dozen fishing poles together," Sparrow was saying, "and then poked at it like a game of renjia?"

"You'd sooner knock the jade back into the sea," Tao said with a snort.

"You know, that's not a bad idea," Sparrow said thoughtfully. "Better the sea have it than the mad chancellor."

"It'll only wash up some other equally destructive way," I said, without bothering to hide my frustration. Leave it to the spirits to raze half a cliff into the sea! I looked out at the black waters and sighed, taking off my weapons. This was not the kind of battle I'd been expecting.

"What are you doing?" Sky's voice was as hostile as the wind.

"What does it look like I'm doing?" I bit back, unfastening my outer cloak. I didn't want anything getting in the way of my mobility.

He grabbed my wrist before I could remove it. "You're not going out there."

I tried to pull away, but his grip was like a manacle. "Do you have a better plan?" I demanded, irked. *Why must I answer to you? Maybe if I were commander, you would finally see me as your equal.*

"Yes," he said. "We leave and come back with more men."

"More men—that's your solution to everything, isn't it?"

"I would never order my men to do anything I wouldn't do myself. You know that." He glared at me. "That's why I'm ordering you *not* to do this."

I tried to jerk out of his grip again. No use. "Sky," I said, lowering my voice. I didn't want our argument attracting an audience. "Don't forget we have the same goals here. You saw what happened at Dian River. The phoenix's seal is far too destructive to be left unaccounted for. If we walk away tonight, someone else will only retrieve it first. None of this ends until Zhuque's jade is destroyed."

"He's right," Sparrow said miserably. "We came here to retrieve the jade. We might as well see it through."

Sky didn't let go of me. "What's in it for you?" he said lowly, his eyes boring into me. "Why are you so willing to throw away your life for this?"

Because my life is forfeit otherwise, I didn't say. *And so is yours.*

"Sacrifices must be made," I said instead, repeating his favorite line back to him.

I could tell from his expression that he saw my logic, despite not wanting to. He released me furiously. "Then I'll go," he said.

"Commander!" Tao protested.

"Don't play the fool. It doesn't suit you," I said coldly. "I'm the lightest one. It should be me."

My bravado left me as I faced the sheer edge of the cliff. The wind buffeted my body, crashing waves shrieking in my ear. It was a very far distance to fall. I peered over the edge, at the jagged rocks that would be my demise. At least my family wouldn't have to see my broken corpse at the end of all this. There would be no body to bury.

I closed my eyes. I imagined Xiuying meeting Sky, the warmth in Sky's voice as he'd called her *Jie* in my vision. Rouha playing in the garden with Sparrow. My family and friends all together, safe and whole. And then there was me—hair loose, sword plain to see. Accepted for who I was. Loved for it. This could be my future. *It will be.*

Evening my breaths, I stretched, practicing my qi gong. *Wood, fire, earth, metal, water.* I cycled through each one, as if simply preparing for a routine sword practice.

"What is he doing?" someone asked. I ignored him.

As my qi activated, warming my body, I stepped out onto the beginning of the ledge, walking forward with slow yet steady steps. Behind me, I heard a collective gasp as the crowd realized I was not bluffing.

I did not pause. Ten steps. Twenty. Fifty. I was halfway there already, and my feet had not faltered once. I stared fixedly at the glowing jade at the end of the cliff, awaiting me. It grew closer and closer, its light so brilliant it burned an afterimage in my vision.

I was going to make it, I realized. Confidence buoyed my steps. Only half a dozen meters left. *Just don't look down, don't look anywhere but the jade—*

A gust of wind knocked directly into me, and despite my qi I lost my balance, teetering on the rock. If the crowd gasped, I could no longer hear them, for out here the wind smothered all sound.

I regained my balance, then bent into a crouch. The stone here was too smooth, slippery as soap. Worn away by water as if over the course of years instead of overnight. Unnatural, all of this. The spirits had a foul sense of humor.

Slowly, I crawled forward, until I could crawl no longer, for the surface was too narrow. I tried reaching for the jade, then cursed my short arms—if only I had Sky's limbs, or better yet, Sparrow's. I would have to stand to get close enough to grasp it.

Why had I decided to crawl earlier? It was so much harder than I'd imagined to rise to my feet, balanced on a ledge no wider than a folded fan. I focused my qi, bringing it into my core, then stood in one swift motion. Without overthinking it, I lunged forward and grasped the jade. The shard of rock bit into my palm, but the cold heft of it brought me keen, searing joy. I screamed out loud from relief, from exhilaration. As I turned, I caught sight of the crowd, cheering from afar. Sky stood apart from the others, arms crossed, expression impossible to determine.

Now all I needed to do was return. Holding my breath, I strode forward, maintaining my balance even as the gale returned, battering my body like a cat playing with its prey. My blood hummed with adrenaline as I walked, a low thrum like the vibration of a gong. I fixed my gaze on my destination, imagining myself reuniting with the others, triumphant, jade in hand.

So I did not heed the slippery patch of rock until my foot twisted and my heel met air. I might've recovered, if not for the wind that finished the job, throwing me entirely off the cliff. I perceived myself falling before I fell, as if my thoughts raced to make up for lost time. The panic threatened to swallow me whole as my stomach dropped, and I felt the wind rush past my ears, my thick hair blinding me to the world. I could not see the waves below, but I could feel them, the sea salt spray and the laughter of the spirits. They had never believed I would make it.

It was spite then, the spite that remained when fear threatened to supersede everything else. In spite, I called upon my ambition, my greed—*my power*. It rose to meet me, a familiar presence like no other, the only thing that had never deserted me. The wave, too, rose, shoving me toward land. I clamped the jade between my teeth, then grasped on to the cliff face, hoisting myself up with painstaking effort. My vision was fogging, my body refusing to cooperate with my mind. The muscles in my arms soon burned with exhaustion, but I could almost see the blurry edge of the summit.

"Sky!" I screamed through the jade. I was shaking uncontrollably now, my adrenaline stretched thin.

He was there in seconds, leaning so far down, my stomach swooped in terror. He reached for me; I lunged for his hand yet missed, unable to see clearly. My muscles blistered in pain and denial.

Sky leaned farther down, and it was this terrifying sight that made me snap out of my daze. I prayed that Tao or Sparrow was holding down his legs, otherwise he was going to careen directly into the sea. I caught his hand at last, then tried to pull myself up, but my strength was pouring out of me like water from a loose net.

"Give me your other hand!" Sky shouted.

My instincts raged at me not to let go. How counterintuitive this felt. But in that moment, I trusted him more than I trusted myself. I let go of the cliff face and he caught my open hand. Then he hauled me up, and I cried in relief as I collapsed on solid ground, spitting out the jade.

Before I could open my eyes, Sky had me in his arms. "I thought I'd lost you," he whispered, his voice breaking. "When you fell—"

"A tree broke my fall," I said hoarsely, betting on the fact that they'd had limited range of sight from their vantage point. "It was sheer luck. I caught on to it, then managed to climb back up."

Sky pulled me closer. "Meilin—"

Someone cleared his throat above us. Belatedly, I realized a hush had fallen over the crowd. I raised my head. My blood ran cold.

Ximing soldiers surrounded us on all sides, their spears pointed at Sky and me. But the sight that made my heart stop was not the soldiers. It was the stranger from the tavern, holding my hard-won jade in the palm of his hand. He wore the same plain robes but now bore twin blades strapped to his back. Lei, he'd called himself. But perhaps that too was a lie.

"*You*—" I started, before a soldier seized me. I tried to twist out of his grip, but two more followed, pinning me down by my arms and legs. I reared upward and sank my teeth into the nearest one, until he struck me in the face, so hard the back of my head met rock. My vision went dark, but I fought for consciousness in the same way I'd clung to that cliff face, my fingertips turning white, refusing to let go. *No*, I thought with tattered desperation, *not when I was so close*.

Across from me, soldiers had stripped Sky of his weapons, then shackled him. He was staring at me—stark terror in his eyes.

I had never seen Sky so afraid.

"Chain the others," Lei ordered, and to my horror I saw that Sparrow and Tao had also been captured.

I'd been bound before and was expecting the usual discomfort, but the raw, devouring pain that seized me was like nothing I'd ever encountered. As they fastened thick iron manacles around my wrists, I gasped, feeling as if I were being slowly suffocated. I would've fallen to my knees if not for the soldier holding me up. What was happening to me? Why was I suddenly so weak?

"Ren!" Sky cried out. "What are you doing to him?"

"Nothing more than what I've done to you," said Lei, raising a brow. To the guards, he added, "Gag them."

I couldn't speak, could barely breathe. The swell of power that had suffused my limbs, strengthening my qi, my ability to move through this world—it all deserted me in one brilliant blow. A killing blow. Emptied, stripped bare; it took everything within me to keep my eyes open, to not collapse before my enemies.

I saw my future stretch out before me, a future I had tried so desperately to resist. Cages—it always ended in cages. No matter which direction I chose, imprisonment became my fate. Tears welled in my eyes. I wanted to scream, but with my gag, even that choice had been taken from me.

"This little rock has caused me an inordinate amount of trouble," Lei mused, turning the jade over in his hand. "I wonder—"

The sound of hoofbeats made him pause. A second battalion of soldiers rode toward us, helmed by a very much alive Chancellor Sima. I was too weary to even summon surprise.

Sima Yi looked pale and, by the way he dismounted, unsteady on his feet. Still, he strode to meet Lei with the same confidence he'd possessed when we'd first met on the night of the harvest moon. I shrank back from him, but he had eyes for no one else, his total attention fixed on the jade in Lei's hand.

"You-you're here," Lei said, his voice startled.

"Of course I'm here," said the chancellor. "Why would I not be? You know very well the jade belongs to me. I have the warlord's authority, do you not recall?"

He'd been poisoned only hours earlier. And yet here he stood, largely unscathed. Was it because of his spirit affinity, I wondered, that he had some sort of resistance to poison?

Lei hesitated, his fingers closing around the jade. Sima's expression darkened as he inhaled slowly. "*Give it to me.*"

A chill ran down my spine. It was, undeniably, compulsion. His voice had strengthened as if another's had echoed his command. The phoenix.

"*Now.*"

Trembling, Lei raised his hand. His mental resistance was remarkable, but it cost him. I could see his expression wavering as he struggled, fighting an internal battle. The presence of lixia intensified as Sima redoubled his efforts, the air growing thin and claustrophobic. At last Lei's eyes went blank, and he dropped the jade into the palm of Sima's outstretched hand. Sparrow shuddered beside me, mouthing a prayer against evil. I looked down at my bound wrists. My hands were shaking.

Sima had directed his compulsion so precisely that it touched only one individual, thereby channeling his lixia with efficiency. If he could effectively use compulsion with only one fragment of his seal, how much stronger was he than I?

Untrained, weaponless, and chained, how could I possibly defeat him?

I forced my eyes shut, trying to calm myself—when I heard cries of awe and alarm.

I raised my head. Chancellor Sima had joined the two pieces of jade in his hand. They blazed brilliantly, obliterating the darkness of the night. The cliffside had been lit aglow, the sea beneath shimmering like polished diamonds. *Breathtaking*, I thought. And perversely unnatural. I watched with horror as Chancellor Sima raised his hand in the air, and the translucent ghost of the phoenix woke. The bird rose from the ashes of her seal, regaining color and verve and light. She unfurled her wings, screaming.

At Sima's command, the phoenix shot living fire into the ocean. Thousands of flames danced across the surface of the water. *Impossible*. Even the very sea could not quench the thirst of that fire, which took and took and took, determined to triumph over its natural enemy.

The air around us crackled with tension, with unadulterated

power. With this much lixia at his fingertips, Sima could raze all of Anlai to the ground. And we were powerless to stop him.

Can't you do something? I begged the sea dragon spirit. *Can't you intervene?*

I heard a low murmur in my head, as if Qinglong was trying to respond, but I could not make out his words. Something had silenced him, so that he could no longer reach me here.

The iron, I realized, looking down at the heavy manacles locked around my wrists. That was why Sima had paid bandits to steal all the iron from our camp. Iron did not simply block the phoenix's power, as I'd assumed.

It blocked *all* spirit power.

"Almost," Sima said, as if to himself. He called back the phoenix, then placed the seal around his neck. Night returned, enveloping us in shadows once more.

I glanced sideways at Lei, who had been largely forgotten. He'd woken from the stupor of compulsion and now appeared furious. Under the moonlight, I watched as rage and desperation flashed across his features, before he quickly schooled his expression into one of cold indifference.

"Prince Liu," Chancellor Sima said, inspecting Sky like a butcher inspecting livestock. "You look just like your father." The chancellor turned toward his general. "Take the prince. Kill the others," he said simply, before mounting his horse and departing.

He hadn't even glanced at me once.

I breathed out a sigh of relief as his figure receded into the distance, before remembering why he was most likely in a hurry—to find the third jade piece. To complete his seal.

I wanted to scream.

"We'll start with you," Sima's general said, advancing toward me. Sky began struggling against his guards, making incoherent sounds through his gag.

"Why don't we take them alive?" Lei broke in. His voice was nonchalant, as if he was suggesting a new type of tea to sample.

"You heard the chancellor's orders," said the general, drawing his sword.

Lei lifted a brow. "And will the chancellor be the one I blame when I speak to my father about this little incident? Or will that be you, General Huyi?" He smiled at the general's answering scowl. "Think about it this way—we can use them to make the prince sing."

Without warning, he turned toward me and kicked me in the gut. I cried out, slumping against the soldier restraining me.

"Should I do that again?" Lei asked Sky. He took me and shoved me to the rock, then put his boot to my neck. I could feel the pressure building at my throat with every passing second. "Do you want me to break his neck?"

Sky tried to speak but couldn't. Lei ordered a soldier to ungag him.

"Take me, and leave the others behind," Sky rasped. "Then I'll do anything you ask."

"Thought so," said Lei, smiling. "Take them all."

"No—" Sky choked as the gag was thrust back into his mouth.

Lei released me, and, not a moment later, I grabbed him by the leg with my bound hands and wrenched, so that he lost his balance and fell. As we rolled toward the edge, I scrabbled for a choke hold, but he was too slippery, and far stronger than I initially assumed. After a chaotic tussle, he managed to extricate himself from my grip, looking unfazed by his proximity to the cliff face. Two soldiers immediately grabbed me from behind.

Lei got to his feet, disheveled but grinning. His loose dark hair framed his face in waves. The fact that I'd previously found him attractive now made me sick. "Hello, Ren. Nice to see you again," he said amicably. "My thanks for retrieving the jade on behalf of Ximing."

Trussed up, bound, and gagged, I glared at him with all the force I could muster.

His smirk only widened. "Pity, I rather liked you," he told me, before turning away. "But I can't stand liars."

THIRTY-THREE

If a spirit seal is like a pair of spectacles, allowing you to see what lies before you, then iron is like a blindfold, inhibiting both physical and spiritual sight.
—LOST JOURNALS OF AN 8TH-CENTURY LIXIA SCHOLAR,
DATE UNKNOWN

WE WERE BLINDFOLDED AND DRUGGED, UNTIL THE WORLD fell away. I dreamed of nothing but viscous, suffocating darkness, clawing at my nose and mouth.

When I awoke, I found myself in an unfamiliar place. I tried to stand before realizing my ankles and wrists were bound in heavy iron manacles. With considerable effort, I raised my head, then breathed in the sickly-sweet odor of my breath. It was not opium poppy, but a similar variant. Against my will, I had consumed that drug. It had altered my mind, tainted me.

Bile rose in my throat. At thirteen, I had sworn never to touch opium. I had seen the drug work its way through my father, like a worm infecting an apple from the inside, turning it rotten at its core. I wanted to rip my brain out of my head to cleanse it. Had the drug distorted my thoughts? Was I on my way to becoming like my father?

I gagged, fighting the urge to retch. I registered a window behind me, and by the sound of the wind buffeting the outside walls,

I guessed we were in some sort of prison tower. I wondered—if I could remove these manacles, should I jump? Give up, like my mother did? And then this would all be over.

"*You are not your mother*," Xiuying had told me. I breathed out, focusing my qi. I was not my mother nor my father. I was more than the inheritance they had left me.

I sat up, wincing as my irons clanked loudly. We were in a circular room made of stone. Sky, Sparrow, and Tao were also bound and chained to the walls, though they had not yet woken. Sky sported a new black eye that I hadn't seen at the cliffs. I wondered if he'd struggled or tried to fight the drug.

Though my limbs were stiff, my nails were no longer than they'd been at Xi Lan, and my cuts hadn't yet scabbed over. Perhaps not much time had passed.

By the sound of the crashing waves outside, we had to still be on the eastern coast. But no such stone towers existed in fishing villages like Xi Lan. *New Quan, then*, I thought. They had taken us back to New Quan.

My eyes fell upon the wooden chair at the center of the room. Then I realized why we were here.

We were to be interrogated.

Beside me, Sky stirred. "Where . . ." His voice was rough with disuse. His gaze fell from the chair to the locked door to me. He put it all together much quicker than I had.

"Meilin," he said. I widened my eyes at him before he realized his mistake. "Ren. You cannot allow them to find out," he said lowly. "They're barbarians. They'll do . . . unspeakable things to you. Whatever happens, don't tell them—"

Footsteps sounded on the stairway outside.

Tao came to as the lock turned in the door. Guards filed inside, led by the general who'd obeyed Chancellor Sima—General Huyi. So neither the chancellor nor Lei had bothered to supervise our interrogation. Perhaps we weren't worth their time.

Or perhaps they were off seeking the third jade piece already, I thought with rising alarm. And who was Lei, for that matter? When I'd met him at the Xi Lan tavern, why had he seemed familiar?

"That one first," General Huyi said, pointing at me. Two guards unchained me from the wall and dragged me toward the center of the room. And I saw that the general was holding two long wooden rods.

I began to tremble. I could not help it. I had never expected such a fate to befall me.

The spirits must be laughing. For I had set this all into motion myself. My betrothed was abusive yet wealthy. Married to Master Zhu, I would have been ensconced far from the cruelties of war. And yet I'd been dissatisfied with my lot in life. There were other girls who had it worse than me. I was by no means the luckiest or unluckiest of women, not exceptional in any way. Why had I aspired to more than my station in life? Why had I dared ask for more?

But I had not asked for more. I had *demanded* it.

They strapped me to the chair. I was shaking so hard that General Huyi laughed. I was a coward, I thought. I was a girl and a coward.

"How did you know about the jade?" the general asked.

"I-I didn't know about it," I stuttered. "We only heard there was treasure..."

"Let's try again, shall we?"

I felt them bind my legs together at the knees and ankles, before understanding what they were about to do. Two guards each held a long wooden rod, which they placed between my legs.

I had heard of leg-twisting before, but only in passing, used in horror stories to scare thieving children from the market. It was a particularly cruel form of torture that often left its victims crippled, their bones dislocated or crushed.

I wished I hadn't known this. *The anticipation is worse than the punishment itself*, I told myself. The expectation of pain, the interminable waiting.

But then the pain came, and I saw how wrong I'd been. I had promised myself I would not cry out. But it took me no longer than a second to break my promise. I screamed as they pressed their rods down, tears leaking from my eyes. I thought I would lose my legs. I thought my legs were missing from my body.

But they had barely begun.

"Who told you about the jade seal?" General Huyi asked again. "Do you have a Ximing informant?"

My vision was coming in and out, my breaths shallow and jagged. "I-I don't know."

They pressed down on the rods once more, so deeply the poles formed an X before me. I let out a strangled cry, too weak to scream any longer. I could barely see anything or anyone beyond the daze of pain, which submerged me whole.

"Who betrayed Chancellor Sima? Who broke the jade seal?"

I was crying softly, unable to respond. He jerked my head up so that I'd pay attention to him. "Answer me!"

"I don't know," I said, half-delirious. "I don't know. I don't know."

"Why did you come to Xi Lan, then?"

"I told you—we only heard there was treasure."

"And what does the prince of Anlai require of treasure?" General Huyi sneered. "You take me for a fool, boy. You will suffer for it."

He nodded to the guards, who lifted the rods once more, then brought them down. The pain knew no end. I was dying but could not die. I lost the ability to scream, to sob, to speak. I balanced on a thread of consciousness, wishing in vain to fall over the edge.

"Please!" I could hear the torment in Sky's voice. "We don't have the answers you seek."

I felt the guards lower their rods, though the pain did not recede.

"Very well," the Ximing general said. I sensed movement above me, but I could not see through the fog of pain. "Why don't we work with you instead, Prince Liu. Perhaps you will prove more forthcoming."

THIRTY-FOUR

Just as spring must wither, and the moon must wane,
so too must a man with happiness encounter sorrow.
For the only state of permanence is impermanence.
—BOOK OF ODES, 856

THEY UNCHAINED ME, BUT I COULD NOT WALK ON MY OWN. I FELL out of the chair, no longer in control of my own body. One of the guards picked me up and deposited me against the wall, out of their way. I lay there like a rag doll, barely breathing, curled in a fetal position.

From afar, I heard the interrogation begin, this time with Prince Liu. I started to cry again. This was my fault. If I hadn't told Sky about Chancellor Sima's power. If I hadn't called upon the sea dragon spirit. If I hadn't let Zilong die. If I hadn't joined the army. If I hadn't left home. If I hadn't given breath to my greed.

If I had simply drowned like my mother, who had not endeavored to change the course of the war and the fate of the Three Kingdoms. If I had only let go.

"That's enough," said General Huyi abruptly, his voice jarring through my thoughts. I heard the guards untie Prince Liu from the interrogation chair. They could not maim or injure him in any serious manner, I saw, because they needed him as their prized hostage.

But they could make do with the rest of us.

I tried to clear my head. Sky was chained to the wall not five feet away, watching me with an intensity that burned. I tried to show him that I was okay, but he did not appear reassured. When General Huyi wasn't looking, he mouthed something to me, but I couldn't understand what he was saying.

They moved on to Tao, then Sparrow. Tao didn't say a word, but Sparrow broke at last.

"It was Ren!" he cried out. "He knew—I don't know how. But he pulled me aside in the middle of the night to ask me to join his secret mission—a mission that would take us deeper into Ximing..." His face contorted as he realized what he'd done. "No!" he screamed. "No! Ren—I'm sorry. I didn't mean—it's not true!"

But the guards were already unhooking him from the interrogation chair. "Ren," Sparrow sobbed. "I-I..."

I felt as if I'd been removed from my body, as if I were watching myself from afar. The guards had to lift me to my feet; I could not stand on my own. As I sank into the chair, I closed my eyes, too weary to even tremble. I felt deadened and numb inside.

But the pain woke me. Pain had a way of doing that. I thought I would be used to it by now, but it astonished me every time. Then I blacked out, which was the most merciful thing my mind could have done for me.

When I awoke, I saw only minutes had passed. I tensed as I readied for a fresh wave of torture. But instead, General Huyi only scrutinized me, a shrewd glint in his eyes. Beyond him, I could see Sky with his head in his hands.

The general undid my chains, knowing I could not flee even if I wished to. "There," he said in a different voice. "Does that feel more comfortable?"

I nodded soundlessly, disturbed by the change in him.

"Here, have some water." I felt him place the rim of a cup to my lips, and I drank greedily despite my distrust. "Thirsty, aren't you?" he remarked. "Would you like some supper?"

I shook my head, apprehensive.

"Eat," he ordered. "You need sustenance to regain your health."

The aroma of shaokao barbecued meat turned my stomach, but I forced a few bites down because I had no choice.

"Now opium," he said, "to help you sleep and recover."

I recoiled in my chair. "No."

"You'll enjoy it," he said smilingly. "All my prisoners beg me for it every night. You're lucky. I only give it when I'm feeling nice."

"I don't want it."

He beckoned to the guard, who brought it in its edible form. I jerked back, gagging at its acrid scent. Now I was shaking again.

"Open your mouth," he commanded.

I turned my face away.

He grabbed me by my jaw. "This is a gift, boy. It's impolite to refuse a gift."

I tried to shake my head, but his grip tightened.

"Open your mouth!" he ordered, his mask of sympathy replaced by irritation.

My ears were roaring. The room disappeared. I only knew one truth—*I will not obey*.

He began to pry open my mouth with his bare hands. He was stronger than me. The smell of opium drew closer. I would not consume it. I would not.

I was powerless. I was a prisoner. My will was not my own.

No. My will was mine and it belonged to me. Qi coursed through my veins as I felt my will depart from my body and expand, the refusal so strong it became visceral, consuming. My spirit power yearned for release, but the iron was like a dam against a river. The waves crashed against the barrier, again and again and again, until I couldn't take it anymore: I blacked out.

"REN!" SOMEONE WAS SHOUTING. "REN!"

I stirred before registering the foul taste in my mouth. I spat. Blood.

The general was staring at me with shock and something else—something familiar—in his eyes. Then I understood: it was fear.

He fears me.

His gaze went from me to my manacles. I looked down. To my surprise, a long but shallow crack ran down the manacle on my left wrist. The fissure was ornamental at most; it would do nothing to free me from my chains. But it had not been there moments ago.

"There's something not quite right about you," General Huyi said, grabbing my face and examining me. His hand lingered on the soft underside of my jaw.

"Chain him," he ordered the guard. "I'll be back tomorrow." Then he patted me on the head as if I were a dog.

The guards shackled me to the wall, then left. Only now did I notice my shackles were thicker and wider in diameter than my companions'. As if . . . as if they already knew.

As the door locked from the outside, I heard a sound like a suppressed sob. I glanced at Sparrow, who hadn't looked at me once. But I could see the shame and guilt written on his face.

"Sparrow, I don't blame you," I said numbly. "I couldn't think through the pain either."

Sparrow sucked in his breath. "But you didn't break," he said in a small voice. "None of you did. Except me."

There was nothing I could say to that. I shifted against the wall, then felt the hard press of jade against my rib cage. I could not see the seal, sewn into the lining of my tunic, but the weight of it was a reminder. If only I could get these iron manacles off me.

Then I laughed at myself, at my own foolishness. If only I could *walk*. With the pain radiating through my legs, I could barely stand on my own. There was no chance of escape, not now.

Was this how my mother had felt, all those years ago? As her mind had deteriorated, she'd become increasingly confined. First to Willow District, then to the house, then to the women's chambers, then to her bed. With every greater restriction imposed, she grew smaller and smaller, until she barely spoke at all. I remembered her voice in those last days, thin and frail as the petals of orchid blossoms.

And yet Sima's comment suggested my mother had not always been this way. *"So she was the one who stole it?"*

Could my mother really have discovered the seal of a Cardinal Spirit? Not just discovered the seal—but stolen it? The nerve required to accomplish something like that. She would have needed to be clever, but also . . . reckless, foolhardy.

Perhaps I take after her, more than I thought.

Unexpectedly, tears pricked my eyes. I had cried many times for the mother I'd lost, stolen by death. But now I cried for the mother I'd never known—not the empty shell of a woman bound to my father, but the reckless, foolhardy girl she'd been before that, years ago.

I cried for her. I cried for the inheritance she'd left me.

THIRTY-FIVE

In his darkest depression, the Great Warrior Guan Yang turned to the Azure Dragon. "Will you help me?" he pleaded. And the dragon replied, "You need only ask." Thus the bargain was struck.

—LEGENDS OF THE MOUNTAINS, 754

IN MY FEVERED STATE, I SLEPT FITFULLY. I FELL ASLEEP FEELING AS IF my skin were on fire, then awoke believing I'd swallowed ice. I sat trembling against the wall, watching thin moonlight coalesce on the stone tiles.

"I'm sorry for how I treated you."

I started. I hadn't known Sky was awake. He sat against the wall with his elbow on one knee. "What do you mean?" I asked quietly, so as not to wake the others.

"That night we fought. I-I was angry. I wasn't thinking. I regret . . . how I behaved."

I nodded. That night, he had patronized me, denigrated me, commanded me to leave and return home. I looked away from him and fidgeted with my manacles. "I'm not any different, you know," I told him. "I'm still the same soldier you used to train with every night."

He smiled ruefully. "I'm trying, Ren." His voice lowered. "I just wish I had . . . more time. To try again with you."

More time. That was what we all wished for, wasn't it? Once, I had wished for only a little more time outside the confines of the women's quarters. In truth, I had not expected to come out of the war alive, though I could not bear to tell Xiuying this. A few months of freedom were all I'd dared ask for. But now I too wanted more. Freedom was like that, my mother had warned me. Once you tasted it, you were hard-pressed to let it go.

The door crashed open, startling the others awake. Given the late hour, I was surprised to see guards troop inside.

I was even more surprised when they came directly for me. They removed the manacles around my ankles, so that I only wore a pair of iron handcuffs.

"Where are you taking me?" I demanded, stumbling forward with rising trepidation.

The guard supporting me sniffed. "The prince requests your presence."

"The prince?" I repeated, glancing over my shoulder at Sky. "Who...?"

"No," Sky said, his voice like I'd never heard it before. "Please, *Ren*—"

I saw the desperation in his eyes and realized—he believed he would never see me again. He thought I was going to my death.

"Sky—" I screamed, before the door slammed shut behind me.

I WAS BLINDFOLDED, THEN FORCED INTO A COVERED WAGON. I LOST ALL sense of my bearings as the wagon departed, jolting on every cobblestone. When we arrived at our destination, I sensed a change in the air. The corridors we walked through smelled of incense and lavender, rather than brine and salt spray.

When my blindfold was removed, I found myself in a decadent keting room with rice paper windows, lacquered furniture, and silk tapestries depicting ancient bamboo forests. Lounging on the platform before me was Ming Lei.

He'd discarded his commoner's guise in favor of embroidered silk robes. Now he wore dangling earrings of gold and onyx and a buyao hairpiece of matching gold. Rings glimmered on his knuckles, one or sometimes two on each finger. He hadn't been lying when he'd described his vanity.

But he'd lied about everything else.

"Your Highness." My guard bowed and released me. I swayed, off-balance. *Your Highness?*

Lei is a prince of Ximing?

He yawned, stretching himself out on the shafa with the grace of a jungle cat. When he turned toward me, it was with the same insouciance he'd displayed in the tavern, as if we were simply sharing another drink in a nondescript fishing village.

"General Huyi informed me of your oddities," he said, toying with a porcelain cup of steaming qingjiu. His gaze dropped to my iron manacles. "I can't say I'm unsurprised."

It took me a moment to figure out what he was saying. The short journey had left me deeply fatigued, and I could barely stand upright on my own. I did not know if my loss of balance was due to my fever and illness or due to my suppressed spirit power.

He sipped his qingjiu, taking his time. When he got to his feet, I saw he'd left his robes partially unbuttoned, revealing the pronounced planes of his chest. I looked away.

"The wise thing to do would be to kill you," he said, and despite myself, the brutality of his words startled me. "It's evident you pose a significant threat."

"Is it?" I lifted my chin, trying to still my trembling. "I'm chained, unarmed, and can barely walk on my own. Do I pose a threat to you?"

"Yes," he said, his dark gaze flicking to me, to my eyes. "Several."

I waited.

He downed another cup of wine, then wiped his mouth. "I'll say this: your existence proves an inconvenient truth. One that I'd rather not be made aware of."

I pressed down on a broken nail. "Then kill me and go on lying to yourself."

He smiled at that. "I told you I can't stand liars."

"Then you must hate yourself."

"With a passion," he said.

He fixed his piercing gaze on me, and this time I refused to look away. A slow fury was spreading through my chest, a bird unfurling its wings.

"Very well," he said, waving his guards forward. "Put him up in the adjoining rooms. Send Autumn to tend to him—he's clearly ill." He looked into my eyes, then away. "And make sure his irons are never removed."

THIRTY-SIX

Even a phoenix in a cage is mocked by sparrows.
—BOOK OF ODES, 856

MY NEW PRISON WAS A BEDCHAMBER AS ORNATE AS THE prince's. A subtle fragrance scented the air—orange blossoms, like the perfume Xiuying used to wear. The reminder made my heart pang. I lay on my impossibly soft bed and closed my eyes. I knew I could not grow complacent here; just because my imprisonment had changed shape did not mean it was no longer a prison cell. I had to scheme and plan... how to break out my friends. How to flee New Quan. There was much work to be done.

But instead, as I told myself to get up and search the room, I found my eyelids growing heavy. I could hear guards outside speaking in hushed voices. I told myself I would lie here for only a moment longer, but that moment became two, then three, until I stopped counting entirely.

"STARS ABOVE! WHY DID YOU KEEP HIM IN SHACKLES?" A STRIDENT voice woke me from my stupor. From afar, a guard mumbled his reasoning.

The woman made a tsking sound. "It's not like he has a chance of escape with all of you crowding around him. The prince sent for me to *heal* him."

Another mumbled reply, this one longer.

"Then at least get rid of the chain!"

I felt the weight binding my hands together removed. Still, they did not detach the irons from my wrists.

"Stars above," the woman murmured. A gentle hand pushed my hair back. "He's very sick. Prepare a bath!"

"Xiuying?" I muttered. "Is that you?"

"You're not going to die," she said. "I'm going to save you."

I drifted into sleep, believing Xiuying had come to me at last.

"YOU HAVE SOME EXPLAINING TO DO," XIUYING SAID TO ME. "MISS."

I stirred, sensed the meaning in her words, then shot upright. Hours or days had passed. I was clean now, with no taste of blood on my tongue. My hand shot immediately to my tunic, before I breathed out a small sigh of relief—I could feel the hard, warm edge of jade, where I'd sewn the stone into the inner lining of my uniform. So my seal was safe. For now.

"Careful," she said, easing me back down onto the pillows. She was decidedly *not* Xiuying. "Take it slow. I just brought you back from the verge of death."

The stranger looked to be Xiuying's age, with thick blue-black hair that cascaded down her back in three long braids. Her complexion was dark, and her sharp, tapered eyes almost violet under the lamplight.

I raised my hand to my face, realizing my fever had broken. My hands were unrestricted now, though an iron band still encircled each wrist. My uniform had been cleaned. And yet . . . my cheeks burned as I realized what this meant, that this woman had stripped, washed, and dressed me.

"Why did you join the army?" she asked. There was no condemnation in her voice, only curiosity. "Do you have a death wish?" She paused. "Or are you a spy?"

I shook my head, which intensified my migraine. "Please don't tell anyone."

"I'm afraid I can't do that," she said. "All I can do is try to keep you alive."

I breathed out, disappointed yet unsurprised. I knew it was already a miracle I'd survived.

"Does the prince know?" I asked.

She mulled this over, as if it were not a simple yes or no answer. "The best I can do for you is hold him off until you recover. Then I must inform him. Otherwise," she smiled grimly, "I'll be out of a job."

"My companions..." I trailed off, afraid of her answer. "Do you know if they're... all right?"

"They're alive," she said. "I don't know much else. And I couldn't tell you more if I did."

I have to get them out, I thought. When the healer stood and moved to the basin, I scanned my surroundings, looking for a possible escape route. There were no windows, and only one door, which I assumed was heavily guarded. How thin were the walls? I couldn't hear any sound from outside, not even the caw of birds. Perhaps I could check the floorboards after she left...

"There are no escape tunnels here, if that's what you're looking for," the healer said, as she returned with a fresh towel. "Don't even think of trying to get out. Your security is nearly impossible as it is. You don't want to hear what kind of argument I had to get the guards out of your bedchamber. How would you like for a whole battalion to watch you bathe?" She raised a brow and I flushed to my neck.

Her touch was gentle as she mopped my forehead and checked my temperature. She frowned, then brewed me tea. It was only after I'd drunk half a cup that I realized the tea was meant to help me sleep. I spat it out, but it was too late.

"You—" My tongue felt as if it were turning to lead.

"My name's Autumn," she said pertly. "Try for civility, please." She hesitated. "What's your name?"

I didn't know what compelled me to speak the truth. Perhaps it was how devastatingly familiar she felt—how much she reminded me of Xiuying. "Meilin," I rasped.

"That's a beautiful name. And rather fitting." She winked at me. "You make a very pretty boy, you know. No wonder our prince was so interested in you."

DAYS PASSED. SLOWLY, I DID HEAL. THOUGH MY LIMP PERSISTED, I RE-gained my ability to walk. The Ximing prince tried to call for me, but Autumn detained him on my behalf, claiming I was unwell. I could hear them bickering by the keting door, but their tones were never serious, only playful. She claimed the mental taxation that came with Prince Cao's conversation was too much for any infirm patient. He claimed he would provide much-needed diversion from her nagging. Autumn insisted. She won.

Then the prince left on an expedition, and I no longer had any visitors at all. I was not permitted outside my quarters. I forgot what natural sunlight felt like, and only saw light under the oil lamps. The momentary glimpses I caught of the outside world came when

Autumn arrived or left my quarters, and in those instances, I could see three guards stationed outside my door. At least the number had gone down from six.

I had already ransacked my bedchamber and sitting room, looking for a way out, but my quarters were impenetrable. It was no ordinary guest room but a well-crafted ruse. Beneath its expensive furniture and elaborate décor, the place was a prison cell, barring all contact to the outside world.

But I could not forget what was happening beyond these walls. Sima was hunting the third jade piece; the war between the Three Kingdoms raged on. Every night, I dreamed of Chuang Ning burning, a glorious vermillion bird raining flames from the sky. Everyone around me died. Only I survived—for I was meant for the cage.

THE XIMING PRINCE RETURNED LATE THE FOLLOWING EVENING. INstead of coming to my door, he relayed a message requesting my presence. Autumn frowned as she read his note, glancing at me with concern in the twist of her mouth. She left abruptly, returning an hour later. I asked her what was wrong.

"Lei seems tired," she admitted, and I was surprised to hear her speak of the prince so casually. "I don't think his trip went very well."

"He's returned?"

She nodded reluctantly. "He wants to see you. He's determined. I couldn't persuade him otherwise."

I looked down. We both knew I had recovered some time ago. Now Autumn was only stalling, for my sake.

The door opened then. A dozen guards trooped into the sitting room.

"A bit much, don't you think?" Autumn quipped. No one smiled.

She hovered near me, making sure my topknot was secure and

my tunic properly buttoned. Her face was clouded with apprehension. "Be careful," she said under her breath. "His moods can change as swiftly as summer rain."

"Do you think he'll have me killed?" I asked, voicing my fears aloud. Her worry intensified my own. When she looked at me like that, with concern in her eyes, it made it near impossible for me to detach myself from my own emotions. In times like these, I missed the numb coldness of the spirit realm.

Autumn tugged at her braids nervously. "He likes you," she said at last. "He wouldn't have kept you alive for this long if he didn't."

But I noted her hesitation.

The iron bands around my wrists went unused as the guards bound my hands with rope. Autumn remained behind as they led me out of my quarters. I glanced back at her, wondering if this was another inevitable goodbye.

For this long, she'd said. How much longer did I have?

THIRTY-SEVEN

> *"Can you play the zither?" asked the princess.*
> *"No," he said.*
> *"Can you sing?" she asked.*
> *"No," he said.*
> *"Can you recite poetry?" she asked.*
> *"No," he said.*
> *At last she cried, "Then what can you do?"*
> *And he bowed low and answered, "Your Highness,*
> *I can teach you to raise a revolution."*
>
> —LEGENDS OF THE MOUNTAINS, 754

THIS TIME, MY GUARDS LED ME PAST THE PRINCE'S SITTING ROOM into his private bedchambers. There I was taken aback to find Lei in the flesh, sitting cross-legged at his low aiji table, drinking sorghum wine. His face was bare and devoid of ornamentation, though he still wore his glittering rings. A fresh cut ran down his left brow, along with a blue-purple bruise mottling his cheekbone.

"Ren," he said, in his deceptively cordial manner. "Come, sit."

The guards let me go. I glanced back at them, but they avoided my gaze. Awkwardly, I walked forward and knelt at the table, my bound hands making even this simple maneuver difficult. His eyes followed me as I moved. I could tell he'd noticed my limp.

"Tea?" he asked. "Or wine?"

I shook my head. It wasn't like I could drink either even if I wished to. The gesture was a farce. Despite his parody of hospitality, my hands were bound, and if I lifted so much as a finger against him, a dozen guards could take off my head in an instant.

"You're looking much improved," said Lei, pouring himself more wine. With how much he drank, it was a wonder he still managed to form complete sentences. "I trust Autumn did her job well."

I looked away, unsettled by the intensity of his gaze. I knew it was irrational, but I feared he could read my mind as he regarded me with those bright copper eyes.

"She was worried for you," he went on. "You left quite an impression, for her to care for you so." He smiled. "I must confess it made me a tad jealous."

Startled, I glanced up at him. He was watching me, waiting for a reaction. Everything was a game to him, wasn't it? His words were like needles, used to penetrate and burrow under my skin.

"She did tell me something rather interesting, though," he said, as he peeled the skin off a grape. "How many secrets are you hiding in that little head of yours, Ren?" He grinned. "But that's not really your name, is it?"

I tensed, trying to hold every muscle in my face still. I could not betray any reaction, not in front of him.

He popped the grape into his mouth, chewing deliberately. When he swallowed, he seemed to make up his mind. "Undress."

A dull roar filled my ears. *He knows*, I thought. *Autumn told him*. My hands strained against my ropes.

"Ah," he said. "Clumsy of me to forget." He removed a knife from his long sleeve and leaned forward. I flinched back, but he only slit my bindings. "Go on."

I flexed my wrists, rubbing at my iron bands out of habit. My heart was lodged in my throat. "No."

"Why not?" he drawled. "Is it because you have something to hide?"

I glanced at my surroundings, at the dozen guards stationed behind me. Was there any way I could get out of this?

"You do not wish an audience?" asked Lei. He shrugged. "I can be generous, when it suits me." He raised his voice. "Guards, leave us."

To my astonishment, they obeyed. Then we were alone.

Can't you do anything? I thought desperately. But the voice in my head remained silent. Even the dragon spirit could not reach me here.

"To tell you the truth, I didn't believe her at first, but now, looking at you, I understand I was wrong." Lei was peeling a citrus fruit, the cloying scent lingering in the air between us. "It's a marvel I didn't notice earlier. Now that I know you, it seems so very obvious." A smirk tugged at his lips. "You are ever-intriguing, *Meilin*."

Autumn had betrayed me. She hadn't only given him my identity, she'd given him my name. My true name.

Tears pricked my eyes; I forced them back. I would not lower myself to cry in front of him.

I was too naive, too gullible. It shouldn't have surprised me—after all, I'd always known Autumn was a Ximing healer, sworn to serve her prince. And yet her kindness had been like an oasis in a sea of sand. And I had come to rely on it.

But I was, and had always been, completely alone.

Lei offered me a citrus slice, which I refused. My eyes trailed down his robes. Though he was dressed casually, as if for bed, I knew now that he was armed; there was probably more than one dagger hidden within his robes.

Could I take him on by brute strength alone? My hands were

unbound, and there were no guards in sight. I was unarmed, without my spirit power, but I was also trained as a soldier. Was he?

I decided to test his reaction. "Aren't you worried I'll kill you?"

He laughed. "I can defend myself against you."

The condescending tone of his voice infuriated me. "Because I'm a woman?"

He took his time to reply, dabbing at his full lips. "Let me give you some advice, *Meilin*." He leaned back on his arms, lounging on the floor. "Don't wear your insecurities on your sleeve. Then scoundrels like me can use them all too easily against you."

I gritted my teeth. "What do you want from me?"

"Easy," he replied. "Undress."

"No."

He arched a brow. "Would you rather I do it for you?" He smiled, his affable expression belying his sinister words. "I can make you."

"Do not—do not touch me," I ordered. But my voice trembled.

He raised a hand in the air; I flinched, only for him to reach deliberately for the wine instead.

"*Be careful*," Autumn had warned me. "*His moods can change as swiftly as summer rain.*"

Lei was playing at niceties now, but how soon would his patience desert him? I began to sweat, imagining the gaping maw of a hungry wolf. Slowly, I unbuttoned my tunic.

I was trembling so hard it took me twice as long as usual. Lei's eyes did not leave my face. My tunic was open now, revealing my chest bindings and my bare stomach.

"Everything," he said, and the command was clear in his voice.

I closed my eyes, took a breath, then forced myself to obey. I stripped off my jacket, then my tunic, then, slowly, my breeches.

"Stand."

I got to my feet. I stood naked before him, vulnerable and defenseless. Though we were in the thick of summer, I shivered beneath his gaze.

He rose, stopping a pace away from me. His eyes were darkened with desire.

"So you are a woman, after all."

"I thought you already knew that," I said, lifting my chin.

He grinned. "Hearing is one thing. Seeing is . . ." His eyes raked over me. Gooseflesh pricked my skin. "Another."

I closed my eyes, knowing what came next. I recalled what Sky had told me, about how the Ximing people were barbarians. He had warned me not to let anyone find out.

I will not let him, I decided then. *I will kill one of us first.*

But instead, he turned away. "Put your clothes back on."

At my look of surprise, he raised a brow. "Unless you'd like to remain as you are?"

I dressed hastily. Meanwhile, he removed his outerwear, opting instead for a robe one would wear to the bathhouses. He didn't bother securing the tie, so that it gaped across his chest, revealing a triangle of bronzed skin. His lack of modesty discomfited me, not that I would ever admit this to him.

On the aiji table, I saw the knife he'd used to slice fruit. While his back was turned, I slipped the knife into my pocket. Then I sat, pretending to reach for the teapot.

He returned his attention to me, laugh lines crinkling his eyes. I felt as though he were constantly laughing at my expense, though I had no idea why. It was impossible to read him.

He took a seat across from me, folding his legs like a dancer. With his topknot undone, his face appeared softer, younger. It was unnerving: how someone so monstrous could appear so lovely.

"Tell me about yourself," he said lightly. "How did you end up here?"

"You summoned me," I bit out. "I'm your prisoner."

He inclined his head in response. "How unfortunate for you," he said. "Forced to bear with my ramblings."

I had the suspicion we would wander in circles all night if he had his way. I set my cup down. "Have you found the third jade piece?" I asked bluntly.

He drank from my teacup. "I was wondering when we'd return to this subject."

THIRTY-EIGHT

I searched the kingdom for a man worthy of my power.
Finding none, I kept it for myself.
  —RECORDS OF THE GRAND HISTORIAN, 489

M Y GAZE FLICKED TO THE BRUISE ON HIS CHEEK. "HAVE YOU?"

"No," Lei said simply. I could not tell if he was lying. "Any chance you know where it is?"

I said nothing. Bound in iron, I could not reach Sima through impulsion. Not that I would divulge this fact to the Ximing prince.

He sighed theatrically. "You do make life so difficult for me, Meilin." As he refilled my cup, I noticed the glint of steel within his trailing sleeve. "It's a pity you're so very lovely, and I'm so very shallow."

"Do you expect me to sympathize with you?" I snapped.

"You could make an effort." He lifted one shoulder. "Most people at least pretend to like me."

"I don't see the point," I said, "seeing as I'm most likely to die either way."

"I'm not going to kill you, Meilin. You're far too valuable for that."

I shuddered. "I'm not going to help you either."

"Why not?" He cocked his head at me. I couldn't believe he had the gall to ask me that. "I can make a very good ally."

"I would *never* work with you," I hissed. "You're a—"

"Barbarian?" he finished, biting out a laugh. "Yes, I heard what your courteous Prince Liu said about us." He began to steep new juhua tea blossoms. "You northerners think we all crawl in the mud like worms. Poor barbarians, they say. Left on their own, they'll eat raw meat with their bare hands." He shot me a caustic smile. "I'm sorry to disappoint you. We actually use chopsticks."

"I don't hate you because you're a southerner," I said, trying to keep my voice level. "I hate you because you had me tortured, humiliated, imprisoned, and brought to the verge of death. If it hadn't been for Autumn, I'd be in the grave right now."

"We don't bury our prisoners," he pointed out, voice wry.

I took a breath. He was sharper than me, faster with words. But I could not let him get under my skin.

"If this is your way of making friends," I said, glaring, "it's no wonder Ximing has no allies."

His eyes darkened. He threw his head back as he finished his drink; I watched the knot in his throat pulse. "Ximing has no allies because our coffers are empty. Because for the past century, we've been subjugated and sucked dry under the Wu Dynasty, while up north, Anlai ate the fats of the emperor's plunder. And they claim there used to be peace."

I absorbed this new piece of information silently. In truth, I did not know much of politics or history, nothing beyond what was taught to Anlai women—which wasn't much. I glanced at Lei out of the corner of my eye. He clearly liked to talk, and even liked talking to *me*, though I couldn't understand why. Perhaps I could use him for information. Then, when I escaped, I'd have something valuable to offer my commanders. This wretched detour wouldn't have been for nothing.

"Is Anlai your primary target, then?" I asked, pouring myself fresh juhua tea to make the question seem casual. "What about Leyuan?"

His eyes crinkled again. He was very handsome when he smiled, I thought; he was very handsome all the time. But that just made it easier for him to deceive.

"A secret for a secret," he proposed, considering me.

I feigned deliberation. This wasn't a fair trade for him, considering he could always torture the information out of me if he wished. But it would be tactless to raise this point. "You first," I said generously.

"Leyuan is crumbling under debt," said Lei. "They won't hold out much longer. And their warlord will soon be deposed."

"I thought Warlord Yuan was the only rightful heir among the Three Kingdoms," I said, remembering what Sky had told me. "Wasn't he a distant cousin of Emperor Wu?"

Lei gave a false laugh. "You'll find that starving villagers care less about blood lineage than they do their crops." The planes of his face glimmered under the lamplight. "Warlord Yuan's greatest mistake lies in underestimating the might of the western rebels in Leyuan. They'll face civil war before they come close to restoring Tianjia."

"Civil war?" My mind was racing. "But I thought—"

"Enough, you busybody," Lei reproved, but he was laughing. He pushed his hair out of his face, then leaned toward me. He'd clearly prepared his question in advance. "Tell me this. Were you born with golden eyes?"

I shifted. "My eyes aren't golden."

He arched a brow before pouring himself another glass. He drained it, then set the cup down harder than he needed to. I tried to recall how much wine he'd already had.

"General Huyi tells me you don't like opium."

I stiffened in shock. I hadn't expected this line of offense.

"Why?" Lei asked. "He meant it as a small mercy."

"It was no mercy to me," I said tightly.

"Someone in your family became slave to the drug," Lei guessed, watching my expression. "Your brother, perhaps. No, your father."

I tried to keep my face still, but Lei was too practiced at reading others. He nodded, satisfied. Then he sat back, his hand absent-mindedly trailing the cut along his brow. "I wish my own father could lose himself to the pipe," he mused.

I stared at him, wondering if I'd misheard. At my look, he smiled. "Then, at the very least, he could leave this kingdom alone."

So Lei does not get along with his father, the warlord of Ximing. The man who had declared himself emperor over Tianjia—and called for war.

"Then . . ." I raised my head. "You did not wish for war?"

He looked amused. "And you did?"

I blushed and shook my head. "Of course not," I said. "I just thought all princes were hungry for power."

He studied me closely, as if I were a riddle. "Power should never be so concentrated in the hands of a few."

I wanted to roll my eyes. I added *hypocrite* to the list of names I called him in my head.

"Unless those hands are your own," I said. "Isn't that what you're thinking?"

He reached for the wine jar again. "Humor me, won't you, Mei-lin?" he said. His voice sounded unchanged, but I could tell by the size of his pupils—he was well inebriated. "Imagine you're a little boy, third or fourth in line to the throne—it matters not—with a concubine for a mother."

His face was unreadable.

"She is the only one you see every day, for you are forbidden from entering the inner palace. Then, when you turn eleven, your father takes note of you during a diplomatic bestowment ceremony. He commands you to live in the imperial palace with the royal family, despite your mother's wishes." His voice grew rueful. "At first, you are greedy and ambitious. You fight to be the best at everything. Your mother warns you not to attract too much attention, but you do not listen. You are a fool.

"The king notices you and favors you. Jealous, the other queens scheme against you. But they do not target you, because you are a prince. They target your mother, because she is a concubine."

I didn't want to hear the rest of this story. I didn't want to see him in this light, as anything less than a monster. "You don't have to—"

He ignored me, his eyes faraway. "Your mother is framed for treason. And your darling father is too vapid and careless to tell lies from truth. At the advice of others, he has your mother skewered and beheaded, and her corpse dragged through the dust by dogs. All the while, he places his dear beloved son in the front row, and orders him to watch with his eyes wide open."

His voice was choked with feeling, but he went on regardless. I didn't know if he saw me as he looked onward, or if he was too caught up in the thralls of wretched memory.

"It is because of power that they did this. Because they had it, and they wanted to hold on to it, or because they didn't have it, and wanted it. And it is because of power that my father, who is the most foolish, irresponsible man I know, can dictate the fate of thousands and determine the course of our kingdom. So ask me again if I believe power should be concentrated in the hands of a few. I do not care who the few are. I am not so naive as to believe I would be any different."

He took a breath at last, then smiled at me, seeming to return to himself. Unsettled, I poured him a cup of tea and pushed it toward him, sliding his wine farther away.

He noted all of this with a grudging smile. "Now you know. There is no love lost between my father and me."

"Is that from your father?" I asked, nodding at the bruise on his cheek. I asked because the mark was intimate—an enemy soldier would not have done such a thing. And because my own father had struck me in the same way, many times before.

He looked at me, the tendons in his neck raised. Slowly, he nodded.

So you can be a prince, I thought, *and still be made to feel powerless.* I looked at him with an odd feeling in my throat.

This provoked him, more than anything else I'd done. He caught my expression and suddenly grew *furious*. His lip curled as he rose to his feet abruptly. Autumn was right; the change was as swift as summer rain. "And does Prince Liu know who you are?" he asked, a lethal undertone to his voice. The air around us crackled with tension.

Bewildered, I stared up at him. "What—"

"He does," Lei said, reading the answer on my face. He laughed; it was not a pleasant sound. "Is that why the prince kept you around? So he could use you as his company whore?"

My vision turned red as I leapt to my feet. "You—"

In that moment, I lost my temper. I forgot about the guards stationed outside and my tenuous status as prisoner. Without any regard for the consequences, I seized the porcelain cup from the table and hurled it at him.

He ducked with lightning reflex. I grabbed another cup, but before I could throw it, he caught my wrist with enough force that I shattered the cup in my hand. The porcelain shards flew through the air, a jagged piece slicing his cheek open.

Blood trickled down his face.

The doors burst open, but Lei ignored his guards. He yanked me back by my arm, then shoved me against the wall. With calm precision, he planted his hands mere inches from my head, caging me in with his arms. We were both trembling. As he leaned down to look at me, I could see his huge, dilated pupils. He was completely drunk.

A thin gash ran across his cheek, to match the bruise and the cut along his brow. The blood seeped down his jaw, and still he did not pause to stanch the wound. Instead he fit his hand against my throat, his fingers curling around the base of my neck in an unequivocal warning.

"Make no mistake," he said lowly. "I am not to be pitied."

"I would sooner pity a viper," I snarled. Then, taking advantage of our close proximity, I spat on him.

He smiled coldly. "We'll have our fun, you and I."

THIRTY-NINE

But don't you know? Mortality is what makes the taste of life so sweet. That is why all spirits crave the taste of human blood.
—BOOK OF CHANGE, 207

My conversation with the Ximing prince renewed my sense of urgency. The next morning, as soon as Autumn entered my rooms, I was ready.

"Autumn," I said. "I-I'm hurt."

She came over at once, dropping her bundles of zongzi glutinous rice by the door. "What happened?"

"Prince Cao lost his temper last night. So . . . did I." I showed her the long cut on my wrist, which ran beneath the iron manacle encircling my left arm. Remembering Xiuying's lessons, I'd narrowly avoided any arteries.

Autumn gasped. "This is serious," she murmured, raising my arm to inspect it. "Lei did this to you? How could he?"

"It was . . . an accident." I avoided her gaze, my eyes instead skipping to my rumpled bed. Hidden beneath my blankets, the fruit knife I'd stolen was still soaked with blood. My blood.

"The iron's rusted here," I continued. "I'm concerned about infection . . ."

"Yes, of course," Autumn said, chewing on her lower lip. "I need to get this cleaned properly."

She tried to adjust the manacle, but it wouldn't budge; it was too tight. I held my breath.

"I need to loosen this a bit," she muttered to herself. "Especially while the wound's open like this."

I nodded, biting my tongue to keep from speaking.

She set my arm down gently, but I still winced as the iron jolted the open gash. "I'll speak with Dian Wei," she said, naming one of the prince's guards. I didn't answer, for fear of showing too great a reaction.

Minutes passed. I eyed the glutinous rice but decided not to eat, pretending instead to nap from exhaustion. I had purposefully fasted and dehydrated myself to look even more pale and sickly than I already was.

When Autumn returned, I could hardly believe it; she held a set of keys in her fist. "I stole these, so we have to be fast about it," she was telling me. "Quick, give me your hand."

I did not need any encouragement. I gave her my left hand quickly, not having to fake the trembling in my bones. "Poor dear," she said, clucking, before unfastening the manacle.

I inhaled sharply; the change was immediate. It felt as if a massive weight had been lifted from my shoulders, one I hadn't even been aware of. I tugged on my lixia experimentally, but my spirit power could not reach me. I had to remove the other one too. This would get ugly.

Autumn had set the keys down to start cleaning my wound. Perhaps I wouldn't have to hurt her after all. I reached for the keys, hoping to appear casual.

"What are you doing?" she asked. I ignored her and fitted the key into the lock.

"Meilin!" she exclaimed.

I exhaled. Before she could cry out and alert the guards, I jabbed her in the diaphragm, hard and fast. She slumped forward, the wind knocked out of her. In a moment, I had the second manacle off.

Lixia flooded through me, followed by a rush of cold exhilaration. Release, I needed release. I sought a target for my power, my first victim.

There would be many today.

Autumn sat up, coughing. I nearly struck her with my lixia before catching myself and slamming a mental shield up. Autumn was backing away from me, terror stark in her eyes. I tried to ignore the answering hurt that sprang up in my chest.

"Go to sleep, Autumn," I told her, holding her gaze. I saw her; I saw her concern for me. I used it against her. *"Go to sleep."*

The power lurched out of me: graceless, inelegant. Still, the lixia took hold. She slumped to the ground as if possessed.

I flexed my wrists, which were deliciously light, unencumbered. *The world is mine*, I thought. *It answers to me.*

I reached under my tunic and grasped my seal. The stone pulsed against me, alight with jagged energy. I pressed it against my wound, letting blood drip through the cloth, onto the jade. The seal hissed. I released my consciousness.

I did not so much as fall into the spirit realm as let it fall into me. Within, the sea dragon was waiting.

"You are testing my patience."

The dragon's cobalt eyes glittered with anger. It had been so long, I'd forgotten what his voice sounded like. It was a cold wind, one that penetrated your very bones.

"I didn't know the iron would affect me too."

"You were incautious. As you are now." He circled me slowly.

"You cannot go through with your plan. Leave the others behind; they will not die here. You must prioritize Zhuque's jade."

I stiffened. So he was reading my mind, at this very moment. He saw my plan—he saw what I intended to do. But it was not an unknowable power, as I'd initially assumed. It was merely impulsion; something I too could access.

"Are you listening to me?" he hissed. "You must escape and retrieve the jade."

I had managed to tune out his voice previously, but now I would have to create a mental shield even more foolproof—so that he could not know my thoughts. I imagined a weeping willow tree, like the ones that grew along my neighborhood riverbank. Then I imagined the branches lengthening, clustering together, forming a secret, impenetrable hiding place. I had hidden beneath one many years ago, the first time my father had struck me.

Uncle Zhou had found me soon after, for the willow branches were sparse at that time of year. But this willow, this tree of my mind, would be impenetrable. There, I collected my innermost thoughts and hid them.

"No," I answered, "I'm not leaving anyone behind."

I felt a presence trying to steal inside; I forced him out, branches unwavering. *You will not know my intentions.*

A brief silence, then: "You've never done that before." Perhaps I had startled Qinglong out of his anger; his tone betrayed only surprise. "You're a quick learner, I'll give you that. Especially with your little mind tricks."

His condescension nettled, but it was too familiar to cut deep. I was used to my father's belittlements, Lieutenant Fang's, and even, to a lesser extent—Sky's. Perhaps my natural talent for mental manipulation stemmed from years of reading Father's moods, in the same way a sailor learns to read the tides. When storms struck, a slow learner became the first to drown.

The dragon sniffed. "But pick your battles wisely, Hai Meilin."

Before, Qinglong's threats might have frightened me. But the fact that he'd waited for me throughout my imprisonment, even after losing his patience, emboldened me. *He needs me*, I realized. Just as I needed him. He could no more choose another vessel than I could choose another spirit. We were bound to each other.

The thought lent me courage. "Either help me or don't," I told him. "But I'm the only one you have."

He scoffed but, as I expected, did not deny this.

I turned away to explore the spirit realm. I found the inverse of the room I was being kept in, and beyond my bedchambers, the palace, the city of New Quan, the ocean. The world was vast, sparkling. But I could not be distracted.

"There's a secret entrance to the prison tower," the dragon said reluctantly. "You'll need to enter through the lower levels of the palace."

I studied the landscape for a moment longer, trying to commit as much as possible to memory. Then I forced myself awake.

Thankfully, Autumn was still fast asleep. She lay slumped over in an unnatural position, her arm bent crooked under her chest. Gently, I turned her so that she lay flat on her back, so she wouldn't be sore when she awoke. Though I knew it would be the least of her concerns.

I grabbed my keys and fruit knife—it had served me well—then stalked quietly through the keting to the front door. I studied the keys first before choosing one that looked like the best fit. No luck. I tried the second one. It entered, but not quietly.

"Autumn?" a guard asked.

"Yes?" I replied, pitching my voice higher.

The door swung open for me. I slammed into the guard with my fruit knife, dragging it across his throat. He fell, choking. The other two guards had both been sitting on the floor, eating breakfast. One had glutinous rice stuck to his chin.

"Sleep," I told them. They blinked at me, confused. I cursed at myself, at my own lack of experience. "*Go to sleep*," I said again, and this time, they both obeyed, albeit less immediately than Autumn had. I breathed out, then stumbled, catching myself against the door. My knees buckled. I was dangerously inexperienced and didn't know how to ration my use of lixia. A simple command like this, and I was already on the verge of collapse?

I armed myself with their weapons, then on second thought took their coil of rope. With that I ran for the nearest source of sunlight. It was an open-air gallery, two floors above ground level. I eyed the distance. There was only one soldier in the courtyard below, his back turned to me. Now, I thought, before they discovered the guards slumped outside my cell.

I knotted the rope to the nearest column, then rappelled down into the courtyard. The guard turned just as I landed, but he was within kicking distance. I spun forward with a roundhouse kick and felt the blow connect to his head. He fell soundlessly. I ran.

Recalling the layout of the palace from the spirit world, I found the tunnel entrance in the cellar near the servants' quarters. The stairs led into shadow, but I had no time to search for a lamp. Gritting my teeth, I descended into darkness before misjudging a step and tumbling down one or two flights of stairs. When I managed to right myself, I checked for broken bones—none, thank the skies. Only a smattering of bruises that would surely cause me trouble later. But for now, adrenaline dulled all pain.

The tunnel meandered, leading up, then down. I passed the first trapdoor, then the second, then the third. At the fifth trapdoor, I heard the distinctive sound of crashing waves.

This must be it. The room I entered was circular, made of hewn stone. I stared up into a familiar set of winding stairs. Relief flooded through me; Sky was here. I would save him.

I took the stairs two at a time before skidding to a sudden halt; I could hear men conversing outside the prison door. Several of them.

"He's to be shipped to Tzu Wan," said General Huyi. "Make sure he's in traveling condition." A note of malice slid into his voice. "The chancellor has a bone to pick with his father. But I'm sure the son will suffice for now."

I counted half a dozen men before me. Even a soldier with Zilong's abilities could not take on six soldiers with a sword alone. But, I reminded myself, I had more than a blade.

Steeling myself, I stepped out into the open. "Go to sleep," I ordered, but this time, my voice came out weak, unsteady. I could perceive its lack of weight.

General Huyi stared at me, shock written across his face. "You," he said softly.

"Go to sleep," I said again, stubbornly, trying to force strength into my words. My head spun as my vision began to flicker.

The soldiers laughed.

With a curse, I gave up and swung my sword at the guard closest to me. In his surprise, he didn't even draw his blade. My sword sank into the soft flesh of his gut. I wrenched it out just in time to meet another guard's spear. I parried his blow but had to disengage when I felt another blade whirling at me from behind. I was surrounded. Someone knocked the sword from my grip. I tried to whip out my dagger, but General Huyi wrapped his hand around my wrist.

"What is it about you?" the general asked lowly, eyeing me. "You're not . . . *right*."

I wasn't—I was wrong. I was an aberration that should not exist. A woman, a warrior, a spirit medium.

Spirit medium, I thought, closing my eyes. Manipulation of the mind came easier to me than elemental magic, perhaps because I had always lived in my head. But it would be foolish of me to ignore such a potent resource, even one I wasn't naturally gifted at; I only needed to look to Chancellor Sima's example to see how much damage could be done with elemental magic alone.

Come to me, I commanded, concentrating on the crashing waves outside the prison tower. *Obey me as you obey the spirit of the sea dragon. For even he listens to me.*

I breathed out, balancing qi and lixia in my being. When I opened my eyes, water droplets hung in the air, trembling with frantic energy. The room smelled of sea brine, of salt. General Huyi was staring at me with naked fear in his eyes.

"He's touched by the gods," someone said, awe in their voice.

I smiled.

The water crystallized into knives of ice. General Huyi was closest; I aimed at his right eye.

His screams echoed against the stone.

Every knife met its mark. As General Huyi lay on the floor, writhing, I snatched the keys off his belt. Behind him, the other men had succumbed to their invisible wounds, blood and water pooling against them.

I stepped over their bodies, trying to ignore the wave of fatigue that pressed up against me. My vision had turned vague; the door split into two doors, both blurry. I forced my feet forward, willing myself not to faint. No more qi left, but I had to keep going. I unlocked the prison door.

"Ren!" Sparrow exclaimed. "What's going on?" He stared at me in horror, and I realized I was covered in blood. Other people's blood. How many had I killed in the span of an hour?

What had I done to them? To myself?

Dizzily, I handed Tao my keys—he was closest to the door—and leaned against the wall as he unlocked his own chains, then freed the others. Sky came to me immediately.

"Where are you bleeding?" he demanded.

"It's-it's not mine." My voice was hoarse beyond recognition, my vision dim and unfocused. "We have to go. Stable—through the tunnels—"

I swayed. Sky caught me before I fell. "Skies," he muttered. "Meilin, you're so cold."

Had my heart stopped pumping blood? I did not know. Sky supported me as we made our way down the stairs, making slow progress. I guided them through the tunnels, toward the stables. The stable hand was only a boy, but I was too weak to compel him. Sparrow knocked him out, but he used too much force. The boy bled out on the ground. He looked barely past childhood.

I tasted salt water on my tongue. Belatedly, I realized I was crying.

"I'm the heaviest," Sparrow was saying, as the others decided what to do with the two mares in the stable. "I'll ride with Ren."

Sky and Tao led the way, breaking into a gallop as soon as we made it out the gates. I clung to Sparrow for dear life as we rode, blinded by the ruthless sunlight reflecting off the sea. Gulls cawed at us from above; I couldn't remember the last time I'd heard birds. Now that I was crying, I couldn't stop. We were *free*.

"Oh, Sparrow," I said, "I'm so happy to see you."

He couldn't hear me over the pounding hoofbeats; we were moving so fast. Then, abruptly, we slowed. I looked up.

All warmth drained from my limbs.

A platoon of soldiers rode toward us from the north, helmed by the Ximing prince. Lei rode faster than the others, pressed against his stallion, his long robes flying behind him. I could not make out his face from here, but I could imagine his expression; he would not let me go peacefully. And we could not outride so many men.

Sparrow pulled on the reins as the guards closed in. I guessed he was considering turning back southward, but the palace would be swarming with soldiers by now.

"Stop," I said with sudden certainty. Sparrow brought the mare to a complete stop, and I jumped off.

"What are you doing?" Sky shouted at me, trying to turn.

"*Go*," I ordered. "I'll hold them off."

I did not know if I compelled him. All I knew was that my resolve was steel. I had nothing but dregs left, but I had learned to feast on dregs.

I'm sorry, I didn't tell him. *I'm sorry I lied to you. I'm sorry this is how you'll learn the truth about me.*

I waited until Lei and his men were close. As expected, I was their priority. I was the one he wanted.

Perhaps he'd known all along. *"Were you born with golden eyes?"* he'd asked me, the night before.

Here was my answer. I invoked what had never forsaken me—not when my father had struck me, not when Master Zhu had bought me with a pair of pigs, not when my mother had turned her face away from me. I invoked my ambition. My greed. My undying belief that I was meant for more than this, that I could do so much more than they all believed. My greed was unending. *An ocean's hunger.*

I called upon the might of the sea. My ambition could match it.

The haixiao wave that rose awed even me, its master. The Xi-ming soldiers stopped in their tracks, their horses rearing in terror. I encouraged the wave, letting it rise higher and higher—

An arrow struck me in the shoulder. I faltered, then stared up at Lei, at the bow in his hands.

I wrenched the arrow out. Of course—it was laced with iron.

I fell.

FORTY

The binary of the living and the dead does not apply to spirits. Rather, all spirits cycle through seasons of strength and weakness, decay and rebirth. In this manner, though Cardinal Spirits tend to disappear from human history for centuries at a time, no spirit creature is ever truly gone from this world.

—LOST JOURNALS OF AN 8TH-CENTURY LIXIA SCHOLAR, DATE UNKNOWN

WITH CONSCIOUSNESS CAME PAIN. I GROANED AS I TRIED TO lift my head; I felt as if I'd been run over by a cartload of bricks. Several carts.

My right shoulder was stiff and impossible to move. Someone had fitted my arm into a sling and bandaged the arrow wound beneath my tunic. But—it wasn't my tunic. My clothes were missing, replaced by simple clean linen garments.

I sat up in raw panic before nearly passing out from the fresh onslaught of pain that came from any movement. My jade—*it was gone.*

I had no spirit power whatsoever. My hands were bound in chains, as were my ankles. All my remaining willpower deserted me; I fell back in bed.

I had been so close to freedom. I had heard gulls flying overhead, felt the rush of wind on my face. I had embraced Sky; he had held me in his arms.

But he was gone now. Or so I hoped.

"You're awake."

Autumn emerged from the keting, her voice devoid of its customary cheeriness. Beyond her, I spotted a guard standing in the keting, *inside* my rooms. Had he been watching me sleep?

I decided to ignore the guard. "What happened to the clothes I was wearing?" I asked Autumn, rubbing my sternum with my free hand. My chest felt hollowed out, empty. Losing the jade was like losing a limb, a critical sense. Without it, I no longer felt whole.

She wrinkled her nose. "Your clothes were soaked in blood, Meilin."

I sat up with some difficulty, trying not to jostle my sling. "What did you do with them?"

"I threw them away."

I gasped. "You didn't."

She looked at me, then shrugged. "I didn't."

"Please," I whispered, not needing to feign the pathetic quality of my voice. "I need my old clothes back. They-they remind me of home," I lied.

"Meilin," said Autumn, steeping tea leaves. "I'm going to be honest with you, as I always have been. You're in no position to make demands right now."

I swallowed. "Just tell me this, please. Did my companions . . . did they escape?"

Autumn would not look me in the eye. But as she set down her teapot, her head bobbed—just a fraction, but unmistakably—yes. *They escaped.*

Gladness unfurled in my chest, followed by a breathless pang like disappointment.

Don't be ridiculous, Meilin. Of course you wanted them to escape.

But why had they not come back for me? Sky . . . I thought Sky of all people would not leave me behind.

No matter. Duty came first for him, as he'd always made clear to me. Soon I would join them of my own volition. I would retrieve my jade, and I would escape this place.

Autumn winced as she sat beside me, her hand instinctively moving to her abdomen. I felt my throat close. "Did I . . . did I hurt you badly?"

She didn't respond, pouring two cups of oolong tea.

"I'm sorry," I whispered.

"Drink this," she said, handing me a cup. "Lei's called for you."

I flinched, my chains rattling in response. "Now?"

She nodded, before reaching over to brush my hair out of my face. "Here," she said, taking a plum blossom hairpin from her own head.

I shrank back. "I don't want it."

"Why?"

"It'll make me look like a girl."

Autumn sighed. "Everybody already knows, Meilin. Your right to privacy's been revoked. There's a guard to be stationed in your room at all times."

With that, she slid the pin into my hair. Horrified, I could do nothing but blink at her.

When Autumn signaled the guard over, he unchained me from the wall, then led me from my rooms. Outside, two additional guards joined us. The chains around my ankles permitted me to walk, albeit with small steps. We made slow progress to Lei's rooms.

I hadn't realized how late it was until I caught a glimpse of the sky above—pitch black, no moon in sight. Was tonight a new moon? Had Sky and Sparrow and Tao traveled in the dark? Had they returned safely? Were they free, as I was not?

"Enter."

Despite the hour, Lei was wide-awake. He sat on his shafa overlooking the balcony, surrounded by haphazardly stacked scrolls. To my surprise, he was reading.

He waved me in carelessly, not looking up from his scroll.

The guards deposited me on the seat across from him. My shoulder wound twinged at the prince's proximity. I recalled the longbow in his hands, the cold, calculating expression on his face. "You said you wouldn't kill me," I burst out, my voice accusatory.

He folded the scroll in his hands before turning to another one. "You're still alive, aren't you?"

"You *shot* me."

"Meilin," he said, sparing me a second's glance, "I never miss."

He was *infuriating*. It was agony to sit across from him, to come and go at his beck and call. "You know what? You're a monster."

He yawned.

Humiliatingly, tears sprang to my eyes. I hated his cold, indifferent expression as much as I hated my own pathetic one. I hated that I was here, captive and alone, after everything I had sacrificed in the pursuit of freedom. I hated that I had helped my friends escape, but there was no one left to help me.

Loneliness and despair wrapped around me like the arms of an old friend: inviting, familiar.

No, I thought, swiping angrily at my tears. I could not allow myself to wallow in my emotions. Instead, I deepened my breathing and sealed them far from myself, as I had long trained myself to do. *You cannot afford to be soft, Meilin.*

I had repeated those words often, so much so that I could not recall their source. Xiuying? Or . . . my mother?

"I underestimated how much trouble you'd be," said the prince. He was watching me, his eyes curious, prying. "Pity you're the one I'm looking for."

I stiffened. "I told you I'd *never* help you." Then I hesitated. There was something I needed from him. "Unless you give me something in return."

"And what would that be?"

I paused, wondering if it was too early to reveal my cards. If I asked him for my uniform, it might alert him to its importance. But I could see no other route. Although he was by no means my ally, he was the only one now who could help me.

"My old uniform," I said carefully. "It reminds me of home."

"Hm," he said. "Humor me and perhaps I'll humor you." He set down the bamboo slip in his hand. "Did you know," he said, his eyes flickering in thought, "only one lixia seal has ever been destroyed in known history?"

I glanced down at the book on the aiji table: *A Comprehensive Overview of Lixia-Induced Disorders*. He must have taken it from that New Quan library the fishermen had spoken of.

"A seal can only be unmade by its own wielder. Powerful, isn't it? A weapon whose only weakness lies in the one person who will never exploit it."

I shifted my right arm in its sling. Despite my intentions, he'd caught my interest. Did the prince mean to imply that only Sima's fire could destroy the phoenix seal?

Come to think of it, why had *Qinglong* never told me how to destroy it?

When I'd asked him in the sea, he'd simply told me to give it to him—that he would take care of the matter himself. I'd obliged, thinking it one fewer concern to worry myself with. But now I wondered . . . had I followed orders too unthinkingly?

Like a woman, I thought, taught to be incurious, pliant, accepting.

"When a woman asks, smile but do not answer."

"The study of lixia is still relatively undeveloped," Lei continued, rousing me from my spiraling thoughts. "Scholars still don't know how to access the spirit realm, or why certain spirit mediums possess greater affinities than others." His eyes cut to mine. "Thirsty?"

I shook my head, though I was. He poured two glasses of sorghum wine anyway, which I was beginning to tell was his preferred beverage. The clear liquid resembled water, though its alcohol content was dangerously high. I didn't touch my glass.

"Jade transfer is uncommon but not unheard of," said Lei, his attention returned to the scroll at hand. I much preferred him this way, with his gaze off me. "If the human host dies, the spirit is weakened and cannot move freely through the physical world, but once they find another vessel, they can return to power."

I sat back, mulling this over. I recalled how surprised Lei had been when the chancellor showed up at the Xi Lan cliffs. Perhaps Lei had been the one to poison him that night—because he coveted his jade.

Had he thought to kill Sima—and steal his jade for himself?

But that didn't make sense. Why had he not chosen to kill me, then, a far easier target? Surely he knew I was a spirit medium too?

Lei was still talking.

"And yet, the relationship is parasitic in nature, for the reverse is not true. If the seal is destroyed, so is its host." He leaned forward, admiration in his voice. "Clever, don't you think? Why else would a lixia seal be so difficult to destroy? Because it stakes its own survival on the most constant nature of humankind—the will to live." He smiled, dropping the scroll on the table. "I almost wish I'd come up with it myself."

I was incapable of speech. I snatched the scroll from the table and began reading furiously. He was not lying, as I had hoped. The one time I wished for a lie, he spoke the truth.

The complexity of my mission multiplied before me. The only one who could destroy Zhuque's seal was its host. Sima Yi. And yet destroying your own seal was suicide, for if your seal perished, so did you.

I would not only have to find the last jade piece before Sima did, but I would also have to bring it to him, then force him to destroy the jade himself. He would never agree to do such a thing, not if he was in his right mind.

Compulsion, I realized. Compulsion was the key.

I looked back at the scroll. *"Though efforts were made in the year of the Monkey Emperor to eradicate all lixia from Tianjia, the campaign was largely unsuccessful, with over a hundred and twenty priests falling prey to spirit power. (See list of victims in the Tiansun Archives.) Even a human host with selfless intentions, hoping to accept the seal with the aim of bringing about its eventual destruction, may find themself vulnerable in the face of lixia. For in accepting the seal and becoming a vessel, a spirit medium embraces not only the abilities of the spirit but also its character and disposition. More often than not, the spirit will overpower its host, assuming control over the medium's body and mind."*

Chills ran down my spine. Was this what Qinglong had been planning for me all along? What he'd already put into action? I thought about the past few weeks—how I'd coveted Sima's jade, focused single-mindedly on retrieving it. I thought of my fear, or lack thereof. I had begun to fully embrace my powers, no longer wary of their effect on me. My old fears had been shoved aside, forgotten.

I was afraid now, that was for certain. Who was my enemy? Was it the Ximing prince? Chancellor Sima? Or . . . Qinglong?

Ice-cold loneliness burrowed in my chest. I'd never felt so lost and alone in this world.

"Drink," said Lei, nodding toward the full glass before me. "It helps."

What did I have to lose? I drained the glass, ignoring the burning sensation, then pushed it back toward him. He did not smile. Instead, he looked strangely sad.

"Even knowing the risks," I asked him, "you still seek the jade for yourself?"

I had accepted Qinglong's power thoughtlessly, without understanding how lixia worked. Yet Lei knew much more than I did. Still, he was willing to sacrifice his freedom—his sanity, even— for jade?

"You tell me," he said. "Is the power worth it?"

He waited, his gaze dismantling me slowly. "I have no power," I answered at last, my voice hoarse. *Not anymore.*

"You're telling the truth this time," he said, with quiet certainty. I met his eyes then. What did he want from me? I couldn't begin to guess his motives.

Before I could speak, someone rapped at the door.

Lei stood. "Enter."

To my surprise, a monk entered with a snow-white lynx at his side. I did not know what company princes kept, but I doubted this was customary. Lei turned and nodded to my guard, who came over and grabbed me at once. I held on to the scroll, and when the guard tried to take it from me, Lei lifted a hand. "Let her have it, and the rest," he said, motioning to the pile of scrolls on the table, which all seemed to be taken from the New Quan library. To me, with a wink: "You could use some light bedtime reading."

"My uniform—" I started, but the guard had already towed me outside. I glanced over my shoulder to see what the monk and lynx would do, but the door slammed in my face.

FORTY-ONE

And when the Great Warrior Guan Yang passed, the people did not know how to mourn him. For although he had accomplished many heroic deeds in his lifetime, his subsequent years were marked by corruption and madness. Despite his many good intentions, the excess lixia ultimately consumed him whole.

—LEGENDS OF THE MOUNTAINS, 754

DESPITE MY CHAINS, I COULDN'T STOP PACING. THE GUARD IN MY keting must've grown tired of the constant clanking, for he'd turned his back to me. With the length of my chain, I could only walk halfway across my bedroom, but I made do with the space I had. Back and forth. Back and forth.

My thoughts traveled many times the distance. I'd already read through all the scrolls given to me, which had only exacerbated my fears of madness. Had Qinglong been manipulating me all along? He had commanded me to find the phoenix's jade, to prevent Zhuque from restoring her seal to wholeness. *"She is our greatest threat,"* he'd told me.

Was she my greatest threat . . . or *his*?

"Fire and water are lifelong rivals," Sima had said, the first time we'd met. *"But, Haiyang, we need not be enemies."*

My emotions roiled. Had I made the wrong choice? No—Sima wanted to raze the Three Kingdoms to ash. If he had his way, everyone I loved would die. I alone would survive—fated for the cage.

I covered my face with my hands. The truth was, I did not know whom to believe. I had so few allies, and enemies at every turn. I understood myself with cruel clarity; I wanted to trust Qinglong, because I wanted to obey orders. The choice had felt safe—and *familiar*. It was what had always been expected of me. Even now I missed the simplicity of army life, the unthinking nature of it. My commander dictating my every decision, from when I rose to when I slept. There was no room for doubt, for regret, for . . . responsibility.

Did I really want to go back?

You could be so much more.

I stilled. Was this Qinglong's influence, or my own? Who could say?

One thing was clear: I needed my jade before I could even consider escaping. Lei obviously wanted something from me, and I would play along, for now. I would be as docile as a trained dog—until I got my uniform back. Then all bets were off.

But what of Sima's jade? It would be nearly impossible to steal the jade off his back, but perhaps I stood a chance at reaching the third jade piece before he did. Unless . . . Sima couldn't have found it already, could he? Surely Qinglong would've mentioned something to me if he had.

Unless Qinglong was playing both sides.

The possibility of his betrayal stung, like an old wound torn open. It was in my nature to trust, to remain loyal, despite having been wronged again and again. How pitiful I was—to long to depend on those around me, to long for their respect and care and affection.

Even here in enemy territory, I had let my guard down. I hadn't known this until I'd felt the knifelike breach of trust, as one-sided as it was. That the prince of Ximing—who I knew with all logic was my enemy—would shoot me in cold blood, without a moment's hesitation. That Autumn the healer—who I knew served the prince—would reveal my identity to him, my most hidden of secrets.

I looked in my reflection and saw myself, and hated what I saw.

In frustration, I kicked at an armchair, before swearing at my stubbed toe and hopping gracelessly to my bed. These excess chains were ridiculous. Lei knew it too: that I could not escape without my jade. Perhaps he'd only added these extra precautions to humiliate me. It would not be unlike him.

The door burst open; it was unusual for Autumn to enter without first knocking. I sat up as General Huyi barged inside, wearing civilian clothes. He looked as if he'd come directly from the infirmary; his complexion was pale, sickly, and his head swathed in bandages. Notably, his right eye had been covered by a thick eye patch. He glared at me with his remaining eye.

"Leave us," he told the guard in the keting.

"Yes, sir." The guard saluted him before retreating.

My hackles rose. "Why are you here? Did Lei send you?"

The general sneered at this. "The prince must learn he can't always get what he wants."

He advanced toward me, and I drew back, before realizing I did not want to be caught on my bed. I reached for the fruit knife I'd stowed beneath my pillow and jumped to my feet.

"From the moment I laid eyes on you... I knew there was something wrong with you." His gaze went from my loose hair to the manacles around my wrists. "To think he means to let *you* live."

"Meilin?" Autumn stood in the doorway, carrying a bowl of steaming rice noodles. She looked between me and the general.

"Leave us," General Huyi growled. When she didn't move, he added, "Now."

"General Huyi." Autumn bowed formally. "I'm very sorry, but under the prince's orders, the prisoner is not to speak to—"

"The princeling oversteps his place," he snarled.

Autumn tried to come between us. "Please, sir, discuss the matter with—"

He slapped her, hard. I shrieked as Autumn flew backward, her porcelain bowl shattering against the floor. I thought of Xiuying on the floor, Father's wine bottles littered in broken shards. My old protective instincts sprang up as Autumn crawled backward on her hands and knees, her palms leaving bloody stains on the floor.

"Leave!" the general shouted, his voice growing increasingly deranged.

"Go," I whispered. She fled.

My chains prevented me from escape. I backed up against the wall, my hand sweating against the hilt of my fruit knife.

"Do you know what you did to me?" he hissed. Tugging the eye patch from his face, he revealed a deeply swollen eye, matted with dried pus and blood. The wound was beyond repair; he would never see from his right side again.

I swallowed.

"For someone like you to possess the power of lixia..." He tried to close the distance between us, but I jerked my chain upward, tripping him. He sprawled forward but dragged me down with him. Panicking, I tried to scramble out of his grasp, but he grabbed my chain, wrenching me to him against my will. My wounded shoulder smacked the bedpost and I cried out in sharp, wretched pain. He laughed, applying pressure to my wound. I gasped for breath, the onslaught of pain unbearable.

"You're a perversion," he said softly, holding me down by my throat. I met his eyes and saw his gaze, thick with hatred, and something else—*lust*. In desperation, I tried to stab him in the side, but my chains made me slow; he caught my wrist before the knife met flesh.

He stole the blade from me, then grazed its tip against my cheek. "Should I remove your eyes first? Or perhaps your mouth?" He traced the knife against my lower lip. "Repulsive," he whispered, so close I could feel his hot breath on my face. "Disgusting." But his excitement was overt, his hardening member pressed against my hip.

"Already in chains," he murmured. "The prince made it so very easy."

He shifted to undo his belt. Momentarily freed, I kneed him in the groin, then tried to strangle him with my chains. He grabbed my free arm and wrenched it back; I screamed as my elbow fractured into pieces. Tears blurred my vision as I felt the general lower himself over me, holding me down by my broken bones. Darkness pressed in.

Suddenly he was thrown off me, flung against the wall with a resounding crack. Immobilized by pain, I could not so much as react. I watched in a stupor as Lei withdrew a curved dagger and, with little ceremony, gouged out the general's other eye.

General Huyi screamed and screamed. I too would have screamed, if I could speak, for the sight was horrid. When Lei released him, he slumped to the floor, barely breathing. Blood poured from his ruined eye socket.

A familiar hand turned my face away. "Where are you hurt?" Autumn asked me, running a deft hand across my body. I gasped as she grazed my broken elbow, the sharp spike of pain nearly sending me into oblivion.

"I need you to stay awake, Meilin," she said urgently. "There might be internal bleeding. You can't go under."

Someone else crouched beside me. Jasmine and cedar, I thought distantly; the scent permeated the hallway. As if from a faraway memory.

"I can't lift her," Autumn said to him.

He was gentle, impossibly gentle. Still, the consequent pain spilled tears down my cheeks, my breaths turning short and shallow. As he lifted me in his arms and carried me outside, I wondered if this was, at last, how I would die.

Autumn ran to keep pace with us. "Hold on, Meilin!" she was saying. "Open your eyes. Look at me."

But I could not see her from here. As I opened my eyes, all I could see was the Ximing prince, his eyes hard and glinting, his mouth set in a thin line.

In the infirmary, he set me down on a stretcher. Autumn worked ceaselessly as I drifted in and out of consciousness. She gave me potion after potion, each one for some different purpose, and the pain was so unbearable I could not even mind the fact that I'd been drugged.

I did not know how much time had passed, but when I stirred, I became aware of both my arms restricted in tight slings. I could barely lift my head, yet I felt the presence of another beside me. "Will I die?" I asked Autumn.

The voice that answered was not the one I'd been expecting. "No," said Lei. "You will not." I could not see his face, but I could hear the lethal emotion in his voice. "I protect what's mine."

FORTY-TWO

The Ruan, an ethnic minority group mostly located on the southwestern peninsula of Ximing, are renowned for their fabled clairvoyants. During the unified days of the early Wu Dynasty, many would travel from as far as Leyuan to the seaside village of Yihei, in order to have their fortunes told—for a hefty price.

—REMEMBERING THE WU DYNASTY, 913

I SPENT THE NEXT WEEK IN THE INFIRMARY, ATTENDED TO BY Autumn. Mired with exhaustion, I barely spoke at all, my mind dull as if blanketed by a dense fog. When I was finally deemed fit to leave the infirmary and return to my quarters, I noticed my former chains did not make a reappearance. The only ones that remained were the thin iron bands encircling my wrists. Autumn said nothing about this improvement, though I saw her glance darkly at my irons once or twice.

I did not mention the change either, though it crossed my mind, late at night when the fog temporarily lifted. I had hated the physical weight of my chains, the constant restriction of movement. Yet I had not perceived the mental weight, the invisible toll the iron had taken on my thoughts and emotions. Even now I felt it—the subtle strain, smothering my lixia, and by result, my qi. For the two were intertwined now.

In the prison tower, I'd succeeded in creating a thin fissure in my manacles. Could I do it again? With enough willpower, could I shatter my chains and escape this place?

The idea left me profoundly exhausted. First, I had to heal. I could not use my arms at all and had to be fed like a child. I no longer required a guard, for I could not even open a door on my own. Autumn said the healing process would take three months, but privately, I hoped for three weeks, even with iron blocking my powers. I'd seen firsthand how Sima had recovered overnight from deadly poison. Every night, alone, I willed my bones to heal, to knit back together like jade seeking wholeness. I prayed to no gods, for I knew that even if they existed, they were merciless.

LEI MADE AN APPEARANCE ON THE TENTH DAY, ENTERING MY ROOM IN discreet riding clothes, twin blades strapped to his back. Autumn, who was in the midst of changing my bandages, looked equally startled by his visit.

"I have a lead on the jade," said Lei, eyes bright and watchful. I knew he awaited my reaction, so I did not give him one.

He raised a brow at my silence, then said to Autumn: "Pack whatever potions she requires for a three-day journey."

"Are you mad?" Autumn started. "You can't bring her along—have you seen the state of her?" She cut the bandage, then gestured to my useless arms.

Lei turned to me. "Would you rather I take you with me, or leave you behind?"

There was no question when it came to the jade. "Take me with you."

WE RODE WITH A SMALL CONTINGENT OF GUARDS, ALONG WITH THE monk and his oddly intelligent lynx. Even more oddly, the lynx was the one who led the way, taking us through thick jungle deeper south.

As I could not ride alone, Lei rode with me, his strong arms encircling my useless ones. He did not talk much, and he seemed constantly on edge, as if waiting for something momentous.

At the end of our second day, we arrived at a small lighthouse surrounded by rock-strewn tide pools. Under the shadow of the lighthouse sat a nondescript straw hut, barely larger than the size of my New Quan prison cell.

The lynx went berserk, yipping and making high-pitched sounds that seemed like a cross between a laugh and a scream. The monk silenced the creature, nodding at the Ximing prince. Lei dismounted, then lifted me off his horse.

Two guards had gone inside the straw hut before emerging with an old man, his face sagging with wrinkles and sun exposure. "Your-Your Highness!" he exclaimed, falling to the black sand in a deep kowtow.

"Rise." Lei went to him and lifted him by his shoulders. "There's no need for that."

"You've come a long way to Ben Niu," the lighthouse keeper said, voice thick with reverence. "You must be weary. Please, come and have tea. I know my home is unbefitting your—"

"Not at all," Lei cut in. "I'd be delighted."

He followed the old man inside, without looking back at me. I dawdled for a few moments, considering my options. Attempt escape? I almost laughed at the idea, glancing at the guards surrounding the lighthouse. Search for Sima's jade? Could it be somewhere in the black water, or had it already washed ashore? I could comb the beach; then, if I struck lucky, I could hide the jade somewhere no one else would find it.

But of course, Sima would find it. As soon as his jade reached land, he would perceive it, no matter the distance.

What had Lei been thinking? His quest was foolish, and by having me accompany him, he made us both fools. Still, I thought, looking at the lighthouse keeper's hut, if the prince had actually discovered the third jade piece, I didn't want him pocketing it without my knowledge. I followed.

Inside, the hut smelled of decomposing fish and earthy ginseng root. I had to suppress a cough, but the prince didn't seem to care. He sat on the dirt as if it were as comfortable as his silk sofa, nodding agreeably at the old man.

"I'd meant to make the journey to Tzu Wan tomorrow, to sell it at the public market. It felt like a favor from the gods, at long last. I'm an old man, with humble ambitions. I only wanted a little coin to leave to my children. They live in the capital, you see. You know how difficult it is to make ends meet in the city."

He exhaled then and, with notable reluctance, withdrew a tiny piece of jade, no larger than a lychee seed. My chest constricted at the sight of that fiery jade, pulsating like a living creature. The final piece of Zhuque's seal. The sea had given it up, at last.

Is this how it all ends?

"Of course," said the lighthouse keeper, his expression torn. "I would be honored to pass it on to you, my prince."

But his hands shook as he slowly, painfully dropped the bead into Lei's outstretched palm. How hard it was to relinquish jade, even as an old man with little ambition.

"You have my thanks," Lei said, leaning forward, and I could see the man attuning to the prince's charisma, like flowers toward sun. "Your children will be handsomely rewarded for your noble deed. As for you—"

The old man's eyes bulged as he choked, foam rising from his lips. I started forward from the doorway, but what could I do? I looked from the lighthouse keeper to the prince, then caught the prince's expression: unfeeling.

He'd poisoned the man himself.

I took an unconscious step back. Lei had been kind to me these past few days. But I could not forget the truth of him: a beautiful face, belying a heart of stone.

The lighthouse keeper died in seconds, curled up on his side like a child afraid of the dark. Lei rose, examining the jade between his fingertips. His utter lack of contrition enraged me.

"How could you?" I asked, unable to curb my tongue. "He was innocent—he even offered you the jade willingly! You—why?"

Lei's eyes fell upon me. They were as cold and distant as the black sea. "He would've left a trail for the chancellor to follow," he said bluntly. "You saw Sima's powers of mental manipulation yourself. He would've extracted the memory from his mind—and learned that I possess the jade he seeks."

"You fool," I swore. "Sima will know regardless—you think he can't sense his own seal?"

Lei smiled then. "He can sense some things, and not others," he said cryptically. "Soon he'll find himself on a wild-goose chase from Ben Niu to Mount Fuxi."

He stepped around me out of the hut, striding toward the monk. I swore again but followed, stopping short as I caught sight of the glint of iron in the monk's hands. I backed away, thinking it was intended for me, before the monk took the thin strip of iron and folded it. I gasped. In his hands, the iron bore the viscosity of honey and folded as easily as soft clay. He worked his hands deftly around the stone, then murmured a prayer and handed the miniature ball of iron back to the prince. It was altogether no larger than a butterfly's wing.

I could not see the jade anywhere. Then I realized—it was hidden inside the iron.

Lei had found a way to block spirit mediums from perceiving their own jade.

"How..." I trailed off as the lynx dived into the water and the monk chased after his animal. He was young, hardly past adolescence. Were monks usually so young?

Come to think of it, I couldn't recall the last time I'd seen a monk. After Warlord Liu had deemed all religious movements seditious, they'd been exiled from Anlai or forced to go into hiding.

The world outside my Chuang Ning home was far wider than I could've ever imagined. Were there other forms of magic beyond the jade seals? Other ways of manipulating elements, communing with spirits? There was so much I still did not know.

I watched as the monk returned to us, his wet robes flapping in the breeze. "Do you have your own seal?" I asked boldly, because I had nothing to lose. And yet if he had his own seal, how in the world could he manipulate iron?

The monk did not answer. He merely looked at me, then turned away as his lynx began to mew.

"Don't take it personally," said Lei, from behind me. "He's taken a vow of silence."

Irritated, I whirled on him. "How in the skies is this possible? Seal magic shouldn't be able to manipulate iron."

Lei considered this, as if the fact had not occurred to him. "There are more than a few ways to harness lixia," he said at last. "Your kingdom has crippled itself in choosing to deny the existence of the spirit realm. But the rest of the world will not abandon its progress on account of one warlord's mandate."

As much as it pained me to admit it, Lei was right. Given my mother's influence, I knew more about the spirit realm than most in Anlai. And yet, here in Ximing, a chancellor with a spirit seal could be called blessed. A scholar in New Quan could study the psychosomatic effects of lixia. And a prince, with time, money, and an extensive network of spies, could even find a way to manipulate one form of lixia against another.

Despite Anlai's superior wealth and natural resources, our own fear and denial of lixia had set us back in this war. And this choice could cost us our lives.

Never had I so wished to speak with Sky—to pull him aside, to discuss matters in private within the quiet of our training ring. I had no head for politics, for military strategies at a scale larger than my own squad. Now I wanted Sky to tell me what to do, to take charge, as he'd done with the threat of malaria, and the bandits' ambush, and even Chancellor Sima's missing seal.

But Sky was not here.

I exhaled. "Is that why you wish to conquer the Three Kingdoms?" I asked Lei. "Because of Warlord Liu's mandate against lixia?"

Lei's smile was enigmatic and entirely unsatisfying. He turned away from me.

"Destroy the evidence," Lei called, commanding his men. "Chancellor Sima will arrive shortly; if the body is examined, it must look like a failure of the heart."

What did the prince plan to do? I wondered, watching his back. I was no closer to figuring out his schemes than I had been weeks ago. Meanwhile, the war hurtled forward, unceasing, while my useless body took its damned time to heal. *I will escape*, I repeated, over and over like a prayer. *I will return to Sky, to my army*.

I would return to my power.

I did not know if Qinglong was using me, but it did not matter. I had to use him. We were too deeply embroiled in this war of humans and spirits, and the stakes were too high. I would drag the sea dragon with me—to victory or to ruin.

There was a terrible wrongness to the scene before me: guards trampling through the lighthouse keeper's hut with little respect to his home, pouring poisoned tea out into the black sea like a libation. The old man would not even receive a proper burial. By the time Sima arrived, his body would have begun to decay.

"How gratifying," said Lei, glancing back at me. "Your face is, as always, wonderfully expressive."

"You *are* evil," I spat out.

"And you are not?" He raised a brow. "Tell me, my little saint, how many men have you killed since the start of the war?"

I fell silent. I had lost count.

Lei attached the iron-encased jade to a chain around his throat. An unimaginative hiding spot, I thought, though my own cleverness had not rewarded me. My old clothes were lost to me in New Quan. Perhaps some unfortunate palace servant had discovered my jade. Perhaps it had traded hands several times already. Lei had agreed to send word to New Quan—to look for it—but I did not lend much weight to his promise.

No matter. Once we returned to New Quan, I would find a way to remove my irons. I would track down the keeper of my jade, and I would take it from them—by persuasion or by force. Lei was right; I was no saint.

The sun had hidden itself beneath the tree line, and now we only had the echoes of its glimmering rays to guide our path. One of Lei's most trusted guards, Dian Wei, called him away in an urgent voice that made my ears prickle. Shortly afterward, the lynx, in a foul temper, decided to bite one of the mares, causing a ruckus among the remaining men. Now was my chance. With my useless arms and feeble build, no soldier had deemed me a threat worth guarding. Amid the chaos, I stole across the sand toward Lei and Dian Wei, taking small, discreet steps to compensate for my lack of balance. They'd gone behind the lighthouse and were now no more than two tall silhouettes cloaked in darkness.

"The entire delta's blocked off by Zihuan's fleet," Dian Wei was saying.

Zihuan? I hadn't heard that name before.

"How many vessels did he bring?" asked Lei.

"The entire national fleet, by the looks of it. Over a thousand combat ships."

I swallowed a curse. If Zihuan was one of Ximing's men, then their navy was vastly more formidable than anyone in Anlai suspected.

"He succeeded, then," said Lei. "For that was not his alone to command."

Dian Wei made a noise of assent. "Some of the flying barques still bear the insignia of Prince Ang." A beat of silence. "I'm sorry, Ming Lei. I know you two were close."

Lei's tone was as impassive as always, divulging nothing. "Da Ge had it coming to him. At first I believed it was kindness that made him trust and forgive Zihuan. But by the third attack, I knew it for what it was—*idiocy*."

"He was a good man."

"And now a dead man." Lei let out a long breath. "Regardless, the hour is late. This changes things."

"The siege . . ." Dian Wei said something else, too low for me to discern.

"It's all moving faster than I thought," said Lei. He seemed to hesitate before making his final decision.

"Inform the others," said the prince at last. "We ride for Tzu Wan."

The southmost city of the Three Kingdoms, I realized. *And the capital of Ximing.*

FORTY-THREE

*Zihuan may be many things, but he is not power-hungry.
He does not covet my crown; far from it, he has faithfully
served as my right-hand man in battle.*

—CAO ANG, IN A PRIVATE MISSIVE TO CAO LEI, 923

W E REACHED TZU WAN AT DAYBREAK. BUILT INTO THE CREST of a cliff, the Ximing imperial palace overlooked the vast expanse of sea, which glittered under the glow of dawn. As we neared the entrance hall of the palace, beams of morning sunlight caught the deep red and gold hues of the three-tiered pagodas, accentuating the intricate phoenix statues mounted on the tiled eaves above us.

To my surprise, Autumn awaited us in the entrance hall. Lei crossed the courtyard as soon as he spotted her, leaving me behind with his soldiers. In the hallway, I watched as the two of them spoke to each other in lowered voices. I couldn't make out their words, but I could see the way Lei's face softened when he spoke to her, laughing with an ease I rarely saw in him. Autumn, too, appeared lighter, freer. She cackled at something he said, before flushing and lowering her voice.

I looked away. The intimacy they shared . . . it wasn't my business. I was alone, without genuine friendship to rely on. My own friends were far from this place, fighting for survival. I thought of Sparrow and Zilong drunkenly singing by the campfire, their faces merry against the flickering firelight. I thought of dueling Sky in the training ring, his muttered curses as I knocked his practice sword out of his grasp.

"You're supposed to get good. But not better than me," he would complain, in his good-natured way. *"I'm training my own rival."*

I missed all of them, dearly. I missed our hard-won intimacy, the lack of deceit between us. But that too was a lie, because there'd always been some level of deception between us—the pretense that *I* had crafted, a spider's web of lies.

And like a spiderweb, it was all so easy to tear apart.

If I returned—no, *when* I returned—would my friends welcome me home?

"Let's head to your quarters," Autumn called, trotting over to me as Lei disappeared farther into the palace. "I need to rewrap your bandages."

Trailed by the same contingent of guards, Autumn led me to my new prison cell, a room just as lavish as my former accommodations, and equally confining. There was one door, heavily guarded, and no windows. I hissed with frustration.

Autumn ignored me, marveling at the progress of my recovery. "I've never seen anything like it before!" she exclaimed, after undressing my shoulder wound. She shot me an admiring look. "No wonder Lei says you're special."

Has she not guessed at the cause behind my abnormal recovery? I returned her gaze with difficulty. Perhaps, her mind dulled by pain, Autumn had not recalled my act of compulsion against her, my black magic. For surely she would not treat me with such kindness and affection if she knew the truth of what I'd done.

General Huyi had called me repulsive, disgusting. Because I was a woman? Or because I wielded lixia? Or both? Was this how Sky too saw me—now that he'd witnessed my spirit power?

I never wanted to be special, I thought, *I only wanted to belong.* Or was that also a lie? Did I even know my own desires, the sheer depths of them? Perhaps now that the dragon no longer whispered in my ear, I no longer knew what I wanted.

Trying to feign calm, I asked, "At this rate, when can I use my arms again?"

"Perhaps even two weeks," Autumn said, appraising me. "You're a marvel, Meilin."

I clenched my jaw and did not answer. She would not say such things if she knew the truth.

ONE WEEK PASSED AND I REMOVED MY SLINGS MYSELF, DESPITE Autumn's orders. My limbs were stiff and my muscles shrunken, but my desperation greater than ever before. Every night, I dreamed of iron gates, barring my path to the spirit realm. I tried again and again to harness my lixia, but it felt like trying to light a fire in a rainstorm. The iron gates absorbed every ounce of my power, until I was left bereft, emptied—a carcass fit only for crows.

ON MY NINTH DAY IN TZU WAN, AUTUMN INFORMED ME THAT LEI HAD returned to the imperial palace.

"Where did he go?" I demanded. I'd wondered why he hadn't called for me, if he'd simply lost interest. When she didn't answer, I added, "And where is Chancellor Sima?"

"You know I can't tell you that," she said gaily.

"What of my uniform?" I asked hurriedly, as Autumn opened the door and beckoned the waiting guards inside. "Any word from New Quan?"

"We're expecting another shipment in the next day or so. I'll bring your old clothes over once they're delivered." She sniffed. "They were a hassle to track down, you know. But the prince ordered it done, so what could I do?"

Lei had held true to his word. "Thank you."

Soon my jade would be mine again. Soon I would have my means of escape.

She fixed my hair, then shooed me away. "Go. You're to meet him at the lotus-viewing pavilion."

But by the time my guards led me there, someone else had already occupied the pavilion. Spotting the stranger, my guards slowed, indecision on their faces. The man was drinking pu'erh tea with several elegantly dressed courtesans, the distinctive bitter scent wafting across the pavilion. Despite the morning breeze, he had eunuchs fanning him from every side, as well as courtesans peeling mandarins for him.

Someone tapped me on the shoulder; I jumped. "Let's go somewhere else," said Lei, motioning for my guards to release me. He pulled me behind the jiashan rock garden, out of sight from the pavilion.

"Are you hiding from that man?" I asked him.

He cocked a brow. "Unfortunately, he already knows of my existence. I'm hiding *you* from that man."

Lei was in a curiously good mood today. I wondered what he'd accomplished during his recent travels.

His eyes swept over me. "I see you refused my gifts."

Upon my arrival in the capital, my wardrobe had been stocked full of extravagant dresses. I had not touched any of the garments, much preferring my simple men's clothes. "Did you really think I'd wear a gift of yours?"

Lei settled himself on a limestone rock and looked up at me, perfectly at ease. "How can I win you over?" he mused, as if to himself.

I glared down at him. "You can let me go," I said through gritted teeth. If not for the Ximing prince, I would have long escaped with the others. It was because of his malicious schemes that I was still here, farther from my people than I'd ever been, doubting my kingdom, my allies, even myself. He'd asked too many prying questions, raised too many prickling doubts, and now I could no longer parse fact from fiction.

I will escape this place, I promised myself. *But I'll come back for you one day—and take my revenge then.*

He smiled. "I have no doubt you'll be the death of me someday."

I blinked. Had he read my mind? Or were my expressions so transparent, as he claimed?

"I don't understand you," I bit out, but my words were lost in the growing din of cicadas.

Lei rose to his feet. "I cannot release you, but I can give you something else you desire." He removed his bejeweled hair ornament and handed it to his guard.

I stared at him, uncomprehending.

"Fight me," he said, smirking. "I think it would be fun to be bested by a woman."

"Fun?" I repeated. "You have a very twisted sense of enjoyment."

He shot me an insufferable grin. "But I think you do too." He cracked his neck. "In fact, I think you will find this quite enjoyable as well."

Despite my scowl, he was right. After so much pointless conversation, I was itching for a fight. "Don't underestimate me," I snarled, stretching my newly freed arms.

"Your Highness," Lei's guard interrupted, "do you think it wise—"

"We'll be careful, Dian Wei. No need to worry." Dian Wei still looked aghast. *Lei can be careful*, I thought. *I will not be*.

"No weapons," Lei said to me. "First to concede loses."

Blood rushed through my veins. The terrain was impractical; we were confined by the jiashan rock garden, the bridge, and the three-bay hall overlooking the water lily pond. Nevertheless, I could fight anywhere.

We circled. Immediately, I could tell by his mantis stance that he was trained in kung fu. But so was I.

I lunged at him first, flipping through the air. I remembered his lightning reflexes from earlier and feinted before knocking him off his feet in a surprise double maneuver. I felt his sharp exhale before we both fell. As we rolled across the cobblestones, I scrambled for the upper hand. He tried to pin me with his superior weight, but he was clearly holding back. *I warned you not to underestimate me*.

We had devolved from traditional kung fu. I did not care for honor or tradition but thought only of pain, of inflicting it. As if this were a street fight between commoners, I swiped at his face and felt my nails dig into his jaw. He swore under his breath and tried to twist my arms behind my back. I wriggled out from beneath him, using my qi to twist and jump to my feet. We were near the water's edge now.

Lei was bleeding, his hair loose and his robes creased. I didn't know what I looked like, but I didn't care. I ran toward him, aiming a butterfly twist kick at him. He dodged and grabbed my leg in the air, then slammed me to the ground. My breath whooshed out of me. He pressed his elbow against my throat. "Concede?" he grinned, breathing heavily.

My chest hummed, responding to something both distant and near. I knew that sound, that feeling, like the vibration of an internal gong. I looked down at his exposed arm pressed against my throat—his long sleeves had fallen back amid the fight—and caught a glimpse of the bracelet around his wrist. A single iron pendant hung off the band. It was larger than the one he wore around his neck—perhaps because it hid a full seal, and not a broken one.

He'd known all along about my seal. He'd *stolen* it.

Only a second had passed. I leaned forward and bit him, sinking my teeth into his arm. Startled, he relaxed his hold for an instant. I shot to my feet, dodged his attack, then ran at him full speed.

We crashed toward the pond's edge, but I stopped us moments before we fell in. I had my boot to his sternum this time, a killing blow if I had a blade. I pushed my boot a little harder than I needed to, so that his breath was constricted. I knew that I was pressing my luck with all these watching guards, but I was feeling spiteful, angry.

"Your turn," I said, panting. "Concede, Your Highness."

"It's my honor to concede to you," he replied, but there was a twinkle of amusement in his eye. Turning, he wrenched my leg with him as he pitched himself into the water.

I sank with him, sputtering as we plunged to the floor of the pond. The pond water was muddy and full of algae. Through the green haze, I saw Lei push off the ground to return to the surface. But when I tried to follow, I found my leg trapped. There was some sort of netting on the pond rocks, and my trouser leg had affixed to it. I had not taken a breath before sinking into the water, and as I panicked, trying to untangle the wires, I lost more air.

Someone touched my shoulder. I looked up to see that Lei had returned for me, a knife in his hand. Calmly, he batted my hands away and used his knife to cut the wires from my bleeding ankle.

Then we both swam to the surface.

I broke through the water and gulped down fresh air, before turning to Lei in outrage. "You—that's cheating!"

"You bit me, Meilin." Lei was treading water, out of breath and still wheezing with laughter. "You're not one to talk."

I pushed myself out of the pond, then wrung out my dripping hair. Strangely, even with the newfound knowledge of my jade, I felt lighter than I had this morning. I'd craved the thrill of a fight, the release of it. And, even more than the adrenaline, I'd missed the ability to move my limbs freely, unencumbered by pain and injury. *I'll never again take this for granted*, I promised myself, relishing the impossible health of my body. I was in such a good mood I almost wanted to laugh.

"What in the skies?"

Autumn crossed the bridge toward us, shaking her head at our bedraggled appearances. Lei offered me a hand, which I refused, climbing over the bank retaining wall myself.

"Do I want to know?" Autumn asked Lei.

"It's such a hot summer morning." Lei tried for seriousness but could not hide the mirth from his eyes. "We decided to go for a swim."

"In the water lily pond?" Autumn surveyed him with her hands on her hips. "You look like the toad prince from the Legend of the Twelve Maples."

I glanced at Lei, and involuntarily a smile tugged at my lips. Lei's usually impeccable appearance was marred by a long clump of algae perched in his hair, which fell over his forehead to resemble a rather ungainly hat. His eye makeup had smeared, coming down his cheekbones like inky black tears, and his fine indigo robes were bedraggled and dripping pond water.

"The toad prince?" Lei repeated in disbelief, his vain expression entirely at odds with his disheveled appearance. I laughed out loud.

Autumn and Lei both turned to stare at me. Hastily, I remembered myself and clapped a hand over my mouth.

But Lei was smiling, his eyes crinkling at the corners. He tugged my hand from my face. "You're lovely when you laugh," he said quietly.

I searched his copper eyes, unsure if this was another one of his games. He made everything sound like a riddle, and I was incapable of guessing the correct answer.

"No flirting!" Autumn interrupted, breaking us apart. "You already possess an excess of beautiful women in your life, Your Highness."

Lei threw an arm around Autumn, dripping pond water onto her unspoiled clothes. She tried to shove him off, to no avail. "There is no such thing as too many beautiful women," he said. "And I have a very generous heart, Autumn. There is enough room for everyone."

"Please," she said, rolling her eyes. She wriggled out of his grip and took my arm, leading me away. "There's only one person in your heart, Your Highness, and that's yourself."

We heard Lei's answering laugh even as we crossed the bridge.

FORTY-FOUR

And when you choose your friends, remember the Noble Commandant Chen Wu, who survived countless wars only to be felled by his brother-in-arms, the traitor Fan Li, against whom he did not even lift his blade.

—ANALECTS OF ZHU YUAN, 889

"YOUR UNIFORM'S ARRIVED!" AUTUMN ANNOUNCED IN MY QUARters, handing me my useless clothes. "I had a servant wash the blood out for you. Do you want to try it on?"

I shook my head in barely veiled disinterest. Autumn left me, promising to return with supper. Alone, I paced the confines of my bedchambers.

So the prince had known about my jade all along. He'd worn it in front of me for weeks, taking me for a fool.

No matter. This would only simplify things. I would use Lei's hubris against him; I would compel him, stealing both Sima's jade and my own in one fell swoop.

But how could I access my lixia? I stared at the now-familiar sight of my manacled wrists. My vision narrowed as I willed the iron to break, to bend.

Nothing happened. I'd only succeeded in giving myself a migraine.

I still had no more spirit power than the guard outside my door.

And I was still a prisoner.

I cried out in frustration and punched the wall next to me. The wood didn't budge, and the painting beside it merely wobbled. Still, my knuckles throbbed—they'd bruise. Lei would notice and likely make some unfunny remark about my temper.

I slid to the floor, pulling my knees to my chest. Lei noticed every little thing about me. He could catch the merest hint of emotion in my eyes—and guess the truth accordingly.

So why hasn't he pressed me? He could have had me interrogated, punished, tortured. Instead, he'd chosen to banter, to make small talk about mostly nothing at all. Was it because he pitied me? Or because he wished to win me over without coercion?

I recalled the steely glint of desire in his eyes. Perhaps the prince was interested in me. At times, it even felt like more than mere curiosity. This fascination . . . I could exploit it. If I did not have my sword, my lixia, I would have to rely on my other assets. Manipulate *him*, the master manipulator.

The door opened and Autumn poked her head in. She scanned the walls, looking for new damage. "Please don't destroy the painting," she said. "It's one of my favorites."

The watercolor depicted birds roosting along a plum blossom branch, with water cascading in the background. I thought it rather meaningless but kept my opinion to myself.

"You don't like it," Autumn inferred.

I shrugged.

She motioned for the servants to enter with supper. "It'll be gone soon anyway," she said with a yawn.

"Why?"

"Oh, we're removing all valuables before the . . ." Her face reddened. "Anyway, enjoy it while you can."

Before the . . . what? Were Prince Liu and his men coming here? To Tzu Wan?

"Is the palace preparing for a siege?"

Autumn batted her hands at me as if trying to bat away a fly.

"Why would Lei try to lure the Anlai army *here*, of all places?" I wondered aloud. "And where is he going instead?"

"Stop using that little head of yours!" Autumn tried to giggle, but she couldn't hide her still-flushed cheeks. "Eat your dinner while it's hot. It's Chef Min's huotui noodle soup—your favorite."

"How do you know it's my favorite?"

"Because it's the only time you actually clean your bowl," she said, in a chiding way that reminded me awfully of Xiuying. I had to take a breath at that one. *You cannot afford to be soft, Meilin.*

I blew on the steaming broth to cool it. In the army, I'd developed an enormous appetite, rivaling even Zilong in how many noodles I could consume. It was just another part of me that had withered away under captivity, along with my drive, my former zeal.

I gripped my porcelain spoon harder than I needed to. I would get it back, I promised. I would take back all that he had stolen from me, and more.

I started to eat, before stopping short. "Hm?" said Autumn, but I was lost in thought. I considered the aroma of the broth, its rich, flavorful pork painstakingly salted, dried, and fermented in a time-consuming process. The period of fermentation took a minimum of two weeks, and every chef had their own way of aging the meat. I was sure a palace chef like Chef Min had his particular way of doing it and would take great offense at buying another chef's huotui in the marketplace.

I took a huge gulp of soup, then breathed out in satisfaction. "Delicious," I said, in between enthusiastic bites. "Can you ask Chef Min to make huotui again?"

Autumn smiled at the sight of me slurping down my noodles

and only belatedly thought my request over. "I can, but he probably won't be able to finish fermenting the pork before..."

"Before?"

Autumn avoided my gaze. "This time of year, there's just a lot of change happening around the palace!" she explained, her voice pitched higher than usual. "Chef Min may be going on holiday."

A lie, I saw. A plain lie.

They were laying a trap for the Anlai army—one that would take place in less than two weeks.

Dian Wei had mentioned plans for a siege, I recalled, at Ben Niu.

"*This changes things*," Lei had said. "*It's all moving faster than I thought.*"

Indeed, I agreed, trying not to panic. Depending on where Sky's camp was now stationed in Ximing, it could take me anywhere from three to twelve days to find them on foot. That left me with only about a day's leeway to warn Sky of the impending trap. And that was all only if I managed to escape *now*.

I turned away from my bowl to think, only for my attention to snag on the brass mirror behind me, which I'd studiously avoided looking at. My eyes... they were dark. Dull.

Do they no longer shine gold?

"Meilin, are you listening?"

I blinked at Autumn. "Sorry?"

She sighed. "Did you need anything else? If not, I'll be back in three days. I have to settle some personal affairs."

Because she was preparing to leave Tzu Wan.

Time, I thought desperately. *Time is always against me.*

"Actually, I had a question," I said. I went to the wardrobe and rifled through the colorful silks. "What kind of dress does the prince favor?"

Autumn eyed me before parsing through the clothes. "This

one," she said, holding out a dark red silk with a low back. It was an unusual style, not in vogue in Chuang Ning. "It shows off the neck," she explained, running a hand over the dress's collar. "He's fond of such things. Don't ask me how I know." Her nose crinkled.

I remembered standing before him in his bedchamber, his eyes snagging on my exposed throat. He had been drunk that night. If I could get him drunk again...

"You have a slender, elegant neck," remarked Autumn. "One must take advantage of youth, as they say. Beauty is the—"

"—wisdom of women. I know."

She set the dress down on my bed. Up close, I saw that her expression was pained. I wondered if this hurt her; if my presence, somehow, was hurting her.

"Autumn. I never meant to—to get in the way between you two."

Her brows dipped. "What do you mean?"

My cheeks burned. "I know you and the prince are... close..."

To my surprise, Autumn giggled. "The prince is like a brother to me, Meilin. He's actually my di di's age." She sat back on the bed. "He's only twenty-two, you know."

Twenty-two? That meant he was only four years older than me. And yet the confidence with which he carried himself lent him an air of maturity. *A false one*, I thought, *like everything else about him*.

"Actually," she said, lowering her voice, "I don't lean that way."

"You don't lean...?"

"I don't like men."

"Oh... oh!" I clapped my hands over my mouth, then glanced at the door to the keting. "Sorry, I-I didn't mean to pry—"

"It's all right," she said. "If I didn't want to tell you, I wouldn't have."

It all sounded very simple when she put it that way. "My mother too . . ." An unnamed instinct compelled me to speak. "She was like you. She once told me she loved women too."

"You two must be very close, for her to tell her own daughter this."

"My parents had a . . . loveless marriage. It was no secret," I said. I did not think my mother and I particularly close, and I hated for Autumn to assume so.

She frowned. She opened her mouth, and I knew she was about to say something kind or comforting, and I could not bear it. I did not know why I'd bothered to tell her this, when I knew she would only feed it to Lei, to serve as further ammunition against me.

"I'll try on the dress," I said. "If it's not too much to ask, could you let the prince know I'd like to see him tonight?"

"He's gone out into the city," Autumn said. She hesitated, her teeth worrying at her bottom lip. "He won't be back until late tonight."

Sima had two pieces of his seal already, and Lei had the third. I was running out of time. No, I was entirely out of time. "I can wait up," I said. "If he's willing to see me."

"I'm sure he's willing," Autumn replied. "He enjoys spending time with you, you know." Her eyes were dark, imbued with meaning.

I looked away. Lei did not care for me, I reminded myself. He was obsessed with me, which was not the same thing. I was nothing more than a novelty to him. A girl who could wield a sword, like a monkey who could dance or sing songs.

Autumn had said it best: there was only one person in his heart, and that was himself.

And yet, as I ran a hand along the dress, I recalled what Lei had said about his mother. His mother had been taken from him too, though she had not wished to go. She had wanted her son; she had loved him. And he had been forced to watch her gruesome execution from the front row. His father had ordered him not to look away.

But I could not pity him. I tried on the dress, then studied my reflection.

He was my enemy, and when the time came, I would kill him.

FORTY-FIVE

*How can a sparrow understand the grace of an ibis? How can
a common man understand the strength of Prince Zihuan?*
—CHRONICLES OF THE THREE KINGDOMS, 954

MY DRESS LOOKED LIKE SOMETHING AN IMPERIAL COURTESAN might wear. My robes were filmy and diaphanous, befitting the sultry summer air, with a near-transparent silk sash wrapped around my bare shoulders, highlighting the swell of my breasts.

If Xiuying saw me like this, she would be appalled. But if I did not do this, she would never see me at all. I tinted my lips to match my scarlet dress, then pinned up my hair with a simple wooden hairpiece. Within the coils of my long hair, I hid my knife.

Lei called for me long after sundown. I wondered what he'd been doing out in the city, this late at night. I would have to gauge his temper, reading his mood to inform how I would act. And yet I was well accustomed to doing this, for I had lived with my father for eighteen years.

"Bring her in."

The prince's voice was low and rasping, like the crackle of a dying fire. My stomach swooped at the sound. It was nerves, I told myself. I was merely nervous.

I entered the prince's sitting room. My guards remained at the door, fanning out in a uniform line. There were three of them by the entrance, and three by the door leading to Lei's bedchamber. I wondered if there were more stationed inside, guards I could not see. This would prove inconvenient.

Lei emerged from his bedchamber, leaving his door open. I could see an open-air balcony opposite his bed, overlooking the sea. His rooms were peaceful, luxurious. Of course. He was a prince. He lived a spoiled, privileged life. He wore silks and sapphires. Beautiful women likely visited him every night.

But tonight, there was only me. I straightened as he crossed the threshold, unbuttoning his riding cloak. His hair had been tied up in a topknot, though a few strands had escaped during the night's activities. A streak of dirt smudged his cheekbone, and his usually immaculate nails were caked with dried blood.

As I inspected him, he afforded me equal attention. A smile opened his face as his eyes skipped from my tinted lips to my bare shoulders, to the column of my exposed neck. Involuntarily, I touched a hand to my throat.

"I knew red was your color," he said. "Your beauty rivals the moon, fair Meilin."

I ignored this. "Where were you?" I asked, taking a step toward him. None of his guards moved. *So they will allow me to approach him like this.* "I was waiting for you."

"Out and about," he answered vaguely, dipping his hands in a porcelain water basin. Blood and debris dispersed in the water. "Apologies for keeping you waiting."

"Let me help you," I said, coming up beside him. My heart hammering in my chest, I took his hands in mine. His touch was surprisingly cold, as if he'd been out in the snow. I dipped his hand back into the basin and gently washed the dirt and dust from his skin.

I noticed a jagged cut trailing up his left arm. I began to roll up his sleeve before he stopped me, placing his hand over mine. *So my jade remains on his left arm.*

He was watching me, his eyes flickering like flames in the wind. "You're feeling particularly charitable today." Up close, he smelled of sweat and cedar. It was not an unpleasant scent.

"When the mood strikes," I replied, feigning nonchalance. I dried his hands, then moved toward the table. "Would you like a drink?"

"Only if you drink with me."

I poured him a full cup. "I don't believe in surrendering to vices."

"Ah," he said, taking the wine jug from my hands and pouring a second glass. "But life is too short not to spend it enjoying oneself." He offered me the glass he'd poured. "Just one drink, Meilin, in honor of your beauty."

I accepted it, clinking glasses with him, then pretending to take a sip. "Is it my beauty," I asked, trying to temper my curiosity, "that intrigues you?"

"One of many things."

"It was my eyes," I remembered. "That was why you first noticed me. Back in Xi Lan." His cup was empty, so I filled it again. "Why?"

His expression turned inward. He accepted the drink and threw it back in one fluid motion. "I've told you of my mother," he answered at last. "But what I told you—"

The door crashed open. I shot to my feet. *Who would dare barge in on the prince?* I wondered, turning to stare at the intruder.

The man wore more jewelry than anyone I'd ever seen. Gold diamonds dripped from his ears, matching the equally loud collar at his neck. His long silky hair was done up in an elaborate buyao pin of lapis lazuli, which complemented the hue of his satin robes. With all the jewelry he wore, I thought, it was a wonder he could lift his head at all.

I'd seen him before, I recalled, at the lotus-viewing pavilion. He was the man Lei had been trying to avoid.

"Leave us," the intruder commanded the guards. To my astonishment, they obeyed.

"Zihuan," said Lei, rising. He bowed in deference, yet somehow managed to make even this gesture appear mocking. "Or should I call you Crown Prince now?"

This man is the crown prince of Ximing?

"Why not *Ge*?" Cao Zihuan said smilingly. "How close we used to be. Though you were always closer with First Brother."

Abruptly, the crown prince turned to me. "Who's this?" he asked, inspecting me with a look that left me cold. He took a step forward and I went stiff with fear, my body recalling General Huyi in a way my mind could not.

Lei slipped between us, offering his brother a drink. "An old friend," he said. "She's a poison master."

Zihuan wrinkled his nose in distaste, taking several pronounced steps away from me. "I never understand you and your hobbies, Di," he said, shooting me a very different look now, this one accompanied by a shudder. He sipped his wine, then clapped Lei on the back with a grin. "At least you have a pretty face to look at as you bleed out on the floor."

Lei gave him a practiced smile. "She trains me well."

I adjusted my trailing sleeves, making sure my iron bands were hidden beneath the gauze. I did not trust Lei, but I trusted his brother even less. Without making a sound, I offered the crown prince a low bow, which he did not acknowledge. Then I took several steps back to stand against the wall, trying to hide my nerves. How long would the crown prince stay?

Zihuan selected a plump golden mandarin from the fruit platter on the aiji table. "Peel this," he ordered me, before hesitating. He seemed to recall my supposed profession and scowled. "Never mind," he said, choosing a slice of pale dragon fruit instead.

I watched the corner of Lei's mouth twitch, before he hid his smile beneath a mask of calm. "To what do I owe the pleasure of your company, Ge?"

"I was bored," Zihuan said, collapsing on the silk shafa on the dais. "I wanted to see you before I leave." He yawned. "I heard you got your hands on a new spirit medium from Anlai... where is he?"

Lei didn't bat an eye. "Dead," he said without hesitation. "He cracked too easily under interrogation. I barely lifted a finger."

"Pity," said Zihuan. "He could've proven useful if he'd turned." He bit into another slice of dragon fruit, then, with his mouth full, said, "Next time, Di, be more careful. When we play our cards right, the Anlai practitioners are more than happy to betray their kingdom. Particularly after their own warlord's declared he'll feed them to the dogs."

Lei's expression was one of mild regret. "There was nothing to be done in this case, unfortunately. The boy went mad." He chose a seat that kept both his brother and me within his line of sight. "They usually do."

Zihuan raised his cup at that. "Sima's certainly well on his way," he quipped, and the two brothers laughed together.

The back of my neck crawled.

"You know, he wrote me a deranged letter the other day, demanding we delay our attack on Chuang Ning until his seal's made whole. What nonsense," Zihuan said, scoffing. "The fool wants to wait until we're old and gray and half in the grave. Sometimes I wonder if he truly wants his revenge on the Liu clan, or if even that's only talk."

"Well, the old man has waited for ten years," said Lei, voice wry.

Zihuan shook his head with disdain. "You probably haven't yet heard—we finally came to an agreement today. Thank the skies Father sided with me. Sima will be off on his inane scavenger hunt, but at least he's agreed to assist from his little hidey-hole." He sneered. "As for me, I set sail for the siege tomorrow. Finally."

I inhaled sharply. The crown prince would set sail *tomorrow*? To lay siege to the capital of Anlai?

Qinglong was not lying to me, I realized with a pang. There *was* a future where Chuang Ning burned. An increasingly likely future.

Xiuying would take the kids and run, I told myself. She would read the signs and know to escape to the countryside.

Or would she? Xiuying had never witnessed the power of lixia, never learned anything about spirit mediums except their supposed extinction. And most Chuang Ning residents believed their walls impenetrable. The Anlai capital had only been breached once in known history; even then, the walls had never fallen. Rebel spies had simply infiltrated the Forbidden City, then opened the gates from within.

Ximing could not possibly breach Chuang Ning with its meager forces. Only through the phoenix's seal did they stand a chance. How much power had Sima accumulated in my absence? I wondered. And why did he seek revenge on the Liu clan?

Old memories took on new meaning. "*You look just like your father,*" the chancellor had told Sky at Xi Lan, his voice threaded with bitterness. I'd always known that Sima had incited this war for the sake of personal vengeance, following the death of his wife and child. And yet, though it was obvious in hindsight, the connection had slipped my mind until now. But of course—Sima's target was the warlord of Anlai. Sky's father. That was why he fought for Ximing.

I had failed to connect the dots because I did not wish to. For I could clearly recall Sima's memories—the brutality of that general, the things he had done to an innocent mother and child. They were not things I wished to associate with Sky.

Sky, who was softhearted and kind. Sky, who would never commit such atrocities.

But my traitorous mind conjured the sound of Sky's blade whizzing through the air, the sight of his stony indifference as he killed a man in cold blood. He was kind until he was not. Soft until he was not.

Would he make a good leader for his people? Or would he never become ruler at all—would it be his father and older brothers who ruled? Was Anlai any better than its neighboring kingdoms, or did it only possess greater resources due to luck rather than divine favor?

My head hurt from the enormity of these questions. These were matters beyond me, I reminded myself, beyond the scope of my concern. The only thing I cared about was the safety and well-being of those I loved. It did not matter who ruled the Three Kingdoms, if Tianjia remained separated or united. Other men, men with cleverer words and sharper eyes, could answer such questions. As for me, I would secure my own freedom, and live as I wished to.

All these thoughts came and went in a matter of seconds. When I remembered myself, I looked up to find both Zihuan and Lei staring at me. Had they asked me something?

"Come here," Zihuan said impatiently, as if not for the first time.

Uncertainly, I looked to Lei, which only served to further incense the crown prince. "Now," he added.

I approached with caution. I kept my head down but could feel his lecherous eyes inspecting my body. For an irrational moment, I thought of gouging out his eye, just as I'd done to General Huyi back in the prison tower. But I'd had power then.

I was powerless now.

"Sit," he said, grabbing my arm and yanking me beside him on the shafa. "How long has he been keeping you here, my pet?" he asked me, though he easily could've asked Lei instead.

I could smell the opium on him, a different variety than the kind my father favored. Still, the noxious scent left me faint. I took a shallow breath, careful not to inhale through my nose.

"Look at me," he commanded, and I flinched but obeyed. Under the candlelight, his eyes were as light as his brother's, so pale they looked as though they could see straight through you. Yet unlike Lei's, they betrayed his every emotion. I could see his greed. He coveted what his brother possessed.

He leaned toward me, his eyes closing as he inhaled. "How does poison always smell so sweet?" he murmured. Then he kissed me.

I was so shocked I reacted without thinking—and bit him.

My heart stopped at my own daring. Zihuan swore, shoving me back against the shafa as he checked his lip for blood. Beyond him, I saw Lei standing now, eyes flashing. Zihuan appeared not to notice his brother. Instead, pinning me down, he reached for the candle on the aiji table. With a sneer, he dripped the hot wax onto my exposed collarbones.

I screamed, first in surprise, then in pain. The burning wax pooled in the hollow of my collarbones as I struggled against him.

Suddenly, his weight was lifted off me. Lei had an arm around his brother but wore a smiling expression, as if this were but a joke.

THE NIGHT ENDS WITH FIRE

With a quick jerk of his head, he motioned for me to go into the adjoining room.

I fled, the skin on my collarbones still blistering with heat.

"Ge, forgive me. You know I don't like to share," said Lei lightly, sounding both unassuming and firm at the same time.

Despite my fear, I lingered in the keting doorway, eyeing the two brothers standing beside each other. All their earlier ease had belied a now obvious truth: the two of them were not friends.

"Behave, Di Di." Zihuan still held the burning candle in his left hand. Now he closed the gap between them and pressed the candle flame directly against Lei's throat. I choked down a gasp as Lei stood, unmoving, his skin kindling beneath the flame. How could his own brother do this to him?

Several eternally long seconds passed. Zihuan watched, waiting for a sound, a look, anything. The hot wax had begun to drip down Lei's throat to his chest, under his robes. How much pain he must be in, and yet his half-lidded eyes made him look merely bored. Only his posture gave him away—his back ramrod straight, unbending.

Time seemed to slow. At last Zihuan released him, frowning at the angry red marks left in his wake. "You know Rea's betrothal ceremony is coming up soon," Zihuan told him, the threat palpable in his voice. "You've worked so tirelessly to keep her safe. Such a pity if it all came to naught."

Carelessly, the crown prince dropped the burning candle on the floor. Lei stepped on the flame, snuffing it out before it could spread.

"I look forward to seeing you in Anlai," Zihuan said with a smirk. "You can address me as Your Majesty then."

With that, the crown prince took his leave.

FORTY-SIX

Her beauty was so startling that birds would fall from the sky, and fish forget to swim.
—CHRONICLES OF THE THREE KINGDOMS, 954

I RAN TO LEI, NOT NEEDING TO FEIGN MY CONCERN AS I SURVEYED his extensive burns.

"I'll call for Autumn," I said, turning to the door to summon the guards outside. But Lei stopped me.

"There's no need," he said evenly. "It'll only worry her. I can deal with something like this on my own."

I swallowed, not trusting myself to answer. How strange that he would think of Autumn's well-being before his own, even at a time like this. Stranger still that someone could be both kind *and* despicable; that someone could hold these dualities separate.

Lei left my side, opening a lacquered cabinet that I'd assumed held his wine jars. Instead, he unrolled a swath of bandages. I went to him and took his place, finding all sorts of medical supplies hidden within. Recalling what Xiuying had taught me, I dampened a washcloth with water, then motioned for him to sit.

He appraised me silently before obeying. The night had taken a turn I hadn't expected, but I was still here to get in his good graces. I sat beside him and pressed the cold compress against his raw, blistering skin, then fumbled with the ties of his robes, trying to inspect the damage beneath. He hesitated, and for a moment I thought he would push me away. But he only undid the ties himself, revealing a spectacular array of old and new scars. It was a sight unbefitting a pampered prince, one who supposedly spent all his time drinking and flirting.

"Who did this to you?" I asked quietly. "Your brother?"

Lei's smile was rueful. This time, he drank directly from the wine jar. "He had help."

Your father, I thought but did not say. How horrific. Lei had grown up a prince, but in a palace of vipers.

Neither of us speaking, I cleaned his wounds and made an ointment of honey and peiji root, applying the salve to his throat and chest. Lei watched me as I worked, but his gaze no longer discomforted me. I had greater concerns on my mind.

Lei's personal guards have not yet returned. And he is on his third jar of wine.

I finished my work, dabbing my hands on the used washcloth. Before I could rise, Lei caught my wrist. "Thank you," he said. "*Meilin.*"

Heat bloomed across my stomach at the way his voice curled around my name. He saw my expression and brought his lips to the inside of my wrist. *Cedar and jasmine, like a dream.* I did not know if I wished to push him away or draw him closer.

Lightly, he ran his fingertips over my exposed collarbones, then rested his hand gently against my throat. I shuddered despite myself, gooseflesh breaking out across my skin. My own burns had been negligible, for the hot wax had only touched me momentarily. But you could still see the faint pinkish vestiges left by the candle, which Lei now traced with his delicate touch. I looked at the prince's face, impossibly beautiful.

He was not pure evil as I'd initially thought, but that did not make him *good*. In fact, it was only in relation to these other monsters that I viewed him in any positive light at all. And yet, even knowing all this, I could not deny the way his presence aroused something within me, a low tug in my gut.

He cupped the back of my neck and, involuntarily, I closed my eyes. But instead of our lips meeting, he merely kissed me on the forehead, then on the rim of my ear, my neck. I felt my insides turn to hot liquid. I was enjoying this too much, I thought, bemused and conflicted and furious all at once. This close to him, I could feel his warmth enveloping me, and instead of feeling repulsion I only craved more of it. How was I able to enjoy this, I wondered, when the fate of all that I loved was at stake?

Because you're selfish, the voice in my head whispered. *You're selfish and self-absorbed like your mother. You're greedy and overindulgent like your father.*

I forced my eyes open and looked up at Lei, at last admitting my attraction to him. There was less separating us than I'd thought. Undeniably, I was drawn to him—for we shared the same warped greed within us.

Lei pulled away. He was waiting for me, I recognized. But waiting for me to do what?

"You intervened, with your brother." My voice came out unexpectedly hoarse. "For my sake."

His eyes darkened, his pupils huge and dilated. "You are not his to toy with."

I studied him, using silence as my weapon.

"You are mine," he said, and this time, it felt like a confession.

The corner of my mouth twitched. He was thoroughly drunk, I could tell. "You must earn my trust first," I told him.

His fingers wound through my loose hair. "And what have I been doing, all this time?"

I thought of our sparring contest at the lotus pavilion, the many dresses and meaningless gifts he'd showered upon me. "Fooling around."

His smile was like a honed blade. "Was it not to your liking?"

"I am a difficult prisoner to please."

"You don't have to be a prisoner," he said quietly. "There are other choices afforded to you."

"Like your lap dog?" I asked, a challenge in my voice.

"I would like you in my lap." He grinned. "But no. I could offer you far more distinguished positions. You could make a very competent general, Meilin."

"Impossible." It was a bald lie.

"Because you're a woman?" He raised a brow. "Not every empire need be so misogynistic, you know. I see the potential in you, even if your Anlai prince does not."

Don't bring Sky into this, I wanted to say, anger rising in my throat. But anger hardened my resolve. So instead, I kissed him.

I heard a sound of low surprise at the back of his throat. Then he recovered himself, lowering us both to the sofa. He kissed me back, and I was reminded again of how much more experienced he was than I. His hands moved deftly across my stomach, around my waist. His tongue soon followed, and I gasped, out of breath, quivering with suppressed anticipation.

"Cao Ming Lei," I whispered, and I watched the knot at his throat lift in response. He pressed his lips to the rim of my ear, then the hollow of my neck, and I felt feverish warmth sweep across my skin.

"*You have a very twisted sense of enjoyment,*" I'd told him, in the jiashan rock garden. But apparently so did I.

His hand slid lower, slipping beneath the folds of my dress. I gasped in shock as I felt the foreign weight of his palm against my breast, then gasped from a different sort of emotion as his finger traced teasing patterns against my prickling skin. As if lowering himself before a shrine, he bowed his head and fit his full lips over my breast, his tongue moving so expertly I thought I might implode with feeling. Teeth soon followed, until I squirmed with want.

He could feel my urgency, but he only smiled, enjoying himself, enjoying me. The way he smiled—like he had wanted to do this for a very long time. He brought his mouth back to mine, deepening our kiss; I could taste the wine on his tongue. Meanwhile, his hands ventured farther south, lifting the hem of my skirt until it rode up my stomach. Gently, he brushed his thumb against the inside of my thigh, and I felt my entire being tremble in expectation. I could feel heat spiraling in my core, made worse by the way his fingers carefully circled the apex of my legs, coming not too close, nor too far. I couldn't help myself; I let out a strangled sound, of pain or pleasure I couldn't quite tell.

He raised his head momentarily, a small smile flitting across his mouth. With his ink-black hair askew, his full lips swollen, and his pale eyes brightened with desire, I had never seen anyone so beautiful. My hands tightened around him, wishing he could be mine. Wishing this could be real.

But it was not.

I closed my eyes, breathed in, breathed out. Then my eyes flicked open.

Lei said my name softly, murmuring admirations. I allowed my hands to explore the broad expanse of his shoulders, his chest, until they lingered at the back of his neck. Fiddling with the clasp of his necklace.

Lei shifted, but I pressed my mouth more firmly against his, holding him in place. *There.* I felt the clasp come undone, then wrenched the chain from his neck. In a flash, I twisted, one hand seizing his bracelet, the other pressing a knife against his throat.

Lei grimaced in pain but did not try to move. The skin at his throat had already been scraped raw from flame, and now I had a blade pressed against his still-open wounds. I met his eyes coldly, burying any feeling for him.

"How long have you known?" he rasped, his eyes flitting to the broken bracelet I'd wrenched from his arm.

"That you stole my jade?" I asked. His lack of contrition infuriated me. "Since our duel."

"Ah," he said. His throat bobbed against my knife. "I've been careless with you."

He said something else, but I did not hear him. Gripping my long-lost jade in one hand, I willed my iron cuffs to bend, to break. *Wood, fire, earth, metal, water.* I cycled through each element, again and again. *I have so much to give you*, I thought desperately. I tried channeling lixia until I tasted blood on my tongue.

I looked down at my irons. Only a tiny, narrow fissure had appeared. It made no difference at all.

I swallowed a curse. I could not get through the palace guards without lixia, and even then, I doubted I had the ability to compel so many in so little time.

Where did that leave me? I would have to resort to traditional methods.

A gust of wind blew in through the open balcony, setting the gauzy curtains aflutter. I could not see the sea below, but I could hear its rumbling tides, a sound so constant I'd begun to tune it out. A thrill of fear stirred in my chest. A plan took root in my mind.

But what about Lei? The strategic move would be to kill him. Either now, or later, for he would have to die. And when would I get another opportunity like this, with the Ximing prince weaponless and inebriated, fully at my mercy?

And yet I hesitated. Lei saw my hesitation.

"Guards!" he shouted. I swore, dragging him up with me.

Dian Wei entered first, rushing inside before freezing at the sight of my knife pressed to Lei's throat.

"If you take so much as a step toward me, I will slit your prince's throat. I swear it," I said, my voice ringing out into the silence. I pushed down on the edge of my knife and heard Lei's audible intake of breath. A trickle of blood ran down his skin, smearing against my hand. Dian Wei did not move.

I forced Lei toward the balcony. "If you wanted to look at the stars, Meilin, you could've just asked," he muttered. It was like him to try for levity, even now.

Outside, the night sky was awash in moonlight and stars. The full moon was almost upon us. In Anlai, many believed in using the constellations to decide the course of one's future. Even my mother's matchmaker had once called upon the stars to align the fate of my parents. To decide the date of their matrimony, and the date of their firstborn's arrival. The stars had predicted I would be a boy. The stars were wrong.

"I don't believe in stargazing," I told him. *I believe in making my own fate.*

I smashed the hilt of the knife against his temple, leapt onto the railing, and prayed to my ancestors, to the mother I'd lost. She who had once been as wild as me, as reckless.

I could hear guards scrambling toward the balcony, drawing their swords. Below me, the crashing waves of the sea sounded eerily similar to the screams of men.

"Don't—" Lei stirred, his voice hoarse. "Meilin, it's too dangerous—"

It *was* dangerous. But so was my entire existence.

"I told you not to underestimate me," I said.

Then I jumped.

PART III

FORTY-SEVEN

In the beginning, before Zhuque had grown accustomed to the mortality of men, she formed an attachment to her first human vessel, caring for him as a mother would a son. And when that vessel fell ill to madness, she wept for him on the Red Mountains, her tears born of selfless love. Those tears transformed into an eternal spring, healing the son she'd grown to love, and yet taking him from her all the same. To this day, pilgrims believe that an ancient spring can be found within the Red Mountains, and if a fortuitous traveler finds it, they will be forever cleansed.

—A HISTORY OF LIXIA, 762

Falling into the water felt like slamming into a brick wall. My body screamed in protest as I plunged into the churning waves, sinking into the sea. Despite the oppressive heat of summer, the water was frigid. My limbs grew numb and unresponsive, my brain slowing from lack of air.

"Fire and water are lifelong rivals. But, Haiyang, we need not be enemies."

My countless choices rippled out before me. Even in retrospect, it was impossible to know if I'd made the right decisions.

"Would you surrender yourself to the world, or would you make the world yours?"

"How long were you planning to get away with this? Your crimes are punishable by death!"

"Tell me, my little saint, how many men have you killed since the start of the war?"

"More often than not, the spirit will overpower its host, assuming control over the medium's body and mind."

"From the moment I laid eyes on you . . . I knew there was something wrong with you."

I sank, deeper and deeper.

"They would never let a woman get away with something like this."

"Something like what?"

"They would never let a woman hold on to power."

I had been so young then, impossibly young. I had ventured out into the world believing in the possibility of wonder, the possibility that life outside my bedroom walls could be more tremendous than anything I could imagine at home. It was tremendous, yes, and wretched, and senseless, and savage.

And still I wanted more of it.

My hunger roused me. In the depths of the sea, I drew upon my greed, my insatiable ambition. I cried out to my shadow self, my truest self, and reached for her through her iron imprisonment. I understood now why I was called a perversion. It was unnatural for a woman to have this kind of ambition, and yet *I existed*. My existence was my birthright, and it would be my justification.

My manacles fell apart, as malleable as the monk's iron, which he'd folded with his bare hands. I focused my qi, blood pounding as if laced with a drug, and honed my lixia against my jade. The iron encasement did not so much crumble as explode, shards flying in every direction in the dark water. A sharp, lancing pain went through me, so acute I felt as if my bones were breaking. I cried out, but my joy was so great it overcame the pain. For the sea dragon's jade—*my* jade—flared in the water, a brilliant, intimate blue.

I could feel my qi waning, overwhelmed by the sheer flood of lixia. I knew, somehow, that something core within me was broken, irrevocably so. No matter. *My power*, I thought, *how I have missed you.*

"*You survived*," breathed Qinglong, startling me. I'd forgotten what it was like to have his presence in my mind.

"I always do."

I felt his flicker of pride. He was pleased with me, I could tell, but I did not return his affection. Imagining the willow trees of my youth, I forced my guard up, hiding what I'd learned in imprisonment. Just as he could keep secrets, so could I.

In the depths of the sea, my senses returned to me in full force. I willed my eyes open and began to swim with vehemence. The tides spurred me onward, propelling me with a speed I could not hope to achieve on my own.

Awake and whole, I felt my memories return to me tinged with a surreal quality, as if they'd occurred to someone else. Someone who'd lost the shape of her dreams, her desires. Someone who'd come to accept her own passivity, like a sated pig accustomed to the chopping block. I clenched my jade in my fist, reveling in its quiet yet constant pulse.

I won't be imprisoned like that ever again. I had lost myself in captivity. I had grown soft, callow, enamored with my captor like a child who mistakes a viper for a pet. I swallowed the lump in my throat and made another promise then: the prince would pay.

THE WAVES DEPOSITED ME AT THE NORTHERN TIP OF THE WANGZHI Belt. From there, I tracked the Anlai army through word of mouth, relying on my fragmented memory of Sky's military strategy. I was careful to steal a disguise my first night, and from then on, I stayed away from large ports and metropolises. Though I doubted word from the Ximing capital had traveled quickly, still I erred on the side of caution.

I had never worn so much jade. Without a needle and thread, I kept my own seal stored deep in my pocket, unable to sew it into the lining of my tunic. As for Sima's jade, I reclasped the prince's chain and wore it around my neck. My iron resistance had increased during my time in Tzu Wan, but it was not infallible. It pained me to wear Sima's iron-encased jade, but I could see no other alternatives. Even with my own jade freed, the minuscule amount of iron I wore around my neck prevented me from using compulsion, unless I wished to bring myself to the verge of collapse. Elemental magic, always my weakness, was now entirely inaccessible. So I resorted to my former techniques. Stealing and hiding, lying and running away. Eating and drinking only enough to keep me alive.

On the dawn of the sixth day, I came upon my camp. Adrenaline and triumph rushed through me as I shouted my name and position to the patrol guards, emphasizing my northern Chuang Ning accent. Little Pig recognized me, lowering his bow.

"Ren?" he asked in disbelief. "I'll take you to the commander's tent right away."

My exhilaration faded as I recalled the circumstances in which Sky and I had parted ways. He knew the truth of me now.

"Is the commander awake?" Little Pig asked the guard stationed outside Sky's tent.

He nodded. "He's preparing for the council meeting in an hour." He eyed me skeptically. "Can this wait?"

I touched my topknot self-consciously. I hadn't washed in days, and my clothes looked as if I'd taken a tumble down a hill. Which I had. Twice.

"I can come back later," I said, my cheeks flushing.

"Wait." The familiarity of Sky's voice set my nerves on fire. "Who's there?"

I opened my mouth, then closed it. "H-Hai Ren . . . sir."

There was a long, fatal silence. I stared at the grass, willing my eyes not to well. *Sky most likely wants nothing to do with me.*

Only now, when the possibility of this loss felt real and immediate, did I recognize how much my affection for him had grown. If he turned me away, the hurt would be enormous. *Again*, I thought, *again I have made myself vulnerable.*

"Come in."

Palms slick with sweat, I entered Sky's tent. I did not know if I tripped or simply collapsed, but somehow I fell to my knees, prostrating myself before my prince. The one who had believed in me. Who had called me his friend before anyone else had.

Tears pricked the back of my eyes. "Your Highness," I said, forehead pressed to the ground. "I beg forgiveness for my deceit, for—"

Sky cut me off, lifting me and wrapping me in his arms. "Meilin," he murmured, and his voice was so familiar I started to sob uncontrollably. "It is I who must ask for your forgiveness."

Am I dreaming? I wondered deliriously. Or had I compelled him somehow, without knowing it? I had tried to envision the worst possible outcome many times on my journey, to prepare myself, to harden my heart. I had imagined a screaming argument, a cold-blooded arrest, an unforgiving execution. But never had I let myself imagine this: *forgiveness.*

I drew back. "But . . . you know, don't you?" The walls of my throat thickened as I tried to bring myself to speak the words. "You know about my . . . black magic?"

Sky wiped wetness from my cheeks. "I am not my father, Meilin."

I stared at him in wonder. "H-how?"

"Commander!" Someone called from outside the tent walls. "General Yu requests an audience."

Sky sighed, releasing me. "Not now!" he shouted, in a different tone of voice. To me, he said, "We should talk to Winter."

I shot him a bemused look. "Your brother?"

Sky rubbed the back of his neck. "It's true I was raised to be ... less than accepting of spirit power. And perhaps I would have been, if not for Winter."

"I-I don't understand."

He lowered his voice. "Let's just say you're not the first person I know to hide a certain affinity."

I absorbed this silently, rendered speechless. Once, I had glimpsed a figure like Winter's in the spirit realm but had thought nothing of it, distracted by Chancellor Sima at the time. Was Winter a dreamer like me, wandering the in-between realm without a spirit seal?

"Commander! The horses are standing. Do you have any final messages for the scouts to deliver?"

Sky began to strap on his blades, forehead furrowing in thought. "No," he said, before opening the tent flap. "I'll reconvene with them outside Tzu Wan."

That shook me out of my daze. "Tzu Wan? Why ..."

I trailed off as Sky glanced at me, raising a brow. I knew it wasn't my place to question his orders, especially not in public, but we had to speak candidly, and soon. With growing impatience, I listened as the soldier rattled off a never-ending list of items Sky had to attend to. I shot Sky a pointed look; he nodded.

"Call for Wang Sparrow of Third Platoon and Luo Tao from my personal guard," Sky interrupted. "Have them meet us at Winter's tent. I owe my brother a visit."

"Yes, sir."

"What's going on?" I asked him, just as the patrol gong sounded, marking the hour. Sky swore under his breath. "And postpone the council meeting!" he called after his guard.

It was unlike Sky to forget even minor details. *The strain must be getting to him.*

"Ren," he began, as we crossed the campgrounds. "It's been... madness lately. We've taken most of Ximing, but they've wrought equal destruction on the southern border. And our victories have not been half as lucrative. While they've stolen our steel, impressed our men, and sated themselves on our crops, we've obtained nothing but waste. In the Yun region, they even went so far as to contaminate their own canal. Can you imagine? The savagery of it, to poison your own land and people."

As he spoke, I took a closer look at his face. Dark circles ringed his eyes, and his cheekbones looked razor-sharp, birdlike. How bad was his insomnia getting?

We stopped in front of another tent, this one even larger than Sky's. "Make sure we're not interrupted," Sky instructed the guards stationed outside.

"Yes, sir."

Sky held the tent flap open for me. I stepped inside, then startled to find Winter standing in the entrance, much closer than I'd expected. I attempted a graceless, ungainly bow, unsure if I should salute him as my commander, or bow to him as my prince.

"Hai Ren, is it?" he asked, ignoring my clumsiness.

"Yes, sir."

"There is power in a name," he said lightly. I looked up at him, meeting his gaze.

Winter was as pale as his namesake, his skin as white and clear as fresh snow. I had no idea how he maintained his complexion with all the marching we had done under the southern sun. Perhaps he simply remained in his palanquin all day, refusing to leave the shade even for battle.

For that matter, I could not imagine him engaging in warfare. His nails were perfectly polished, each filed to a uniform length. His hands were unscarred, long and delicate as a musician's. He was tall, the same height as Sky, yet slender, statuesque. His features were androgynous, as was his clothing.

Sky noticed me staring and cleared his throat. I blushed and backed away. Why did this tent feel awfully small?

"Ge, I was thinking," said Sky, taking a seat. "What if you wrote a letter to Father, explaining the advantages of lixia, particularly in this climate?" His brows drew inward. "Father won't be happy about it, but he may acquiesce."

"Father won't be happy about a lot of things, particularly if I am involved," Winter said, with an unconcerned air. At my look of confusion, he added, "Our father is not very fond of his sixth son."

His bluntness unnerved me. "Because you don't fight?" I asked, before immediately regretting my choice of words.

He was unfazed. "Because I don't enjoy violence, yes, but also because I dabble in . . . deviant affairs."

He met my eyes then, and I felt my cheeks heat. I did not know what he was referring to, but it felt illicit all the same.

"Father knows of the Ximing chancellor already, but I don't know if he comprehends the magnitude of the threat."

"Typical," said Winter, with a certain disdain. "Does he know about Ren?"

Sky's gaze flicked to me. "Not yet. But . . ."

"Ren." Winter leaned toward me. "Do you think you can handle the chancellor?"

I fingered the chain of Sima's necklace, his iron-encased jade tucked beneath my tunic. *As long as I have his jade*, I thought, *he does not*. The thought filled me with grim relish.

Sima was far more experienced than I was, far older and wiser. But his powers were incomplete, and while I lived, they would remain so.

"We're out of options, aren't we?" I asked Winter, with more bravado than I felt. "I'm the only one who can stand a chance against him."

I looked between Sky and Winter, making sure they registered the meaning of my words. I needed the princes to understand my role in this war, to be on my side when I made my case before their father. If I won this war for Anlai, if I saved the Liu clan from Chancellor Sima's retribution, they would have to repay me. They would have to acknowledge me, even if I told them the truth of who I was. The *full* truth.

Then, everything out in the open, I would ask for only one thing: freedom.

But don't you want more? It was not the sea dragon's voice I heard, but another, more insidious one. My own. *Think of what you could do with your power. With Sima eliminated, no one could stand in your way.*

My cheeks heated from my absurd thoughts, but no one noticed because Sparrow and Tao chose that moment to enter. They bowed to the princes first before acknowledging me. Sparrow shot me a grin, but he couldn't quite hide the apprehension in his eyes, as if at any moment he expected me to sprout wings or breathe fire. Tao, on the other hand, made no attempts to hide his unease, sitting as far from me as possible.

Sky watched this exchange with an inscrutable expression. "I've ordered them to tell no one of your abilities," he said to me. I nodded, but inwardly, my heart sank. Sparrow had the biggest mouth of anyone I knew. How many people in our platoon had already begun to despise me?

Why do you care, Meilin?

"We march for Tzu Wan tomorrow," Sky said, his voice imbued with a commander's authority. "We've just received approval from my father. Once the Ximing capital is overtaken and the warlord and chancellor disposed of, we'll declare victory over Ximing. We can negotiate a treaty from there."

He made it sound so very easy, as if this would be over in a day. Had he forgotten Sima's obscene power at Xi Lan?

But I recalled his own words, so many months ago in training: *"It's easy to forget, when no one wants to remember reality."*

I shook my head. "With all due respect, Commander, you're falling into their trap. Storming the palace will not ensure victory over Ximing. They mean for us to come."

Now I understood what Autumn had been referring to, when she'd mentioned the transfer of the plum blossom painting. They were removing all palace valuables before the Anlai army arrived. So that when we came, all that remained would be a decoy. A trap.

Sky shook his head. "The warlord—"

"—will not be there." I cut him off. Tao shot me a warning look, which I ignored. "I told you, they *mean* for you to come. Whatever signals they've sent you are false."

Sky's face twisted. Clearly, Zihuan and Lei had baited him somehow. Sky was honorable, and duty-bound, two characteristics that made him far too easy to manipulate. But I was neither.

"Listen," I said, pressing my advantage. "Leyuan is crumbling under debt and civil war—"

"We know this—" Sky growled, his frustration growing.

"—and Ximing knows too. They're targeting Chuang Ning instead." The elder Prince Liu sucked in his breath. "Power has changed hands within the Ximing court. The former crown prince is dead. He's been replaced by Second Prince Cao Zihuan—who has no interest in diplomacy. You need to send the army back to Chuang Ning to defend our capital. Immediately."

"That's a bluff," said Sky stubbornly. "Chuang Ning's walls have never before fallen. Only a fool would—"

"Do you think I lie?" I cried out, vexed. I thought of Qinglong's terrible vision, of Sky bleeding out on the floor of the imperial palace, a blade in his gut. "They've already left!"

Sky clenched his jaw. "Then we will meet them on their way—"

"They're traveling by water," I hissed. "Zihuan's navy now counts over a thousand combat vessels. We're no match for them at sea."

Even Sky fell silent now. His scouts were bound to land, like the rest of our army. Ximing's strength lay in its naval fleet. And yet they were forsaking this advantage to lay siege on landlocked Chuang Ning. Because the phoenix's power upended all our hands.

Sky rubbed his eyes as if trying to dig them out of their sockets. I wondered how much sleep he'd gotten lately. Knowing him, not much.

Abruptly, he raised his head. "You expect me to turn our entire force around on the faith of one word—"

A coldness seeped through me, the same coldness that had led me to kiss the Ximing prince and, in the same breath, bring a blade to his injured throat. For Cao Ming Lei had changed me. "I lived at the mercy of a Ximing prince for *forty-two* days. And despite everything he did to me, I endured. I escaped. And now you dare claim you don't believe me?"

"*Di*," said Winter, turning to his younger brother. "Our family is there. We cannot risk it."

Sky kneaded his jaw. Loyalty to your blood went unquestioned, I knew. Sky could not forsake his family, any more than he could forsake his own limbs.

His nostrils flared. "Very well. Then we'll reverse course," he decided. "I'll lead Third and Fourth Company to defend the city—"

"No," I said. "You cannot go."

"What do you want from me, Ren?" he exploded. Our easy solidarity had been short-lived.

"This is what I propose," I said, crouching in the sand. "Send the majority of your forces to Chuang Ning, to defend the city and hold off Ximing. But keep in mind this is no conventional battle. We cannot overwhelm them with our numbers alone. The phoenix does not heed the might of men. Zhuque slaughters all, without discrimination."

Sparrow shuddered. We were all remembering the phoenix's brilliant flames lighting the waves, unquenched by even the sea. It had been a wasteful show of force on Sima's part. The most frightening aspect—it had cost him nothing.

I felt my face harden. "In order to win this war, we need to target Chancellor Sima. We need to destroy his jade seal."

"What do you think I've been trying to do all this time?" Sky demanded. "While you've been gone, I've been searching—"

"Wouldn't the chancellor be at Chuang Ning?" Sparrow interjected. "How can they hope to destroy the walls, if not through black magic?"

I paused before answering, laying out a plan that I'd been turning over in my head for the past few hours. "During my time in imprisonment, I learned of the infighting between Chancellor Sima and the new crown prince. The chancellor, unlike the prince, intends to find and unite his jade before launching an attack on

Chuang Ning. If my suspicions are correct, Sima will be chasing a lead on Mount Fuxi right now in search of his seal. At the same time, he can still assist in the Ximing warlord's campaign. That must be the understanding they came to."

"Sima will be off on his inane scavenger hunt, but at least he's agreed to assist from his little hidey-hole."

I used my knife to draw a rough map of Anlai in the dirt, with Chuang Ning in one corner and Mount Fuxi in the other.

"Chancellor Sima attacked our forces during the battle at Dian River," I said. "And yet, he was nowhere near the Dian when the fires began. Remember, this was only with one piece of his seal. I imagine his range has doubled with the cumulative power of the second jade piece. The more complete the seal, the more power he amasses."

"Convenient," said Winter wryly, eyeing my map. "Mount Fuxi is the closest peak to Chuang Ning. Apart from the Red Mountains in Leyuan, it has the highest elevation in the Three Kingdoms. Zhuque's power will not only be within range but will be more potent than if Sima stood before the gates of Chuang Ning himself."

"How is that possible?" Sky asked.

I thought of how I'd called upon the might of the sea as I'd helped my companions escape their New Quan prison. I thought of how elemental magic, though never wholly cooperative with me, had been somehow less challenging to summon by the sea.

"Perhaps Zhuque's seal draws its energy from the sun," I said. "The closer her jade is to the sun, the stronger the power."

Winter frowned. "It's almost as if this 'lead' planned for the chancellor to assist in the siege."

What is Lei planning? I wondered, for the hundredth time. I could never begin to decipher his motives, and it drove me mad. His deceptions were endless. He was playing Chancellor Sima; he was playing the crown prince; he was possibly even still playing me. In going to Mount Fuxi, was I falling into his trap?

I shook my head; Lei's schemes for power no longer applied to me. As far as I was concerned, Sima would go to Mount Fuxi, seeking his jade, so I would go to Mount Fuxi, seeking *him*.

My goals were twofold: kill Sima, but first, compel him. Using mental manipulation, I would force him to destroy his own seal. Only in this way could the chain be broken and Zhuque's power obliterated in the human realm.

Then I would be alone, the last one standing, the only one alive who bore the power of lixia.

From far away, I sensed the dragon's purr.

"I'll assemble a platoon to ride to Mount Fuxi," Sky announced. "If we make haste, we can reach the base of the mountain in eight days."

"Eight days?" I repeated. We would need horses, I thought. All of us.

Sky nodded. "The former emperor built hidden escape tunnels out of the summer palace, in case of insurrection. Father had those tunnels fortified. We can use them to break into the palace." He turned to his brother. "Winter, you must lead the army to defend Chuang Ning. General Sun will support you."

Winter's face was drawn. "And you?"

"I must go with Ren," said Sky. "The chancellor will fall beneath my blade."

You'll have to get in line, I thought grimly. *The chancellor's mine.*

Qinglong stirred within me, approving. At last, I was out for blood.

FORTY-EIGHT

Why some possess greater spirit affinity than others has been the subject of much dispute. Though there appears to be some correlation with blood lineage, it is not, in fact, a direct connection as the Quan scholars believed. Such is the case with the Great Warrior Guan Yang, who was born from two parents with weak affinity.

—LOST JOURNALS OF AN 8TH-CENTURY LIXIA SCHOLAR, DATE UNKNOWN

THE DAY PASSED IN A BLUR AS WE MADE BRISK PREPARATIONS FOR our departure. Only at sundown did I finally catch a moment to rest. Sky was locked away in council meetings, which he hadn't bothered to invite me to. Our platoon had been assembled; we would ride at dawn.

I sat near the edge of camp before a dying fire. Only its embers still glowed, slowly suffocating under heaps of ash. My comrades had not bullied me, had not called me names as they used to. And yet their trepidation was palpable, an invisible barrier I could not cross. I could see the fear in their eyes, the agitation. I did not know if Sparrow had shared with them the extent of my transgressions, or if the simple fact that I'd returned whole and hale from imprisonment in Ximing was enough to set them on edge.

I had been wrong to think I could ever belong.

The last ember flickered out. Now my only source of light came from the campfires beyond, near the tent line. I could hear Sparrow's rowdy, drunken singing in the distance.

"I've been looking for you."

I raised my head. Sky stood above me, his silhouette shadowed against the half-light. He took a seat across from me, the extinguished fire between us. I watched him frown at the pit, a silent reproach at me.

He cleared his throat. I noticed he was holding a jug of wine in one hand. I wondered if he'd been drinking too. It was out of character for him.

"Why are you hiding out here all alone?" he asked, in his infuriatingly condescending way.

"I'm not *hiding*," I snapped, cracking a twig beneath my boot. I paused. "You used to invite me to council meetings."

The remark surprised even me, its speaker. This detail had nettled me, yes, but I didn't see the point in raising the issue with him. And yet the words had slipped off my tongue.

Sky raised a brow. "You never went when I did."

"But now you don't invite me at all. Is it because you know who I am now? Because you no longer trust me?"

He shot me a baleful look. "That's not it."

I glared back at him. "Then what is it?"

"I don't want you attracting unneeded attention!"

I rose to my feet. "You don't want me amassing my own power," I hissed. "You want me under your—"

He reached out and grabbed my wrist. "Meilin," he said softly. "What happened to you?"

The shift in his voice startled me. Numbly, I sat beside him, covering my face with my hands. What was I saying? I knew Sky didn't think that way. Sky wasn't any of those things—power-hungry, manipulative, trying to possess me. He'd only been worried for my safety.

I'd conflated him with someone else. Someone I couldn't get out of my head.

Hesitantly, Sky put his hand on my shoulder. I realized then how close we were sitting. Touch was unnatural for us, foreign. If someone saw us together like this, there'd be gossip. But I was tired of being cautious. Lei was right in his own twisted way—sometimes life was too short to give a damn.

"What did he do to you?" Sky asked. "He hurt you, didn't he?"

I shook my head, too weary to explain. Lei's mind games were vastly different from the traditional forms of torture Sky likely had in mind.

"I wanted to go back for you," Sky said, his voice thick. "I tried, Meilin. I—"

"I know," I said wearily. "You couldn't help it. You had to lead your men. You had . . . your duty . . ."

He swallowed hard. I tracked the knot of his throat as it rose and fell. "I thought of you. Every day. No, every hour. It killed me. I couldn't bear to think . . ."

His expression had turned inward: bleak, self-loathing. I felt a pang in my chest—I recognized that look—and took his face in my hands. "Sky, I'm right here. I'm with you. It's okay."

He took my hands in his, his eyes searching mine.

"I will heal," I said, as much to him as to myself. "In time."

"Meilin," he said lowly. "There's been something . . . I've been meaning to tell you. Well, you've probably guessed already."

I waited. A faint blush rose on his cheeks.

He exhaled. "I . . . I have feelings for you."

I blinked, not comprehending, then dropped his hands as if scalded. "You don't know that," I said, more sharply than I'd intended.

Guilt twisted my stomach. The shame was hot and sickening. Shame because only a few days ago, I'd been kissing another prince, drawn to him and the attraction between us. And all that time, Sky had been worried sick for me.

"Listen to me," Sky continued, his eyes wide. "After this war is over, I want to ask for your hand—"

"You've been drinking, haven't you?"

He sighed. "I'm telling the truth, Meilin, whether you believe me or not. It's been this way for quite some time now."

I snatched the wine jug from him in lieu of an answer, taking a generous swig. He frowned at me. I took another drink, just to provoke him.

"You are maddening, Meilin."

I wiped the back of my mouth and handed him the wine. "The usual compliments from you," I said wryly. But I smiled.

He drank with me. Between the two of us, we finished the jug. Both of us were going to have a splitting headache tomorrow. But tomorrow felt so very far away.

"The day we met," I said, some time later. Somehow, we'd both ended up lying on the ground, looking up at the thin piece of sky that pierced through the forest canopy overhead. "The day we met, I was spying on my betrothed."

Sky barely moved. I wondered if he was asleep. It was certainly late enough.

I continued regardless, alcohol loosening my tongue. "I watched him strike a serving girl. The same way my father had always hit me." Unexpectedly, my breath caught in my throat. As if no time had passed, I recalled what my life had been like before the war. I felt the claustrophobia of living under my father's roof. The total powerlessness, knowing I was subject to his capricious whims. "I considered jumping from the rooftops then."

A hand found its way into mine. I turned my head to the side. Sky was watching me, his eyes flickering in the dark. I was glad he didn't speak then.

"I considered it, but I didn't. Because I knew I couldn't abandon my family the same way my mother had abandoned me. And because I was scared. I was scared to die."

His fingers were drawing patterns on my arm now. It felt nice, and I didn't want him to stop.

"I've never told anyone that before," I admitted, the choky feeling still in my throat. "Sometimes, I'm afraid that everything I do is because of my fear. Because I'm afraid of returning to that . . . that helpless—"

My voice broke and Sky pulled me into his chest. "That won't happen again," he said quietly, but with the authority of his commander's voice. He wrapped his arm around my shoulder, and I rested my head against his chest. We fit like that, surprisingly well. As if we'd done this before. And perhaps, I amended, thinking of the nights Sky had nursed me back to health, perhaps we had.

"You're the strongest person I know," he said. "And the most foolish, sometimes."

I smiled, and he laughed softly, his breath tickling my hair. Was this what safety felt like? I wondered, for the notion was foreign to me.

Perhaps he was thinking the same thing. "I won't allow you to return to your father," Sky said, his arm tightening around me. "After the war. Meilin, I swear to protect you . . ."

He was too serious for a night like this. "Enough," I said, making a sound between a sigh and a laugh.

"Why are you so afraid of the future?"

I wrinkled my nose. "I'm not afraid of it—"

"You don't wish me to speak of it," Sky pointed out, the stickler he was.

The truth was, I could not bear to think of my future, as uncertain as it was. If it was wretched, I did not wish to know. And if it was sweet, how much more painful to have it stolen from me?

I knew this: the crown prince of Ximing was sailing for Chuang Ning as we spoke. The sea dragon's vision had been set into motion, each piece of the puzzle fitting into place. And yet, while I lived—Rouha would not die in the flames. Xiuying would not watch her own child be taken from her, fire drowning out the sounds of her screams. This vision would not come to pass. I would save my family.

I would defeat Chancellor Sima, I told myself, with sheer stubbornness. I would defeat him and claim my reward: freedom.

But did I even want that anymore?

It was what I had desired in the past: the ability to live as my own person, answering to no one and nothing. And yet the future that had once appeared so enticing now seemed to have lost its luster.

"*I could offer you far more distinguished positions,*" Lei had told me. "*You could make a very competent general, Meilin.*"

He had been lying, of course, but his lies had taken root in my mind. Could I become a general? A commander of men? Perhaps even a warlord? And what if . . . what if Sky was the key? Sky, who was a clear contender for the throne? Could I help him . . . and help myself in the process?

Could I take the throne through him?

The thought was so foreign I flinched. *This is Qinglong speaking,* I realized, *not me.* With growing unease, I realized I could no longer distinguish the dragon's influence from my own. When had this begun? When Xiuying had first given me my mother's necklace, the dragon's thoughts had felt wholly separate to me, foreign.

But when I'd accepted his seal, when I'd become his vessel—perhaps then our two consciousnesses had begun to merge.

"*For in accepting the seal and becoming a vessel, a spirit medium em-*

braces not only the abilities of the spirit but also its character and disposition. More often than not, the spirit will overpower its host, assuming control over the medium's body and mind."

I shivered with cold dread. I had been avoiding the spirit realm, avoiding the dragon. This could not go on much longer. I would have to exploit Qinglong's power in order to defeat Chancellor Sima. I would have to use him.

But he was also using me.

I closed my eyes. Sometimes, when the fear was overpowering, my future became nothing more than a pitch-black nothingness. *There can be no happiness for someone like you*, a voice in my head whispered. Repulsive. Disgusting. A perversion.

"Meilin," Sky asked. "What's wrong?"

I shook myself out of my stupor and rolled on top of him, so that we were eye to eye. "Kiss me," I said. The wine made me bold. "I want to know what it feels like."

I want to know what it feels like, I didn't say, *with someone other than* him.

Sky's brows furrowed. "They might see..."

"You don't wish to?"

He made a sound of exasperation. "Meilin—"

I kissed him, just one small peck. But then he clasped the back of my neck and returned the kiss, deepening it. He tasted of wine and salt, of yearning. I had imagined this moment so many times in my dreams, and now, I did not know if I was awake or dreaming. He turned me so that I was beneath him, our bodies flush against each other. My hands trembling, I began to unbutton my clothes.

Sky seized my hand, stopping me. His voice was rough, his breaths uneven. "Meilin," he bit out. "Stop."

"Why?" I asked, trying not to sound as though I was whining. I didn't see the point in holding back. Not when we set off for Mount Fuxi in a few hours. Not when I saw a future where he died before my eyes. Not when every day might be our last.

"If we start . . ." Sky swallowed. "I'm afraid I won't be able to stop."

Wasn't that the point? "Then why stop?"

He groaned and moved off me. In his wake, I felt the coldness of the night press against me.

He propped himself up on one elbow to look at me. "I want to treat you right, Meilin."

I looked pointedly away. Who decided what "right" was, anyway? It certainly wasn't me.

Sky reached out to brush my hair from my face. I sighed, relenting; it took too much effort to hold a grudge against him. I knew Sky cared about honor and duty above all else; he wasn't about to have a romp in the forest on the eve of battle. But still . . . I glanced at him and smiled. It would've been fun.

An answering smile lit his face. He traced a finger around my mouth, to my cheekbone and temple. "You're the most beautiful woman I've ever seen," he said quietly.

Now I rolled my eyes in earnest. "I'm the *only* woman you've seen in months."

He laughed softly. For once, I slept without nightmares.

FORTY-NINE

Like the fall of first snow, their army spread across the field, covering every patch of grass from sight. A white flag waved from the center of the army, with one word written on both sides: Vengeance.
—CHRONICLES OF THE THREE KINGDOMS, 954

WHEN I AWOKE, I FELT AS IF SOMETHING HAD DIED IN MY mouth. My back was stiff from sleeping on the forest floor. I blinked open one eye to find Sky watching me, his expression soft.

He sat back as if struck. "I didn't do anything," he said quickly.

I snorted and got to my feet. "What time is it?"

"An hour till dawn," he said, standing and regaining composure. "We should check the horses."

And just like that, Sky had returned to Prince Liu, commander of Seventh Company. I peered at him, and a flush rose to his cheeks, before he turned away, withdrawing to his duties.

I regretted last night's wine immediately. Squinting through a pounding migraine, I stumbled to the latrine. I cursed Sky for having a higher alcohol tolerance than I did. I couldn't even complain to him, because he'd warned me of this fact. Several times.

At dawn, a few army officials rose to see us off. To my surprise, Lieutenant Fang came forward, bowing not only to Sky, but also to me. Most of Third Platoon would ride to Chuang Ning to defend the capital. I hadn't expected to see Fang ever again.

"This is a family heirloom," he said, presenting an unusual armlet made of iron. With a pang, I recognized the heirloom from months ago, when Sparrow had stolen his armlet out of spite. *How petty our squad rivalries now seem*, I thought.

"My family used to hunt black magic practitioners," Fang explained. "This armlet has been passed down to the eldest son of each generation in my clan. It may be of use against the Ximing chancellor."

Sky shrugged and accepted the armlet. "My thanks, Lieutenant."

Perhaps we could use it against Chancellor Sima, I thought, to incapacitate him. But I certainly could not be the one to carry it. I looked at the heft of that thick iron and shuddered.

As Winter arrived, Lieutenant Fang bowed and left. Despite the early hour, Winter looked as composed as ever, his long hair pinned up in an elegant coil.

"Take more men with you," Winter said to Sky, in a way that made me think this was not their first time discussing this. "Father's returning to Chuang Ning this week. He'll bring all of First Battalion with him."

Sky shook his head. "We don't have enough horses. One platoon will have to do."

"But—"

"Speed is of the essence," Sky said, in a voice that was final. "Stars go with you, Ge."

Winter nodded, dissatisfied yet resigned. Their dynamic was odd. I knew Sky deeply respected his brother, though it didn't often show on the battlefield. Sky had once mentioned how their roles had reversed in wartime. Back in court, Winter looked after Sky. But in war, Sky was the protector, the leader of the two.

"Ren," Winter said to me. "I'm sorry we did not have more time together. We'll talk when you return," he said, before leaning in and whispering in my ear, "Just remember—you want Sima's jade destroyed, not handed off to another." He hesitated. "Timing is everything."

Did he know about Lei and his schemes for power? Or was he speaking of someone else, something else? I did not find out. The horses were standing; we departed immediately.

AS WE CROSSED THE BORDER INTO ANLAI, I WAS SHAKEN BY THE TOtal destruction wrought by war. The lush farmlands we'd passed on our way south were now ravaged by fire and bloodshed. Oncebustling villages had transformed into empty corpses, ghost towns. The few survivors we saw emerged from hiding once they realized we were not Ximing soldiers. At the first village, Sky let us stop and speak with them. They spoke of a phoenix blazing across the sky, enacting her wrath on humanity. "This is the gods' judgment," one grandmother warned us gravely. "They are punishing us—for denying them offerings."

Their accounts diverged. Some said the phoenix was the size of a bear; others said the bird was as huge as a body of water, enveloping the sky. The only thing they agreed on was the fire itself. It had incinerated everything within its grasp, burning so ferociously and swiftly it could be no natural wildfire.

Our platoon was disturbed. They had heard the rumors—everyone had—but most had not seen the consequences of Zhuque's power up close. Even if we came to a cease-fire, I thought, we would see the ramifications of this war for years to come.

Meanwhile, the siege on Chuang Ning had begun. According to gossip, the outer walls had fallen within a day.

After hearing news of the siege, we didn't stop again. Sky set us on a torturous pace, so that we made it to the base of Mount Fuxi by the night of the seventh day. As the mountain's shadow descended over our camp, I gazed up at the looming peak and wondered what awaited us there.

Sky pulled me aside before our evening meal. His face was bleak.

"What is it?" I asked, my stomach sinking.

"My scouts just returned. The tunnels are sealed," he said, not one for mincing words. "I don't know how the chancellor found out about them."

"There are no escape tunnels here, if that's what you're looking for," Autumn had told me. And if Autumn knew about the Wu Dynasty practice of hidden tunnels, then Lei certainly did as well.

Could Cao Ming Lei also be on Mount Fuxi? A shudder traveled down my spine. Fear and . . . *anticipation*. I shook my head. I was imagining things.

"That leaves us with one option," said Sky. "There's too much visibility on the top of the mountain. They'll see us as soon as we ascend, regardless of whether we try to hide." His jaw clenched. "We'll have to storm the summer palace."

My mouth fell open. "That's suicide."

"Not necessarily," said Sky, though his expression was bleak. "We have fifty good men with us. The palace is well fortified, but their forces are not large. My scouts report less than a hundred and fifty soldiers—"

"A hundred and fifty?" I screeched. "Those are *not* good odds, Sky."

"What do you propose, then, Meilin? I've tried to think of another option. *Any* option. But if we send for reinforcements, it'll take at least two weeks before a company from Chuang Ning can hope to reach Fuxi. And that's only on horseback. I doubt my father has that many mounts to spare."

"There must be a better way," I said, turning away from him. *What would Lei do?* I wondered, the thought snagging in my mind like a loose thread. The Ximing prince would be shrewd, sly. He would never tackle any problem head-on. Rather, he would get what he wanted through deception and subterfuge.

"Are they allowing visitors into the palace?" I asked.

Sky scoffed. "Yes, I'm sure I'll be well received if I just announce my—"

"Not you," I said. "At least, not you acting as *you*."

"Who else could I be? The prince of Ximing?"

I blanched. "Not him either. What about a traveling merchant, or . . ."

He sneered with derision. "Ren—Meilin—this is war. All businesses cease in war. Besides, Sima hasn't exactly made his takeover of the summer palace a secret. Any Anlai merchant would have a death wish to visit the Ximing chancellor."

"What about someone who wasn't going there willingly?"

"A prisoner?" His brows folded. "Meilin, don't even think of—"

"No," I said impatiently, waving his warning away like an irksome mosquito. "I wouldn't go as myself. I would go as . . ." The idea struck me. "A *concubine*."

I recalled the courtesans at the lotus-viewing pavilion, drinking tea with the crown prince of Ximing. I turned to Sky with grim triumph. "Not all businesses cease in war."

Sky's eyes went black. "No."

"Sky—"

"No." His voice was much louder than it needed to be. "I won't let you do this, Meilin."

"You have to admit this is the superior plan—"

"It's madness!" The stark fury and despair emanating from him made me take a step back. "You'll die."

"No, I won't," I said. "You'll dress as wardens escorting me to Chancellor Sima. If the guards ask, you'll say the chancellor requested a new concubine from Chuang Ning. A captured imperial courtesan," I added frivolously. "One who used to serve the Anlai warlord himself."

"Imperial or not, what kind of courtesan requires fifty wardens?"

"Not fifty," I clarified. "Three. Tao, Sparrow, and you."

Sky fell silent. He could tell I was being serious.

"Then I'll be allowed into Sima's private quarters. While I'm inside, you'll find a way to let the others in secretly in the night. Maybe you can unseal the tunnels. Or you can convince the guards to open the gates." I would have to find some way to transport the iron without touching it, I realized belatedly. Sima would need to first restore his seal, then destroy it. But I could not compel him while wearing iron.

I could feel an oncoming headache.

Sky currently wore the necklace Lei had fashioned, with the iron-encased jade around his neck. I had not wished to alert Sima to the presence of his jade, and so I had decided not to remove the iron encasement. And yet I would have to transport the necklace on my own somehow, without Sky's assistance. I could wear it upon entering, and then perhaps hide it somewhere, within reach.

"*Timing is everything*," Winter had said.

"As a courtesan and a prisoner, you won't be allowed any weapons," Sky cut in. "They'll search your body."

"I don't need a blade," I said. "All I need is my jade."

Sky looked like he hated this idea. Like there was no idea he hated more. I watched him struggle to rein in his emotions. "There are so many ways this could go wrong." He started to pace, the epitome of unhappiness. "He could steal your jade—"

"I'll kill him before he gets that far."

"Meilin."

"You don't want me to kill him?"

He seized me by the shoulders. "I can't lose you," he said, his voice taut with barely suppressed emotion. "I can't." He pressed his forehead to mine, and I softened. I let my eyes fall shut. I was shaking too, with nerves and adrenaline.

"I'll survive," I said, as much to him as to myself. "I always do."

FIFTY

For all spirit summoners, lixia corruption is as inevitable as the waning of the moon. Rather than choosing ignorance, the prudent medium can take certain steps to defer its arrival.

—LOST JOURNALS OF AN 8TH-CENTURY LIXIA SCHOLAR, DATE UNKNOWN

W E SPLIT UP. SKY WENT TO SPEAK WITH LIEUTENANT KUO, who would lead the platoon in his absence, and await his signal from Mount Fuxi. I went to find Tao and Sparrow. We would have to ride to Shizhao, the closest neighboring village, to find workable disguises. From that point on, I would remain separate from the platoon, for no one could recognize me as Hai Ren, the soldier they had trained and fought with for the past six months. No one save Tao and Sparrow. For this plan to work, they would have to know.

I led them both out of earshot, away from camp, then laid out the plan for them.

"A courtesan?" Sparrow asked. "Maybe that could work to get through the palace gates, but in the bedchamber, how could you fool..."

"I wouldn't need to fool the chancellor," I said, spelling it out with difficulty. "Because I am a woman."

I said the words quickly, as if the faster I said them, the faster we could get through this. But of course, my words left a hanging silence. I listened to the caw of thrushes in the trees and wondered if I'd just made a fatal mistake.

"Impossible," Sparrow said at last. "You-you're Ren. We've slept in the same tent for months. You fight better than me, than most of our platoon. You—"

"Does the prince know?" Tao interjected.

"Of course," I said. "He's always known," I added, lying through my teeth. I hoped the fact that Sky had accepted me would make Tao do the same.

Tao did not speak, but I could feel his animosity like a scream.

Meanwhile, Sparrow had begun fidgeting. "No way," he was saying. "I don't believe you. That can't be true." But then he stopped. "That night at the Ji Zong hot springs. That's why you didn't want us to come near you! Because you weren't wearing clothes. And your-your—"

His eyes shot to my chest before his face turned the color of a ripe tomato. I tried to laugh. "Yes," I said. "That is why."

"What have you done to the prince?" Tao hissed.

"What-what do you mean?"

His eyes narrowed like an attack dog's. "Have you bewitched him?"

I stared at him as if he were joking. But he was not. "Tao," I tried, "I'm still the same person. I've never lied about anything else—"

"No," he said, "you've only lied about everything."

He stormed off, before turning back to face Sparrow. "I'm heading into town for our supplies. Are you coming?"

"Sparrow—" I started, reaching for him.

"Don't touch me!" he burst out, and his voice betrayed not anger, but fear. My hand fell limply to my side. I could feel hot tears welling in my eyes.

"Don't forget the disguises!" I called, watching their figures recede into the distance.

That night, as I drifted off to sleep, a vague premonition took root in my thoughts. Tomorrow, I would fail. I would be imprisoned, stripped of my sword and my seal and all my powers. I would become as weak and vulnerable as Father had tried all his life to make me.

Alone, in the dark, I would kill myself as my mother had.

The fears grew larger and brighter in my mind, distorting reality. I felt as if I had no control over my own limbs, as if my body would jump off the nearest cliff even if my mind screamed at it not to. I wanted to bind my ankles together, shackle my hands. Perhaps my life was best spent as a prisoner, when I could not be trusted to control myself. This was my inheritance, despite everything I had done to escape it.

Madness.

I SHOT UP IN MY PALLET, SWEATING FROM A NIGHTMARE I COULD NO longer recall. The sun was still low in the sky, and the high mountain air unreasonably cold for late summer. Shivering, I jogged to the cover of the trees to relieve myself.

When I returned to our campsite, Tao and Sparrow were awake. Last night, they'd returned from Shizhao successful, with appropriate disguises for all of us. Then we'd said our goodbyes to the platoon and made our way up the mountain alone.

More goodbyes were ahead. Soon I would part ways with the others, as only I would be allowed into Sima's quarters. I didn't want to leave things as they were, with bad blood between us. So I approached, cautiously, trying to appear calm.

Tao had his elbows on his knees, his face moody. Sparrow was eating dried pork floss with grim determination, a slight pucker to his mouth.

Hesitantly, I chose my seat next to them. Near enough that we could talk, but far enough that I wouldn't unsettle them.

"I'm sorry," I said, clearing my throat. "I hadn't meant to keep it from you for so long—"

Tao got up wordlessly, then walked into the forest. He kept his eyes averted from me, as if my face were disfigured.

Offended, I looked to Sparrow. He flushed, fidgeting with his food. Stuffing the rest of the dried pork in his mouth, he wiped his hands with exaggerated motions, then pointed at Tao's receding back. "I should . . . go," Sparrow mumbled.

I nodded, blinking back tears. Sparrow followed Tao into the woods, not meeting my eyes once.

Our hard-won friendship had dissolved overnight. We had gone through battle together, even imprisonment. They had trusted me, and I had trusted them. And still, this was how they responded when they learned the truth of me? Would everyone else react this way too?

"They'll come around." Sky sat next to me, sleep still in his eyes. He peered into my face, then saw my suppressed tears. The corners of his mouth turned downward. "It'll just take some time. That's all. I mean, look at me. Remember how it went down when I found out?" He laughed softly. "I tried to force you to desert just so I could stop going out of my mind."

I turned to him, incredulous. He saw he'd caught my attention and smiled ruefully. "And then we fought, remember? I swear I still have bruises from that night." He wiped a stray tear from my cheek.

"Why?" I asked hoarsely.

"Why what?"

"Why are you so . . . accepting?"

He frowned. "That you're a woman?"

"No," I said, because he hadn't been accepting of that. Not for a while. "I mean, about the fact that I'm a... spirit medium. I thought you would loathe black magic." I swallowed. "Or, at least, I thought you'd be surprised."

He leaned back, looking up at the lightening sky. At last he admitted, "I had my suspicions."

"You mean, before New Quan?"

He nodded, and I sat up, astonished.

"Winter told me he'd seen you before, in the realm between humans and spirits. I think he could feel your spirit affinity, how strong it was. Though I don't think any of us suspected you had your own seal." He shot me a sidelong glance. "You really know how to keep a secret, Soldier Hai."

"Apparently not," I said begrudgingly, "if you already knew."

Sky stretched, cracking his neck. "It was for the best," he said with a yawn. "Winter told me to look after you. That you could become Anlai's most important weapon one day."

My shoulders stiffened. "Is that what I am to you?" I asked him. "A weapon for Anlai?"

Sky chuckled, before looking over at me and realizing I was serious. "Of course not," he said quickly. "Meilin, you know I—"

"I need to get dressed," I told him, stalking away.

FIFTY-ONE

The renowned summer palace on Mount Fuxi cost over a hundred thousand gold taels to complete. It was commissioned by Emperor Wu for his favorite courtesan, Tang Huifei; there is said to be no place on earth as conducive for falling in love.

—REMEMBERING THE WU DYNASTY, 913

B Y THE TIME WE REACHED THE PALACE GATES, I WAS SHIVERING. My thin silk dress did little against the biting mountain air, and the lack of trees left the wind fierce and unobstructed. My teeth chattered as I huddled closer to Sky, who held one end of a rope binding my wrists together. The knot was loose, superficial; I could easily break free from it, should I need to.

The knot was superficial, but the iron pendant hidden within the lining of my skirt was not. Ironic that I'd bound myself, voluntarily. But I'd seen no way around it, not unless I wanted to alert Sima to the presence of his own jade.

I stumbled on a loose rock, my bound hands upsetting my sense of balance. Sky reached out to catch me, before his eyes went up to the Ximing archers posted along the gates, watching. I righted myself and kept going, eyes trained on the dirt. Wearing iron, my senses had grown dull, muted. But, I thought, there was one benefit.

The dragon could not know of my true plans now.

Above us, I could see the tower pagoda of the summer palace

piercing the white sky, its eaves tapering with each level until it narrowed to a golden baoding crown at the top. Each level was painted brilliant colors of red and yellow, symbolizing prosperity and fortune.

I looked up at the looming gates, feeling very small. Framing the palace entrance was a pair of ornamental pillars, made of pure white marble. Intricate lotus blossoms were carved into their bases, and clouds floated up the lengths of the columns. At the head, a statue of a stone lion balanced atop each pillar. Legend said these stone lions were to watch and wait for the emperor's return, calling him back if he strayed too far from the palace. But the Wu Dynasty had fallen more than sixteen years ago. I wondered if the stone lions were still waiting for their emperor to return.

As we approached the palace guards, my heart rammed against my rib cage, but Sparrow sauntered up to them with relaxed confidence. We had unanimously dubbed Sparrow our spokesperson. Not only would his appearance raise the least suspicion, but also his southern accent sounded most similar to the distinctive Ximing lilt.

"The chancellor's expecting us," Sparrow said, slipping into dialect. He leaned forward as if offering a secret to the guard. "She's straight from the Chuang Ning Forbidden City. One of the warlord's former concubines."

I cringed, sensing no one would believe that. My complexion was not pale as snow but tan, like rusted copper. My skin was not soft as a ripe peach, but calloused and scarred. My dress was made of silk, but the thread was of low caliber, and it lacked fine embroidery.

"Another one?" the guard asked, eyeing me. "We just had two new arrivals last week."

Dread lurched in my stomach. Sparrow only laughed. "The chancellor's got a healthy appetite, then."

The guard nodded and let us through. But we'd barely made it into the outer courtyard when we were stopped again.

"Wait. Only the whore's allowed in."

Sky stiffened noticeably. I turned toward my companions in shock. They weren't even allowed into the outer palace? How could they stand a chance at unsealing the tunnels, which were connected to the emperor's former rooms?

"According to our instructions," Sky began. His voice was all wrong, I thought. Too refined, too imperial. "We were told we'd receive compensation—"

The guard nodded. "You'll receive your reward in the magistrate's hall. The chancellor doesn't want any commoners entering the palace grounds. Follow me and I'll take you there now."

Sky's eyes flashed. "The girl—"

"She goes with them."

A guard touched my arm, but I jerked out of his grip, panicking. How was this going to work if they couldn't get in the palace?

"Come along now," said the guard, not unkindly. He was young, probably my age. He untied my ropes and took me by the arm. "I'm just bringing you to the other girls. You'll have the days to yourself and the nights with the chancellor." He lowered his voice. "It's not bad, honestly. You're lucky to have gotten out of Chuang Ning when you did."

As we crossed the threshold, I forced down the urge to glance back over my shoulder. I had to trust Sky to complete his end of the mission. I was on my own now.

The courtesans lived in the outer palace. From the layout of their rooms, I understood that the new blood and old blood were kept separate. The old blood consisted of Ximing courtesans, who had followed the chancellor from the Tzu Wan palace. These courtesans were elevated in status and familiar with most of the servants and guards, even going so far as to boss them around. Meanwhile, the new girls were all Anlai prisoners of war. They had been captured and brought here like me. Well, I thought, not exactly.

In the sitting room, a curly-haired girl pounced on me as soon as I entered. "I'm Peizhi," she said, her voice a stage whisper. "That's Diaochan over there." She pointed at a pale girl looking out the window. "What's your name?"

A name. I needed a name. "Mulan."

Her nose crinkled as she smiled. "I'm so happy you've joined us! It was getting so boring—Diaochan doesn't really talk." Peizhi glanced again at the screen door dividing our room from the Ximing courtesans.

"Courtesan Du is taking a nap," Peizhi explained, still whispering. "Do you want to go for a walk in the gardens?"

I glanced at the door. I had noted guards stationed along every corridor. "We're allowed to walk freely here?"

She giggled. "Of course. We just can't leave the palace. Not a bad arrangement, don't you think?"

Across the room, Diaochan made a sound like a scoff.

"She's unhappy because she had to leave her sisters behind in Chuang Ning," Peizhi told me. "They're back at the Plum Blossom Pavilion in East End. Where are you from?"

I recognized the Plum Blossom Pavilion as one of the most widely known pleasure houses in East End. But beyond the most famous establishments, I knew nothing about the workings of pleasure houses. Father had frequented a few, but he'd obviously never been vocal on the subject with his daughter.

Peizhi shrugged, mistaking my silence for reticence. "I'm from the Thousand Crane Palace. It's not as well known as Plum Blossom Pavilion, but it's decent enough. Obviously, nowhere near as nice as this. But I don't have any family—well, my family sold me off as a baby—so it's not like I have anyone to mourn." Her smile was patently false. "Poor Diaochan, though. All her sisters are trapped in the city, and they're Ruan, so they stick together. Where did you say you were from again?"

"Ch-Chuang Ning," I got out.

"That's what I thought! Do you have news of the war?"

Diaochan looked away from the window. "You're from the capital too?" she asked, crossing the floor toward us. When she neared, I saw she was almost a head taller than me.

I nodded.

"Have the walls fallen?" she demanded. Her accent was surprisingly southern, but I understood why she had been bought by the Plum Blossom Pavilion, which was probably the most selective pleasure house in all of East End. Despite her bloodshot eyes—she'd been crying—and her untidy hair, she was startlingly beautiful. Her skin was like alabaster, and her amber eyes slender and tapered, giving her the appearance of clear intelligence. Her mouth was tiny, the size of a rosebud, painted a pale pink hue.

"I saw the chancellor's black magic on my second day here," she said, as if to herself. "The phoenix he conjured from thin air, with that skies-awful jade . . ." Her eyes filled again. "They don't stand a chance, do they?"

"The last I heard, only the outer walls have fallen," I answered. "But I left over a week ago. I'm sorry about your sisters." I paused. "I have sisters of my own."

She nodded wordlessly.

"At least we're safe, right?" said Peizhi, in an attempt at optimism.

"Safe?" Diaochan sneered. "No one is safe with that *demon*—"

"Shh!" Peizhi interrupted, glancing at the adjoining door. "Why don't we go for a walk outside?"

"I'd love to see the gardens," I said. The more I could discover, the better.

Diaochan sighed with marked reluctance but followed us. Once we were out in the open-air gallery, Peizhi breathed easier. "Courtesan Du is in such a foul mood today. She asked me to clip her toenails and yelled at me when I cut one too short."

"Couldn't the servants do that?" I asked.

"She likes to pick on me." Peizhi scowled. "I think it's because the chancellor favors me. He chose me last night."

"He *chose* you?" I repeated, taken aback. "You mean, you aren't called every night?"

Peizhi chuckled. "Of course not. Even emperors don't have that much of an appetite. There are over half a dozen courtesans already, and now you've just arrived. He picks who he wants depending on his mood. He never keeps us long, though, and he's never violent. You should've seen some of my customers at Thousand Cranes."

What if the chancellor doesn't choose me? Sky, Sparrow, and Tao would act *tonight*. They would find a way to let our platoon into the palace and meet me in Sima's rooms at an hour past midnight, after I'd supposedly assassinated him. But what if I didn't succeed? What if Sima didn't choose me? What if Sky couldn't even get his men in?

Instinctively, my hand went to my chest, where I'd sewn my jade into the ruching at the bust. *There are so many variables that could go wrong*, I thought. *So many ways this could end in fire*.

"Let's go to the moon-viewing pavilion," said Peizhi, oblivious to my inner turmoil. "It's pretty empty at this time of day."

Guards smiled at us as we walked down the corridor. Some even called out greetings to Peizhi, who seemed to have settled in despite being here for less than a week.

"Little dumpling," one guard called, winking at Peizhi. "You're looking as—" He stopped short and saluted as a retinue of guards turned the corner, their strides long and their pace swift. Peizhi pulled Diaochan and me out of the way. She moved to bow, and that was when I recognized who stood at the head of the guards. It was Cao Ming Lei.

FIFTY-TWO

There are those with strong affinity and those with weak affinity. But even less is known about a third category: those with no spirit disposition at all. This rare class of people cannot perceive or possess spirit power in any capacity. Whether this is a blessing or a curse remains the topic of much debate. For while they cannot hope to gain the seductive power of lixia, they can also be assured they will never be corrupted by it.
—LOST JOURNALS OF AN 8TH-CENTURY LIXIA SCHOLAR, DATE UNKNOWN

THE XIMING PRINCE LOOKED EXACTLY AS HE HAD IN MY NIGHT-mares. Glossy hair, high cheekbones, a face like a painting. My eyes lingered on his full lips, before I caught myself staring and swallowed.

A cough escaped my throat. I tried to cover it, which naturally only made me cough harder. I bent over, choking, then turned toward the wall to avoid being seen.

"Are you okay?" Peizhi asked. "Mulan?"

I felt Lei's eyes slide over me. I cowered against the wall, covering my face as best I could. My eyes watered and I desperately tried to swallow my cough. My heart was beating so fast in my chest I thought I might faint.

Then their footsteps receded, and they were past us, down the hall. I straightened, my throat scraped raw.

"Heavens!" Peizhi said, as soon as we were out of earshot. "Was that the third prince of Ximing?"

Diaochan nodded disdainfully. I wiped at my leaking eyes.

Peizhi patted my back, making sympathetic cooing noises. "Are you all right?" she asked. Giggling, she added, "Are you allergic to the prince?"

Diaochan eyed the receding guards in the distance, frowning.

"My, he's handsome, isn't he?" Peizhi whispered. "I hope we run into him again. I've never seen anyone so good-looking."

"How long has he been here?" I asked.

"He arrived today, I think," said Peizhi.

"He was here last week too," Diaochan remarked. "I heard Courtesan Du talking about it. He's always coming and going."

My thoughts spun. Why was Lei here? Had I somehow fallen into his trap, in coming to Mount Fuxi? Was I still a pawn in someone else's game, to be used and discarded?

No, I told myself, things were different now. I had my own strength, my own power.

But perhaps that only made me a more valuable tool.

"Winter told me to look after you. That you could become Anlai's most important weapon one day."

Sky's words had stung more than I'd cared to admit. Couldn't he see that my loyalty was not to Anlai but to him?

Couldn't he see that I wished to be more than a weapon?

Perhaps once, I would have been satisfied with less. But I was not the girl who'd left Chuang Ning six months ago. I was hungrier now, greedier.

Unbidden, my last conversation with Xiuying came to mind.

"Sister, I know all these things," I'd pleaded with her. *"My ambitions are small. I only wish to have a little more time. A few months, maybe more. Then I will be satisfied."*

"You would rather death out there in the wild, than death here, enslaved," she'd said, understanding. *"And I will never see you again."*

Xiuying was a commoner marrying into a noble family, expecting to have her happy ending, only to be left penniless and ridden with debt. With an opium-addled husband to rely on, she'd run our entire household on her own, bargaining with loan sharks, distracting Father from gambling, overseeing the education of not only Plum but Rouha too. On the side, she'd even earned a bit of coin selling her herbal remedies to our wealthy neighbors. Her father back in Huang Ju was the town herbalist, and she had taught me what he had once taught her. Xiuying was the strongest woman I knew—the strongest person I knew. I only had to follow her example.

I straightened, wiping away my remaining tears. "Is there an herb garden around here?" I asked. "I'll brew some tea for us." I forced my eyes from blinking, as I always did before I lied. "It helps keep your skin radiant."

BACK IN OUR PERSONAL QUARTERS, I INGRATIATED MYSELF WITH THE other courtesans. I kowtowed before the four Ximing concubines and expressed my delight at learning from their mentorship. They were older than us Anlai girls, in their twenties and thirties. Courtesan Du was clearly their ringleader. As Peizhi eagerly and loudly anticipated my herbal tea, Courtesan Du asked what I was making.

I bowed to her. "I was trained in herbal medicine from a young age. This is an expensive tea I've brewed often for ladies such as yourself. It helps keep your skin supple by removing impurities from your pores."

Courtesan Du's eyes narrowed. When the tea leaves finished steeping, she reached for the first cup before Peizhi could.

Peizhi pouted but could not protest, given Courtesan Du's seniority. I assured everyone I would brew two pots, enough for all of us.

Everyone drank readily, everyone except Diaochan.

"It's bitter," Diaochan commented, taking only a small sip. After Courtesan Du had pretended to enjoy it, no one else dared complain. Diaochan set her cup down.

"You're beautiful enough as it is," Peizhi said, drinking Diaochan's share along with her own. "You don't need to put in the extra work."

Bitter was an understatement. The tea was not meant to be pleasant; rather, it was used as a laxative. Xiuying's father had made it for her grandparents every week to help with their constipation. Which, judging by the empty cups all around, the other courtesans would be finding out soon enough.

Courtesan Du insisted on another batch, which I happily obliged. These women were willing to suffer for their beauty. They were used to burning their skin to remove blemishes and tightening their waists to the point of fainting. In comparison to these practices, an unpalatable tea was the least of their concerns.

"My skin already feels softer," Peizhi remarked, after an hour. The sky was darkening, and I was growing impatient.

Diaochan sneered. "You drank all that water in your tea, what did you expect? It's mere hydration."

As evening fell, I began to worry that I hadn't brewed enough tea, until Courtesan Du let out an exclamation behind the screen door, rushing to the washroom. Minutes later, everyone followed.

Leaving Diaochan and me behind.

Diaochan glanced over at me, a silent question in her eyes. "We should get ready," she said. "They'll come for us soon. The chancellor doesn't like to be kept waiting."

FIFTY-THREE

Some say the dragon and phoenix were once lovers, in a time so long ago that history was not yet born. Qinglong and Zhuque were antithetical in nature, but in their differences, they came together. Peace did not last. Zhuque's jealous disposition made her hostile, and Qinglong's hunger for more made him unfaithful. Realizing they were better suited as enemies, the two swore an oath to never let peace come between them again.

—A HISTORY OF LIXIA, 762

DIAOCHAN OFFERED ME ONE OF HER DRESSES, WHICH I REFUSED. Compared to her fine silks, my robes were less than lovely, I knew, but I could not go without them. I checked to make sure my alterations were in place, my seal safely secured. As for Sima's jade, I now removed it from my skirt, choosing to wear it as a necklace tucked within my bodice. Once I entered Sima's private chambers, I would have to remove it from my body, then compel him to destroy it.

I took a deep breath. *Timing is everything.*

Following Diaochan's lead, I lined my eyes with kohl and dusted my face with ground pearl powder. She clucked at my amateur attempts and redid my makeup, choosing a paint the color of dried rose petals for my lips.

I stared at my reflection in the looking glass. With Diaochan's skill, I was unrecognizable, even to myself. I had no idea how I'd appeared to Sima in the spirit realm, but surely, it had not been like this.

Still, out of an abundance of caution, I chose a conservative headdress from the courtesans' communal wardrobe, one with beaded silk tassels that hung down in front of my face, forming a veil. By Anlai tradition, these headdresses were worn by virgins on their wedding night. But I hoped Chancellor Sima would either not know of this Anlai custom or not care.

"Despite your complexion, you have nice features," said Diaochan. "Why hide your face?"

I could not think of a plausible lie, so I said nothing.

She came closer, parting the tassels of my headdress. "Strange that your capital accent is impeccable, but your skin is so dark." She peered at me. "Which house did you say you were from again?"

Beneath the intensity of her gaze, I could barely think straight. "Palace of Peonies," I said, choosing the first name I could think of. Father had once tried to redeem one of the courtesans there, believing he'd fallen in love. But that was a long time ago, before he'd truly fallen in love with opium.

She smiled without mirth. "The Palace of Peonies is right across from me," she said. "I know every girl there. I never saw you."

"I was new," I said, a flush creeping up my neck.

"You're too old to be new," said Diaochan. "You're at least eighteen."

"I *am* eighteen."

"I wasn't born yesterday, Mulan. Why are you really here?"

I assessed her the same way she assessed me. I knew that Diaochan recognized Sima's power. She might have reason to shift alliances to the winning side in order to survive. Peizhi certainly seemed to be attempting this strategy. She could turn me in right now, and curry favor with the chancellor.

And yet, I thought, Diaochan was also a prisoner of war. Her family was still in Chuang Ning.

I followed my instincts. "Can I trust you?" I asked.

Her eyes widened. "Are you planning to assassinate the chancellor?"

How did she figure it out so quickly?

Her lips twitched into a grin as she unfurled my palm. "Your scars," she explained. "You have the hands of a sword dancer." Her voice dropped to a heated whisper. "I've dreamed of killing that bastard every night since I got here," she said. "Peizhi claims what he's doing is acceptable because he's given us silks to wear and food to eat. But I'll be damned," she hissed, "if I have to suck the cock of my sister's murderer for the rest of my life."

Before I could respond, a knock sounded at the door. Hurriedly, I removed Lei's necklace and handed it to Diaochan. "I can't explain right now," I told her quickly, "but I need you to wear this. When the time is right, I'll ask you to give it back to me."

Confused, she put it on as guards filed into the room. I tucked the pendant beneath her bodice, so that only the cord was visible.

She nodded at me, her eyes bright with rage. I, too, felt my own rage crystallizing in the absence of iron, hardening my resolve. Silently, I called upon my dormant lixia. *Wood, fire, earth, metal, water.* My qi woke slowly, flowing through me, unencumbered.

"Ladies." I recognized the guard as the one who'd called Peizhi a dumpling this morning. He looked around. "Where are the others?"

"Lady issues," I said, at the exact moment Diaochan said, "Diarrhea."

The guard blanched. "Well, then."

"There was an issue with our supper," Diaochan continued, accusation tightening her voice. "Courtesan Du is not pleased."

He muttered something about speaking with the chef before hastily leading us toward Sima's quarters.

Through my swaying tassels, I looked out at the summer palace, which was even more beautiful at night. Bamboo forests oscillated in the evening breeze, their leaves rustling in unison like the swish of silk fans. They bordered a shallow pond flecked with lily pads, whose pale purple blossoms curled inward as if resting before dawn. A family of mandarin ducks had gathered at the pond's edge, folding their wings delicately like courtesans plumping their skirts. Beneath the warm glow of hanging lanterns, I could even see koi fish, the brilliant speckles of color on their scales gleaming against the dark. The palace was deceptively serene. For now.

While the outside air was cold, inside, Sima's rooms were warm and aromatic. The fireplace blazed with warmth, and candles flickered from every table and windowsill. The air smelled of lavender, thick and redolent.

The guards led us past the keting into the bedchamber. Sima had not yet arrived, but the guards left us alone. I could hear them waiting in the hallway.

Diaochan turned to me. "I can convince him to let both of us—" She stopped abruptly as the front door opened. We both heard Sima cross the sitting room.

My heart raced. It was time.

Sima entered, and I bowed deeply, my beaded tassels clacking at my every movement. Keeping my head down, I peered up at him through my lashes. Sima Yi looked handsome in the candlelight. His beard was trimmed and groomed, framing his square jawline. He did not appear as he had in my dreams, maddened by grief and rage. Instead, he looked calm now, features tinged only by fatigue.

My gaze dropped to his left hand. On his middle finger he wore a striking jade ring—Zhuque's seal.

What conceit, I thought.

"You're new," Sima remarked. His voice sounded exactly as it had in the spirit realm. "You're from the Anlai capital?"

I bobbed my head, feigning demureness. Would he recognize my voice too?

"What is your name?"

Why do you wish to know? I wondered. "Hong Mulan, my lord," I said, pitching my voice at a higher octave.

He nodded, removing his sword, then his outer robe. "You," he said, nodding at Diaochan. "You can go."

Instead of heeding his command, Diaochan glided to his side, resting her hand against his chest. "Why not both?" she murmured.

He smiled but shook his head. "I am a simple man."

"You do not enjoy a challenge?" Diaochan raised a brow.

I tried to smile at him through my veil. It might have looked more like a grimace, because he frowned.

"You can also watch," Diaochan said, letting go of him to slide her hand along my neck. She fixed her eyes on me; I blushed beneath her cool gaze.

Sima watched with vague curiosity before shutting the door. We were truly alone now, no guards within earshot.

Diaochan went to the keting, where she poured him a glass of the sweet plum wine sitting on the aiji table. Sima refused the glass and instead, to my surprise, opened a secret cabinet behind his wardrobe, taking out another jar of wine.

"Drink with me," he suggested, pouring us both a glass.

I only pretended to drink, but Diaochan downed her wine, reaching for more and toasting to his health. They clinked glasses, smiling.

Only a few steps away, I stood awkwardly by myself, arms hanging by my sides. *Timing is everything*, I repeated to myself. But I did not know when to act.

Diaochan removed her shawl, baring her soft, pale shoulders. Sima turned to me. "Take off your headdress."

Would he know my face? But with Diaochan's makeup abilities,

I was hardly recognizable to myself. With trembling hands, I removed my veil, my head feeling immediately lighter.

Sima blinked and took a step toward me, but Diaochan surprised us both by forcing her lips onto his. The act was so sudden he lost his balance, and the two of them tipped back onto his bed. Giggling, Diaochan climbed on top of him, barely coming up for air. Was she drunk, mad, or . . . trying to distract him?

Now, I thought. The time was now. I slowed my breathing, focusing my qi. I felt my field of vision narrow as it did before battle. I would have to channel *all* my lixia toward him, toward compelling him. I could not afford to fail.

But before I could speak, Sima shot upright. "What is this?" he growled, his tone entirely changed.

Diaochan sat up, sensing the shift in the air. Sima was holding something in his hand, his other hand clenched around her shoulder. I crossed the room, then froze.

It was Lei's necklace.

The iron pendant had come loose in their foreplay. Sima wrenched it from Diaochan's neck, then dropped it with a hiss.

"What is the meaning of this?" he snarled, and the hairs on the back of my neck rose.

Now. Now. Now.

"*Sima Yi*," I said slowly, imbuing power into my voice, "*give me your jade.*"

His mouth dropped open. But this time was not like the last. This time, his guard was up. He went still, his body humming with lixia, and I felt an invisible shield slide into place in his mind, like a door sliding shut, trapping out all light.

"Haiyang," he said slowly, with effort. Beads of sweat pricked his temples. "So this is how we meet." He swallowed. "There was so much I wished to teach you."

My own body trembled with exertion. How could he withstand the power of my compulsion? "I learned from your mistakes," I hissed, through gritted teeth. *"Give me your jade."*

His hand convulsed, just one twitch, but we both saw that he was weakening. His jade ring caught the lamplight, quivering. I smiled, until he said, *"You will obey me."*

The power of his compulsion racked through my body like a wave of flame, burning me with its intention. The intention felt like my own, like I wished to obey myself. I thought of the willow tree, the willow tree, the willow tree. *Do not forget yourself, Hai Meilin—*

Memories flashed through my mind. My mother, reciting poetry on the eve of her death. My father, on the rare days he missed her, asking me to recount those verses. Xiuying and Rouha, inventing bedtime stories about the world beyond our walls. Sky, dueling me under the flickering oil lamps. The clash of our swords like song.

They were not enough. The memories were not enough. I began to lose myself under the weight of Sima's compulsion, the need to obey, to follow. I was a woman; I was bound to obey. I was a woman, a perversion—made of want.

My want defined me; it swallowed me. I remembered myself, lifting my head. "No," I answered, my breaths uneven. *"Give me your jade."*

Our gazes struck like steel against steel. We were locked in a stalemate, I saw, our mutual energies unable to tip the balance. Despite my animosity toward him, I'd never felt closer to anyone before. I could feel his fire and metal swirling through me, just as he felt my water and wood. In the end, I realized, we were all made of the same five elements. We were more alike than disparate.

Sima, too, sensed the stalemate, his eyes narrowing. But he found a weakness I had not. "Shi Diaochan," he said, and I recognized then why he'd asked me my name. *There is power in a name.* "Kill yourself."

I cried out, thrown off guard. Diaochan's eyes went blank as she reached for Sima's discarded blade and brought it to her throat without hesitation. "No, Diaochan!" I screamed, forgetting myself and breaking concentration. I lunged for her and tried to tug the hilt from her hands, but she fought me, swinging the blade at my face. I dodged her attack but forgot my true enemy, who struck me from behind, so that I fell, descending into the gaping maw of darkness.

THE RELIEF WAS MOMENTARY. I AWOKE TO PAIN, AND—*HORROR*. SIMA had clasped iron manacles around my wrists and gagged my mouth so tightly I could hardly swallow. His expression was cold and distant as he seized my robes and ripped them into shreds, exposing my undergarments. Diaochan shrieked in protest, but guards had entered while I'd been unconscious, and now one of them held her hostage.

I burned with shame as Sima tore even my undergarments off my body, searching for my spirit seal. Stripping me naked, he growled in frustration as he found no hidden jade on my person. "Skies, did you swallow the damn thing?" he demanded, above the sound of hammering in the room. "How?"

Diaochan's eyes went from me to my dress, lying limply on the floor. *A woman would know*, I thought with hate, glaring up at him. *Pity you're not one.*

"I tried," he told me under his breath, and at last, beneath his mask of indifference, I sensed his suppressed rage. Rage at me, at my warlord, and perhaps even at the spirits, pulling us like puppets. "I tried to offer you a different fate."

Tears of hot indignation spilled across my cheeks, blurring my vision, as I tried again and again to speak. I wanted to tell him he was wrong. He did not get to have it both ways. He was no different from the warlord he so despised.

Sima dropped me and I fell to the ground, my bound wrists unable to catch my fall. I tried to crawl toward my fallen dress, but a guard seized me by my manacles and used them to chain me to the wall. I had been stripped of my jade, my sword, even my clothes, I realized. Qinglong's vision was coming to pass.

The hammering in the room suddenly ceased. Turning, I saw a blacksmith in the keting, at work on something on the aiji table. *Lei's necklace.*

"It's done," said the blacksmith.

The magnitude of my failure crashed through me. Sima cradled the exposed jade in his hand, his expression impassive but his eyes flaring with triumph. I wanted to cry, to scream, to throw something. But I could only watch.

As the jade pieces merged in Sima's hand, Zhuque's seal glowed, emitting a soft hiss of excess lixia. A brilliant shock went through my body, like an imperial gong struck in my eardrums. I could feel the phoenix's power knitting back together, expanding, strengthening. My breaths turned shallow. As if in regaining its own life, the jade was leaching mine.

I needed the sea dragon's voice. I needed him to tell me what to do.

But I had shut him out. And now, bound in iron, I was truly alone. He could no longer reach me.

Sima's entire body convulsed. As if ripped from him, a giant shadow of a flaming bird emerged from his chest, rearing into the night sky. The bird screamed and screamed, but beneath Zhuque's cries, I heard another voice, overshadowed but still audible—Sima's.

How much of you is still left? I wondered, overcome by unexpected pity.

As if Sima sensed my remorse, he came to my side, where I sat huddled against the wall. Up close, his face now appeared years younger, fuller. Color had returned to his complexion, and his eyes, once dull, now sparkled under the light.

"You hate me," he said quietly, "but you're the only one who understands me. Do you know—the greatest injustice the warlord did to me was not in murdering my family. It was in letting me live." His hand tightened around Zhuque's seal. "Do you know what agony it is to live at the expense of others? No? I will show you."

I struggled against my shackles as Sima walked away from me. He was going to Chuang Ning now. The dragon had warned me this would happen. Everyone I loved would die. Only I would be spared—for I was meant for the cage.

Could I kill myself? I wondered desperately. Could I follow in my mother's footsteps?

The doors crashed open. Lei appeared in the doorway, his hair tousled and windswept, his robes soiled from riding. Two curved steel blades were strapped across his back. His sharp gaze went from the chancellor standing on the balcony, to the guards, to me.

He crossed the room in my direction, and I shrank back, until he removed his cloak and wrapped it around my bare shoulders. "You fool," he hissed, crouching before me to remove the gag from my mouth.

Then he got to his feet. "Chancellor," Lei said, raising his voice. Yet Sima Yi did not so much as turn. I peered at his still figure on the balcony, surrounded by guards yet unmoving, and made the connection. Sima was conversing with Zhuque in the spirit realm.

In frustration, Lei went to one of his guards, Dian Wei, and began to give instructions in a low voice impossible to overhear. I tried to swallow and was immediately struck by a coughing fit.

"Give her something to drink," Diaochan called. "Please."

To my surprise, one of the guards obeyed, pouring me a glass of plum wine from the aiji table. I did not usually drink, but I'd never needed alcohol more. I brought the wine to my lips as Lei whirled around, his eyes widening. He crossed the room faster than I thought possible and knocked the glass from my hand. The violet liquid sloshed onto the rug, the glass shattering into delicate shards.

"Don't drink that," he snarled, clearly angry with me. It was as if I'd failed him somehow, in a game I didn't know I was playing.

He exhaled. His voice dropped in despair: "It's laced with fine iron."

I gaped at him, astonished. His expression was one I'd never seen on him before. It reminded me of Sky's face as he'd watched the guards lead me away from the dungeons. Xiuying's eyes as she'd told me goodbye.

Hopelessness, I thought. Utter hopelessness.

A lightning bolt of recognition split my chest. I recalled Sima's memories, the subtle fragrance of cedar and jasmine left in the thief's wake. Had *Cao Ming Lei* been the one to steal the phoenix's seal, all those months ago? Had he been the one trying to destroy it?

I recalled the man I'd seen on the Yun mountaintop, the night of the harvest moon. That tall, broad-shouldered figure, twin blades strapped across his back. Even then he'd been following Chancellor Sima. Biding his time. Waiting to strike.

All this time, I'd been convinced Lei was after the jade for himself—because he coveted the chancellor's lixia. For why else would he seek the jade?

"*It is because of power that they did this,*" Lei had told me, back in

New Quan. *"Because they had it, and they wanted to hold on to it, or because they didn't have it, and wanted it. And it is because of power that my father, who is the most foolish, irresponsible man I know, can dictate the fate of thousands and determine the course of our kingdom. So ask me again if I believe power should be concentrated in the hands of a few. I do not care who the few are. I am not so naive as to believe I would be any different."*

He'd been trying to tell me, in his own way. But I had not understood him then.

"Lei," I said hoarsely, my thoughts whirring. He did not want Ximing to win this war, I realized. Or, he did not want his father to win this war. "Unchain me. I can destroy Sima's seal."

"You already failed," he said bluntly.

I glared at him. "It's not over until I say it is."

A ghost of a grin flickered across his lips.

"Trust me—just this once," I said lowly, trying to figure out how to best persuade him. "For-for Rea's sake." I did not know who Rea was, but I recalled how the crown prince had used her upcoming betrothal against him.

Lei's face hardened, and I thought I'd lost him, but then he released a hard breath and pulled a key from his sleeve. As he silently fit the key into my lock, I caught Diaochan's eye from across the room, then jerked my head toward my fallen dress, which was closest to her. She gave a tiny nod.

Adrenaline surged through me as my manacles fell away. Before the irons even hit the floor, I was up and running, sprinting toward the balcony. At the same time, Diaochan twisted and kneed her guard in the groin, then lunged for my dress and threw it at me. I caught it, caught my jade lodged in the bodice, then felt the lixia rush through me, lacing my bloodstream with cold, cruel intention.

I pushed through the balcony doors, biting my tongue hard enough to draw blood, then spat on my jade. I did not so much as touch Sima as collide directly with him. Distantly, I heard guards shout and try to separate us, but Lei had followed in my wake, drawing his sword. The clash of steel dimmed as we both fell, and fell, and fell.

"Why are you here?" asked Sima Yi, surprised.

I blinked, looking around. I'd brought us not into the spirit realm but somehow into a third realm, one I'd never seen before. This world appeared like a shadow realm of our own, carved out of darkness.

It did not matter where we were, I reminded myself. I had but one objective.

I brought the darkness to life with my lixia, blazing light out of absence. I searched for water in this dreamscape and found it deep within the earth, drawing upon it with my greed. I called and called and it answered.

Sima lashed out with fire, turning the air between us into thick steam. I froze the water pooled on the ground and skidded toward him, barreling recklessly forward as I aimed ice crystals at his eyes. He dodged and tried to grab my throat, missing but striking my arm instead. I cried out as his touch burned my skin, hot enough to reach bone.

He drew a ring of fire, hemming me in. I summoned knifelike hail from the sky. He tried to shield with flame, but he wasn't fast enough. Tiny knives sliced open his skin, flaying his face, shoulders, and arms with thousands of shallow cuts.

I raised my arms toward the black sky, reveling in my power. In the human realm, elemental magic was my weakness, but here, it came as naturally as employing a limb.

Sima growled in anger. Blood trickled down his face as he tackled me with brute force, his hands clenched into fists of flame. To my surprise and delight, his physical strength matched mine in this strange realm, giving neither of us the advantage. We rolled across the ground, each trying to get the other into a choke hold. On and on we went, no closer or farther from victory.

We're too evenly matched, I understood, sweat pouring down my back. *This will only end in both our deaths.*

I broke apart, putting distance between us before he could attack again. "We are fools, both of us," I snarled. "What do you think your hard-won victory will cost you?"

He only smiled. This was no surprise to him. "It will cost me my life," he acknowledged. "But my life is already forfeit."

I spat at his words. The idea that his victory meant nothing to him only further enraged me. Perhaps because it came at such great cost to my future. Perhaps because my own life meant everything to me.

I took a deep, steadying breath. I had tried compulsion back in the human realm, but even then, we had come to a deadlock. Haiyang and Taiyang. The sea and the sun. Our spirit affinities matched each other like twins, neither greater nor lesser. And yet, thinking of Lei and his careful manipulations, I wondered if I had somehow missed the point. Brute force was never as effective as gentle persuasion. The trick with compulsion was frighteningly simple: make it come from within.

I studied the pulsating light of his spirit seal. Although in the human realm our seals had manifested as jade stones, here our seals appeared within us, glowing more brilliantly than any light in this place of shadow. I could see his seal within his chest, throbbing to the rapid beat of his heart.

"Think of what you're enabling the Ximing warlord to accomplish with your power," I said, my voice coming out unsteady. "Think of what he'll do to other families like your own." Hesitantly, I took one step toward him. "You can end this, by destroying Zhuque's seal."

I saw the razor edge of his smile moments before he blasted me with an arc of living flame. I swore and rolled to the ground, my right leg blistering with heat. I hissed as I watched the skin crinkle and flake off, revealing charred bone.

"Do you think I care about those other families?" Sima asked me. "I am neither noble nor kind. We're selfish creatures, you and I."

The words stung; they stung because of how true they were. I bit my tongue and forced myself upright, withholding pressure from my right leg. If I were to do this, I needed to convince not only him, but myself.

What would make me destroy my own seal?

The idea felt *viscerally* wrong. Destroy the only thing that lent me power? That made others heed me? That offered me a chance at freedom?

But, I thought, there was a part of me that wished I'd never inherited my mother's necklace. That wished my mother had never gone mad. That wished I could have grown up with a family.

I looked across the vast distance at Sima Yi. Again, though we had just tried to kill each other, I had the sense that I'd never felt closer to another. I felt I knew him, in a way that went beyond words.

I knew his qi. His life force.

"*The greatest injustice the warlord did to me was not in murdering my family. It was in letting me live,*" Sima Yi had said. "*Do you know what agony it is to live at the expense of others? No? I will show you.*"

"You seek understanding from me," I realized. "That's why you want me to suffer." His hands began to glow red, yet I kept going. "You think it'll make you just a little less lonely."

Twin ropes of burning flame lashed out at me; I tried to duck, but the second one caught me on the back like the switch of a burning whip. I fell, but he did not press his advantage, merely watching as I rose unsteadily to my feet. I grew a bubble of cold water, pressing it against my wounds as a temporary salve.

"Getting your revenge won't make you any less lonely," I rasped through the pain. "Nothing you do will bring your family back, Yi. *Nothing.*"

He went still. I saw I had him then.

"Your vengeance only makes you more of a slave to Zhuque's whims." I lowered my voice, as if she might overhear us in this strange in-between world. "Do you remember who you were before you found her seal?"

Did I remember who I was before I inherited my mother's necklace?

Hesitantly, his eyes rose to meet mine. He did remember, I saw. A man vastly different from who he was now. A man, perhaps, who could've been my friend.

"*Destroy the seal,*" I said, my voice echoing with lixia. "*Not because you want to. Not because you're noble, or kind. But because you once were.*" My voice was choked with tears. I no longer knew whom I was addressing. "*Do it for the boy you once were.*"

His hand twitched. Once, twice, three times. At last, he reached into his chest and pulled out his spirit seal. It pulsated wildly, matching the rhythm of his own heart. Afraid, in danger of losing its life. Yi's own survival instinct reared, refusing his intent. But I saw his eyes; I saw his thoughts. Impulsion had always come most naturally to me.

He has to pay. Yi's thoughts were like a pounding drum, incessant. *I need to live—to make him pay.*

Then, a quieter voice—*Would Limei be ashamed of me? Would she even recognize me . . . in the afterlife?*

Or would she turn her face away from me?

Look at the monster I've become—his anger returned. *Li Zhuo must pay for his crimes. I can't let him live, satiated off the fats of his plunder. I will take from him everything he took from me—*

Limei. The quieter voice would not leave him. *And . . . what was my daughter's name? Why can I no longer recall it? Zhuque—she stole it from me. She said it would relieve the pain. I'd wanted her to take away my misery. But her price. Was it too great?*

I don't want this. I don't want this anymore.

I dragged myself out of Sima's spiraling thoughts. "*Destroy the seal,*" I rasped, clinging to my dregs of spirit power, "*and end this.*"

His hands trembled wildly, birds caught in cages. I peered into his golden eyes, so yellow they appeared translucent. Zhuque had nearly eaten him alive.

Little Pearl. Her name was Little Pearl.

"*Ba!*" Her small voice sounded like silver bells. "*Ba, where are you?*"

The tremors in his hands ceased. Now he clenched them into fists, strengthening his mental shields against the Vermillion Bird, but also—against me. I was thrust out of his mind by the force of his will, which felt like an iron brand against my skin. Pressing his advantage, he acted at once.

Sima Yi blew a flame so hot it turned blue in the palm of his hand. In the distance, we both heard the screech of the Vermillion Bird, her shrieking, panicked protests as she caught on to what was happening. Her screams traveled all the way from the spirit realm as she threatened him, cajoled him, whispered promises to him—promises she could not keep. He ignored her, watching as his seal burned away, first to a molten core, then to ash. And, like the seal, Yi himself faded, disintegrating into ash. Tears streamed down my cheeks.

So it was done.

Zhuque screamed in rage, though her cries were already growing distant as her own flames consumed her. For now, she could no longer exist outside the spirit realm. She could no longer come and go into the world of men.

But I could. And so could Qinglong.

I felt a tug at my gut, an unequivocal command. I had ignored him for so long. Patience had never been one of his virtues.

I closed my eyes and let myself fall into the spirit realm. Blood was hardly in short supply.

"*You deceived me,*" he growled, tail swishing in fury. "*I told you to bring me Zhuque's seal, not destroy it!*"

We stood in a reflection of the summer palace, on a balcony overlooking the Anlai mountain range. Yet there were no stars in the sky here, no light.

"You told me to give it to you so that you could destroy it yourself," I said woodenly. "I simply accomplished your task for you. You should be thanking me."

He hissed, slithering closer to me. "*You're even worse than your mother,*" he said, yellow eyes flashing with venom. "*I should have you die a worse death than her.*"

I went utterly still. "You killed my mother?"

FIFTY-FOUR

Much like an addiction, there comes a turning point when the excess lixia starts to overwhelm the body's somatic system, accelerating its decline. At that point, death is imminent.
—A COMPREHENSIVE OVERVIEW OF LIXIA-INDUCED DISORDERS, 910

BUT THE DRAGON HAD DISAPPEARED. IN HIS PLACE, WATER POURED from every alcove, as if the palace had tipped beneath the sea. I ran, but as I threw open the keting doors, I found the hallway already submerged in water. I started to swim, trying in vain to discover the exit. The waters rose as bloated corpses piled up against the walls and ceilings, bobbing up and down as if they were still sentient. I saw Diaochan's floating body, her head face down in the waves. I cried out and turned her; her lips were blue, her eyes wide open in death. I screamed at the sight, releasing her, then watched as she disappeared beneath the surface, weighed down by jewels.

The water levels continued to rise. My shoulders were already pressed up against the ceiling, only a foot of space left before the room was entirely submerged. I panicked, trapped, forgetting to inhale before the waves closed over me—

A FAMILIAR ARMLET CLOSED AROUND MY WRIST, AND SUDDENLY I WAS dragged back into the human realm.

Lei knelt over me, clasping something against my arm. I looked down and found Lieutenant Fang's iron heirloom. How had Lei gotten this?

Then I saw Sky standing behind him.

Dizzily, I rose to my feet, still in total shock. My hand went to my mouth as I saw the pile of ashes beside me—where Yi's body should have been.

Turning, I retched violently. Water came up. Distantly, I recalled my dream of drowning. But had that been a dream? My cloak was soaked through. I was shivering.

My blood crept as memories returned to me. *"I should have you die a worse death than her."*

I staggered back, lost and disoriented. I barely registered the fight unfolding around me, as more and more Anlai soldiers rappelled up onto the balcony, leaping into combat. I watched numbly as Sky disappeared behind a swarm of Ximing guards. I reached for my sword, then discovered I wasn't wearing one. Beneath my cloak, I wore nothing.

How was I still alive? How was I still alive when Sima Yi was dead? When my mother was dead?

In a fog, I backed away from the fighting, or tried to. I stopped short as I caught sight of Lei near the door.

He was on his knees, disarmed and bleeding. He raised his head as Tao brought his sword down in a killing blow—

I cried out and ran forward, catching Tao's sword with my bare hand before it met Lei's throat. I bit out a scream as the sword sliced the palm of my hand, but still I did not let go. "No," I rasped, trembling with exertion. "No."

Tao lowered his sword, his eyes narrowed. I stared at my bleeding palm, numb with adrenaline. I did not understand why I had just saved him.

"We'll take him as a hostage." I lifted my head to see Sky approach. Tao began binding Lei's arms, wrenching his shoulders back so tightly Lei winced in pain. "His release can be negotiated in the treaty agreement," said Sky.

"How irksome for you," Lei said to Sky. His voice was light, nonchalant, as if he weren't bound and on his knees before us. "You suspect what will happen, don't you? I'll get a little slap on the wrist, spend a night in prison, perhaps two, and then return home. Justice is sweet, is it not?"

Why are you baiting him? I wondered. The Ximing prince bordered on masochistic.

"It is not justice," Sky spit out. "It is your undue privilege as prince, to not experience the consequences of your own actions."

Lei smirked. "I'm sure you don't relate."

I watched the muscles in Sky's face contort. Before I could stop him, he kicked Lei viciously in the face. "Sky!" I cried out. I was certain this went against treaty protocol.

Lei had fallen to the floor. He sat upright with effort, his teeth gritted. He was going to get a very pronounced black eye.

"I said I'd keep you alive," Sky warned, his voice dangerously low. "I said nothing about injuries."

Lei ignored his threat and glanced at me. "He's a real charmer," said Lei. "I can see why you chose him. Though I was much better in bed, wasn't I?"

Sky snarled and lunged at him, but I jumped in his way. "Sky, stop!" I shouted, grabbing him by the shoulders. "Can't you see he's baiting you?"

"It's fun, isn't it?" said Lei from behind me. "Hurting people."

I gripped Sky as tightly as I could. He was breathing hard, his chest heaving. I released him only when I was sure he'd remembered himself.

"Gag him," Sky ordered Tao, his jaw pulsing. "And get him out of my sight."

I exhaled, not daring to meet Lei's eyes. I did not know what I'd find in them, and I did not wish to know. When Lei was gone, Sky turned to me.

"Let's get you changed," he said softly, before noticing the bloody smear on my palm. "And let me bandage your hand."

He started guiding me toward the adjoining room, before I hesitated. "Where's Diaochan?" I asked, looking around. Without their leaders, the remaining Ximing guards had surrendered. Yi's chambers were filled with Anlai soldiers organizing servants and guards into groups. I did not see a girl in their midst.

Sky frowned. "Who?"

"She was wearing blue robes," I said, growing increasingly frantic as I looked over the crowd of people. "She's tall, pale—"

"A girl?" Sky said. "I think I saw one with the bodies."

My heart dropped to the floor. "Where are the bodies?"

"They've brought them out to burn," he said. "We can look later—"

The last dregs of my self-control disintegrated. I slumped against the wall, breaking into suffocating sobs.

Sky crouched beside me. "Meilin?"

"I persuaded her to help me." I could barely speak through my tears. "She had sisters in Chuang Ning, at the Plum Blossom Pavilion. She had sisters like me."

"It's not your fault, Meilin."

But I sensed the lie in his words. It *was* my fault. Diaochan would not have been here tonight if not for me.

Yi had made the selfless choice in choosing to destroy his own seal. I had convinced him, and in doing so, I had nearly convinced myself to do the same. And yet, unlike Yi, I was selfish to my core: rotten, made of want.

I should kill myself, I thought desperately, *so that the dragon can no longer use me.* I was nearing madness, a danger to myself and to others. Perhaps it had not been cowardice that made my mother fly from the rooftops. Perhaps it had been mercy.

Madness, there was so much madness within me. I leaned back and bashed my head against the wall, so hard my forehead split. Blood gushed into my eyes as Sky shouted at me. I tried again, but this time, Sky grabbed me by my wrists, restraining me. I struggled against him, sobbing, as he held me so tightly I could not break free.

"Meilin," he said, "stop. It's over. The war's over."

The war is . . . over?

Giving in to crushing fatigue, I went limp in his arms. He picked me up and led me down the hall, away from the others. "You did it, Meilin," he told me. "You killed the chancellor."

But that wasn't what I'd done at all. I had no tears left in me, so I simply buried my face in his shoulder. "Sky?" I murmured.

"Hm?"

"Stay with me?"

He sighed. "Always."

FIFTY-FIVE

Then the Lord Cao turned to Lord Liu. "You and I," he said, "are the only heroes that will be remembered in this world."
—CHRONICLES OF THE THREE KINGDOMS, 954

IT TOOK US THREE DAYS TO DEPART FROM MOUNT FUXI. I SAW THE Ximing prince only once during the journey to Chuang Ning, when we'd stopped along the way to change horses.

Lei's ropes had been replaced by manacles. His usually flawless appearance was now marred by a black eye.

Still, he smiled as he caught sight of me. On an impulse, I looked around, then approached him. The guards surrounding him recognized me and obeyed as I waved them off. I had changed back into my soldier's uniform and tied back my hair, so that no one in the army knew my true identity, no one save Sky, Sparrow, and Tao.

I stopped a few feet away, not daring to get any closer. Even though he was chained and heavily guarded, I remained afraid of him somehow. It was a conditioned instinct, from weeks in captivity. I resented him for it.

"Why did you do it?" I asked, voicing a question I'd nursed for the past few days. "Months ago, before the war began. You stole Sima's jade from him in his sleep. You tried to destroy the phoenix seal. Why?" Lei could have simply killed him then, I realized, but he'd spared his life instead. It made no sense.

A wry smile tugged at his lips. "I'm assuming you'll never tell me how you figured that out."

I looked away from him, envying his smile, envying the way he always managed to appear as if he had the upper hand.

"So many secrets, *Ren*," he said. I could hear the laughter in his voice. "You always hid so much from me."

"You hid more," I shot back, my composure fraying. "You lied to me. You tortured me. You . . . you played with me."

I did not know why I was losing my temper. He was a prisoner already, for skies' sake. Was I really so naive as to seek an apology from him?

"So I did," he acknowledged. "And still you spared my life."

"It was a life debt, nothing more," I said. "Now that debt is paid. There is nothing between us anymore."

"Is that so?"

I met his eyes fiercely. "Yes," I answered, before turning to go. I did not know what I had been thinking, approaching him like this. I would get no closure from him. I would never understand his intentions, his impenetrable motives.

"I'd been waiting for you for some time, you know," he said offhandedly. I stopped short, unable to resist the pull of answers. "You see, my mother was Ruan, and she had second sight."

I'd read those words somewhere but could not recall what they meant. "What?"

"The ability to foretell the future," said Lei, watching me. Nervously, I twisted the iron armlet against my skin; I had not taken it off since Mount Fuxi.

I had always suspected him of reading my mind.

"But the sight is not as simple as it sounds. Like spirit seals, it follows its own set of arcane rules. My mother foresaw my rise to power. She failed to foresee its cost." His expression turned cold. "Her life."

My throat went dry.

"She told me a girl with golden eyes would have the power to change my fate, and the fate of the Three Kingdoms," he continued. "But she failed to foretell what a little menace you'd be." His eyes sparked. "And how distracting."

Color rose in my cheeks. I was suddenly anxious to get away from him.

"*Ren*," he said, as I waved the other guards back. I realized he was using my false name because of our audience. To protect my identity.

"Be . . . careful." He chose his next words with caution. "You should know not to put your trust so wholeheartedly in others."

This, more than anything else he'd said, infuriated me to my core. His tone was not condescending, but I could take it no other way. I swung back around, glaring at him. "You're worried for *me*? You're the one in chains, Your Highness."

His smile was bitter. "Not all chains are apparent to the eye."

WHEN WE REACHED THE CAPITAL A WEEK LATER, I WAS ANXIOUS TO see my family. Sky assured me he'd send soldiers to check on their safety, but the warlord had sent out an official summons requesting my presence, and I could not refuse. He wanted to see the entire platoon that had ridden out to Mount Fuxi.

The platoon was thrilled at the honor. As we rode through the main thoroughfare, women and children applauded us, cheering, throwing flower petals. The news had spread: a platoon of fifty soldiers had single-handedly turned the tide of the war.

I rode behind Sparrow to the Forbidden City, while Sky rode at the front. At the intersection, I looked longingly toward my home in Willow District but forced myself to follow the others, dismounting at the palace entrance.

"Skies above," Sparrow exclaimed from up ahead, where he was chatting with another soldier whose name I couldn't recall. Sparrow had ignored me for the past week, replacing me with new friends as easily as changing clothes. "It's even grander than the paintings!"

His friend gushed in agreement. And yet I could barely register the opulence of the Forbidden City. *Why don't I feel more excited?* I wondered. The dragon's vision was coming to fruition, just as I'd hoped. I was getting what I wanted, wasn't I? Honor and glory and recognition, from the Imperial Commander himself. I had secured victory for my kingdom and, more importantly, for my family and those I loved. I had proven myself not only to my squad, or to my company, but to the entire Three Kingdoms. I had gotten everything I once wanted.

Why do I still feel so empty inside?

Liu Winter greeted us as we entered the palace, speaking to Sky in hushed tones. Sky glanced back at me before striding into the throne room. I smoothed my topknot to make sure it was secure, then followed a few paces behind the princes.

I had only ever seen the warlord from a distance, and I had certainly never entered the throne room. Now awareness returned to me. I felt like a child again as I stared at my surroundings with equal parts awe and fear. The zaojing ceilings above me depicted a coiled azure dragon with a burnished silver pearl in its mouth. At the far end of the hall, a raised platform elevated the emperor's throne, which was flanked by six marble columns, each engraved with gilded dragons. The throne itself was painted gold and, unsurprisingly, embellished with dragons.

The warlord stood to greet us. We all bowed deeply before him, kowtowing on the ground. I pressed my forehead to the cold glazed tiles, feeling my face heat. Before the warlord himself, my nerves returned to me.

"Rise," he said, his deep voice booming across the open expanse. "I invited you here today to honor and commend you. For my son has informed me of your valor and bravery in battle." His eyes swept over the platoon before landing on me. "Especially you, Hai Ren."

I stiffened, peering up at the warlord. He looked impossibly far away on his dais, unreachable.

"Prince Liu spoke of how you killed Chancellor Sima in single-handed combat. How in the face of crisis you demonstrated composure, courage, and outstanding virtue."

I opened my mouth to protest, then shut it. It was not the honorable battle the warlord imagined. It had been chaotic, frightening, devastating. The phoenix's screams still echoed in my nightmares.

But of course, no one knew what had really happened. No one but three people knew how I'd truly infiltrated the palace. I glanced back at Sparrow, whose face blazed red as he averted his eyes from me. He looked . . . furious.

"For your many accomplishments, you should be appointed to a position of the highest distinction. I would have you lead my battalion, if you accept—"

"Your Imperial Majesty." To my astonishment, Tao stepped forward, bowing before the warlord. As he passed me, he averted his eyes. His face was grim, his back stiff. "I apologize for speaking out of turn. But I cannot allow this travesty to stand."

Sky's face had gone white. "Captain Luo—"

Tao ignored him. "It is a perversion to our kingdom and our social order. Hai Ren is a liar and a traitor." He swallowed thickly. In his hesitation, Sparrow ventured to his side.

"Hai Ren is a woman," said Sparrow. And now I understood why he had not been able to look me in the eye.

For a second, no one spoke. Then Sky shouted obscenities at Tao, Winter grabbed his brother, and the platoon behind me descended into barely veiled whispers.

The warlord fixed his hawklike gaze on me. "Is this true?" he asked, and the fact that he'd asked me first, directly, instead of ordering someone else to speak on my behalf, brought tears to my eyes.

"Yes," I forced out, steadying myself. The warlord would be upset, of course, that I'd broken a cardinal rule. But he'd have to forgive me, for I'd saved his kingdom. His people. His own son.

It is all happening, I thought, *just like in Qinglong's vision*.

The warlord sat back in his throne, studying me.

"Father," Sky spoke up, despite Winter's looks of warning. "She has done much for this—"

"Silence," the warlord snarled, holding up his hand. "If you speak out of turn again, I'll have you removed from the inner palace."

I swayed on my feet, struggling to remain calm.

"Hai Ren, you have a choice," the warlord began, in a placating voice. At his tone, the lump in my throat eased. He was not irrational or impetuous like the warlord of Ximing, I reminded myself. He was Sky's father, and a victorious leader. "You know very well your crime is worthy of execution."

Sky made a strangled noise; Winter clapped his hand over his brother's mouth.

"If not for your wartime deeds, I would send you to the gallows now. But it is true that you have done much for this kingdom." He stroked his beard, then rose to his feet. "And yet, if I allow such a perversion to exist, then I am a hypocrite to call myself a man of honor. So you see, you have placed me in a rather difficult position."

My throat felt coated in dust. It was an effort to swallow.

"I will offer you a choice. You may renounce your ways as a soldier and live as a proper, respectable woman. You will never again lift a sword, and never again leave the confines of the women's quarters. You will submit to your father and, once wed, your husband, and you will never again break the law."

His words echoed as if from across a vast distance. *The sea dragon lied to me*, I realized. I had trusted Qinglong because I'd seen him as an immortal spirit, and, subconsciously, as a god. I'd followed him heedlessly, never questioning his assertions.

Even now, I could feel the dragon's vision lurking at the back of my mind, taunting me. That future would never come to pass as he'd shown me. But of course. I'd wanted everything he'd promised—love, acceptance, freedom, power. I thought I wouldn't have to choose.

But everything had its price.

"Or what?" I said, my voice breaking. "You said you were giving me a choice. What is the choice?"

His eyes narrowed. "If you refuse this mercy, then I will have no alternative but to imprison you."

A dull roar filled my ears. "That is no choice at all. You are offering me a life of captivity, no matter what I decide."

He strode forward, standing at the edge of his dais. "So you refuse to return to the ways of womanhood?"

My chin trembled, but I forced myself to lift my head high. "I could never live like that again."

I could not read the warlord's expression. "Very well." He inclined his head. "Hai Ren, you have endangered the social order, jeopardized the morality of the law, and threatened the welfare of the state. For your crimes, you are sentenced to a lifetime of imprisonment." He raised one hand, his eyes already turning away from me. "Guards."

They grabbed me in seconds; I did not resist. My head had emptied of all sound and sight and meaning. I felt my body being lifted and dragged away like a rag doll.

The light changed around me. Dimly, I registered Sparrow and Tao blocking the gallery outside the throne room. "You must strip her," said Tao, his eyes blazing. "For she carries a demon stone, hidden within her tunic."

I couldn't recognize them anymore. Gone were the companions I'd traveled with, supped with, joked with. And Sparrow—he was finally looking at me now. Looking at me as if I were a stranger.

"Sparrow," I whispered, my voice thin. "Why are you doing this? Is it truly so abhorrent to you that I wish to live freely?" I blinked back unexpected tears. I had no more fight left to give. "I saved your life—I saved all your lives."

Sparrow's voice came out stilted and slow. "What you're doing... it's selfish. It's wrong," he said. "We—I—can't allow it. Then we'd be criminals too."

So this was what they believed. Xiuying's parting words resounded in my head. *"They would never let a woman get away with something like this."*

"Something like what?"

"They would never let a woman hold on to power."

Yet still, despite multiple warnings, despite common sense, I'd tried. I'd tried with guileless desperation to earn their approval, their acceptance, their love. Like a child desperate with thirst, I'd been content to drink whatever was offered to me, even poisoned water. I'd drunk and desired more, learning to crave the venom, to seek out its taste.

Even the Ximing prince had recognized this warped impulse within me. *"You should know not to put your trust so wholeheartedly in others."* He'd seen the writing on the wall. Everyone had. Only I had not.

Despite everything I'd done for this kingdom, despite destroying the phoenix's seal and winning the war, still I was not enough. My mission had been doomed from the start. For there was nothing I could do to make them accept me.

As the Ximing prince had said, no one would ever give up their power. Not willingly.

In the back of my mind, I registered iron manacles being fastened around my wrists and ankles. I felt the damp chill as we descended underground into the palace dungeons. I registered the dearth of sunlight, the death of freedom.

Distantly, I heard someone screaming my name. It was Sky. I caught the sounds of a scuffle, then silence. But I was not worried for him. He was a prince, and I was only a girl.

They shoved me through a door, then locked it behind me.

The war was over now, and so I was rendered useless. All along, I'd only been a glorified tool. A perversion, my *friends* had called me. So a woman who could kill a man was a perversion, I thought, half-amused.

In the dark, I rephrased the Imperial Commander's words:

A woman who could use a blade endangered the social order.

A woman who could think for herself jeopardized the morality of the law.

A woman who could take power away from those who held it threatened the welfare of the state.

I lay back in my prison cell and at last, I let myself laugh. Madness, I knew, was catching. They had locked me away and forced me to submit, and now they believed themselves secure, their power restored, their ways of life cemented in stone. But they did not know: they were not safe.

And I would never relent.

FROM THE ANNALS OF THE IMPERIAL COMMANDER, 923, FOLLOWING THE END OF THE THREE KINGDOMS WAR.

BIOGRAPHIES OF NOTABLE WAR CRIMINALS:

In the year 923, Hai Meilin, eighteen, under the alias Hai Ren, broke contract with her husband (name unknown) by disguising herself as a man and enlisting in the Anlai army during the Three Kingdoms War. In enemy territory, she was quickly discovered as a woman and taken captive to become a consort for the second prince of Ximing, Cao Ming Lei. During her captivity, Hai Meilin disclosed many of Anlai's most confidential military secrets to Ximing. Scholars attribute this betrayal as one of the key factors that enabled Ximing to hold out in the Three Kingdoms War for seven months, despite its significantly weaker forces.

Upon Ximing's eventual defeat, Hai Meilin was discovered at the site of surrender on Mount Fuxi, claiming to have acted out of mental illness and temporary insanity. Tried for her war crimes at high court, she was convicted and imprisoned on grounds of sedition and treason. Though some sources claim the woman was skilled with a sword, these claims remain uncorroborated. Notably, Hai Meilin did not participate in battle.

TO BE CONTINUED...

AUTHOR'S NOTE

To this day, most Westerners are only familiar with the legend of Mulan through its Disney retellings. In Disney's animated version, Mulan gets her cake and eats it too. Upon saving the kingdom, she is praised by the emperor for her brave deeds, welcomed home by her father, and even courted by her army captain and true love.

In many Chinese versions of the legend, Mulan does not fare so well. In *Romance of the Sui and Tang Dynasties*, written in 1695 by Chu Renhao, Mulan is summoned by the emperor to become a concubine after the war. Forced to choose between duty and honor, she commits suicide on her father's grave, thereby preserving her unyielding virtue.

However, what ties all these disparate versions together is a commitment to the status quo. Although Mulan is generally considered a symbol of gender equality—choosing to resist social norms by disguising herself as a man—she does not defy existing structures of power because she is ultimately motivated by her filial piety and duty to her country. Critically, when the war is over and her duties to her father and emperor are fulfilled, she returns home, content to resume life as a conventional woman.

But what would happen to Mulan if she were no longer content? What if, upon experiencing independence and freedom as a man, she no longer wished to confine herself to the restrictive gender boundaries of her society? Would society accept her as she was, or, by transgressing the norm, would they punish her for daring to aspire for more?

With these questions in mind, I set out to write a Mulan retelling with a protagonist who does not dress as a man and join the army out of filial piety, but rather out of her own selfish desire to experience life freely. At the core of *The Night Ends with Fire* is the question: What does our ambition cost us?

At the start of her journey, Meilin is neither confident nor bold. Oppressed as she has been all her life, she does not recognize her ambition for what it is, but instead sees it as an aberration, further proof of her depravity. And yet, over the course of the war, as Meilin gains courage and comes into her own power, she begins to redefine the parameters of her potential and reimagine how far she can go in this world.

I hope you, too, may do the same.

K. X. Song

ACKNOWLEDGMENTS

To my agent extraordinaire, Peter Knapp, and to the brilliant Stuti Telidevara, thank you for championing this book from the beginning. To my tremendous editor, Anne Sowards, thank you for your keen insight and wisdom. To the entire publishing team at Ace and Berkley, particularly: Adam Auerbach for art direction, Daniel Brount for the lovely interior design, production editor Megan Elmore for coordinating the copyediting and proofreading, and to Jessica Plummer, Elisha Katz, Kristin Cipolla, and Stephanie Felty for marketing and publicity. To Victo Ngai, for creating the cover of my dreams. Thank you for shepherding this story into the world so beautifully.

It is a joy to also be a part of the Hodderscape team in the UK. Immense gratitude to Molly Powell, who understood my vision for this book from our very first call, and to everyone at Hodderscape, particularly Sophie Judge, Laura Bartholomew, Kate Keehan, Inayah Sheikh Thomas, and Carrie Hutchison. Thanks to Lydia Blagden and Will Speed for the inspired design, and Matthias Ball for the delightful cover.

ACKNOWLEDGMENTS

And, of course, thanks to Anissa de Gomery. Meeting you was like the start of a magical rom-com. Thank you for reading and loving *The Night Ends with Fire*, for being my fellow love-triangle kindred spirit, and for treating me to the most enchanting afternoon in London (truly like a scene from a movie). Working with Fairy-Loot has been a dream come true like no other, and this couldn't have been possible without the entire extraordinary, fairylike team.

Endless thanks to everyone at Park & Fine for all that you do behind the scenes, particularly: Emily Sweet, Andrea Mai, Ben Kaslow-Zieve, and Danielle Barthel. To Kat Toolan and Abigail Koons, thank you for making foreign editions happen; I couldn't be more thrilled to bring *The Night Ends with Fire* to readers across languages and borders.

To Grace D. Li, next-door neighbor and partner in crime. No one gets living dual lives like you. To Joan He, for reading and believing always. To Adriana De Persia Colón, my perpetual first reader; I trust you with all my words. To Yixuan Jiang, for the wealth of knowledge and all your late-night answers. To Amélie Wen Zhao, for understanding what it's like to live between cultures. To Randy Ribay, for the most incisive questions. To Shelley Parker-Chan, for the master class in writing angst. To Alison Green Myers and George Brown, for all that you do at the Highlights Foundation, where many of the words in this book were written. To Alex Villasante, for the ray of sunshine that you are. To Aleese Lin, for opening your beautiful home to us. To Martha Brockenbrough, for your care and thoughtfulness. To Ploi Pirapokin, for teaching me how to make magic.

To Jacqueline Barnes, for waking up with me during those early-morning hours, before even the sun had risen. Knowing you were waiting for me, I found the motivation to get out of bed. I'm so glad to create worlds alongside you.

ACKNOWLEDGMENTS

To all the booksellers, librarians, and bloggers who championed *An Echo in the City* with such kindness and generosity, including: Holly, Cheenie, Talia, Gerard, Abby, Zsamé, and Veronica. You make me want to keep telling stories.

To my family: my mother and father, who never vilified my ambition and instead encouraged me to dream bigger dreams. To my siblings, for late-night solidarity and emergency french fry runs. To Auntie Kwok, for your above-and-beyond generosity. To Grandma, for everything.

To those who will never be recorded in history, yet your memory and legacy live on. May we remember.

**Forged in battle.
Her legend begins.**

Read the explosive sequel to the *Sunday Times* bestselling fantasy *The Night Ends With Fire.*

Buy *The Dragon Wakes With Thunder* now

Read on for the first chapter of

THE
DRAGON
WAKES
WITH
THUNDER

ONE

You may burn bamboo, but it will still stand straight.
You may shatter jade, but its color will not fade.
—BOOK OF ODES, 856

TIME BORE THE QUALITY OF A TANGLED SPOOL OF THREAD. I could not unravel the knots, could not sense where things ended, could not recall where things began.

I started, like always, from what I knew: I was in the palace dungeons, in the capital city of Anlai, my home. My home when I had no ability to choose where I called home.

I had been here for some time now. I had not tried to count the days, which had bled into weeks or months or years. By the chill in the air, and the fur lining of my jail warden's coat, winter was fast approaching.

Snow would be settling on the branches of Xiuying's beloved plum trees, which she pruned every spring. The snow would spread across the garden like colorless jewels, catching the winter sunlight and refracting it in every direction. Rouha would be chiseling out exuberant ice sculptures, and Plum would be trying to eat snow. Uncle Zhou would be simmering his favorite winter melon soup, which tasted heavenly on a cold snowy morning.

The taste of life had been sweet, hadn't it? But it tasted sweetest when it was taken from you.

I remembered the thrill of unfathomable power surging through my veins, that eddy of sheer delight as roiling waves rose to meet my call. Racing through a darkening forest, fighting side by side with my comrades in arms. Knowing my platoon had my back. Knowing I had friends to call my own.

Friends, they said, before betraying me. But we didn't think about that anymore.

I remembered climbing onto a terrace railing and looking out over the dark expanse of water, the waiting ocean like a well of black, black ink. The recklessness that felt like a drug, better than a drug, the thrill of knowing the waves would catch me. *Will you obey me?* I'd asked the sea. *Will you obey me as you obey the dragon?*

And yet, down here in the dungeons, my memories felt as distant as dreams.

The outer door to my prison cell clanged open. I heard the thud of footsteps, even and heavy. Three sets of them.

"Good evening, sweetheart. Let's continue where we left off last time, shall we?"

My heart began to stutter. A practiced response, a trained step in the choreography. Already I could feel the nerves in my hand tingling, anticipating the pain to come. Perhaps the anticipation was worse than the pain itself, for these days, pain lingered beneath every waking moment. There was the pain of separation: of no longer hearing the dragon's voice. The pain of dependency; I needed lixia in my bloodstream like a person needed water. Then there were the more insidious hurts, carved into me like scars: the marks of betrayal, of loneliness. Of knowing there could be no happiness for someone like me.

A perversion. A threat to the state. A girl who desired more.

"Get up."

I did not move. They unlocked the door to my cell and lifted me. Still I did not resist. I felt them clasp chains around my legs, securing me to the interrogation chair.

"*Your greed is unending*," the dragon had once told me. "*An ocean's hunger.*"

They fit wooden sticks around my fingers, opting for my left hand this time. Slowly, the guards pulled the ropes connecting the sticks, not enough to inflict pain, only discomfort. Ironically, the zanzhi, finger crushing, was a torture method reserved for women, as it was considered more humane than jiagun, leg twisting. But I had endured both.

"Where are the remaining black magic practitioners hiding?" asked Warden Hu.

I tried to speak but no sound emerged. It must have been days since I'd last spoken aloud.

"Give her water."

One of the guards forced a canteen of water down my throat, and I sputtered, coughing.

"Where are the black magic practitioners hiding?" he asked again.

I cleared my throat. "There are no others."

"You lie." He nodded once. My throat tightened with the ropes.

I gasped as the pain came, sharp and staggering. Although the pain was concentrated along the base of my fingers, my entire arm reverberated with feeling. Despite the chill in the air, I was soon sweating.

They released the ropes. I sagged against the chair, my hand throbbing with pain. I stared at the useless appendage as if it belonged to a stranger. My right hand was too sore to use, and now my left would soon follow. How did they expect me to eat and drink? How did they expect me to live?

Or had this been their intention all along? To bide their time until Sky forgot me, until my family forgot me, until I faded into oblivion, an unnamed scratch in the annals of history?

"*The might of the sea,*" Qinglong had said, "*is yours.*"

"Where are the remaining black magic practitioners hiding?" Warden Hu asked a third time, his voice as calm as a still lake.

"I know of no others," I said hoarsely. "But perhaps . . . there could be minor spirit summoners in the south? They are more open to lixia practitioning in Ximing . . ."

"Ximing?" He leaned in. "Is that where—"

"Let me through!"

Warden Hu startled at the sounds of a scuffle. A figure clad in white shoved past the stationed guards, striding toward me like a mirage. His complexion was so fair and his robes so clean, he looked like he belonged in a heavenly realm, one set apart from the filth of this place.

"Warden Hu?" Sky's surprise was evident. "What are you . . . ?"

His eyes flicked to me—and I caught the horror in them. Without meaning to, I shrank from his gaze, as if I had anywhere to hide here. It stung for him to look at me like that, to see me with pity, and beneath it, revulsion.

Sky whirled on the warden. "What are you doing to her?"

Warden Hu straightened his shoulders. "Your Highness—"

"My father strictly forbade torture of any kind!"

"The Imperial Commander authorized me to conduct this interrogation," Warden Hu said, careful to keep his tone neutral.

Sky glared at him. "Then why sneak around like this—in the middle of the night, as if . . ." His face changed as the answer came to him. "To keep me from finding out," he finished flatly.

Sky was always like this, as expressive as an open flame. It endeared him to me, but also, it made me resentful. Because no woman could live like that. No, what we were trained to do was conceal, conceal, conceal. Every emotion flung far beneath a smiling mask of good humor and grace.

"Your father believes you have more pressing matters to attend to, Your Highness. You need not concern yourself with the welfare of a state traitor."

Sky ignored him, seizing the bars of my cell. "Meilin," he said urgently, and up close he was so lovely and clean and pure it was difficult to look at him. He radiated health and vigor, like nothing else in these dungeons. "I'm going to get you out of here. I promise," he said. "Just—hold on a bit longer. I'm sorry."

I did not feel any particular emotion, and yet my eyes filled with tears. I did not know why I was crying.

"Meilin," Sky said again, but his face had become an indistinct blur in my vision.

"*Conserve your qi*," the dragon had warned me. "*You must learn to harness your power.*"

The Azure Dragon had lied about many things, but he had not lied about this. No matter—I had not listened. At first, I'd fled from my power, and when I'd finally embraced it, I'd broken every rule, believing myself the exception. I'd overused my lixia, draining my qi—all to keep going, to keep fighting. For what? To save my family, my kingdom? Yes, I had saved them. Yet still I felt empty. Because all along, what I'd really wanted was to prove myself.

I'd wanted to show everyone that I belonged. No—more than belonged. I'd wanted to become the hero of legend, to have my name whispered through the streets, my deeds etched in the stones of history.

Instead, Warden Hu had informed me I had become a stain in

the war annals, a cautionary tale passed from parent to child. Like my mother before me, my legacy would be one of madness and decay—a rot spreading in dark places, remembered not for what it built but for what it destroyed.

That young girl from a year ago, the one who'd dreamed of adventure, of seeing the world beyond the women's quarters. She had sought wonder, wildness. She had believed in the world's capacity for beauty.

Only a year had passed, and yet I could no longer recall what that felt like. To believe in the goodness of people. To seek justice but live with compassion. To hope for better days.

There was no hope for someone like me.

SOME TIME LATER, I WOKE TO A DARK SILHOUETTE AGAINST MY CELL, slashing the light of the flickering lantern. His long shadow stretched across the length of the corridor like a grasping hand.

"Did I wake you?" the Ximing prince asked. Against the icy air of my cell, his low baritone felt like the crackle of a warm fire.

I pushed myself upright, wincing as I put weight on my throbbing hands. "I no longer sleep these days."

"That doesn't sound healthy," he said, his tone light and teasing.

I was in no mood for his banter. "What do you want, Lei?"

He peered down at me through the bars, his eyes narrowing. "I heard you've been refusing food."

I looked away. "I'm not hungry."

It was a lie. I was hungry all the time. Hungry for lixia, for the intoxicating surge of spirit power in my veins. I needed it, craved it, ached for it all the time. I could feel the nearness of my jade, its energy thrumming just out of reach. The lack left me breathless and off-balance, as if I were missing a vital sense.

"Funny," said Lei, his expression unreadable. "You used to strike me as a survivor."

"What's that supposed to mean?" I snapped, losing my temper. How dare he judge me from his seat of privilege? "Go gloat somewhere else, will you?"

He crouched in front of me, so that we were eye level through the bars. "From one prisoner to the next—" He tilted his head, his amber eyes seeming to absorb the flickering firelight. "If you lose your will to live, it's simple. You die."

With that, he rose to his feet. "Do you want to die? If you die, they win. Remember that."

I STARTED EATING AGAIN. THE FOOD UPSET MY STOMACH, FORCED ME to use my broken hands, and heightened my lixia cravings, but at least I started to feel strong enough to stand again. To take a few steps around my cell. To think beyond the span of a day. Two days, a week—that was the limit of what I could take.

The warden's questions kept coming, though they were no longer accompanied by torture. Vaguely, I wondered what Sky had done to achieve such a feat—what he might have bargained with. For there was always a price. I hadn't known that the first time.

"Though you were initially accused of black magic practitioning," said Warden Hu, watching me, "it seems now your accusers have retracted their allegations. Any guesses as to why?"

I shook my head.

"Let's say you did know a thing or two about black magic," he said. "How might one access such a power?"

I told him nothing more than what was common knowledge.

"But why can only some access such a power?"

I said I didn't understand.

"Why are some stricken with seizure and lunacy when confronted with spirit power, while others retain clarity of mind?"

For the first time in a while, I recalled that strange, rippling haze outside the inn in New Quan. The bandits who had wandered near were drawn by the lure of spirit power, moving toward the portal as if in a trance.

"It is a tear in the veil," the dragon had told me. *"So that any human, not just those with seals, can enter our realm. But only those with strong enough spirit affinity can survive such a place. The rest..."*

The rest lost their minds.

"Are more gates appearing?" I asked, raising my head.

"Gates?"

"Portals into the spirit realm," I clarified.

"What are they caused by?" asked the warden, more urgently now. "Why are they forming?"

"I-I don't know," I said, taken aback. "But I wonder if it has something to do with overuse of lixia," I added quietly, thinking of a similar rippling haze I'd once found in my mother's chambers, which were now sealed and boarded up.

If there were more gates appearing, that meant there were more spirit summoners at work. But who? Chancellor Sima was dead. I was locked away in an iron dungeon. Could there be someone else? Someone who'd been biding their time?

Lately, I'd begun to feel a prickling to my senses, though I'd chalked it up to lixia withdrawal. An uncanny sense, as if the spirit realm were somehow nearing. As if the worlds had begun to merge.

Before I could respond, the passageway door burst open. Sky raced toward us, his face alight with undisguised joy. "Father's agreed!" he exclaimed, skidding to a stop in front of my cell. "Meilin can go free."

I blinked at him, unable to process his words.

"Did you hear me?" he asked. "You can come out with me, now. Your maids are waiting for you—they'll help you wash and prepare for court. I asked Mother to set aside a few dresses for now, but once we get your measurements I'll send for . . ." He trailed off as he took in my expression. "Meilin . . . why are you shaking?"

I could not answer. Cold fear coiled around my neck like an insistent noose.

Sky tried to enter my cell but found it locked. He impatiently motioned for the key before barreling inside. But I shrank from the proximity of him.

"Meilin, what's wrong?" asked Sky, kneeling before me, and his voice was so tender it made my eyes sting. I tried to push him away, but my broken hands were useless, unable to do what I wanted from them.

He caught my left hand and I gasped in pain. Immediately he let go, as if my touch burned him. "Meilin. Speak to me, please." His eyes were wide and filled with feeling. It broke something within me, to see myself through his eyes. A pitiful creature, better left alone in the dark. "Don't you want to be free?"

I was sobbing so hard now that I could not form words. He gave me his handkerchief, but my fingers would not close around it, and the fine cloth fell uselessly to the floor.

"Meilin, I made a promise to you. I want to marry you. Did you think I would go back on my word?"

He tried to draw me into his arms, but I flinched away again. Hurt flashed across his face as he backed away, raking his fingers through his hair. "Please. Tell me what's wrong."

"I-I can't. I can't go to court," I said, and I meant it. I couldn't imagine myself in fine dresses, eyes painted like a doll's, and—like a doll—face vacant but smiling, sitting silently by Sky's side as I'd seen the warlord's consorts do. "I want to . . . to leave this place—"

"I'll take you out of the dungeons," Sky said, but I shook my head.

"No," I rasped. "I want to leave the . . . palace. The city." The world.

His face fell. "My father's terms were for you to remain within the Forbidden City," he admitted, "and to return to the ways of womanhood."

The noose drew tight around my neck. So it was the old offer, made again. I would have to relinquish my sword, my freedom, my knowledge of the world beyond. I could be Sky's pretty ornament, or nothing at all.

Yet memories of the outside world, however undesirable, still called to me. I missed the morning sunlight and the reflection of the moon upon water. I missed my family and the ability to run with the wind at my back. When the Imperial Commander had first offered me this choice, I hadn't understood the stakes. I understood them now.

But there was a third factor I hadn't weighed. Here in the dungeons, I was suffocated by iron. There was no possibility of the dragon's presence, his influence, his sly whispering voice in my head. The last time I'd seen him, he'd tried to kill me. Just like he'd killed my mother.

Perhaps once I was freed, he'd finish the job.

"Meilin? Do you want me to call your maidservants here?"

I shook my head. "Can you . . . can you give me some time?"

I could feel his sadness like a millstone, dragging me beneath its weight.

"I'm sorry, Sky," I said, and the sound of his name hurt us both. "Please go." When he didn't move, I turned my back on him. Eventually, I felt the strength of his presence recede.

I didn't know myself anymore. The girl he'd loved . . . I didn't know if she still existed. So many conflicting desires battled within me at once, until I couldn't make sense of any of them. I wanted to be free—of my loneliness, of my captivity, of my weakness. I wanted to be confined—I couldn't be trusted with power, with responsibility, with choice. And all those people above, judging me, mocking me, wanting something from me . . . the thought made me want to hide forever.

Who was I anymore? And if I couldn't trust myself, who could I possibly trust?

WANT MORE?

If you enjoyed this and would like to find out about similar books we publish, we'd love you to join our online Sci-Fi, Fantasy and Horror community, Hodderscape.

Visit hodderscape.co.uk for exclusive content from our authors, news, competitions and general musings, and feel free to comment, contribute or just keep an eye on what we are up to.

See you there!

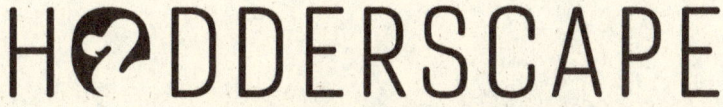

NEVER AFRAID TO BE OUT OF THIS WORLD

@HODDERSCAPE   HODDERSCAPE.CO.UK